image® comics presents

SKULL KICKERS

A DOZEN COUSINS and a CRUMPLED CROWN

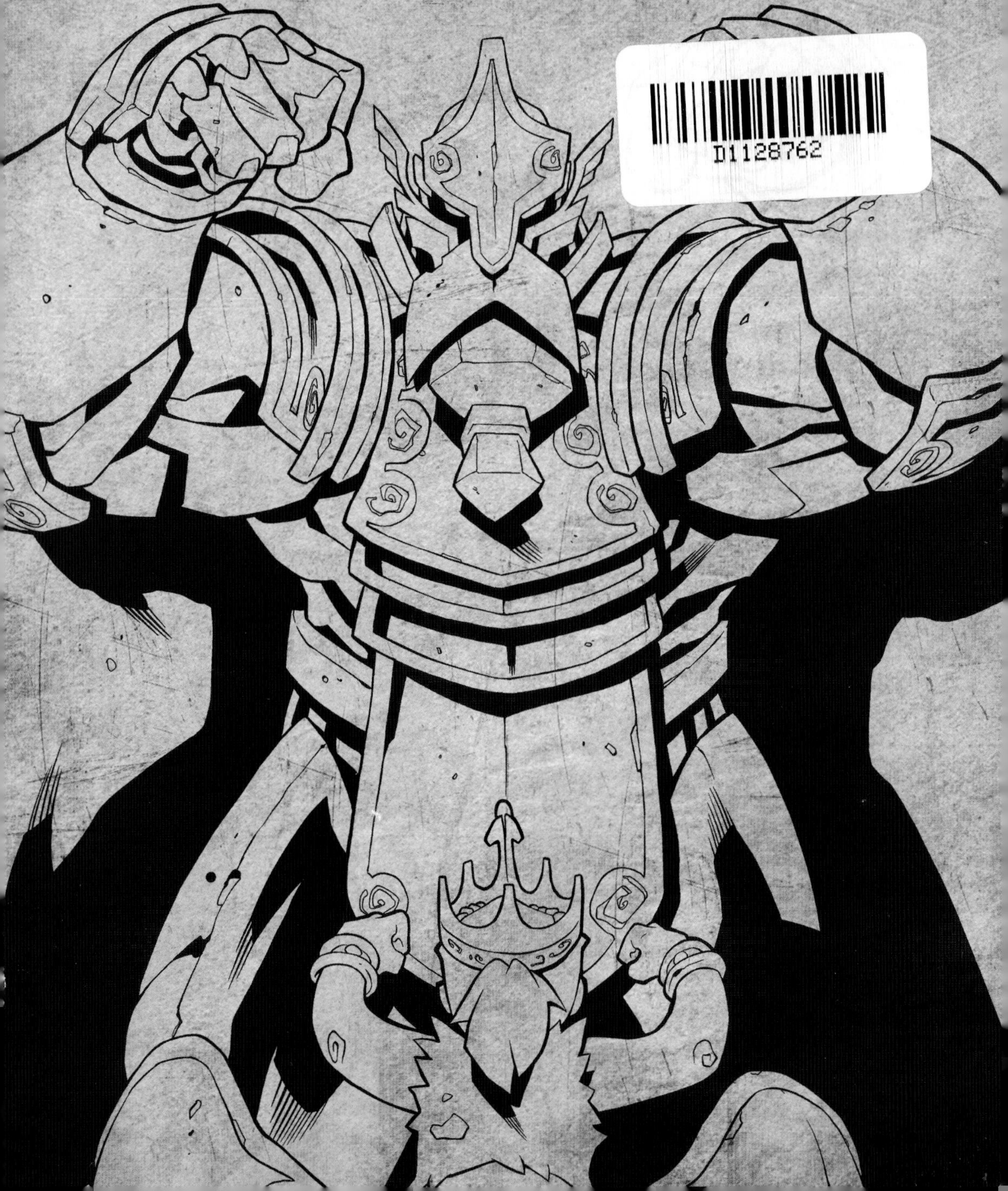

IMAGE COMICS, INC.
Robert Kirkman – Chief Operating Officer
Erik Larsen – Chief Financial Officer
Todd McFarlane – President
Marc Silvestri – Chief Executive Officer
Jim Valentino – Vice-President

Eric Stephenson – Publisher
Ron Richards – Director of Business Development
Jennifer de Guzman – Director of Trade Book Sales
Kat Salazar – Director of PR & Marketing
Corey Murphy – Director of Retail Sales
Jeremy Sullivan – Director of Digital Sales
Emilio Bautista – Sales Assistant
Branwyn Bigglestone – Senior Accounts Manager
Emily Miller – Accounts Manager
Jessica Ambriz – Administrative Assistant
Tyler Shainline – Events Coordinator
David Brothers – Content Manager
Jonathan Chan – Production Manager
Drew Gill – Art Director
Meredith Wallace – Print Manager
Monica Garcia – Senior Production Artist
Jenna Savage – Production Artist
Addison Duke – Production Artist
Tricia Ramos – Production Assistant
IMAGECOMICS.COM

SKULLKICKERS VOLUME 5
ISBN: 978-1-63215-033-2
First Printing

Special Thanks
CARL SMITH
LEGEND COMICS & COFFEE
BEN PENROD
ALL THE DWARVES

Writer
JIM ZUB

Pencils
EDWIN HUANG

Inks
EDWIN HUANG
KEVIN RAGANIT
JOY HAN

Colors
MISTY COATS
ROSS A. CAMPBELL
MIKE LUCKAS

Color Flatting
LUDWIG OLIMBA

Lettering
MARSHALL DILLON

“Tavern Tales” Writers
RON MARZ
ADAM WARREN
TODD DEZAGO
JIM ZUB

“Tavern Tales” Artists
STJEPAN SEJIC
REMY “EISU” MOKHTAR
YINFAOWEI HARRISON
JEFF “CHAMBA” CRUZ
LAR DESOUZA

Issue Covers
EDWIN HUANG
JIM ZUB
JAMES GHIO

Trade Cover
EDWIN HUANG
MISTY COATS

Graphic Design
JIM ZUB

Skullkickers Logo
STEVEN FINCH

Skullkickers Created by
JIM ZUB
CHRIS STEVENS

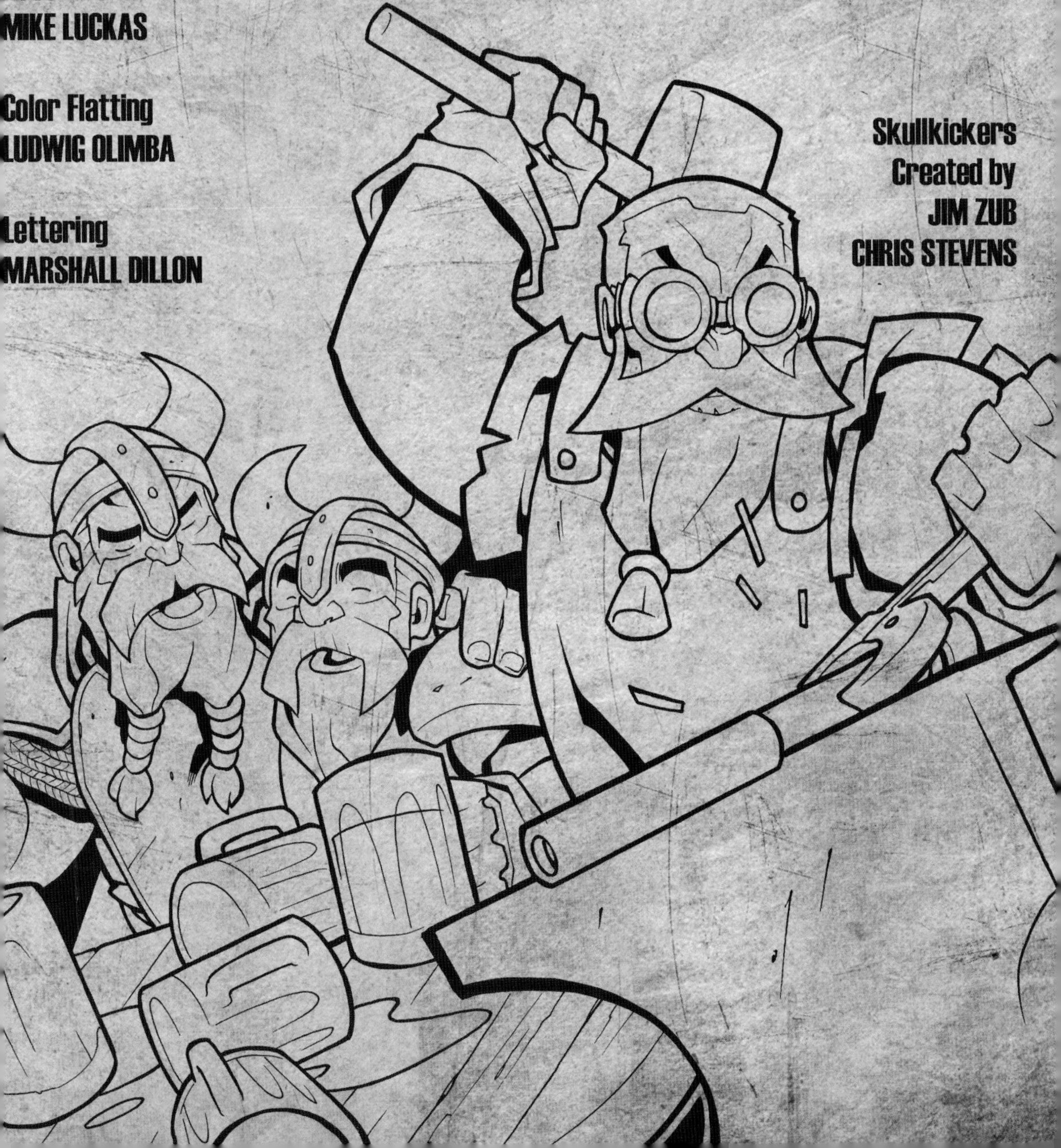

High-Level Storytelling

Over just about 30 issues, Jim Zub's Skullkickers has grown from a straightforward take on fantasy adventure filtered through the comic lens of tabletop roleplaying to a complex, multi-dimensional epic filled with demon lords, doppelgangers, dungeons, and dwarves. Lots and lots of dwarves.

As the overall tale races toward its conclusion, the focus shifts to the dwarf Rolf Copperhead, revealing the past that sent him away from his people and the history of the dwarves themselves that Rolf so greatly affected. Along the way, Zub gives us no fewer than three alternate Rolfs from different dimensions, firmly establishing Skullkickers not just as a riff on the sorts of tabletop roleplaying games Jim played as a kid, but also the Silver and Bronze Age comics that must have shared his allowance with metal Dungeons & Dragons figurines and the latest Monster Manuals.

The adventures of Rolf and Rex—Shorty and Baldy, as they're more commonly known—beat with the energetic pace of a writer paving new and exciting ground, but the fresh ideas resonate so strongly because they're based on a solid foundation of classic tropes from sword & sorcery, gaming, and comics. Every scene plays out with a reverence for the source material only a true fan could pull off, giving Skullkickers a sense of authenticity that will resonate with every dreamer who has ever stayed up too late reading tales of wizards and warriors or throwing funny-shaped dice to imagine them-selves slaying dragons. Jim gets it because he's been there. He's thrown the dice. Because he's sketched out the dungeon maps while he should have been paying closer attention in class. In short, because he's one of us.

In the world of adapting fantasy roleplaying games into fiction the cardinal sin is to write in a way that the reader can "hear the dice falling" with every action in the narrative. Although I can imagine a lot of the things in Skullkickers happening in a fantasy RPG, I confess I cannot hear the mechanical clatter of dice as I read the comics. Instead I hear the real music of an RPG session, the huge guffaws and belly laughs of the players as a hilarious GM sets the scene. Jim's brilliant sound effects ("ominous rumble!", "inanimate object attack!", "ape angst!") sound like something a Game Master would say, conveying in a few words vivid pictures in the minds of the players. His crowd scene asides—probably my favorite of his recurring narrative devices—sometimes read like an RPG adventure's random rumor table.

Hell, with their loose morals, hunger for money, and absolutely gruesome combat prowess, Shorty and Baldy are the quintessential fantasy roleplaying player characters. They even make funny jokes as they rend limbs and heads from the bodies of their opponents. You know, just like you do when you're gaming.

Over scores of issues we've all had the opportunity to sit at Jim Zub's gaming table. Assisted as ever by the enormously talented Edwin Huang and Misty Coats (whose combined powers grow stronger and stronger with every volume), Jim has taken us from muddy village to bustling city to deadly isle to Hell and back. We're just past the half-way point of our journey, and there's dwarves, dimensional doubles, and eldritch horror aplenty up ahead.

I can't wait to discover where the campaign goes next! We couldn't ask for a better GM.

—Erik Mona
August 2014

Erik Mona is the Publisher and Chief Creative Officer of Paizo Inc., publishers of the Pathfinder Roleplaying Game. Mona co-created the Pathfinder world of Golarion, and has written numerous books, adventures, and articles for the game line. He previously edited Dragon, Dungeon, and Polyhedron magazines.

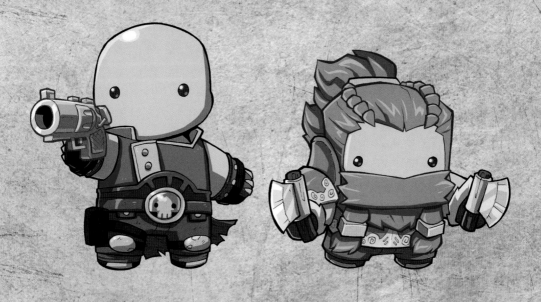

Above: Super cute Skullkickers by Kevin Raganit.

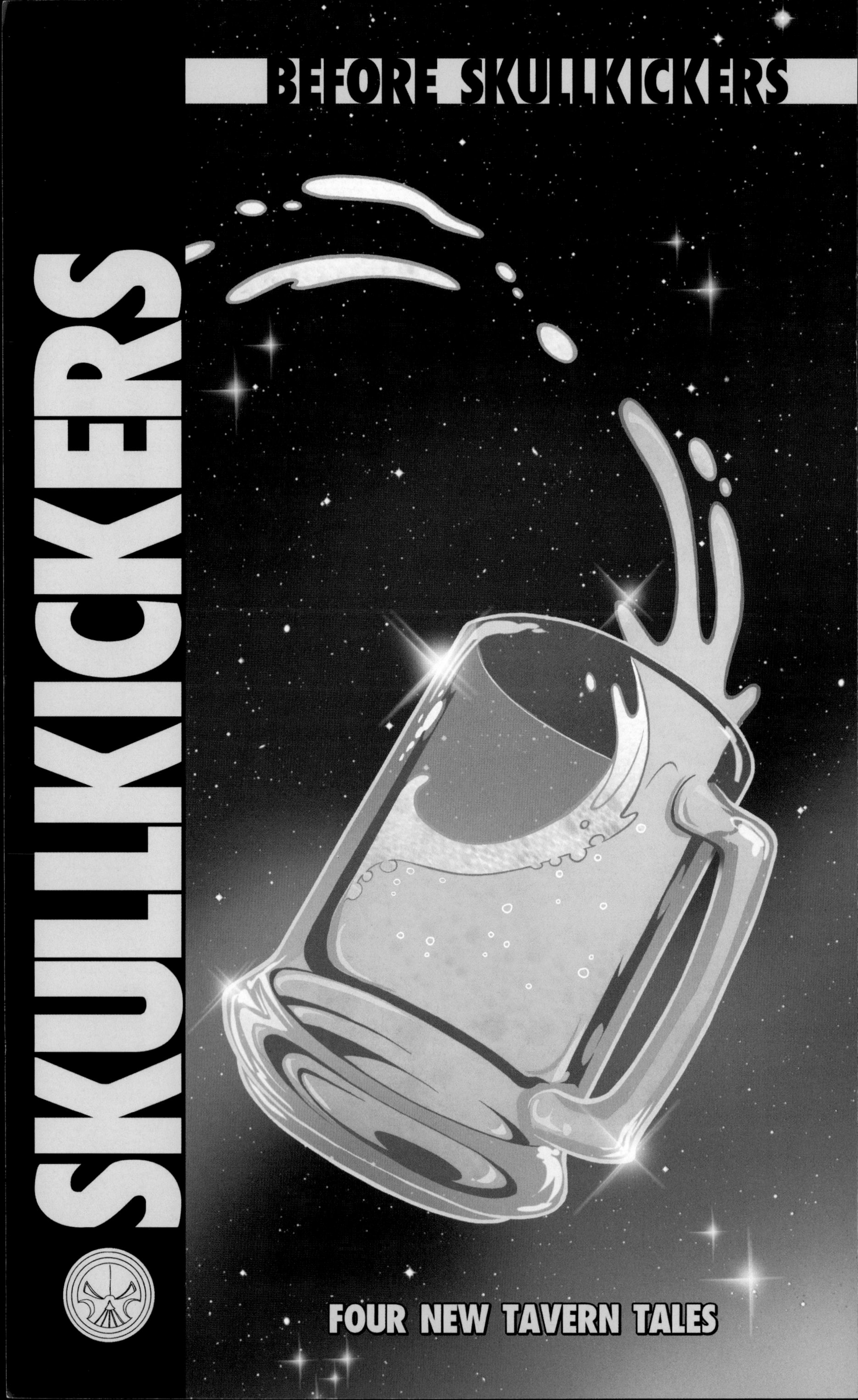
BEFORE SKULLKICKERS
SKULLKICKERS
FOUR NEW TAVERN TALES

BEFORE SKULLKICKERS

People like **prequels**, right? I heard that's a thing people like.

Lately, it seems like everyone is obsessed with the **pre-starting line**. They don't want to see a race anymore, they want to watch someone mulling over which running shoes they should wear before they get to the race track.

You saw our "unbooted" #1's, right? Five new issue 1's in five months. I think it's fair to say that we're here to give the people what they want, even when they're not sure they want it.

I thought the ongoing-moving-forward plot was the thing worth following, but I've been known to be wrong before and didn't want to be wrong again, so I made sure we had a prequel for Skullkickers; Stories that show you who these characters were before they were the ones I wanted you to read about.

Done. Bases covered. <u>Problem solved</u>.

Coming up with a title that felt appropriate but also completely unambiguous about what it entailed was important.

"Pre-Kickers", ""Intact Skulls", "Uninjured Skulls", "Unkicked Skulls", "Issue #0.1", "Issue 0.0"... None of them sounded quite right.

If only there was some way to elegantly explain that the four short stories you're about to read (put together by four top flight creative teams) took place before Skullkickers...

Nope. No way to do it.

Oh well, read on and enjoy.

Elvish Graces

Story by Ron Marz Art by Stjepan Sejic
Lettering by Marshall Dillon

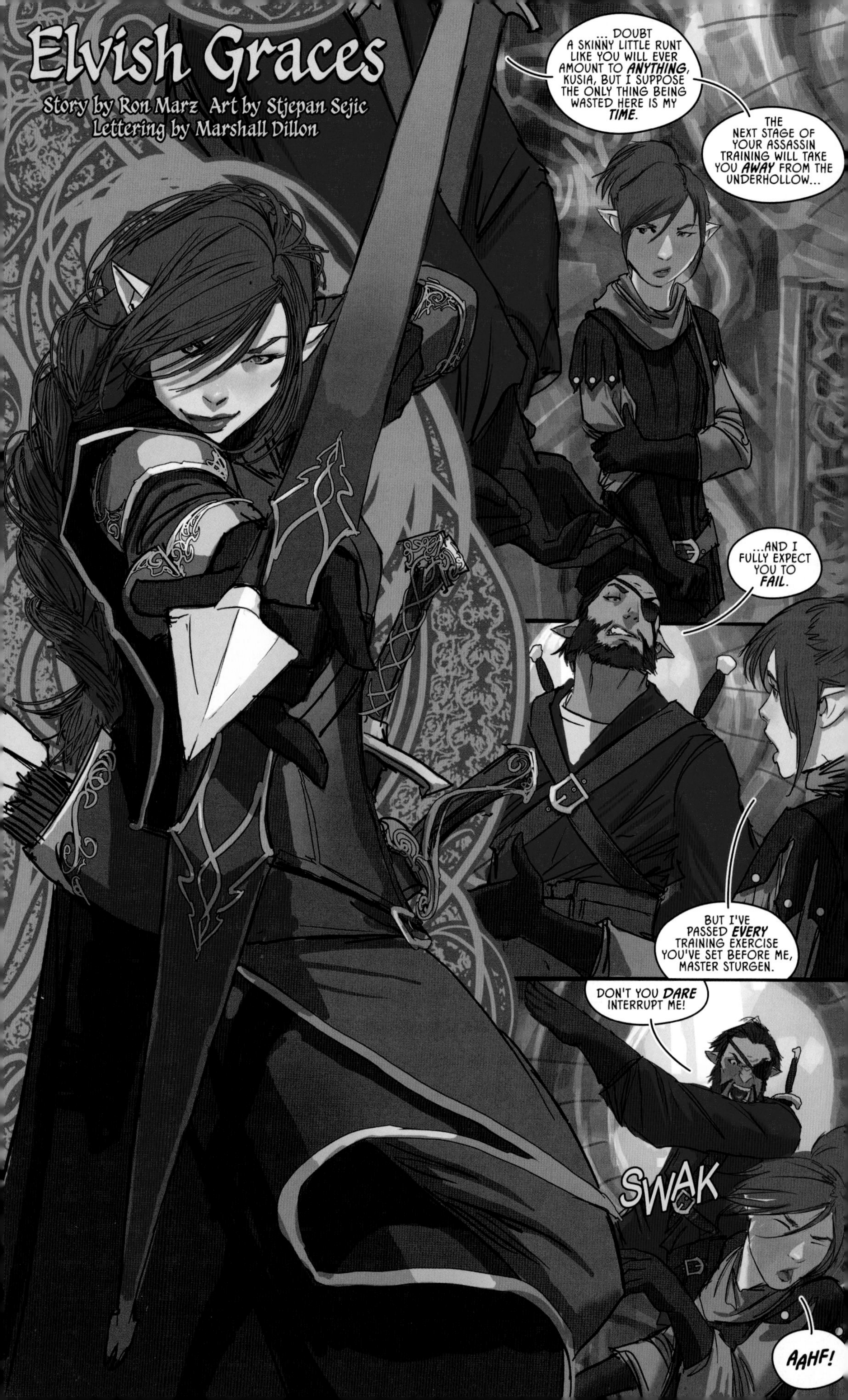
... DOUBT A SKINNY LITTLE RUNT LIKE YOU WILL EVER AMOUNT TO ANYTHING, KUSIA, BUT I SUPPOSE THE ONLY THING BEING WASTED HERE IS MY TIME.
THE NEXT STAGE OF YOUR ASSASSIN TRAINING WILL TAKE YOU AWAY FROM THE UNDERHOLLOW...
...AND I FULLY EXPECT YOU TO FAIL.
BUT I'VE PASSED EVERY TRAINING EXERCISE YOU'VE SET BEFORE ME, MASTER STURGEN.
DON'T YOU DARE INTERRUPT ME!
SWAK
AAHF!

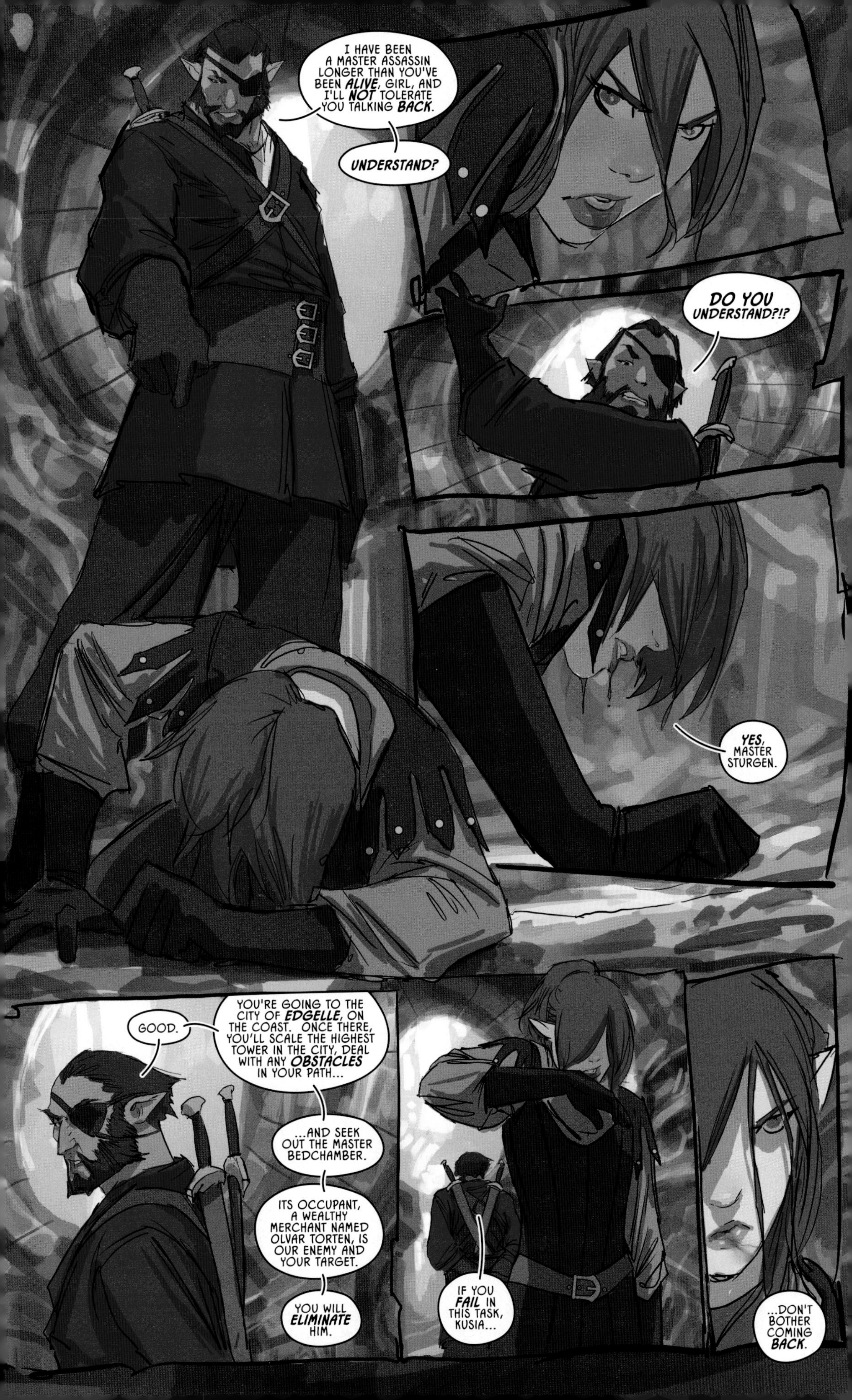
I HAVE BEEN A MASTER ASSASSIN LONGER THAN YOU'VE BEEN ALIVE, GIRL, AND I'LL NOT TOLERATE YOU TALKING BACK.
UNDERSTAND?
DO YOU UNDERSTAND?!?
YES, MASTER STURGEN.
GOOD.
YOU'RE GOING TO THE CITY OF EDGELLE, ON THE COAST. ONCE THERE, YOU'LL SCALE THE HIGHEST TOWER IN THE CITY, DEAL WITH ANY OBSTACLES IN YOUR PATH...
...AND SEEK OUT THE MASTER BEDCHAMBER.
ITS OCCUPANT, A WEALTHY MERCHANT NAMED OLVAR TORTEN, IS OUR ENEMY AND YOUR TARGET.
YOU WILL ELIMINATE HIM.
IF YOU FAIL IN THIS TASK, KUSIA...
...DON'T BOTHER COMING BACK.

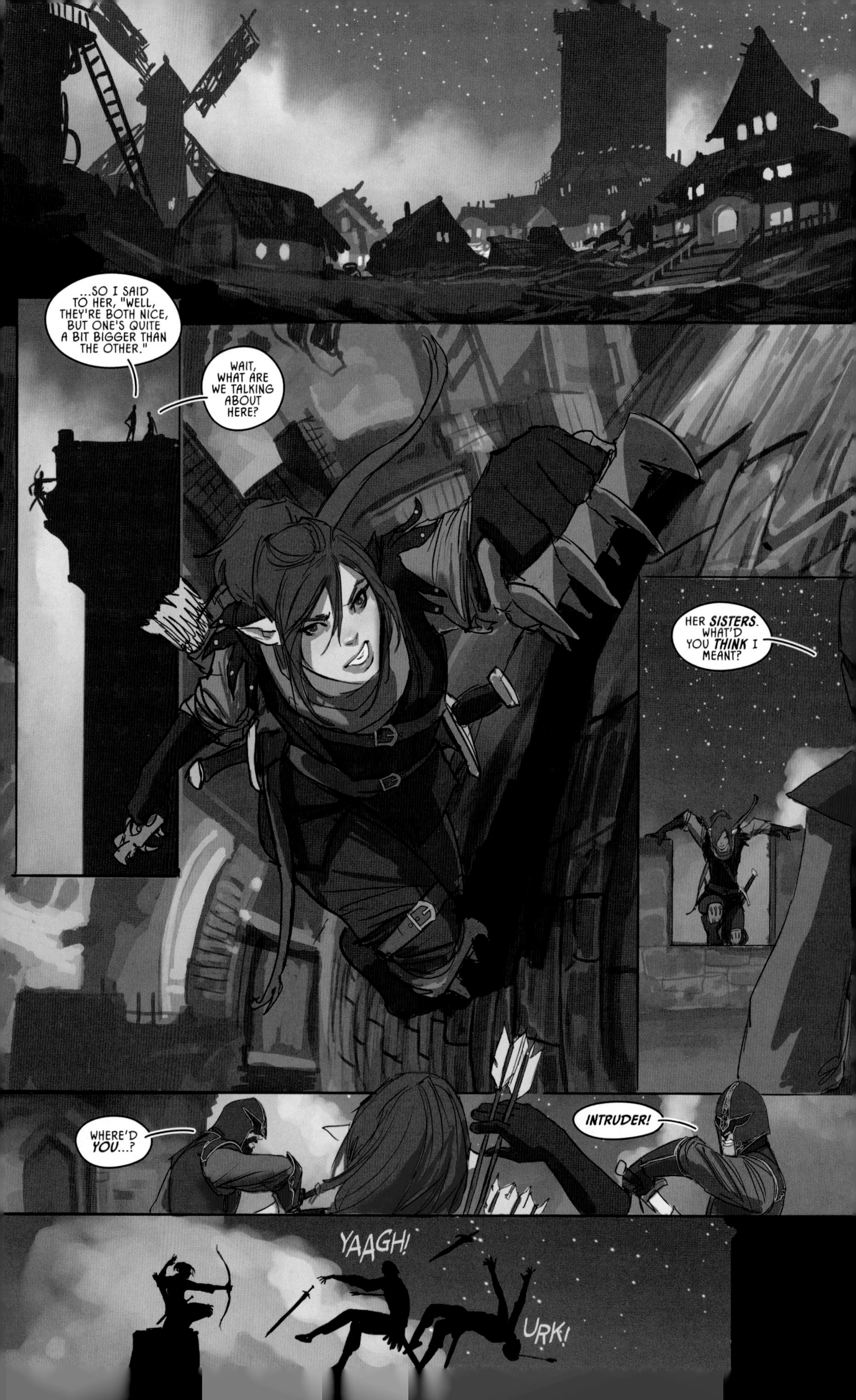
...SO I SAID TO HER, "WELL, THEY'RE BOTH NICE, BUT ONE'S QUITE A BIT BIGGER THAN THE OTHER."
WAIT, WHAT ARE WE TALKING ABOUT HERE?
HER *SISTERS*. WHAT'D YOU *THINK* I MEANT?
WHERE'D *YOU*...?
INTRUDER!
YAAGH!
URK!

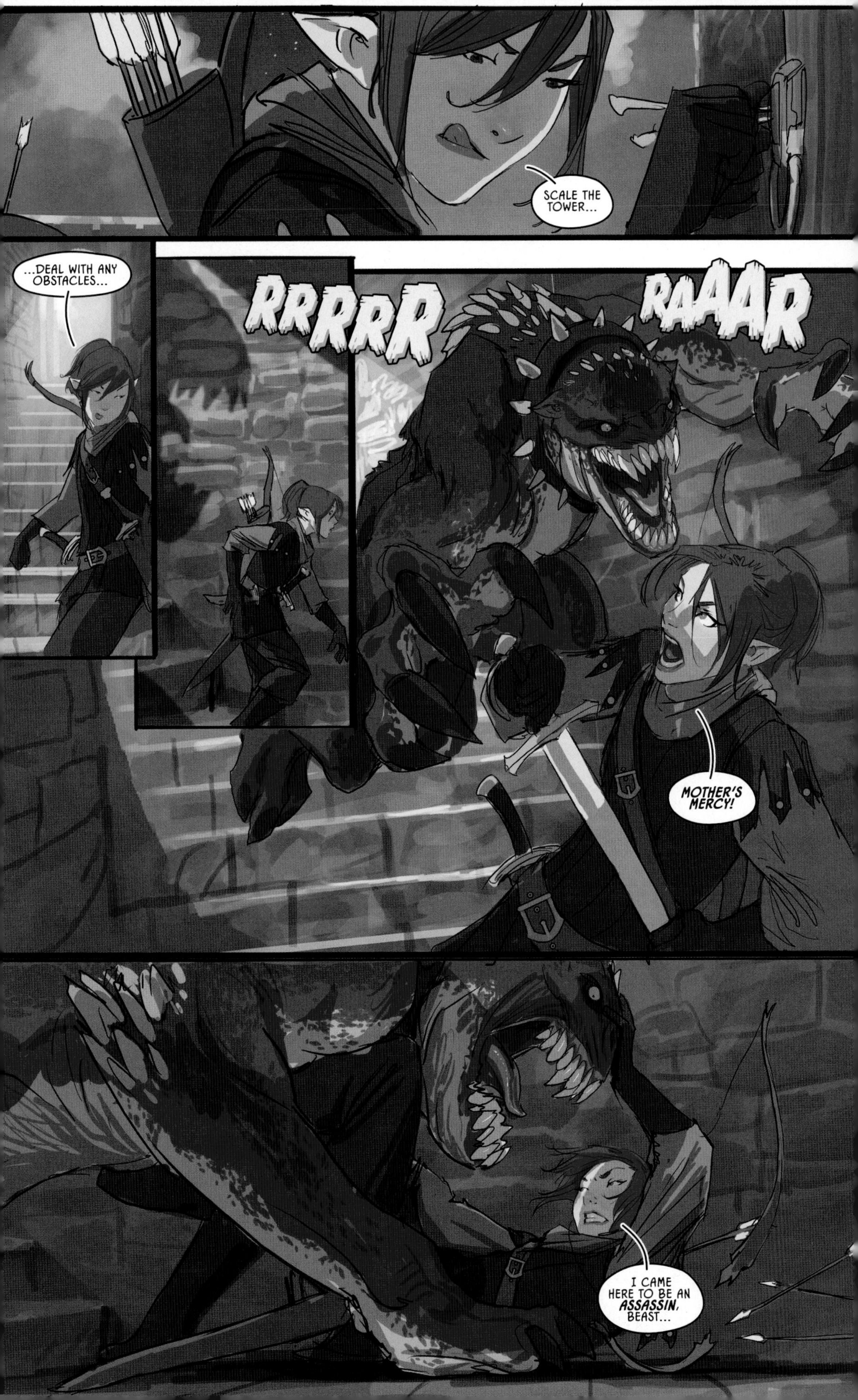
SCALE THE TOWER...
...DEAL WITH ANY OBSTACLES...
RRRRR
RAAAR
MOTHER'S MERCY!
I CAME HERE TO BE AN ASSASSIN, BEAST...

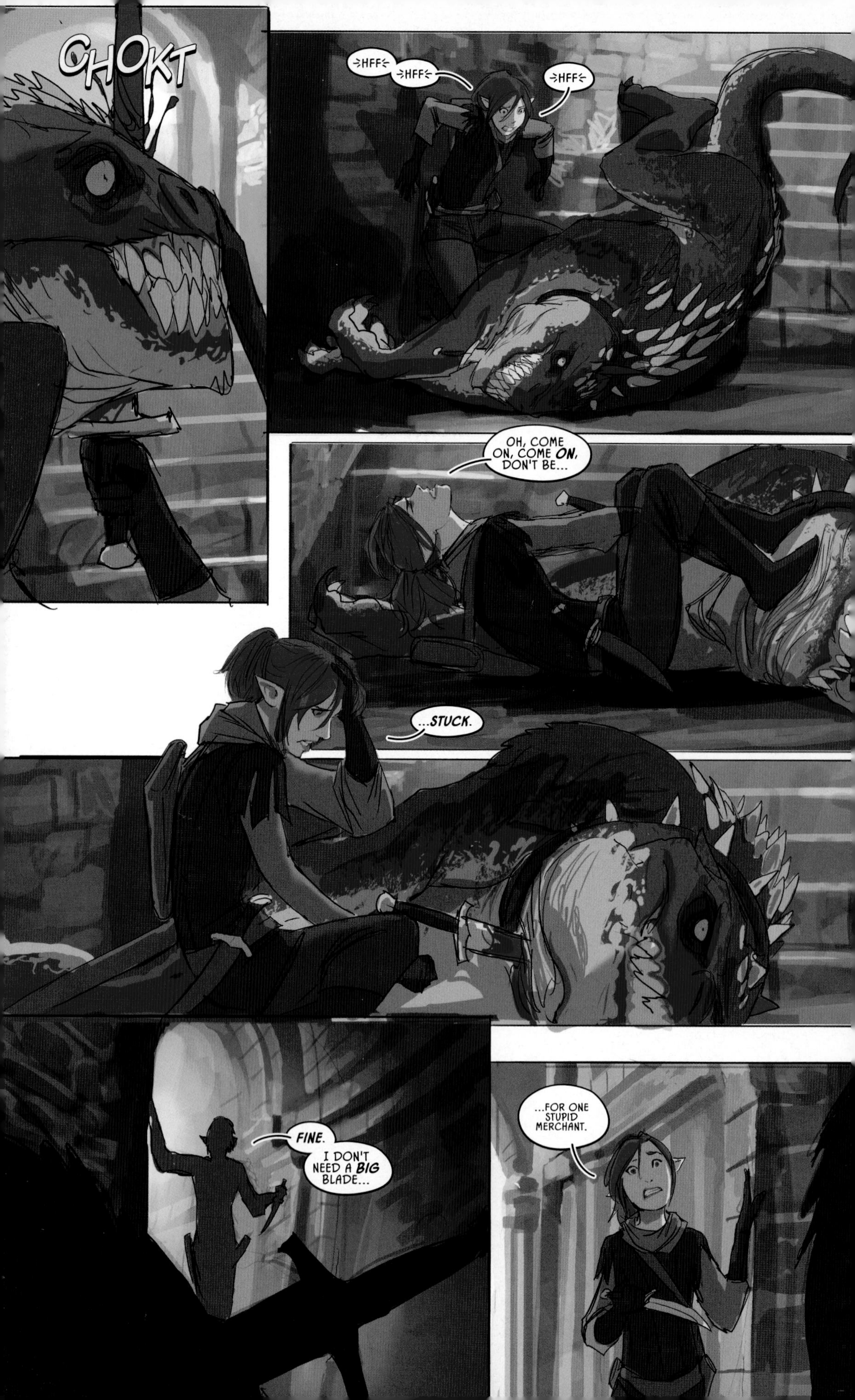
CHOKT
HFF
HFF
HFF
OH, COME ON, COME ON, DON'T BE...
...STUCK.
FINE. I DON'T NEED A BIG BLADE...
...FOR ONE STUPID MERCHANT.

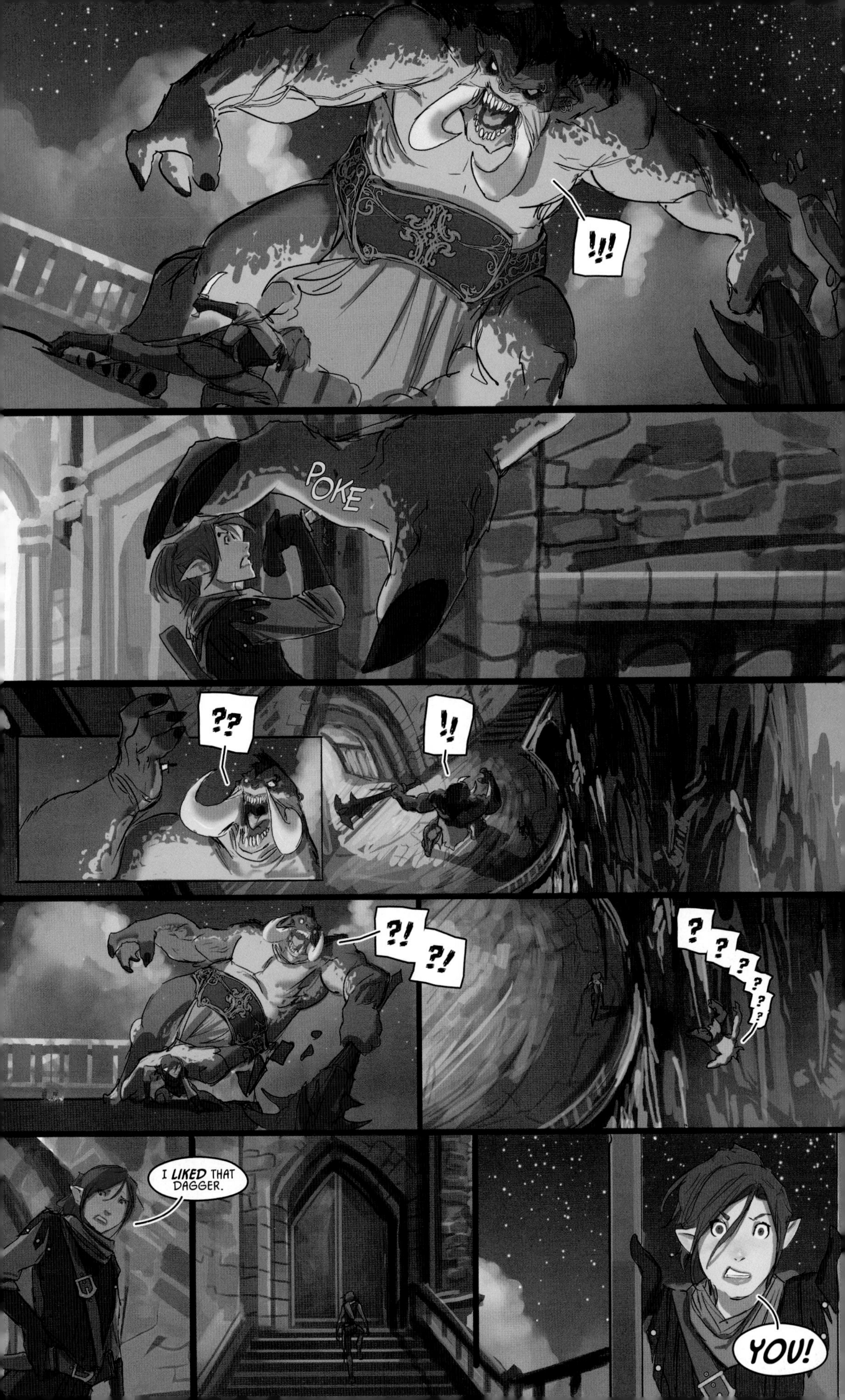
!!!
POKE
??
!!
?!
?!
? ? ? ? ? ? ?
I LIKED THAT DAGGER.
YOU!

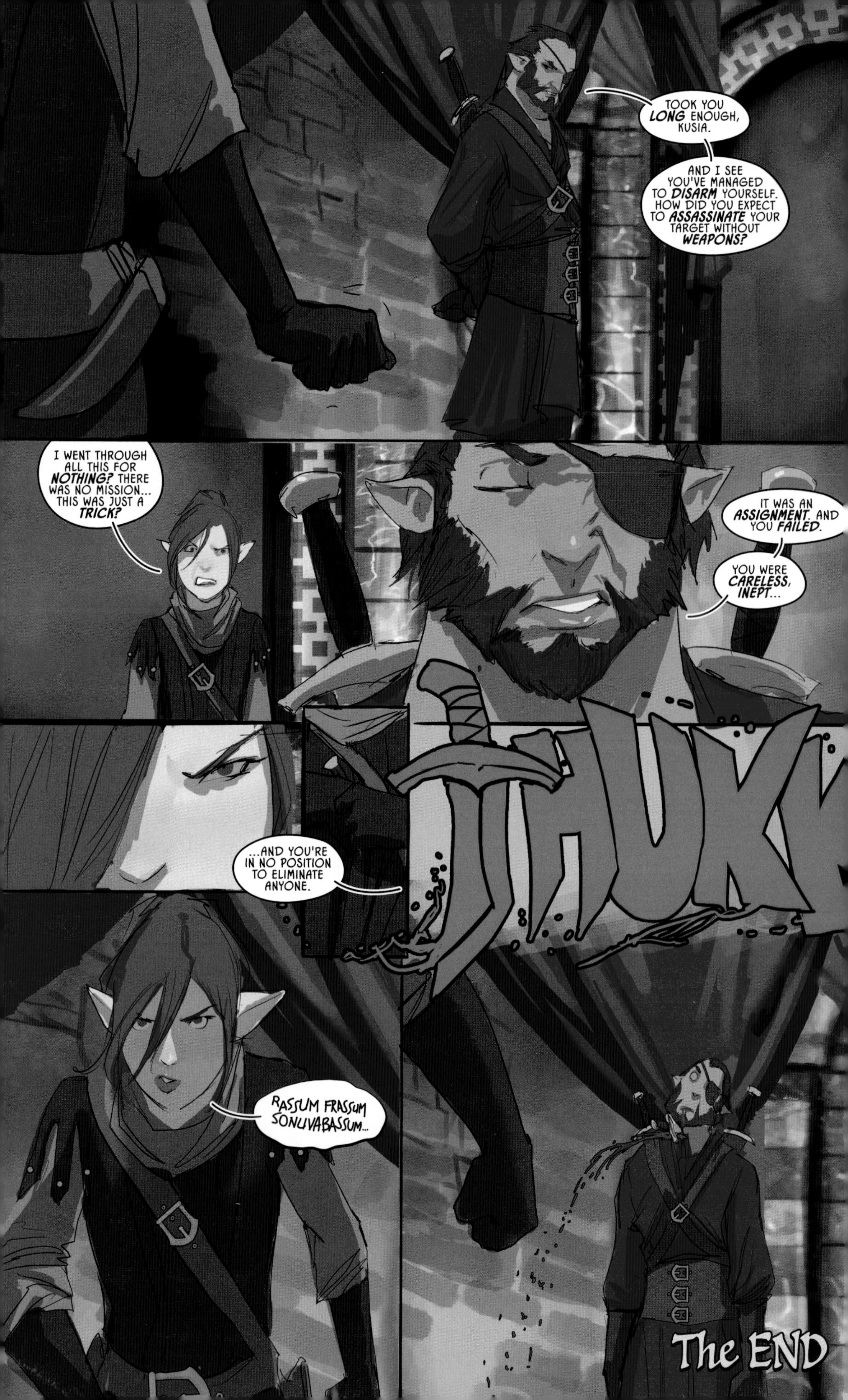
TOOK YOU LONG ENOUGH, KUSIA.
AND I SEE YOU'VE MANAGED TO DISARM YOURSELF. HOW DID YOU EXPECT TO ASSASSINATE YOUR TARGET WITHOUT WEAPONS?
I WENT THROUGH ALL THIS FOR NOTHING? THERE WAS NO MISSION... THIS WAS JUST A TRICK?
IT WAS AN ASSIGNMENT. AND YOU FAILED.
YOU WERE CARELESS, INEPT...
...AND YOU'RE IN NO POSITION TO ELIMINATE ANYONE.
THUK
RASSUM FRASSUM SONUVABASSUM...
The END

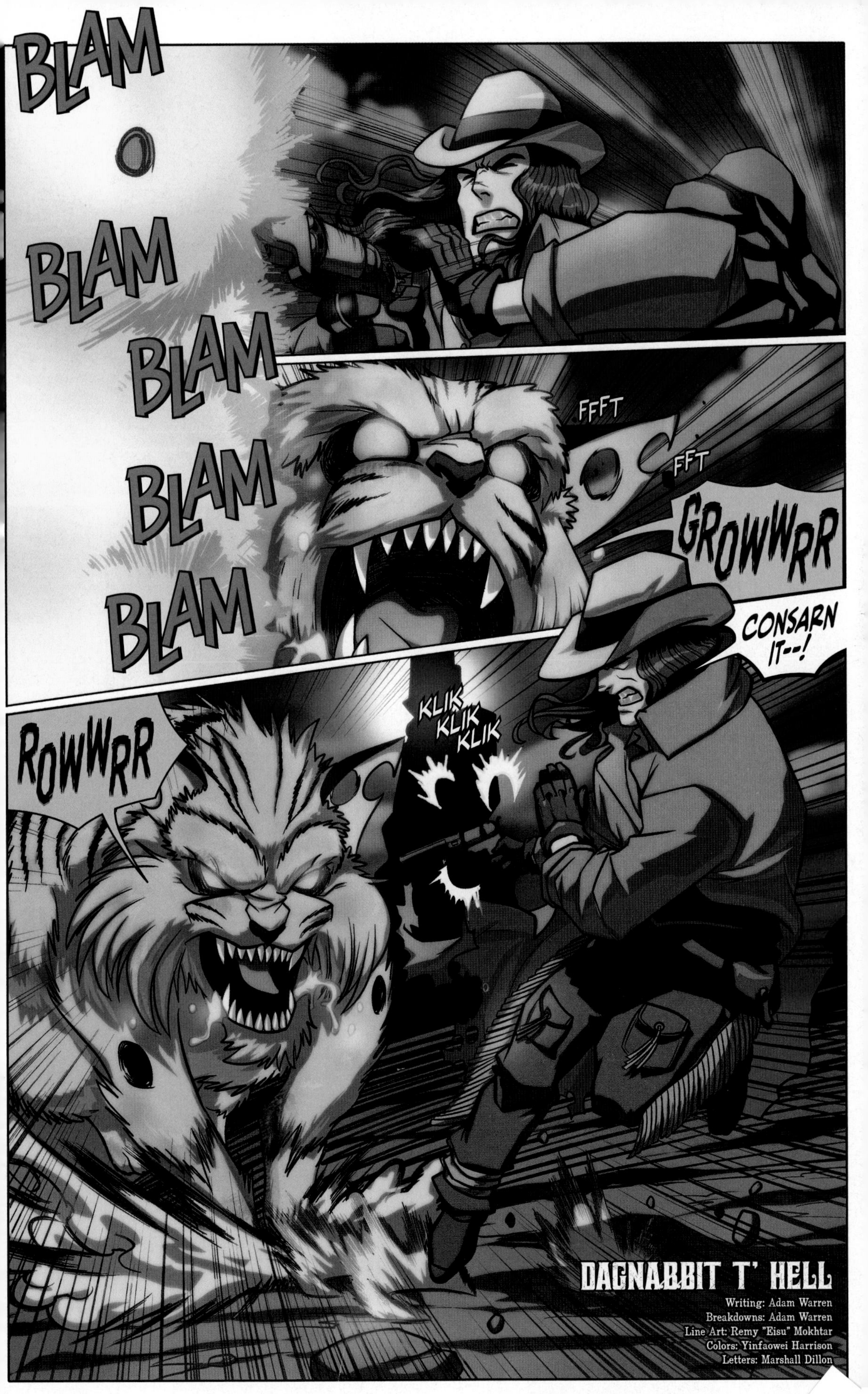

BLAM
BLAM
BLAM
BLAM
BLAM
FFFT
FFT
GROWWRR
CONSARN IT--!
KLIK KLIK KLIK
ROWWRR

DAGNABBIT T' HELL

Writing: Adam Warren
Breakdowns: Adam Warren
Line Art: Remy "Eisu" Mokhtar
Colors: Yinfaowei Harrison
Letters: Marshall Dillon

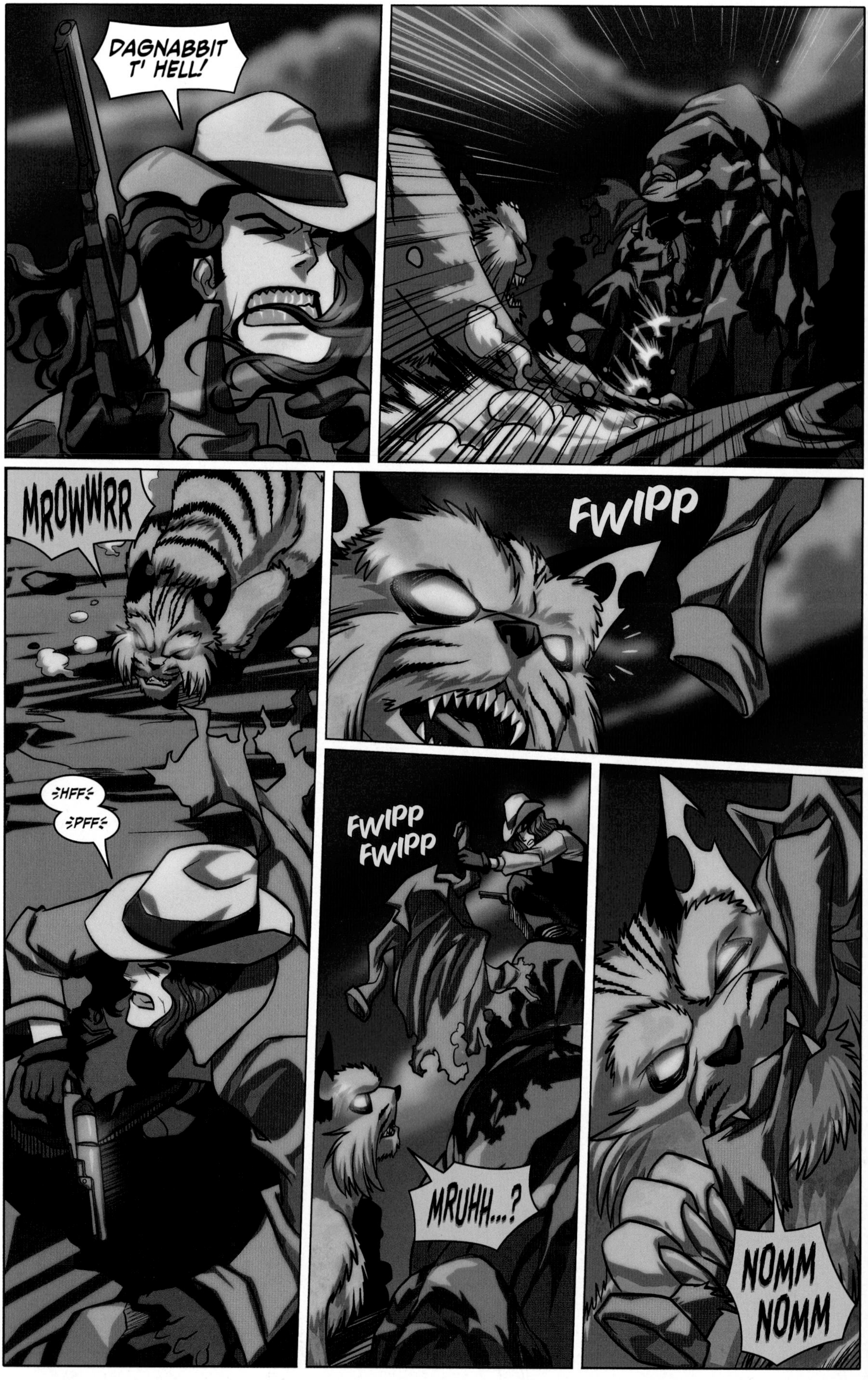
DAGNABBIT T' HELL!
MROWWRR
FWIPP
HFF
PFF
FWIPP FWIPP
MRUHH...?
NOMM NOMM

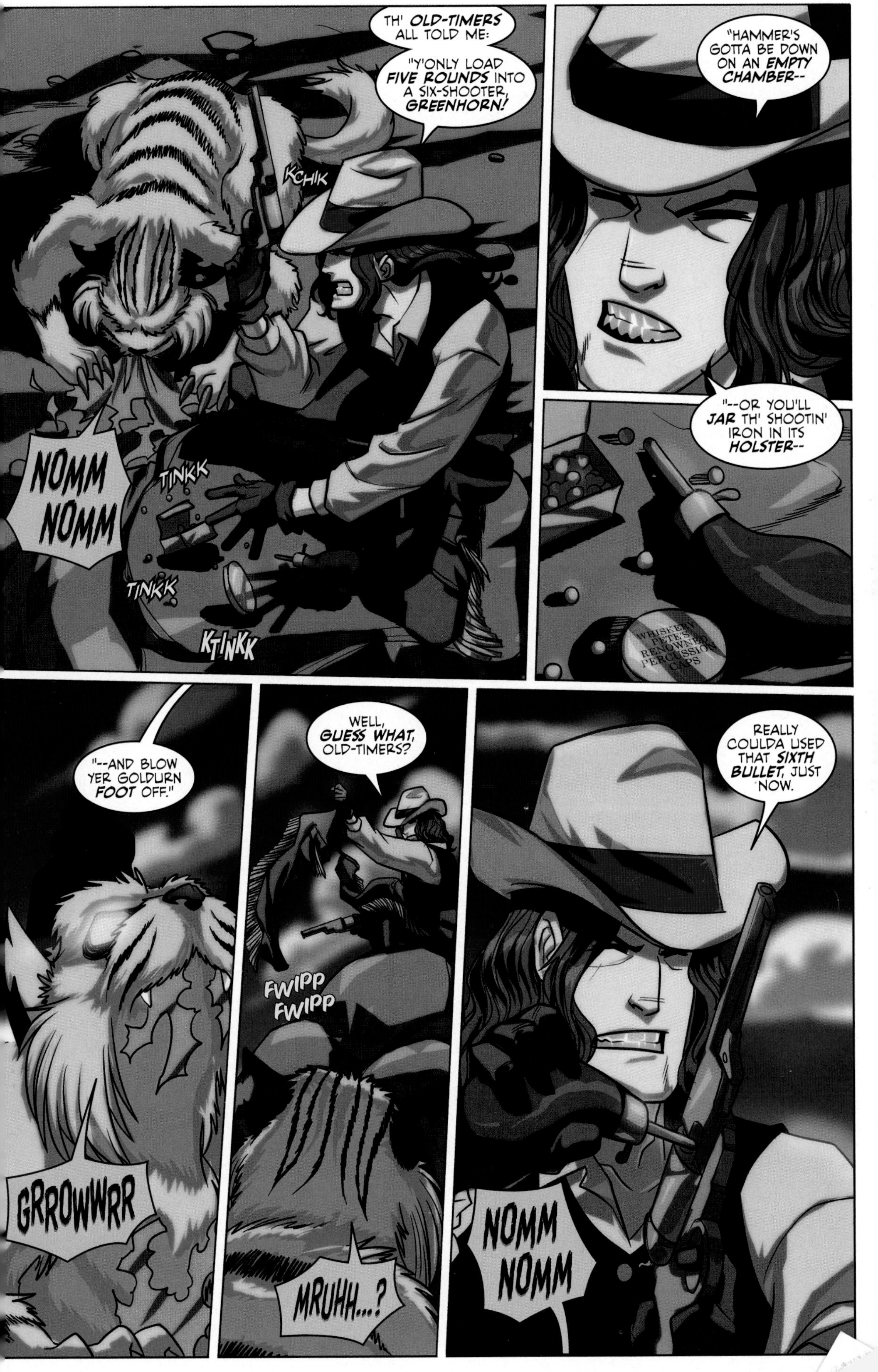

TH' OLD-TIMERS ALL TOLD ME:
"Y'ONLY LOAD FIVE ROUNDS INTO A SIX-SHOOTER, GREENHORN!
KCHIK
NOMM NOMM
TINKK
TINKK
KTINKK
"HAMMER'S GOTTA BE DOWN ON AN EMPTY CHAMBER--
"--OR YOU'LL JAR TH' SHOOTIN' IRON IN ITS HOLSTER--
WHISKEY PETE'S RENOWNED PERCUSSION CAPS
"--AND BLOW YER GOLDURN FOOT OFF."
GRROWWRR
WELL, GUESS WHAT, OLD-TIMERS?
FWIPP FWIPP
MRUHH...?
REALLY COULDA USED THAT SIXTH BULLET, JUST NOW.
NOMM NOMM

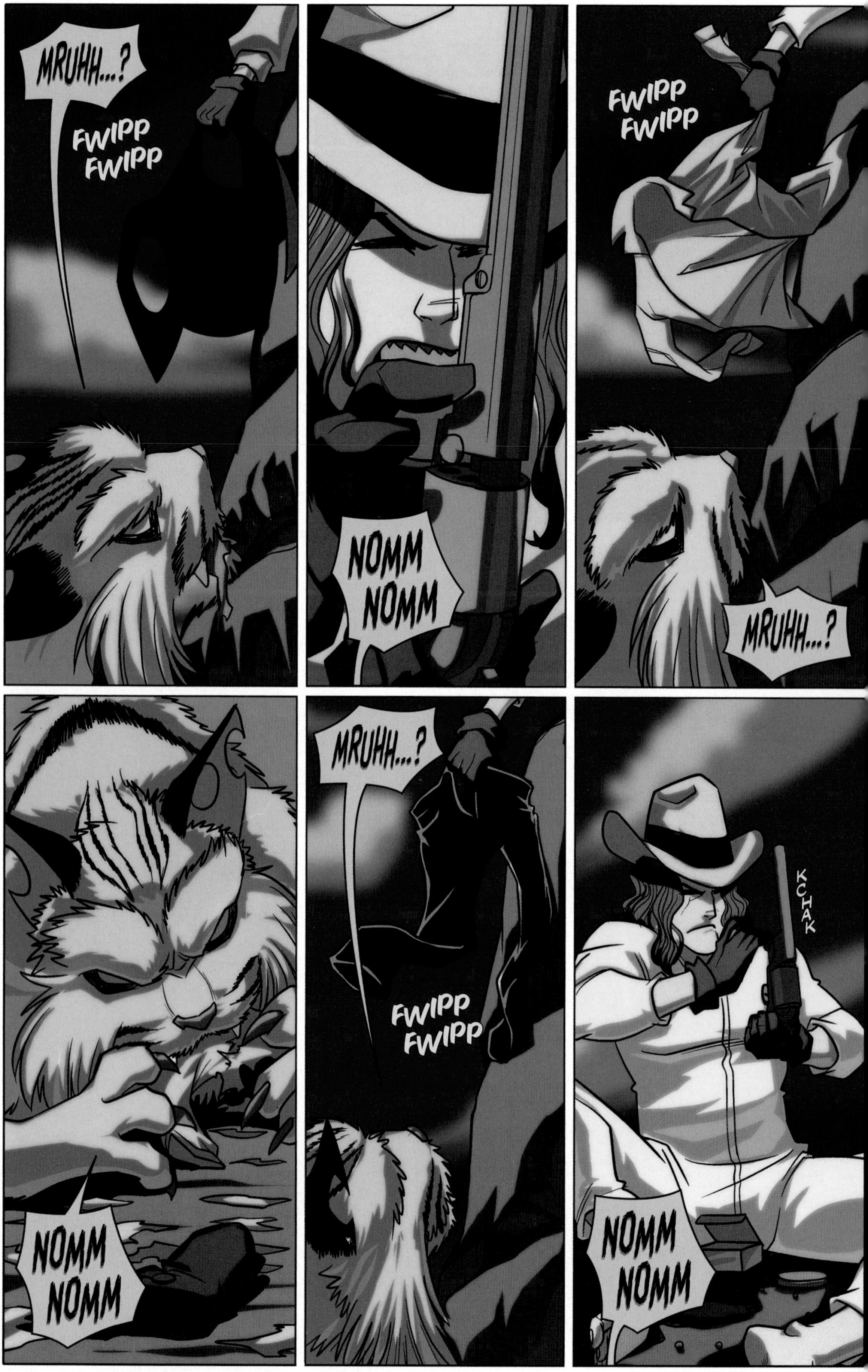
MRUHH...?
FWIPP FWIPP
NOMM NOMM
FWIPP FWIPP
MRUHH...?
NOMM NOMM
MRUHH...?
FWIPP FWIPP
KCHAK
NOMM NOMM

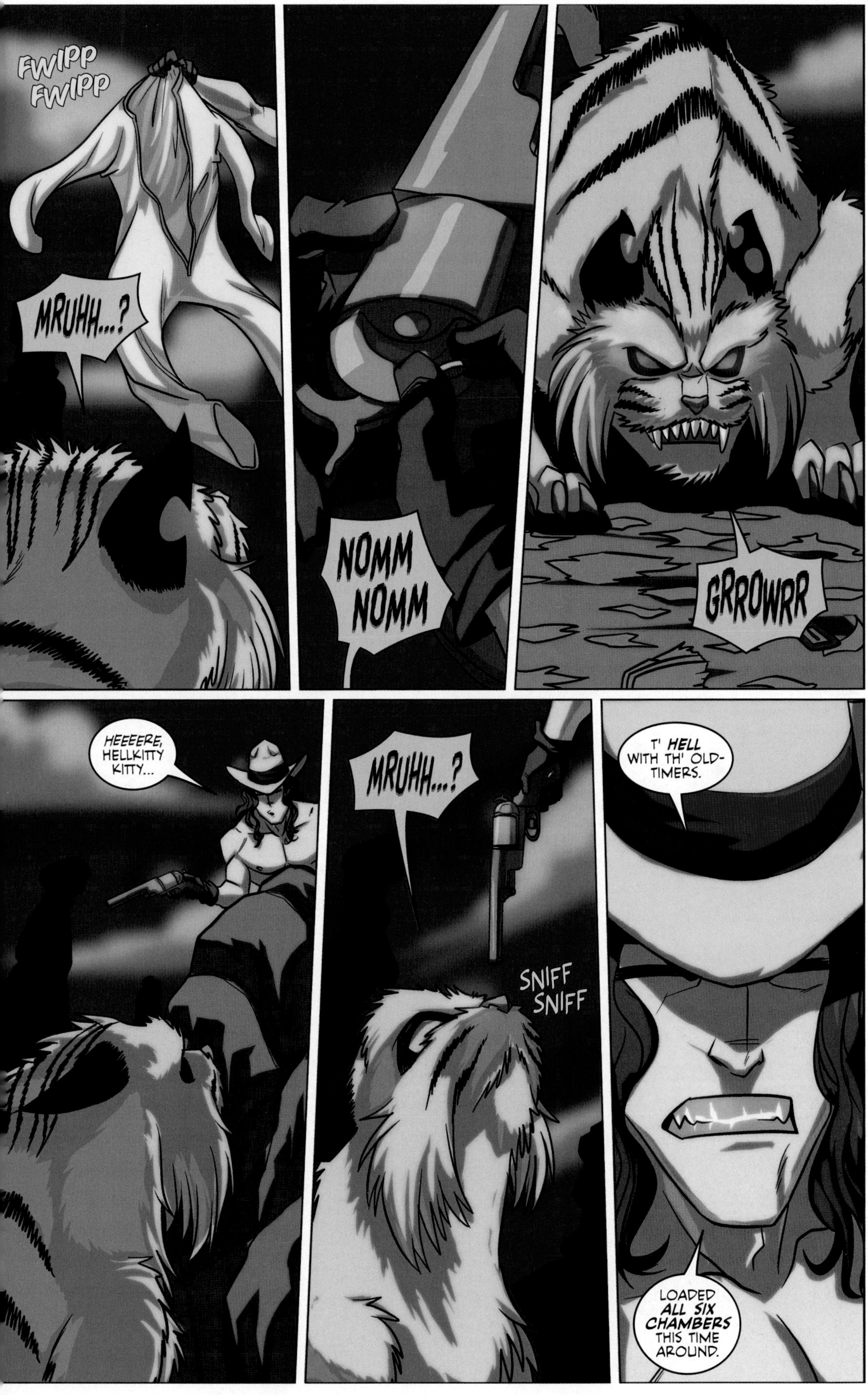
FWIPP
FWIPP
MRUHH...?
NOMM
NOMM
GRROWRR
HEEEERE, HELLKITTY KITTY...
MRUHH...?
SNIFF
SNIFF
T' HELL WITH TH' OLD-TIMERS.
LOADED ALL SIX CHAMBERS THIS TIME AROUND.

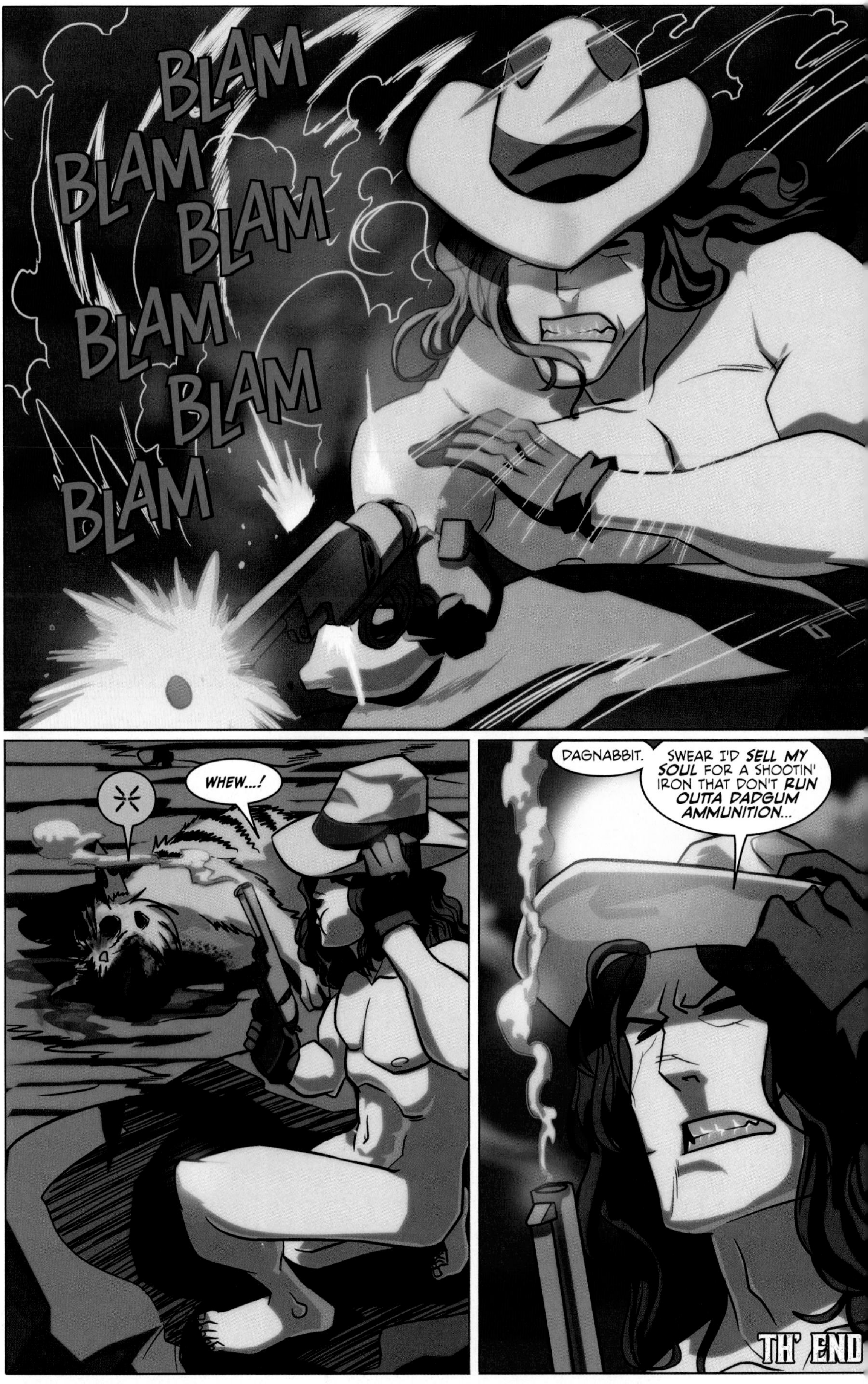
BLAM
BLAM
BLAM
BLAM
BLAM
BLAM
WHEW...!
DAGNABBIT.
SWEAR I'D SELL MY SOUL FOR A SHOOTIN' IRON THAT DON'T RUN OUTTA DADGUM AMMUNITION...
TH' END

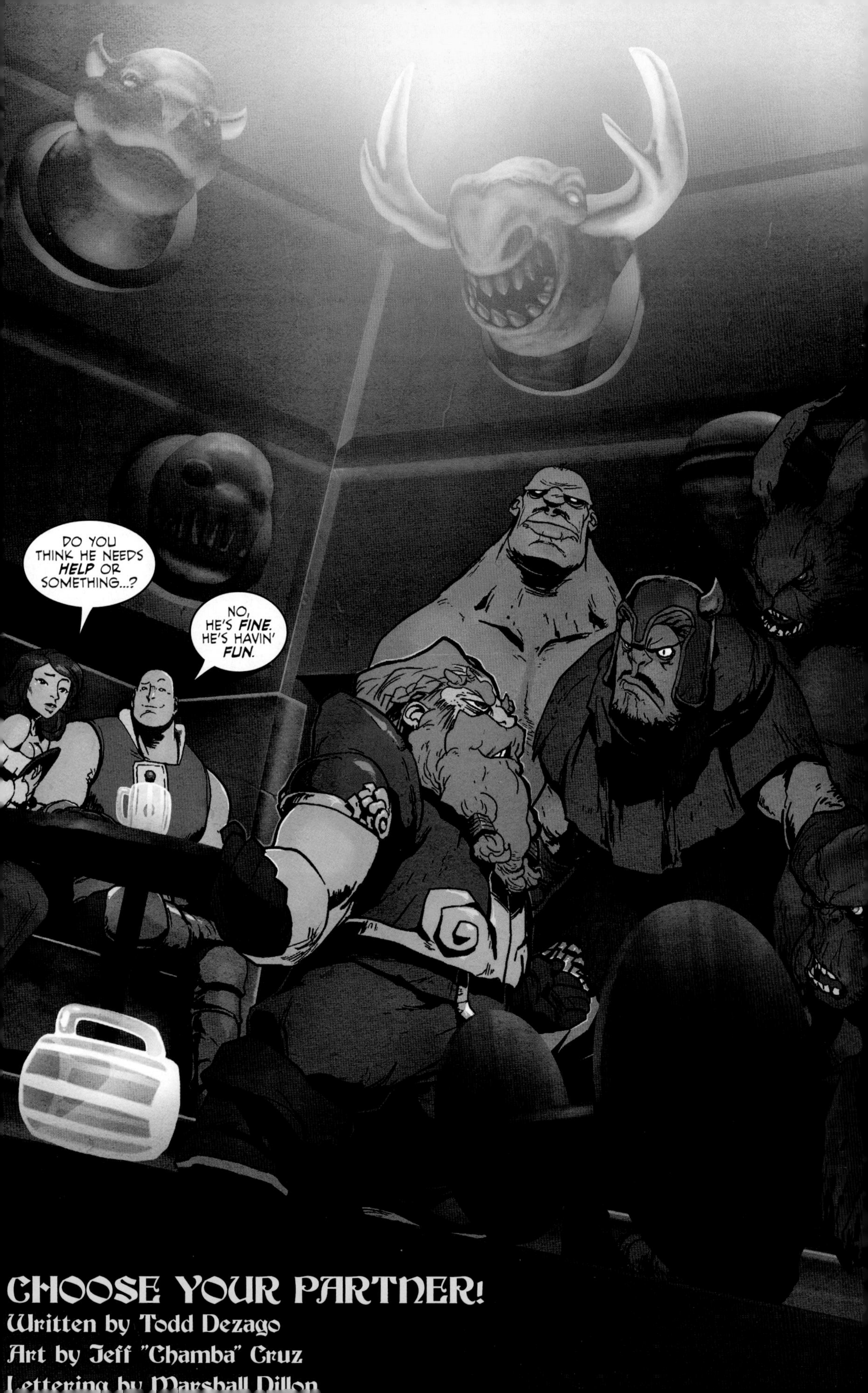
DO YOU THINK HE NEEDS HELP OR SOMETHING...?
NO, HE'S FINE. HE'S HAVIN' FUN.

CHOOSE YOUR PARTNER!

Written by Todd Dezago
Art by Jeff "Chamba" Cruz
Lettering by Marshall Dillon

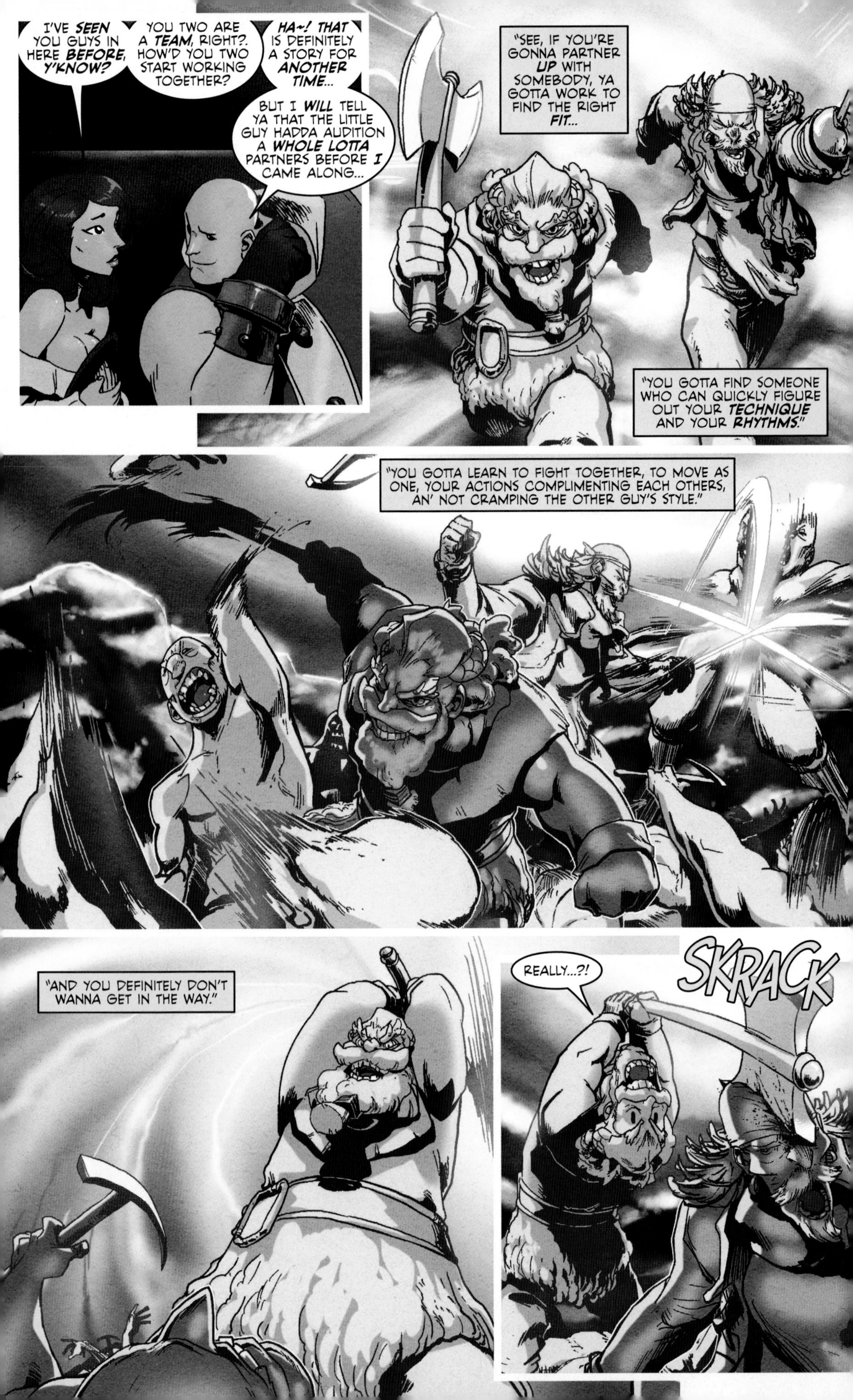
I'VE SEEN YOU GUYS IN HERE BEFORE, Y'KNOW?
YOU TWO ARE A TEAM, RIGHT?. HOW'D YOU TWO START WORKING TOGETHER?
HA~! THAT IS DEFINITELY A STORY FOR ANOTHER TIME...
BUT I WILL TELL YA THAT THE LITTLE GUY HADDA AUDITION A WHOLE LOTTA PARTNERS BEFORE I CAME ALONG...
"SEE, IF YOU'RE GONNA PARTNER UP WITH SOMEBODY, YA GOTTA WORK TO FIND THE RIGHT FIT...
"YOU GOTTA FIND SOMEONE WHO CAN QUICKLY FIGURE OUT YOUR TECHNIQUE AND YOUR RHYTHMS."
"YOU GOTTA LEARN TO FIGHT TOGETHER, TO MOVE AS ONE, YOUR ACTIONS COMPLIMENTING EACH OTHERS, AN' NOT CRAMPING THE OTHER GUY'S STYLE."
"AND YOU DEFINITELY DON'T WANNA GET IN THE WAY."
REALLY...?!
SKRACK

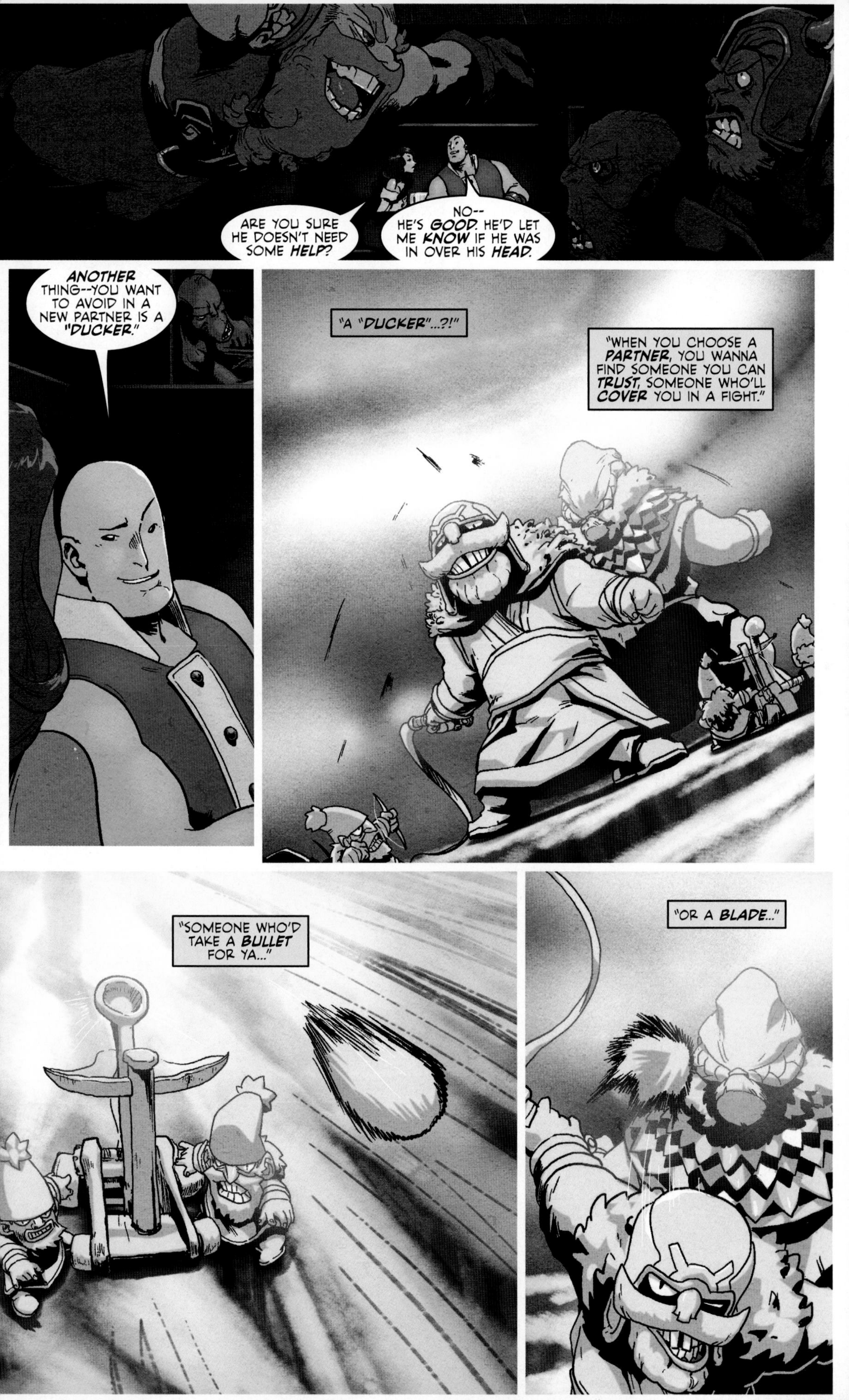
ARE YOU SURE HE DOESN'T NEED SOME HELP?
NO-- HE'S GOOD. HE'D LET ME KNOW IF HE WAS IN OVER HIS HEAD.
ANOTHER THING--YOU WANT TO AVOID IN A NEW PARTNER IS A "DUCKER."
"A "DUCKER"...?!"
"WHEN YOU CHOOSE A PARTNER, YOU WANNA FIND SOMEONE YOU CAN TRUST, SOMEONE WHO'LL COVER YOU IN A FIGHT."
"SOMEONE WHO'D TAKE A BULLET FOR YA..."
"OR A BLADE..."

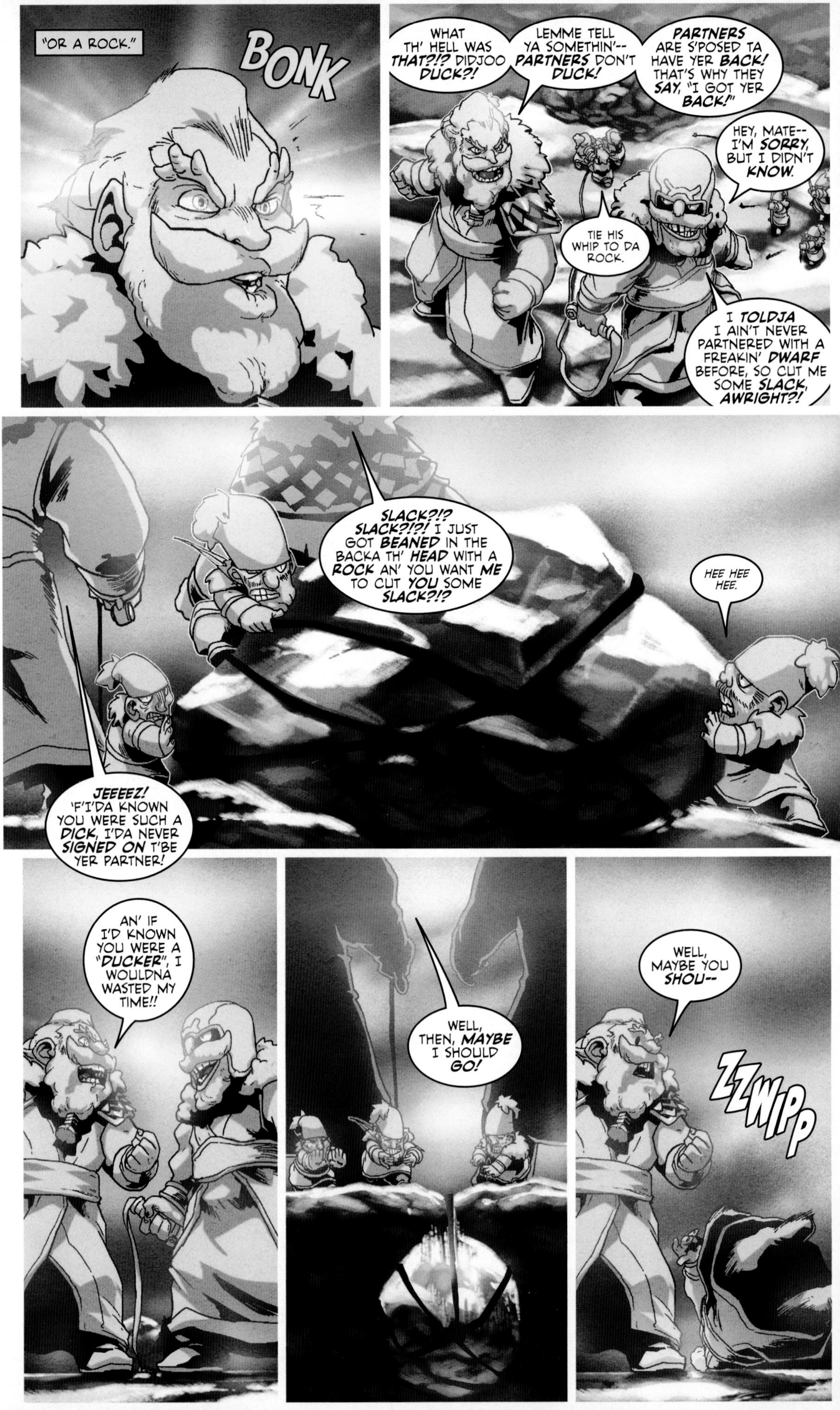
"OR A ROCK."
BONK
WHAT TH' HELL WAS THAT?!? DIDJOO DUCK?!
LEMME TELL YA SOMETHIN'-- PARTNERS DON'T DUCK!
PARTNERS ARE S'POSED TA HAVE YER BACK! THAT'S WHY THEY SAY, "I GOT YER BACK!"
HEY, MATE-- I'M SORRY, BUT I DIDN'T KNOW.
TIE HIS WHIP TO DA ROCK.
I TOLDJA I AIN'T NEVER PARTNERED WITH A FREAKIN' DWARF BEFORE, SO CUT ME SOME SLACK, AWRIGHT?!
SLACK?!? SLACK?!?! I JUST GOT BEANED IN THE BACKA TH' HEAD WITH A ROCK AN' YOU WANT ME TO CUT YOU SOME SLACK?!?
HEE HEE HEE.
JEEEEZ! 'F'I'DA KNOWN YOU WERE SUCH A DICK, I'DA NEVER SIGNED ON T'BE YER PARTNER!
AN' IF I'D KNOWN YOU WERE A "DUCKER", I WOULDNA WASTED MY TIME!!
WELL, THEN, MAYBE I SHOULD GO!
WELL, MAYBE YOU SHOU--
ZZWIPP

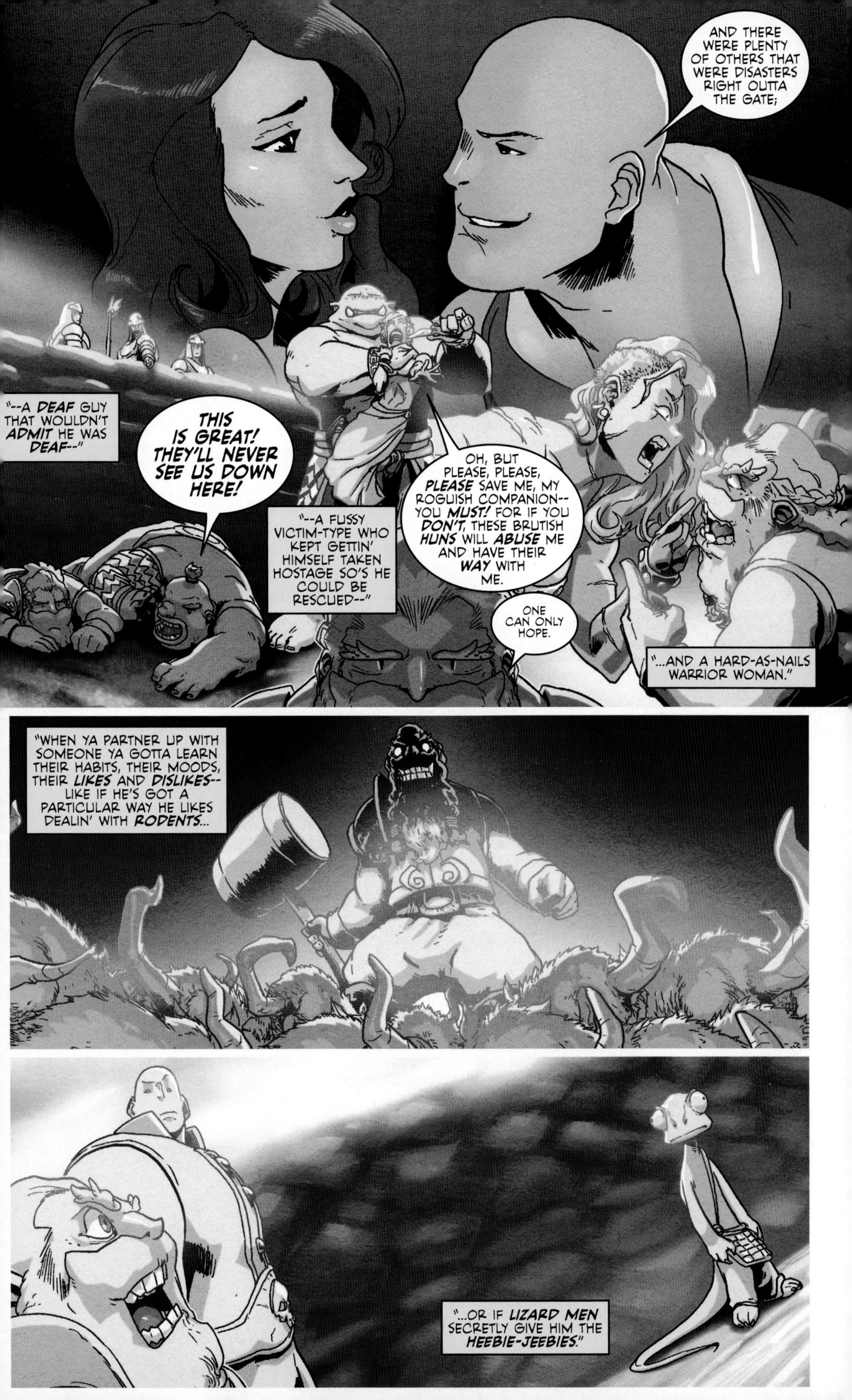
AND THERE WERE PLENTY OF OTHERS THAT WERE DISASTERS RIGHT OUTTA THE GATE;
"--A DEAF GUY THAT WOULDN'T ADMIT HE WAS DEAF--"
THIS IS GREAT! THEY'LL NEVER SEE US DOWN HERE!
"--A FUSSY VICTIM-TYPE WHO KEPT GETTIN' HIMSELF TAKEN HOSTAGE SO'S HE COULD BE RESCUED--"
OH, BUT PLEASE, PLEASE, PLEASE SAVE ME, MY ROGUISH COMPANION-- YOU MUST! FOR IF YOU DON'T, THESE BRUTISH HUNS WILL ABUSE ME AND HAVE THEIR WAY WITH ME.
ONE CAN ONLY HOPE.
"...AND A HARD-AS-NAILS WARRIOR WOMAN."
"WHEN YA PARTNER UP WITH SOMEONE YA GOTTA LEARN THEIR HABITS, THEIR MOODS, THEIR LIKES AND DISLIKES-- LIKE IF HE'S GOT A PARTICULAR WAY HE LIKES DEALIN' WITH RODENTS...
"...OR IF LIZARD MEN SECRETLY GIVE HIM THE HEEBIE-JEEBIES."

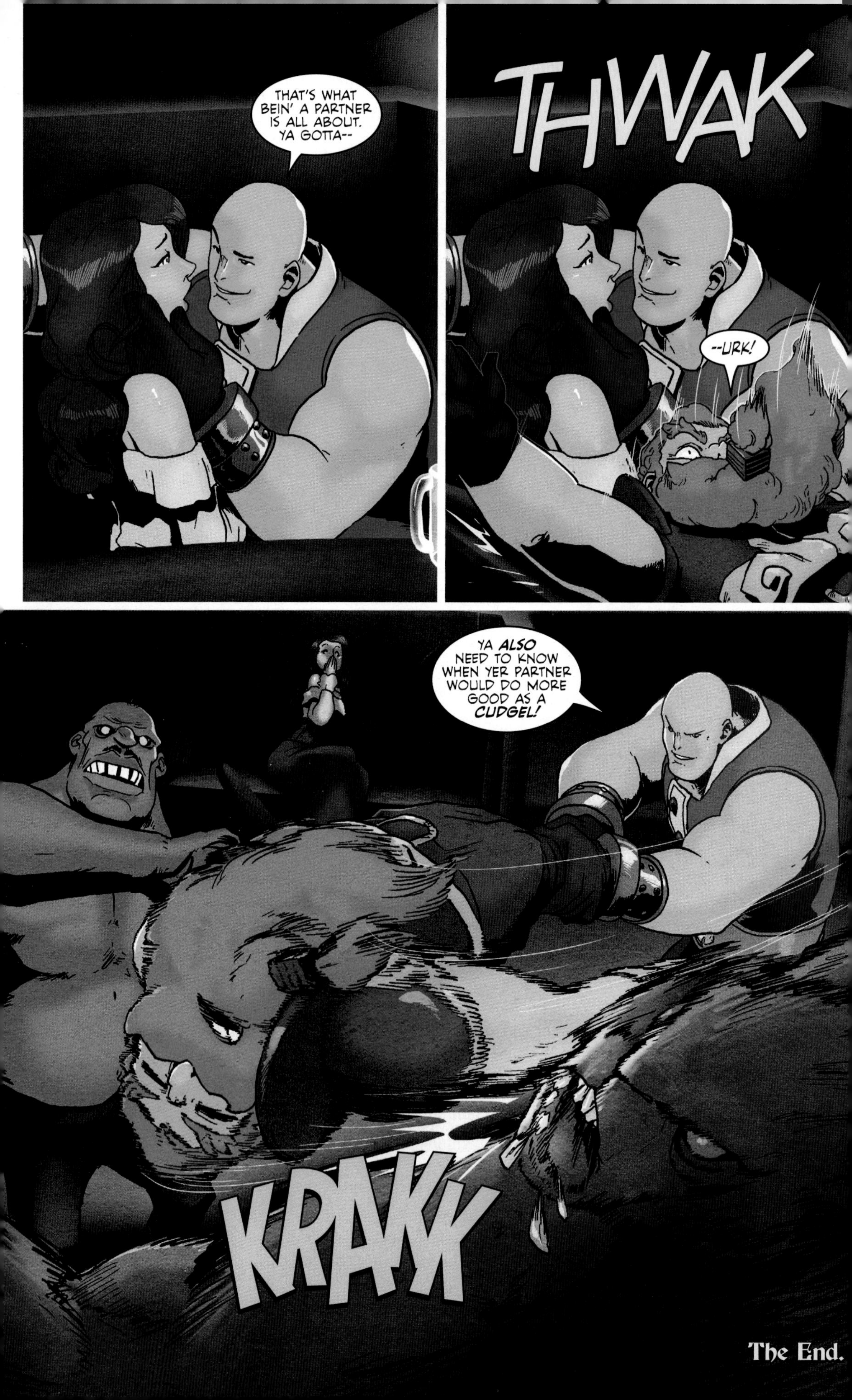
THAT'S WHAT BEIN' A PARTNER IS ALL ABOUT. YA GOTTA--
THWAK
--URK!
YA ALSO NEED TO KNOW WHEN YER PARTNER WOULD DO MORE GOOD AS A CUDGEL!
KRAKK
The End.

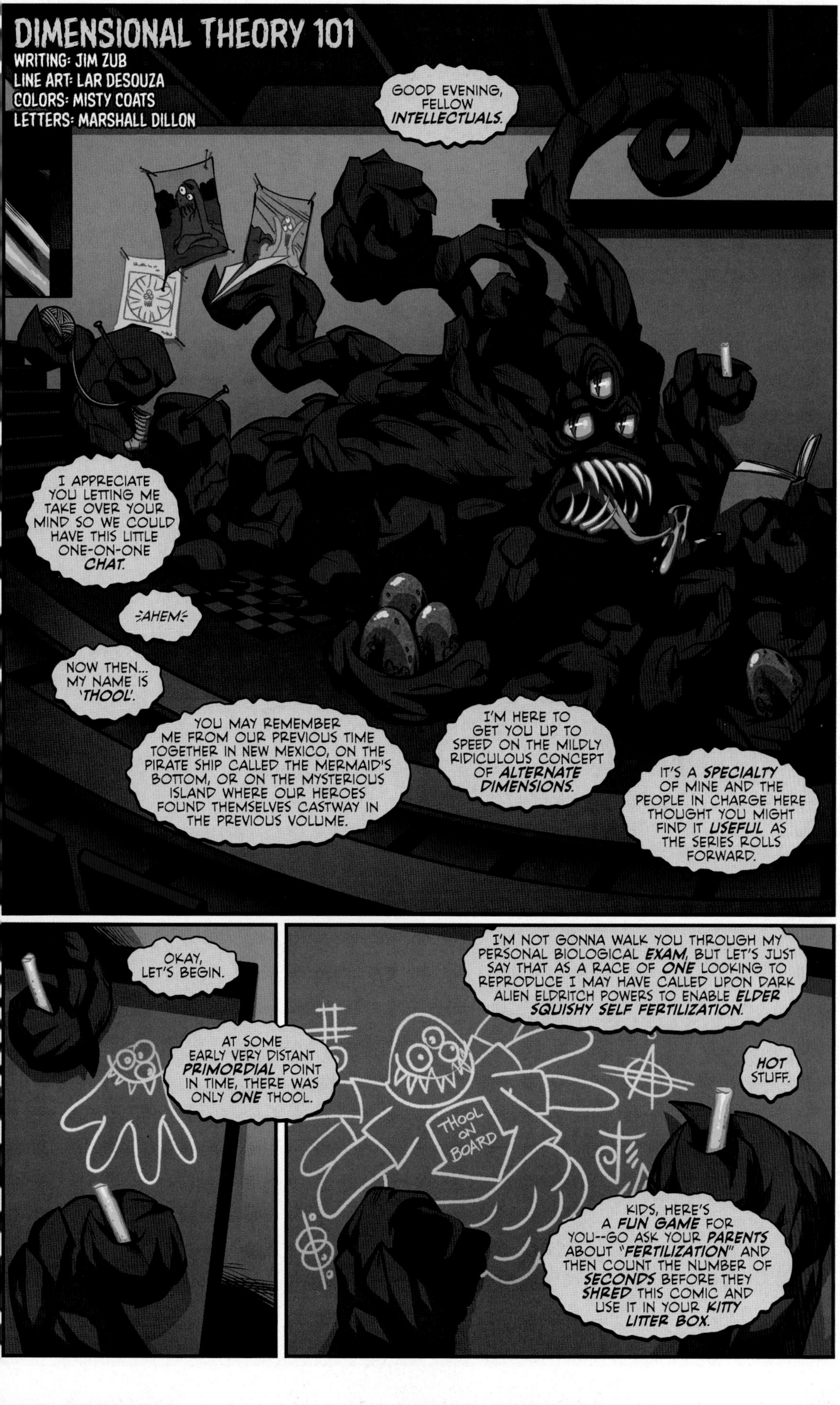
DIMENSIONAL THEORY 101
WRITING: JIM ZUB
LINE ART: LAR DESOUZA
COLORS: MISTY COATS
LETTERS: MARSHALL DILLON
GOOD EVENING, FELLOW INTELLECTUALS.
I APPRECIATE YOU LETTING ME TAKE OVER YOUR MIND SO WE COULD HAVE THIS LITTLE ONE-ON-ONE CHAT.
=AHEM=
NOW THEN... MY NAME IS 'THOOL'.
YOU MAY REMEMBER ME FROM OUR PREVIOUS TIME TOGETHER IN NEW MEXICO, ON THE PIRATE SHIP CALLED THE MERMAID'S BOTTOM, OR ON THE MYSTERIOUS ISLAND WHERE OUR HEROES FOUND THEMSELVES CASTWAY IN THE PREVIOUS VOLUME.
I'M HERE TO GET YOU UP TO SPEED ON THE MILDLY RIDICULOUS CONCEPT OF ALTERNATE DIMENSIONS.
IT'S A SPECIALTY OF MINE AND THE PEOPLE IN CHARGE HERE THOUGHT YOU MIGHT FIND IT USEFUL AS THE SERIES ROLLS FORWARD.
OKAY, LET'S BEGIN.
AT SOME EARLY VERY DISTANT PRIMORDIAL POINT IN TIME, THERE WAS ONLY ONE THOOL.
I'M NOT GONNA WALK YOU THROUGH MY PERSONAL BIOLOGICAL EXAM, BUT LET'S JUST SAY THAT AS A RACE OF ONE LOOKING TO REPRODUCE I MAY HAVE CALLED UPON DARK ALIEN ELDRITCH POWERS TO ENABLE ELDER SQUISHY SELF FERTILIZATION.
HOT STUFF.
THOOL ON BOARD
KIDS, HERE'S A FUN GAME FOR YOU--GO ASK YOUR PARENTS ABOUT "FERTILIZATION" AND THEN COUNT THE NUMBER OF SECONDS BEFORE THEY SHRED THIS COMIC AND USE IT IN YOUR KITTY LITTER BOX.

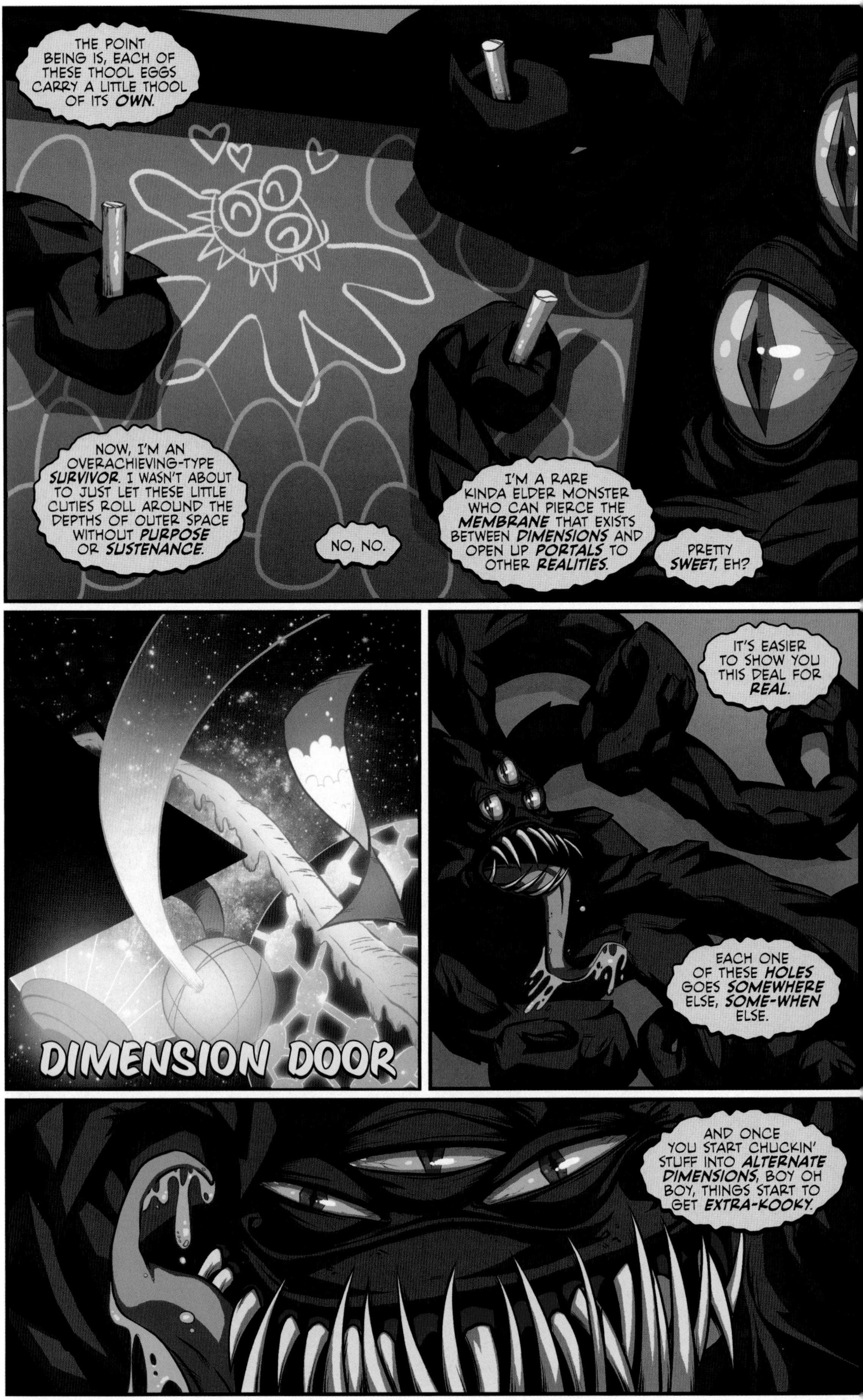
THE POINT BEING IS, EACH OF THESE THOOL EGGS CARRY A LITTLE THOOL OF ITS OWN.
NOW, I'M AN OVERACHIEVING-TYPE SURVIVOR. I WASN'T ABOUT TO JUST LET THESE LITTLE CUTIES ROLL AROUND THE DEPTHS OF OUTER SPACE WITHOUT PURPOSE OR SUSTENANCE.
NO, NO.
I'M A RARE KINDA ELDER MONSTER WHO CAN PIERCE THE MEMBRANE THAT EXISTS BETWEEN DIMENSIONS AND OPEN UP PORTALS TO OTHER REALITIES.
PRETTY SWEET, EH?
DIMENSION DOOR
IT'S EASIER TO SHOW YOU THIS DEAL FOR REAL.
EACH ONE OF THESE HOLES GOES SOMEWHERE ELSE, SOME-WHEN ELSE.
AND ONCE YOU START CHUCKIN' STUFF INTO ALTERNATE DIMENSIONS, BOY OH BOY, THINGS START TO GET EXTRA-KOOKY.

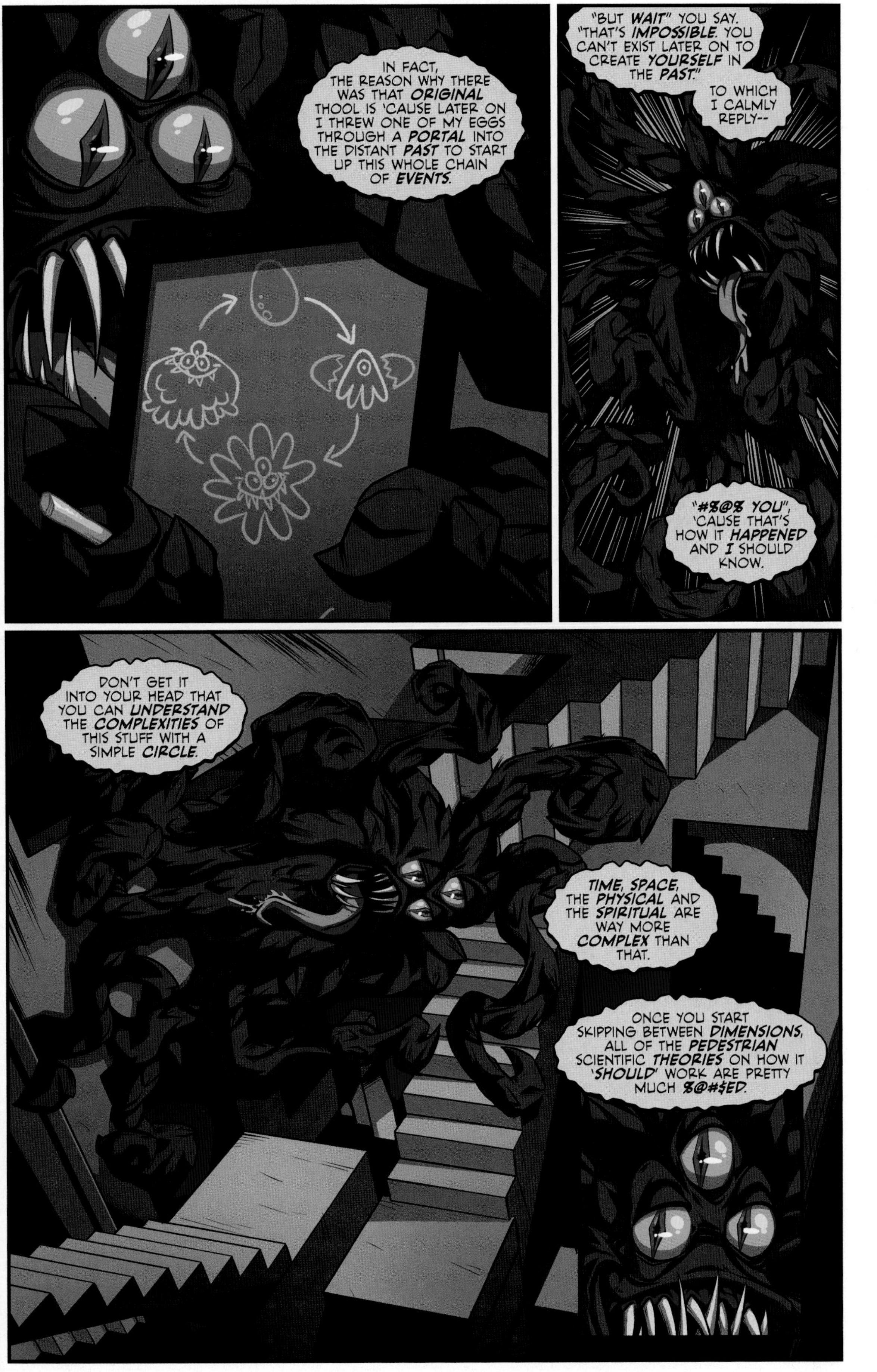

IN FACT, THE REASON WHY THERE WAS THAT ORIGINAL THOOL IS 'CAUSE LATER ON I THREW ONE OF MY EGGS THROUGH A PORTAL INTO THE DISTANT PAST TO START UP THIS WHOLE CHAIN OF EVENTS.
"BUT WAIT" YOU SAY. "THAT'S IMPOSSIBLE. YOU CAN'T EXIST LATER ON TO CREATE YOURSELF IN THE PAST."
TO WHICH I CALMLY REPLY--
"#%@% YOU", 'CAUSE THAT'S HOW IT HAPPENED AND I SHOULD KNOW.
DON'T GET IT INTO YOUR HEAD THAT YOU CAN UNDERSTAND THE COMPLEXITIES OF THIS STUFF WITH A SIMPLE CIRCLE.
TIME, SPACE, THE PHYSICAL AND THE SPIRITUAL ARE WAY MORE COMPLEX THAN THAT.
ONCE YOU START SKIPPING BETWEEN DIMENSIONS, ALL OF THE PEDESTRIAN SCIENTIFIC THEORIES ON HOW IT 'SHOULD' WORK ARE PRETTY MUCH %@#$ED.

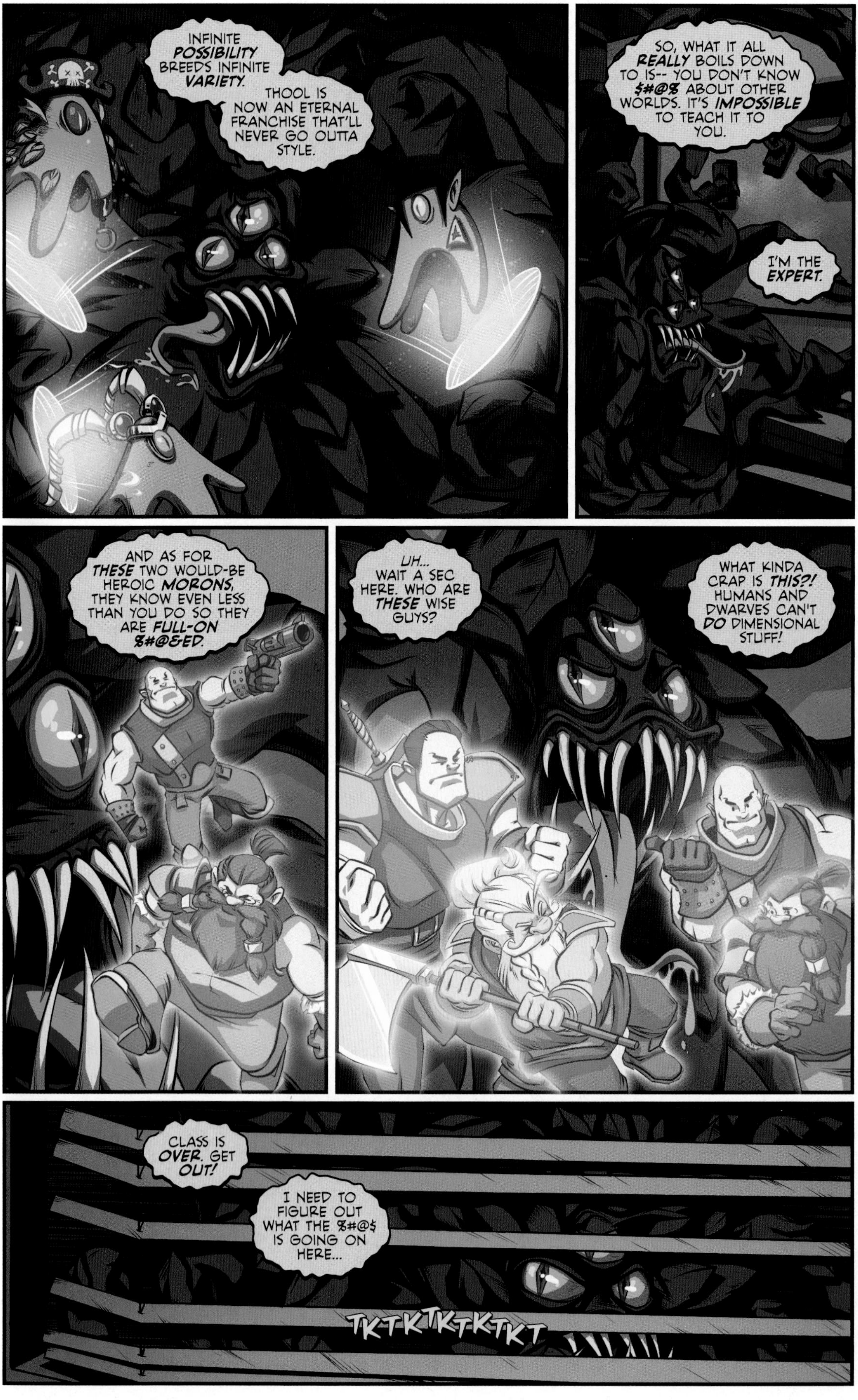
INFINITE POSSIBILITY BREEDS INFINITE VARIETY.
THOOL IS NOW AN ETERNAL FRANCHISE THAT'LL NEVER GO OUTTA STYLE.
SO, WHAT IT ALL REALLY BOILS DOWN TO IS-- YOU DON'T KNOW $#@$ ABOUT OTHER WORLDS. IT'S IMPOSSIBLE TO TEACH IT TO YOU.
I'M THE EXPERT.
AND AS FOR THESE TWO WOULD-BE HEROIC MORONS, THEY KNOW EVEN LESS THAN YOU DO SO THEY ARE FULL-ON %#@&ED.
UH... WAIT A SEC HERE. WHO ARE THESE WISE GUYS?
WHAT KINDA CRAP IS THIS?! HUMANS AND DWARVES CAN'T DO DIMENSIONAL STUFF!
CLASS IS OVER. GET OUT!
I NEED TO FIGURE OUT WHAT THE %#@$ IS GOING ON HERE...
TKTKTKTKTKTKT

CHAPTER ONE

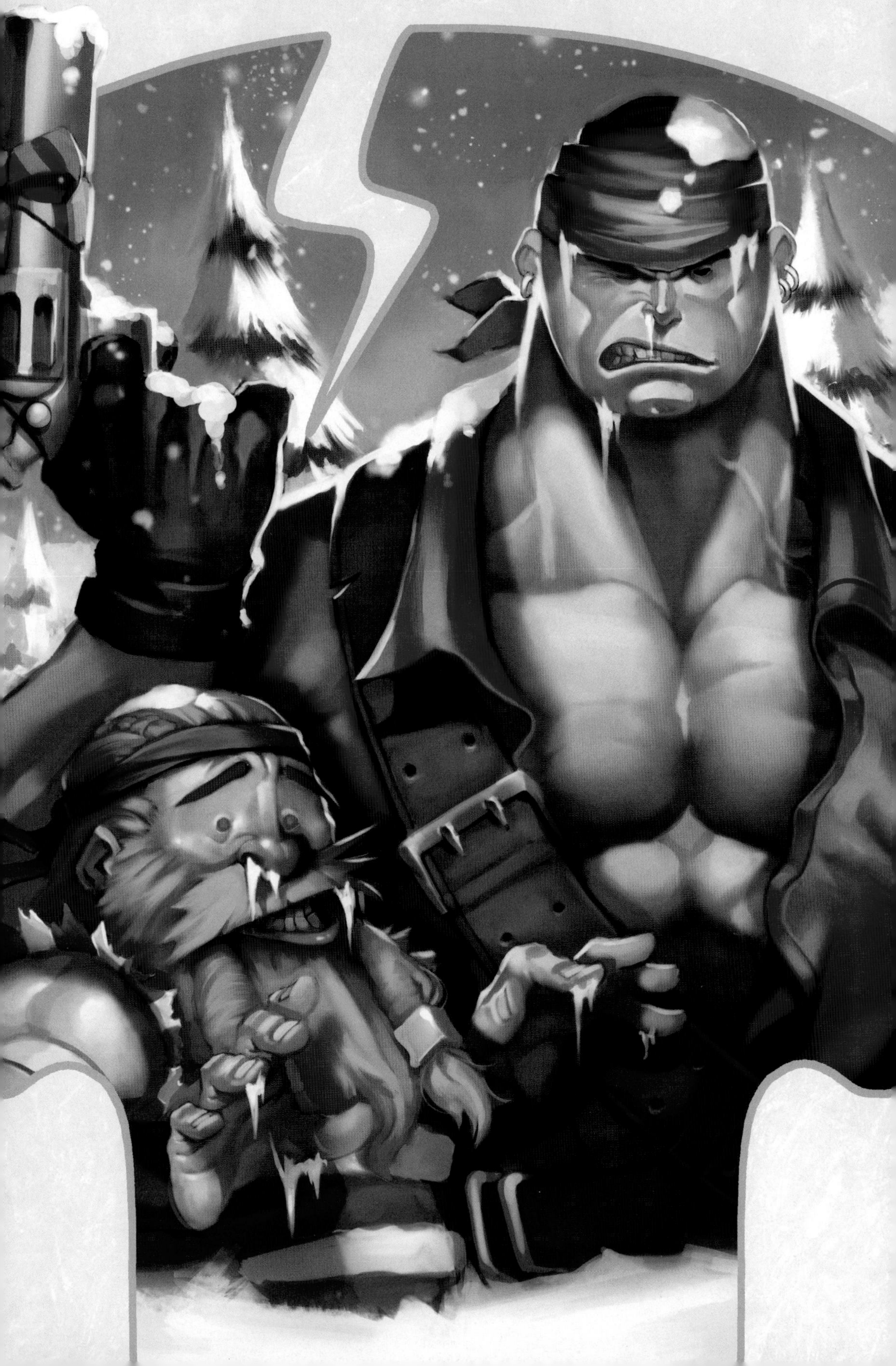

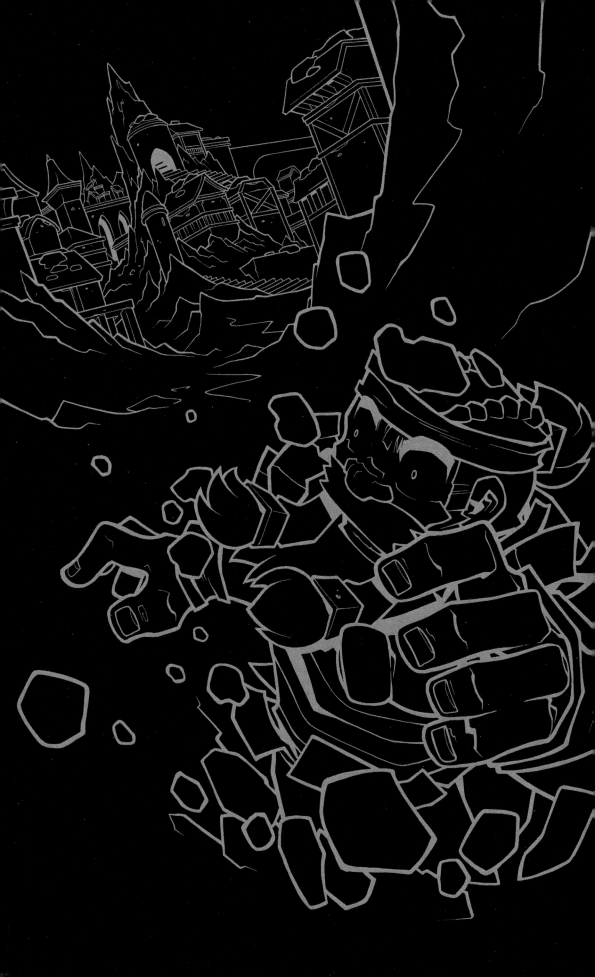

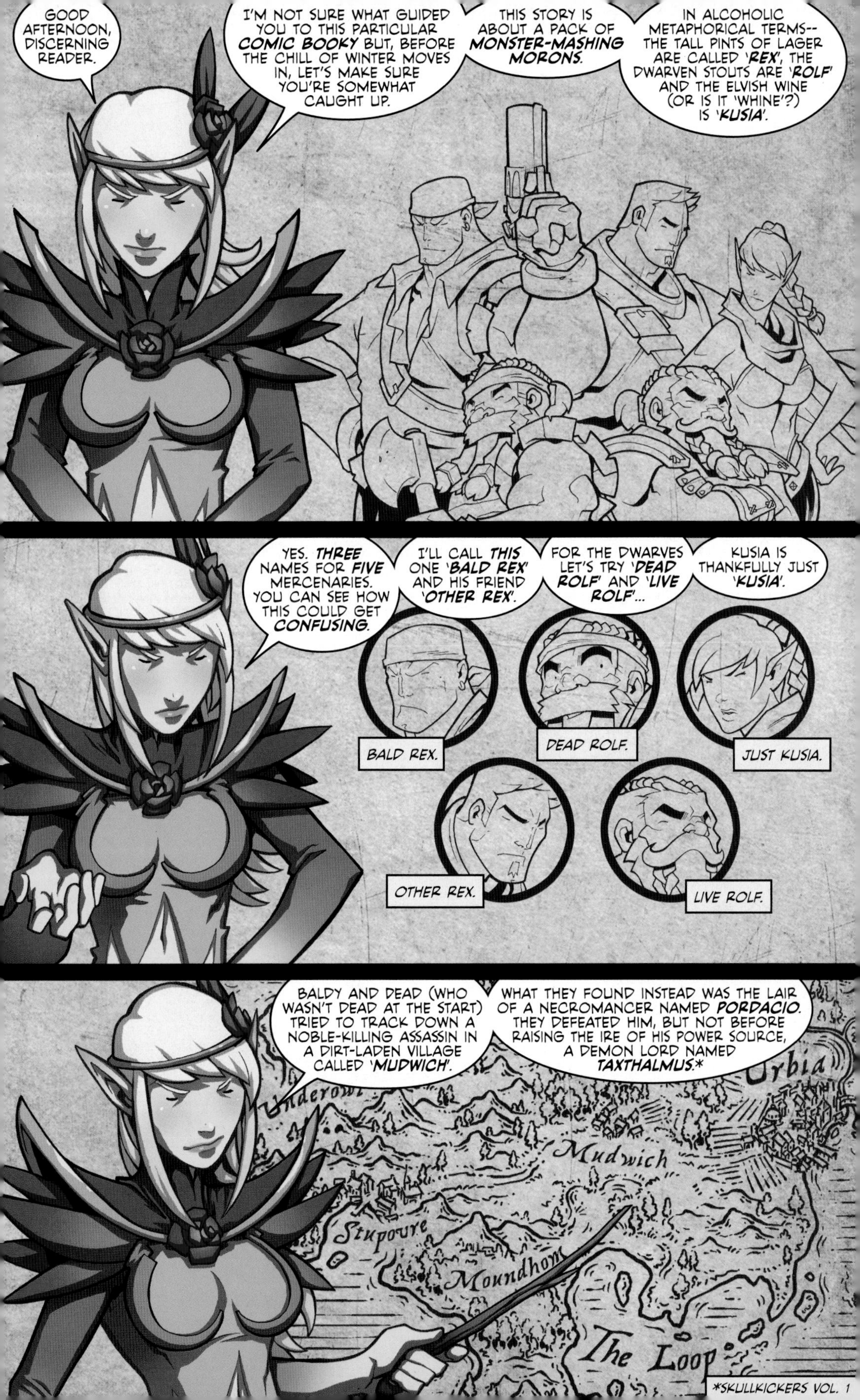
GOOD AFTERNOON, DISCERNING READER.
I'M NOT SURE WHAT GUIDED YOU TO THIS PARTICULAR COMIC BOOKY BUT, BEFORE THE CHILL OF WINTER MOVES IN, LET'S MAKE SURE YOU'RE SOMEWHAT CAUGHT UP.
THIS STORY IS ABOUT A PACK OF MONSTER-MASHING MORONS.
IN ALCOHOLIC METAPHORICAL TERMS-- THE TALL PINTS OF LAGER ARE CALLED 'REX', THE DWARVEN STOUTS ARE 'ROLF' AND THE ELVISH WINE (OR IS IT 'WHINE'?) IS 'KUSIA'.
YES. THREE NAMES FOR FIVE MERCENARIES. YOU CAN SEE HOW THIS COULD GET CONFUSING.
I'LL CALL THIS ONE 'BALD REX' AND HIS FRIEND 'OTHER REX'.
FOR THE DWARVES LET'S TRY 'DEAD ROLF' AND 'LIVE ROLF'...
KUSIA IS THANKFULLY JUST 'KUSIA'.
BALD REX.
DEAD ROLF.
JUST KUSIA.
OTHER REX.
LIVE ROLF.
BALDY AND DEAD (WHO WASN'T DEAD AT THE START) TRIED TO TRACK DOWN A NOBLE-KILLING ASSASSIN IN A DIRT-LADEN VILLAGE CALLED 'MUDWICH'.
WHAT THEY FOUND INSTEAD WAS THE LAIR OF A NECROMANCER NAMED PORDACIO. THEY DEFEATED HIM, BUT NOT BEFORE RAISING THE IRE OF HIS POWER SOURCE, A DEMON LORD NAMED TAXTHALMUS.*
Urbia
Mudwich
Stupoure
Moundhom
The Loop
*SKULLKICKERS VOL. 1

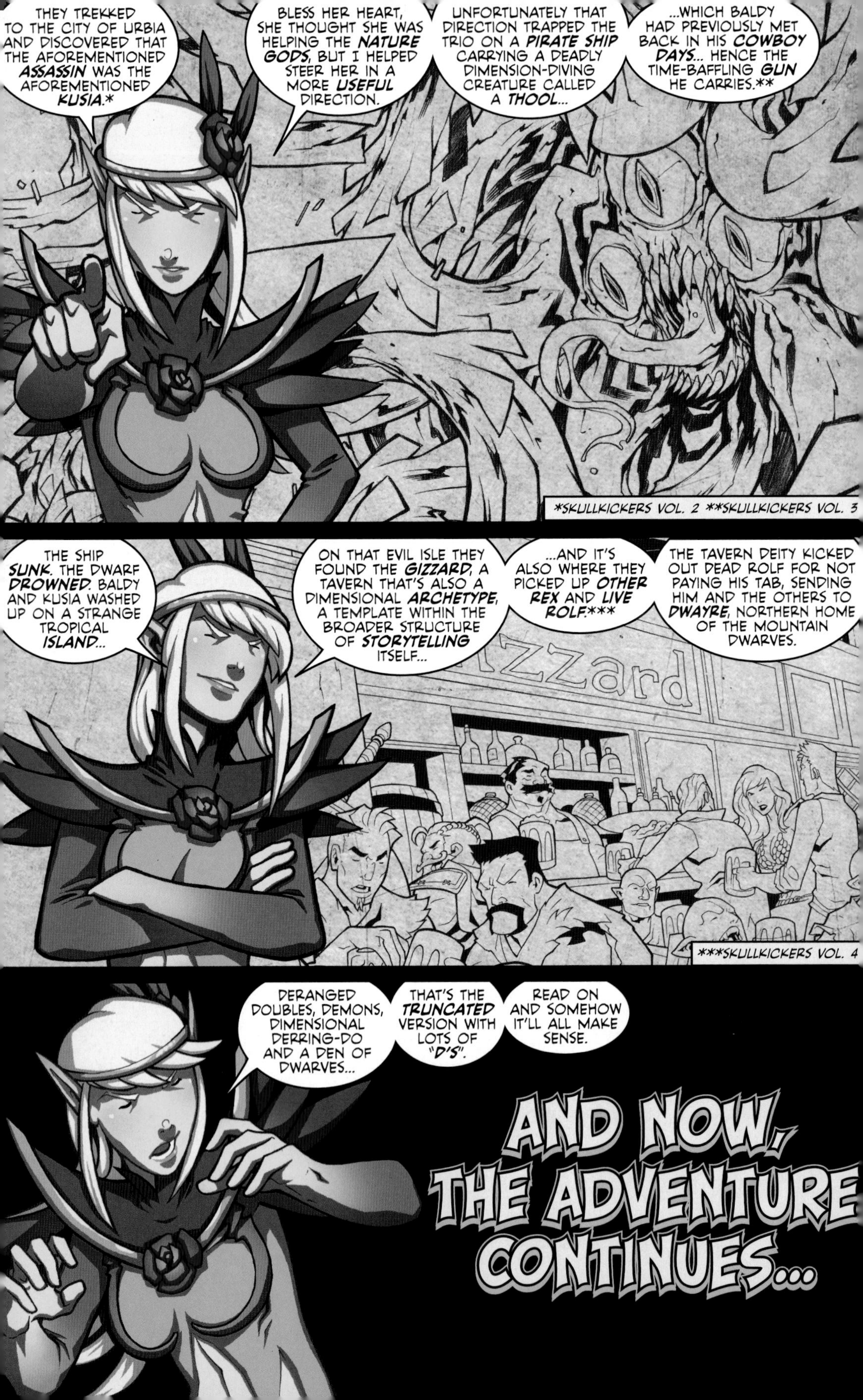
THEY TREKKED TO THE CITY OF URBIA AND DISCOVERED THAT THE AFOREMENTIONED ASSASSIN WAS THE AFOREMENTIONED KUSIA.*
BLESS HER HEART, SHE THOUGHT SHE WAS HELPING THE NATURE GODS, BUT I HELPED STEER HER IN A MORE USEFUL DIRECTION.
UNFORTUNATELY THAT DIRECTION TRAPPED THE TRIO ON A PIRATE SHIP CARRYING A DEADLY DIMENSION-DIVING CREATURE CALLED A THOOL...
...WHICH BALDY HAD PREVIOUSLY MET BACK IN HIS COWBOY DAYS... HENCE THE TIME-BAFFLING GUN HE CARRIES.**
*SKULLKICKERS VOL. 2 **SKULLKICKERS VOL. 3
THE SHIP SUNK. THE DWARF DROWNED. BALDY AND KUSIA WASHED UP ON A STRANGE TROPICAL ISLAND...
ON THAT EVIL ISLE THEY FOUND THE GIZZARD, A TAVERN THAT'S ALSO A DIMENSIONAL ARCHETYPE, A TEMPLATE WITHIN THE BROADER STRUCTURE OF STORYTELLING ITSELF...
...AND IT'S ALSO WHERE THEY PICKED UP OTHER REX AND LIVE ROLF.***
THE TAVERN DEITY KICKED OUT DEAD ROLF FOR NOT PAYING HIS TAB, SENDING HIM AND THE OTHERS TO DWAYRE, NORTHERN HOME OF THE MOUNTAIN DWARVES.
***SKULLKICKERS VOL. 4
DERANGED DOUBLES, DEMONS, DIMENSIONAL DERRING-DO AND A DEN OF DWARVES...
THAT'S THE TRUNCATED VERSION WITH LOTS OF "D'S".
READ ON AND SOMEHOW IT'LL ALL MAKE SENSE.
AND NOW, THE ADVENTURE CONTINUES...

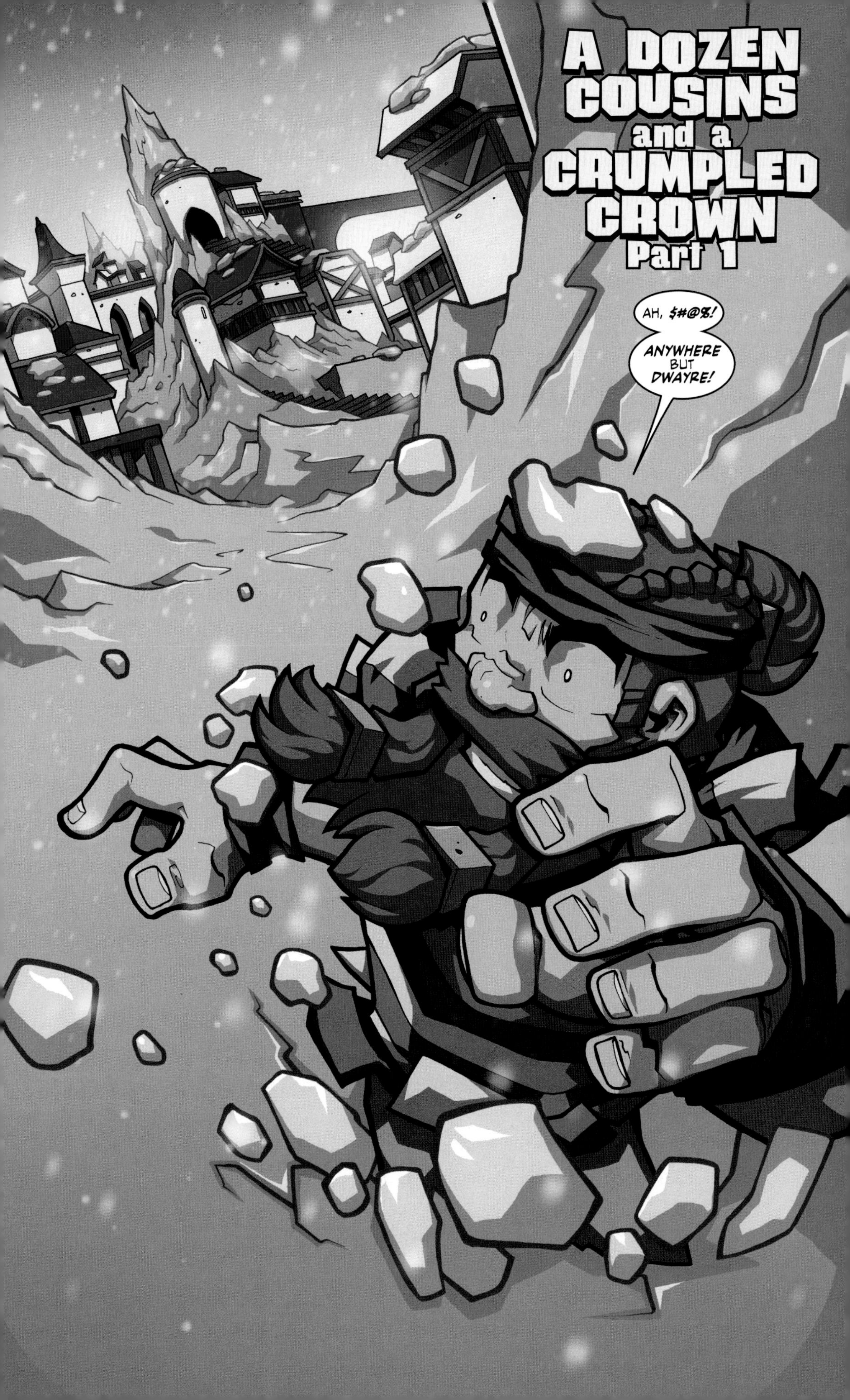
A DOZEN COUSINS and a CRUMPLED CROWN
Part 1
AH, $#@%!
ANYWHERE BUT DWAYRE!

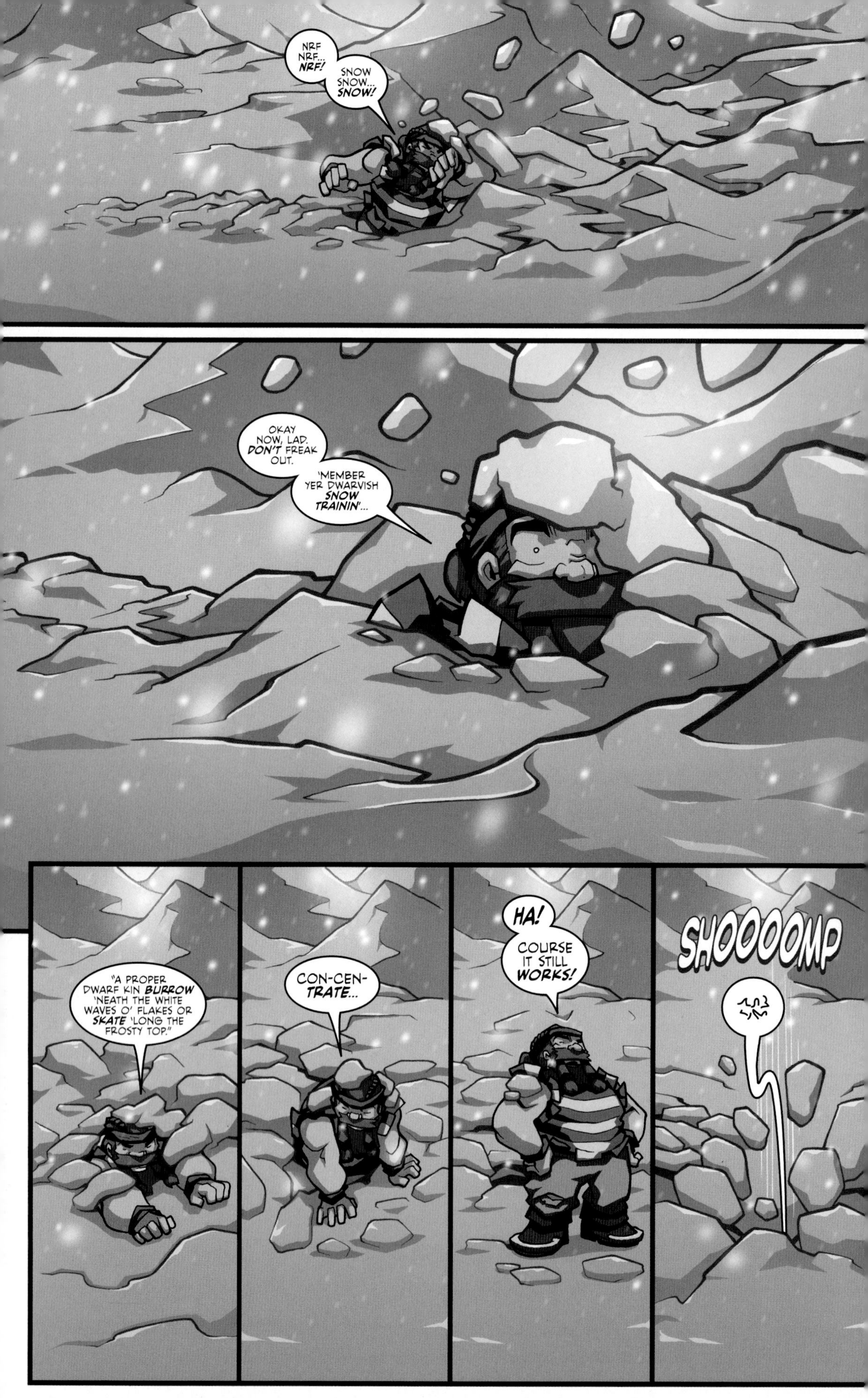
NRF NRF... NRF!
SNOW SNOW... SNOW!
OKAY NOW, LAD. DON'T FREAK OUT.
'MEMBER YER DWARVISH SNOW TRAININ'...
"A PROPER DWARF KIN BURROW 'NEATH THE WHITE WAVES O' FLAKES OR SKATE 'LONG THE FROSTY TOP."
CON-CEN-TRATE...
HA!
COURSE IT STILL WORKS!
SHOOOOMP

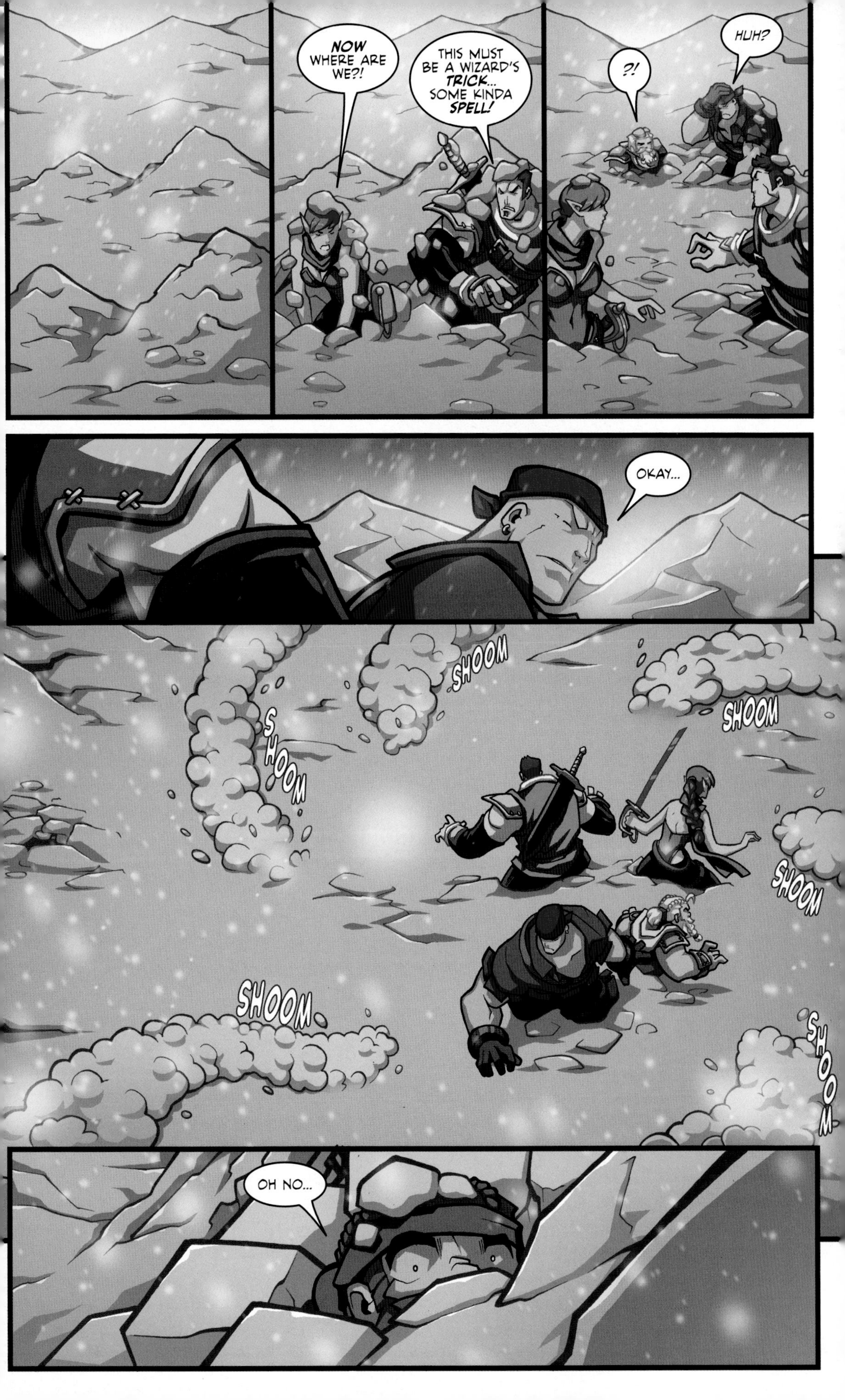
NOW WHERE ARE WE?!
THIS MUST BE A WIZARD'S TRICK... SOME KINDA SPELL!
?!
HUH?
OKAY...
SHOOM
SHOOM
SHOOM
SHOOM
SHOOM
SHOOM
OH NO...

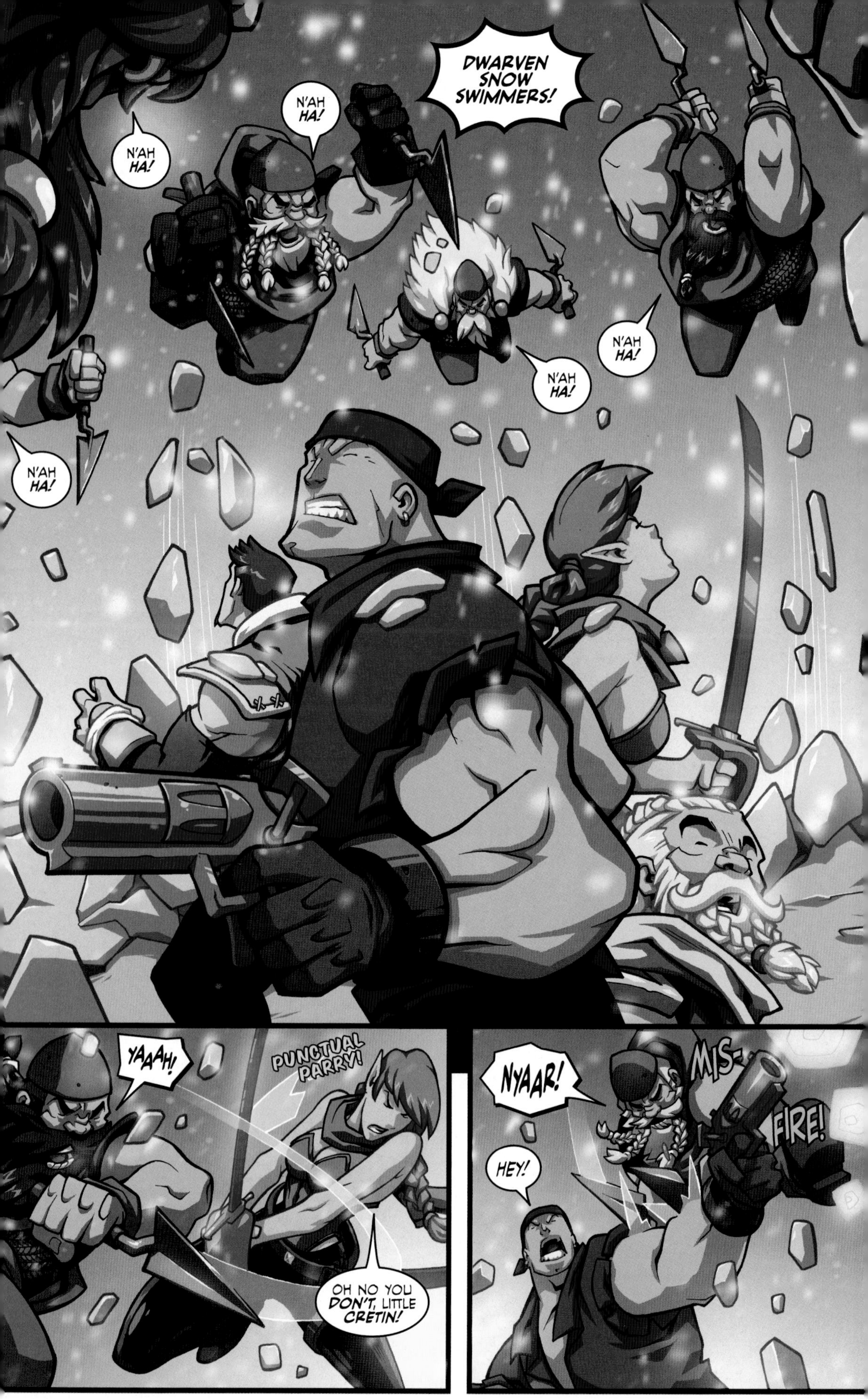
DWARVEN SNOW SWIMMERS!
N'AH HA!
N'AH HA!
N'AH HA!
N'AH HA!
N'AH HA!
YAAAH!
PUNCTUAL PARRY!
OH NO YOU DON'T, LITTLE CRETIN!
NYAAR!
MIS-
FIRE!
HEY!

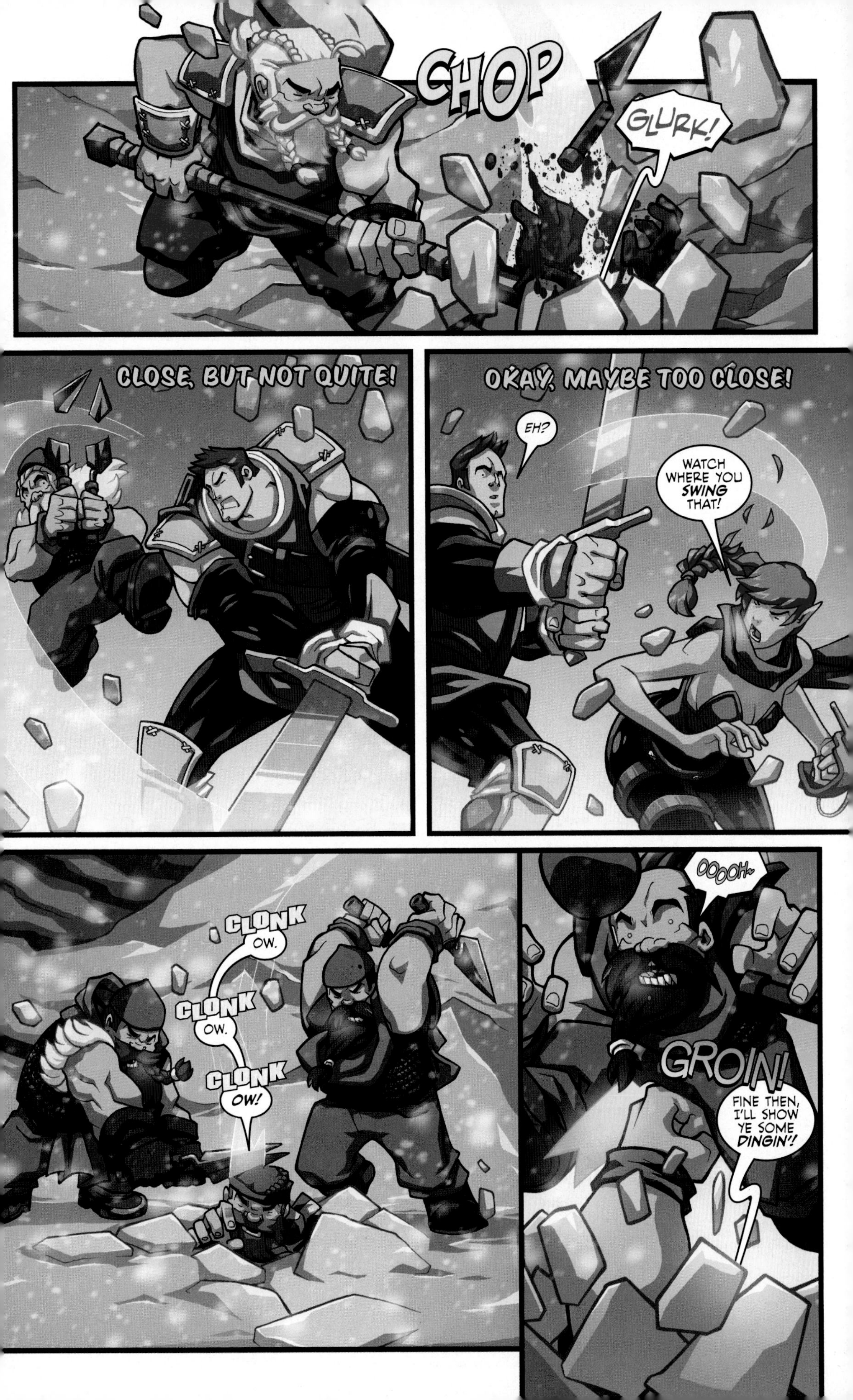
CHOP
GLURK!
CLOSE, BUT NOT QUITE!
OKAY, MAYBE TOO CLOSE!
EH?
WATCH WHERE YOU SWING THAT!
CLONK
OW.
CLONK
OW.
CLONK
OW!
OOOOH~
GROIN!
FINE THEN, I'LL SHOW YE SOME DINGIN'!

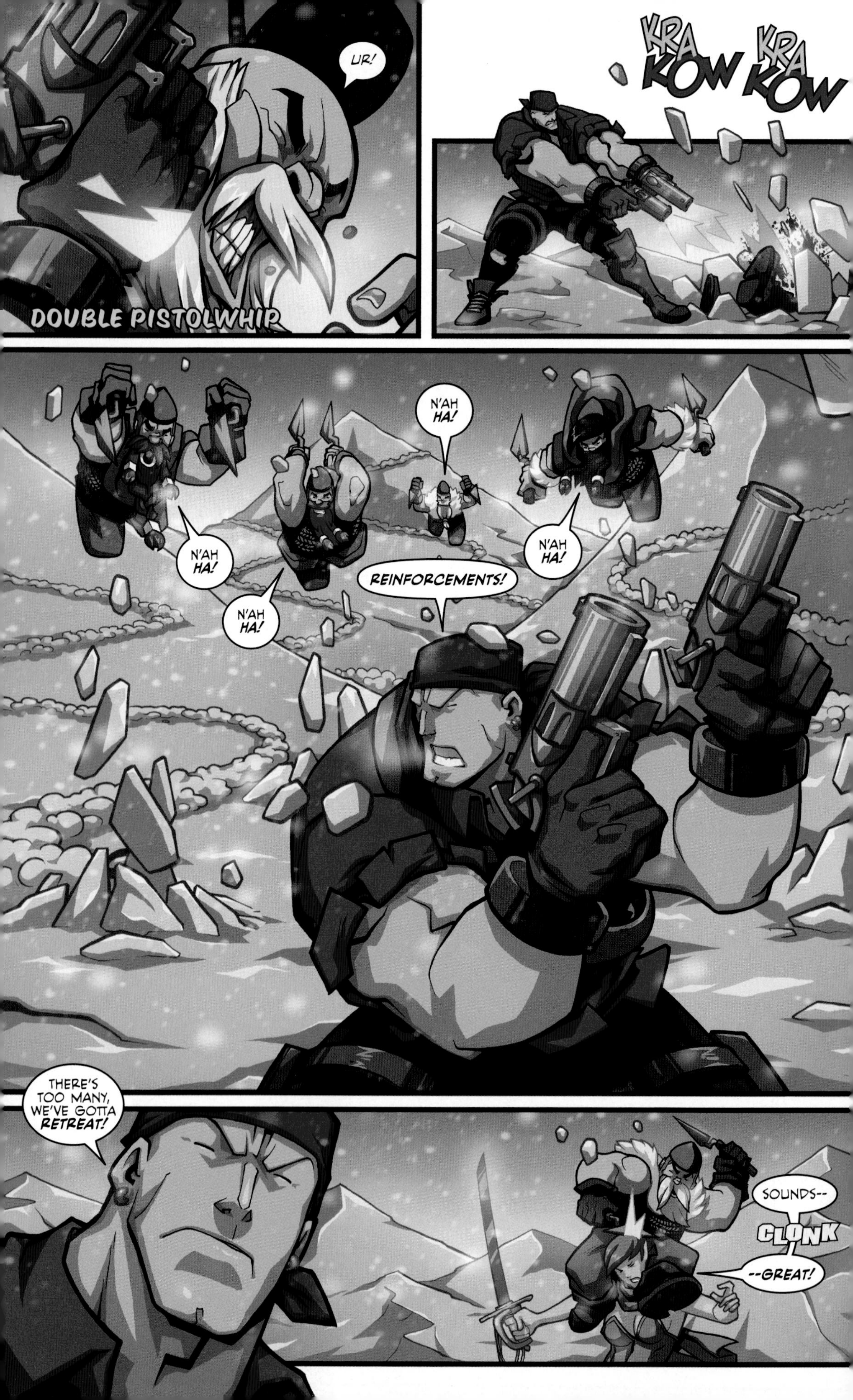
UR!
DOUBLE PISTOLWHIP
KRA KOW KRA KOW
N'AH HA!
N'AH HA!
N'AH HA!
N'AH HA!
REINFORCEMENTS!
THERE'S TOO MANY, WE'VE GOTTA RETREAT!
SOUNDS--
CLONK
--GREAT!

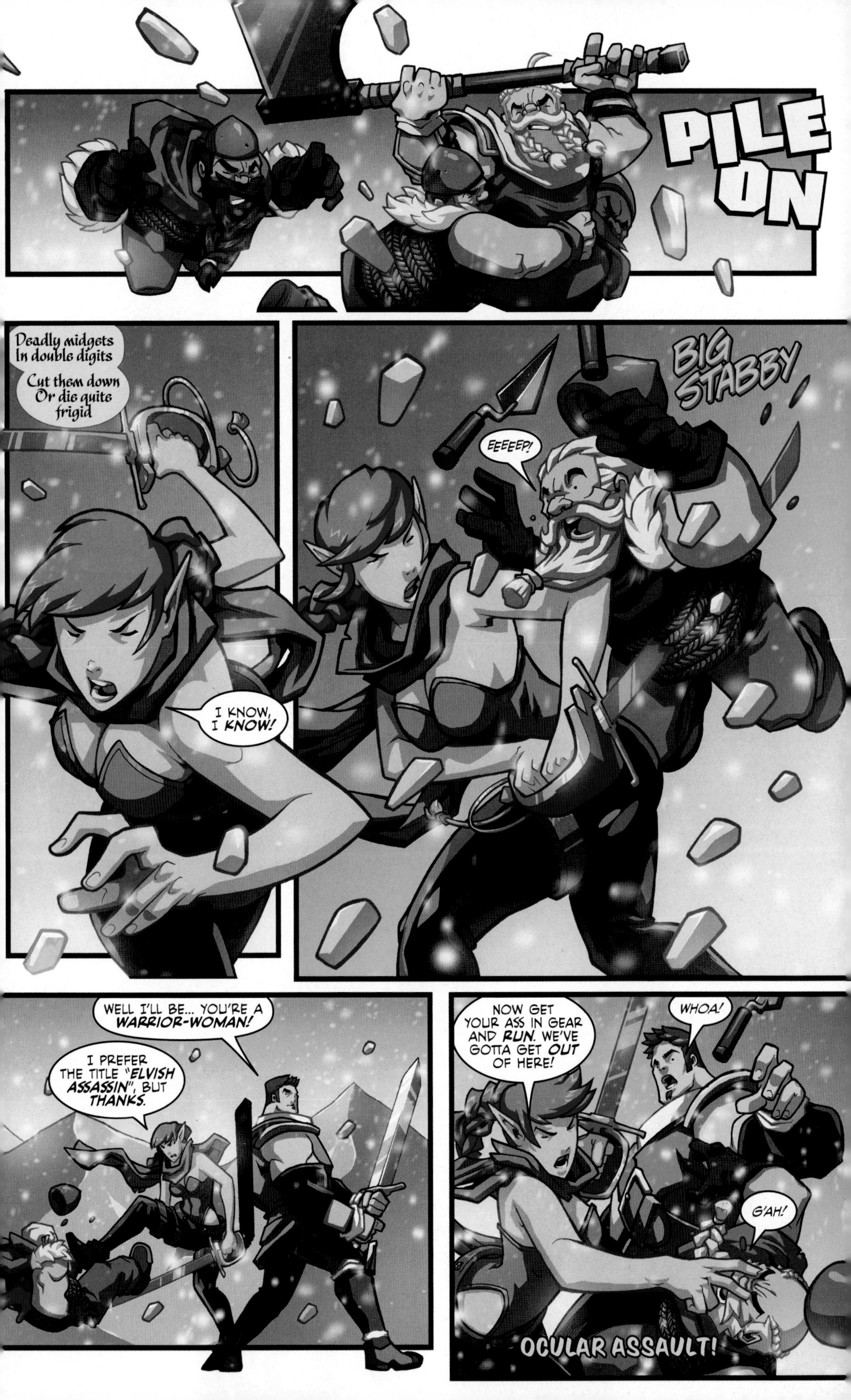
PILE ON
Deadly midgets
In double digits
Cut them down
Or die quite
frigid
BIG STABBY
EEEEEP!
I KNOW, I KNOW!
WELL I'LL BE... YOU'RE A WARRIOR-WOMAN!
I PREFER THE TITLE "ELVISH ASSASSIN", BUT THANKS.
NOW GET YOUR ASS IN GEAR AND RUN. WE'VE GOTTA GET OUT OF HERE!
WHOA!
G'AH!
OCULAR ASSAULT!

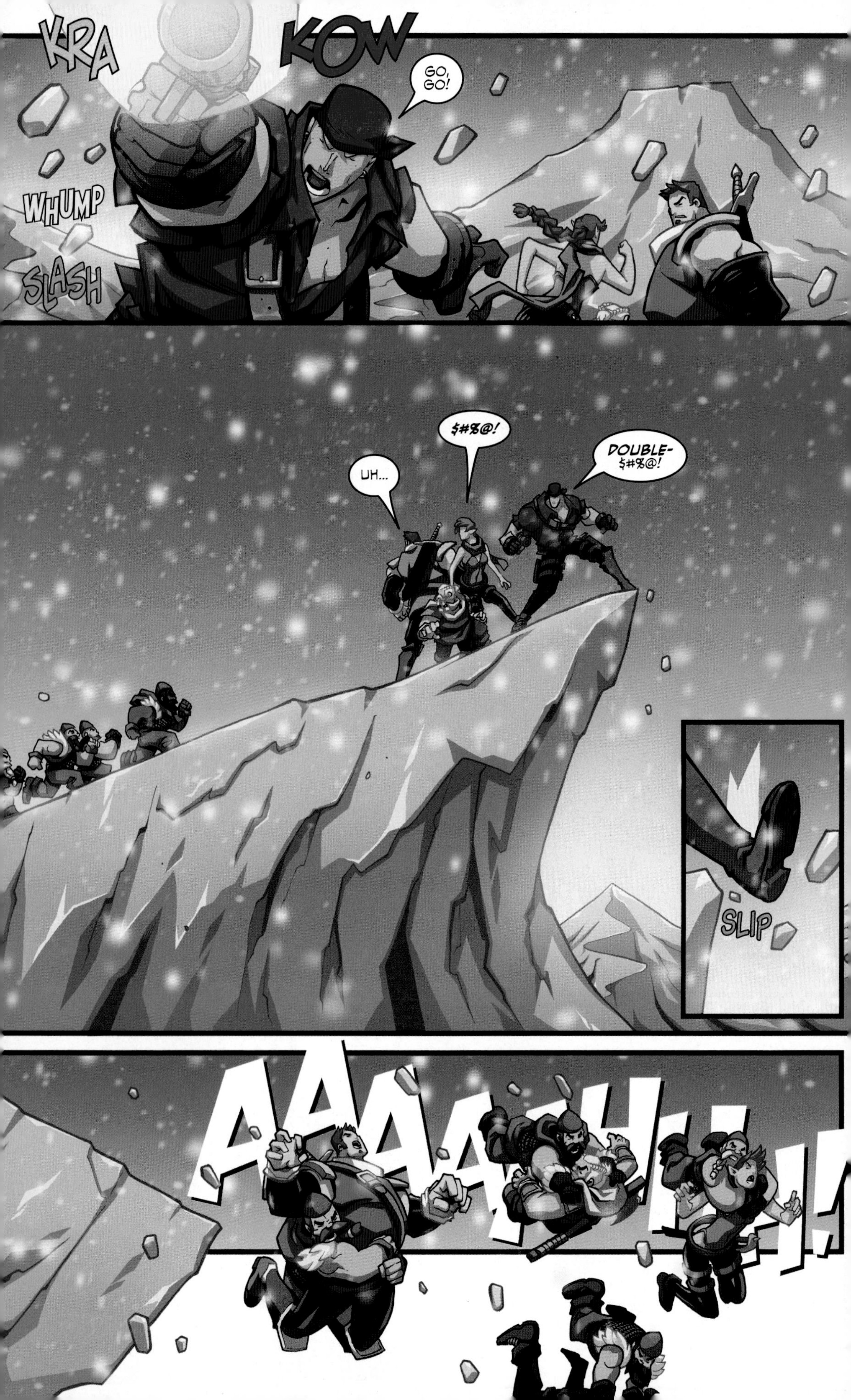
KRA
KOW
GO, GO!
WHUMP
SLASH
UH...
$#%@!
DOUBLE-$#%@!
SLIP
AAAAHHH!

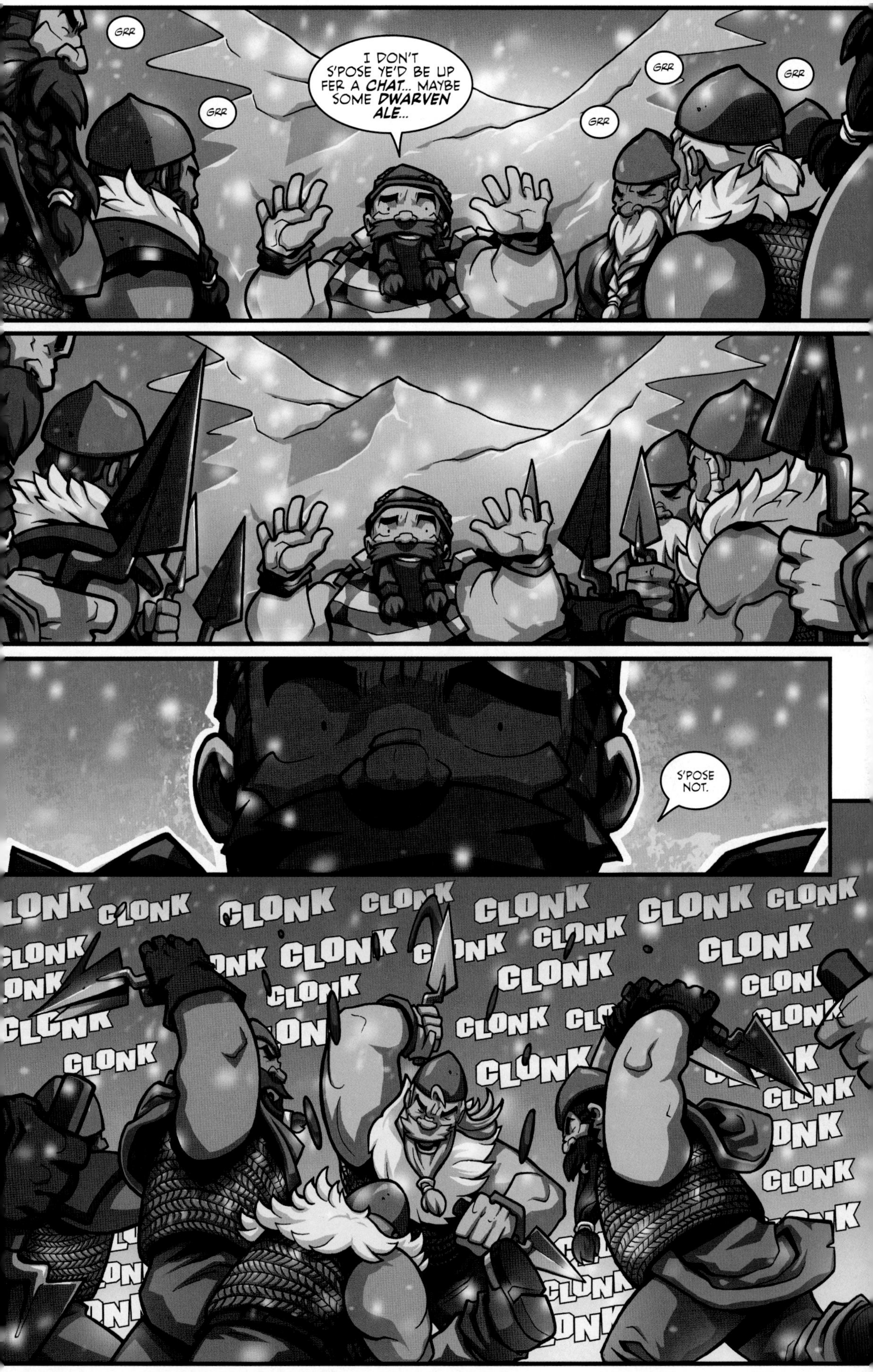
GRR
GRR
I DON'T S'POSE YE'D BE UP FER A *CHAT*... MAYBE SOME ***DWARVEN ALE***...
GRR
GRR
GRR
S'POSE NOT.
CLONK
CLONK
CLONK
CLONK
CLONK
CLONK
CLONK
CLONK
CLONK
CLONK
CLONK
CLONK
CLONK

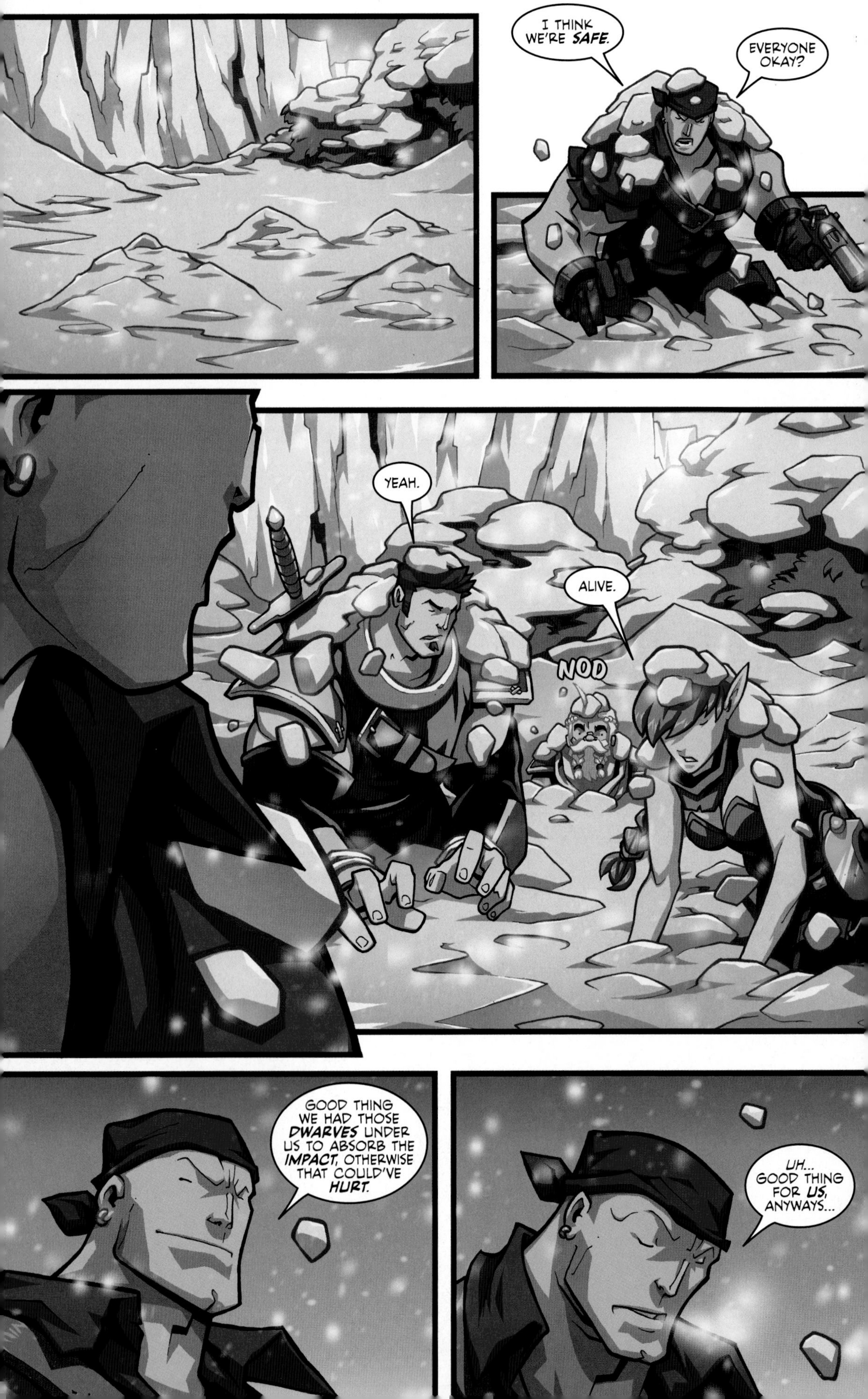

I THINK WE'RE *SAFE*.
EVERYONE OKAY?
YEAH.
ALIVE.
NOD
GOOD THING WE HAD THOSE *DWARVES* UNDER US TO ABSORB THE *IMPACT*, OTHERWISE THAT COULD'VE *HURT*.
UH... GOOD THING FOR *US*, ANYWAYS...

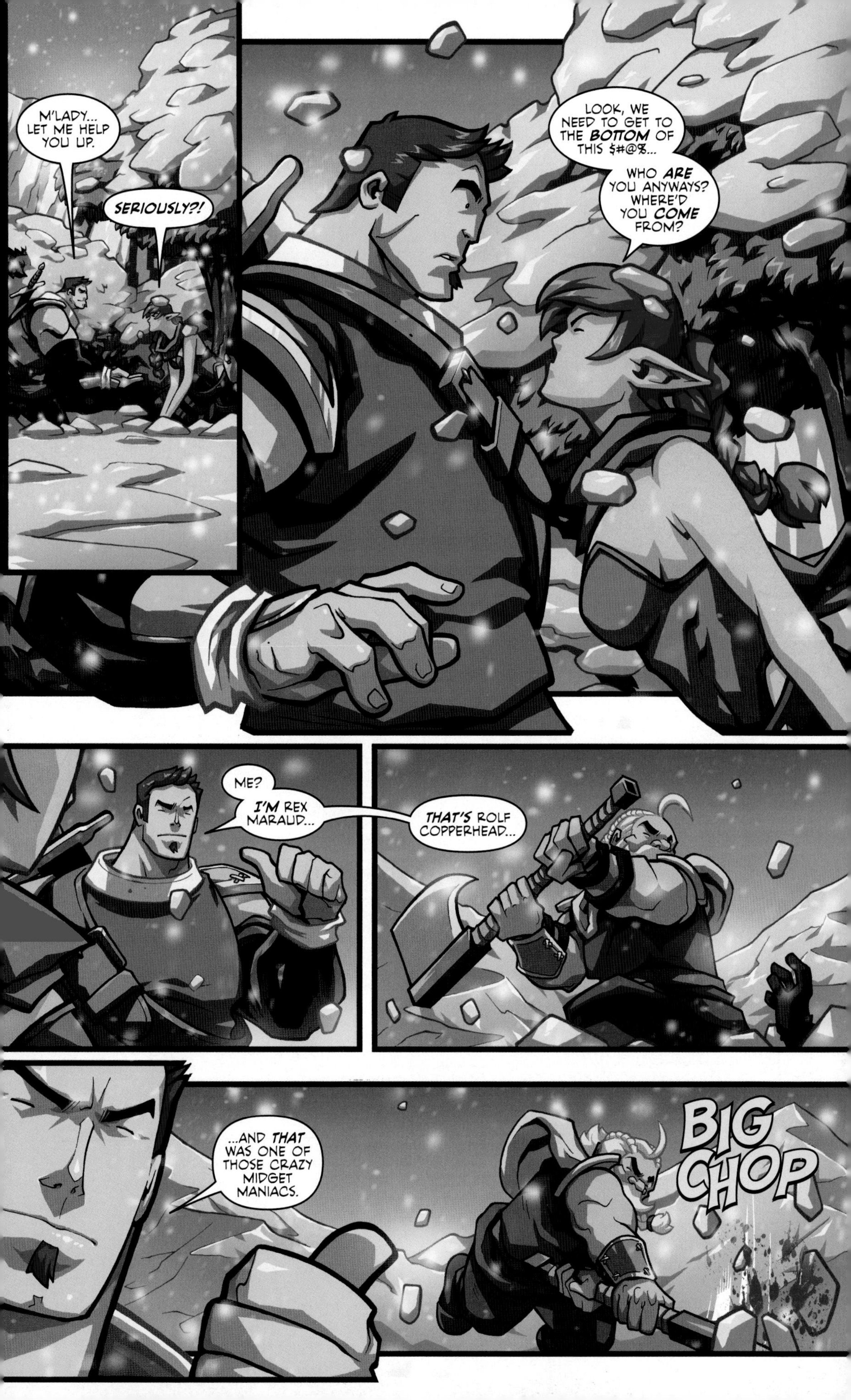
M'LADY... LET ME HELP YOU UP.
SERIOUSLY?!
LOOK, WE NEED TO GET TO THE BOTTOM OF THIS $#@%...
WHO ARE YOU ANYWAYS? WHERE'D YOU COME FROM?
ME? I'M REX MARAUD...
THAT'S ROLF COPPERHEAD...
...AND THAT WAS ONE OF THOSE CRAZY MIDGET MANIACS.
BIG CHOP

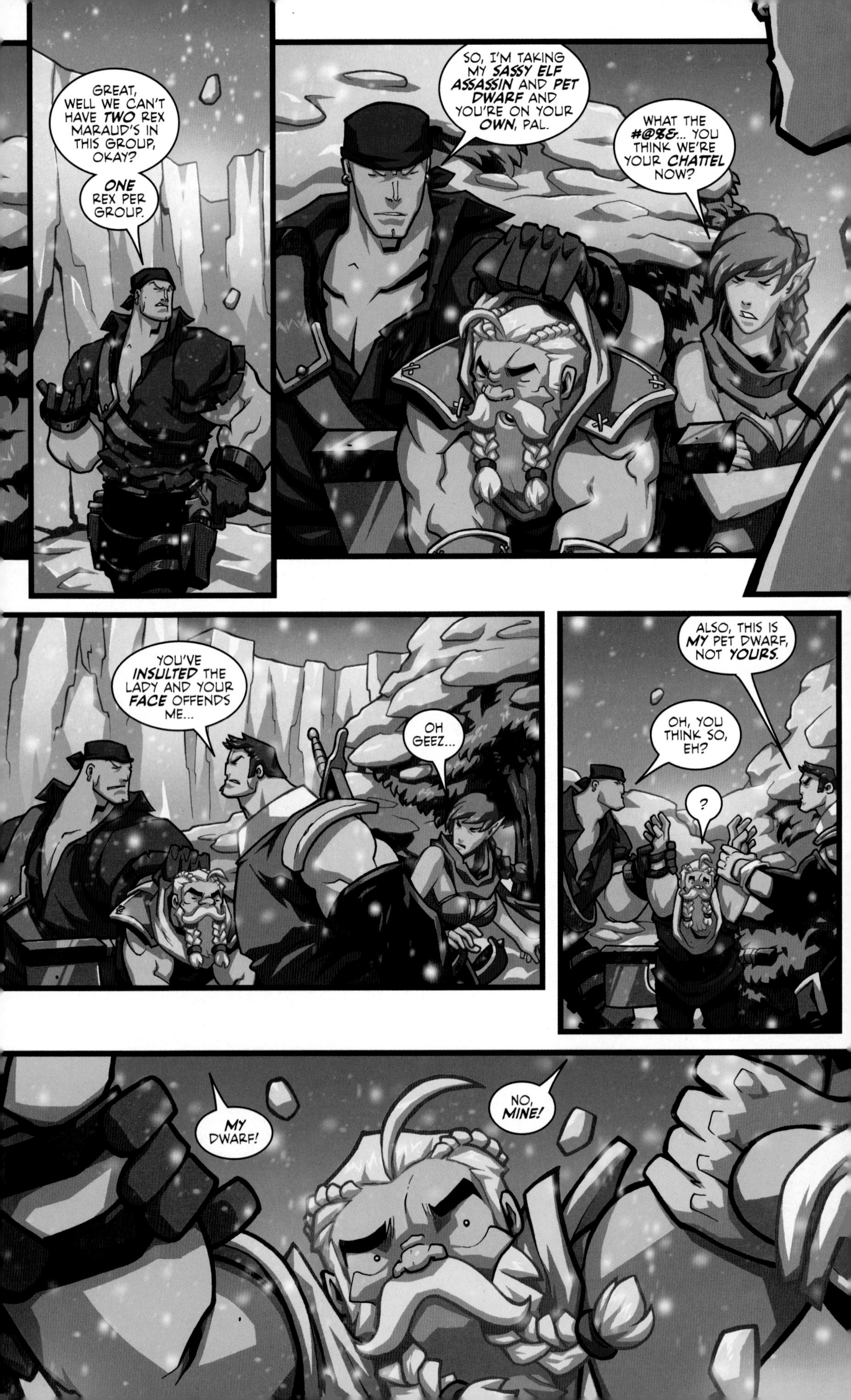
GREAT, WELL WE CAN'T HAVE TWO REX MARAUD'S IN THIS GROUP, OKAY?
ONE REX PER GROUP.
SO, I'M TAKING MY SASSY ELF ASSASSIN AND PET DWARF AND YOU'RE ON YOUR OWN, PAL.
WHAT THE #@%&... YOU THINK WE'RE YOUR CHATTEL NOW?
YOU'VE INSULTED THE LADY AND YOUR FACE OFFENDS ME...
OH GEEZ...
ALSO, THIS IS MY PET DWARF, NOT YOURS.
OH, YOU THINK SO, EH?
?
MY DWARF!
NO, MINE!

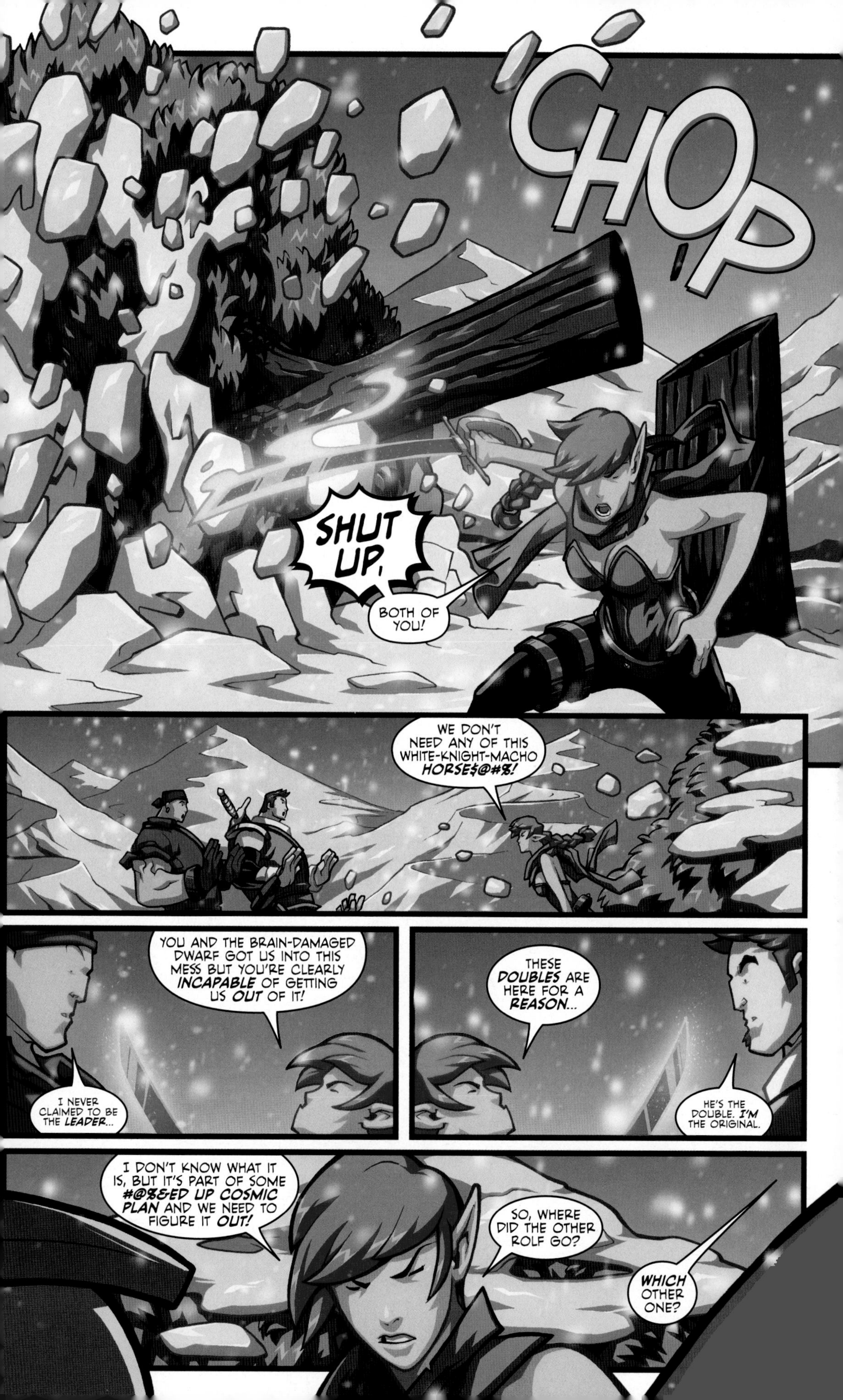
CHOP
SHUT UP,
BOTH OF YOU!
WE DON'T NEED ANY OF THIS WHITE-KNIGHT-MACHO HORSE$@#%!
YOU AND THE BRAIN-DAMAGED DWARF GOT US INTO THIS MESS BUT YOU'RE CLEARLY INCAPABLE OF GETTING US OUT OF IT!
I NEVER CLAIMED TO BE THE LEADER...
THESE DOUBLES ARE HERE FOR A REASON...
HE'S THE DOUBLE. I'M THE ORIGINAL.
I DON'T KNOW WHAT IT IS, BUT IT'S PART OF SOME #@%&ED UP COSMIC PLAN AND WE NEED TO FIGURE IT OUT!
SO, WHERE DID THE OTHER ROLF GO?
WHICH OTHER ONE?

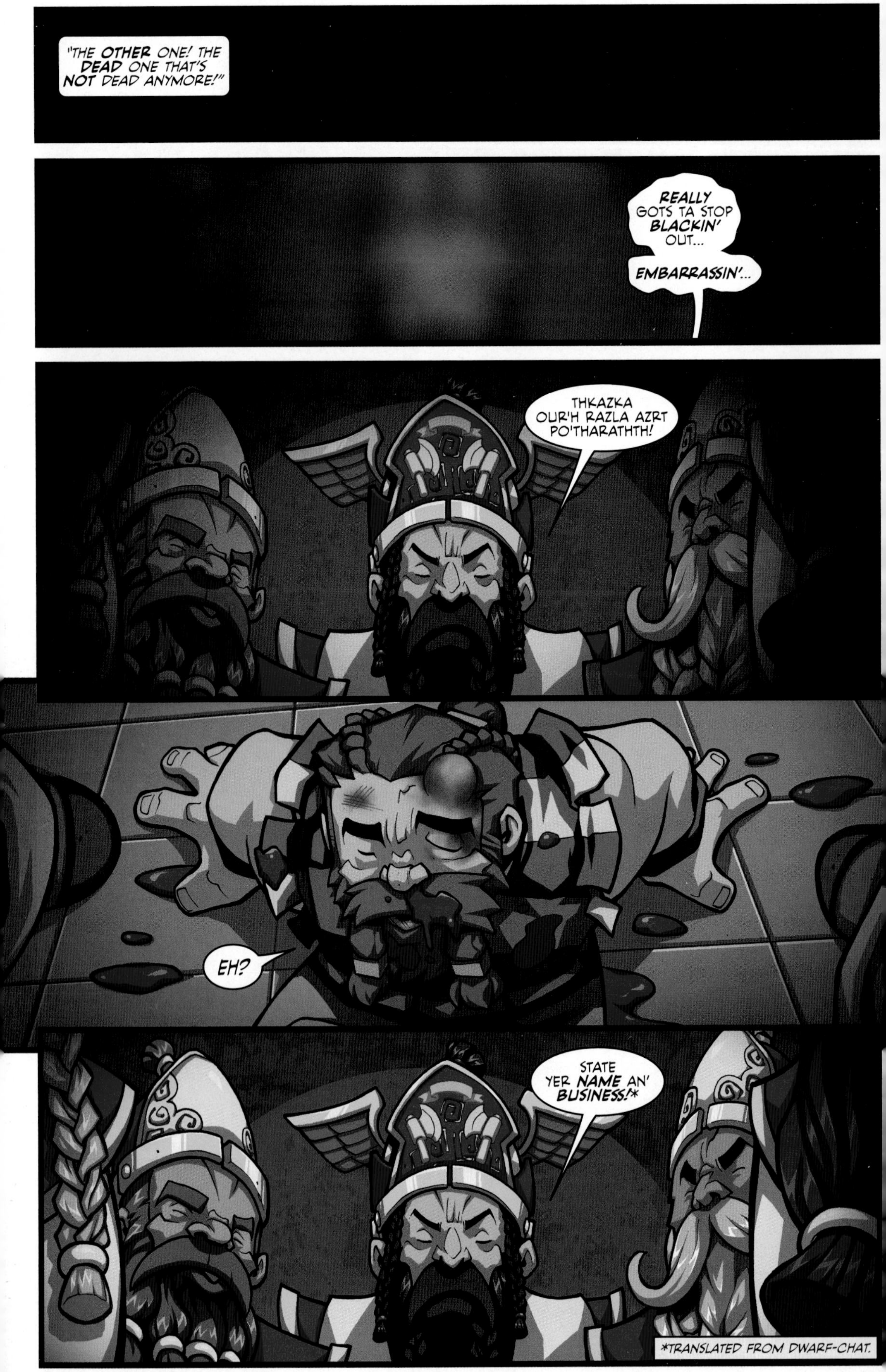
"THE OTHER ONE! THE DEAD ONE THAT'S NOT DEAD ANYMORE!"
REALLY GOTS TA STOP BLACKIN' OUT...
EMBARRASSIN'...
THKAZKA OUR'H RAZLA AZRT PO'THARATHTH!
EH?
STATE YER NAME AN' BUSINESS!*
*TRANSLATED FROM DWARF-CHAT.

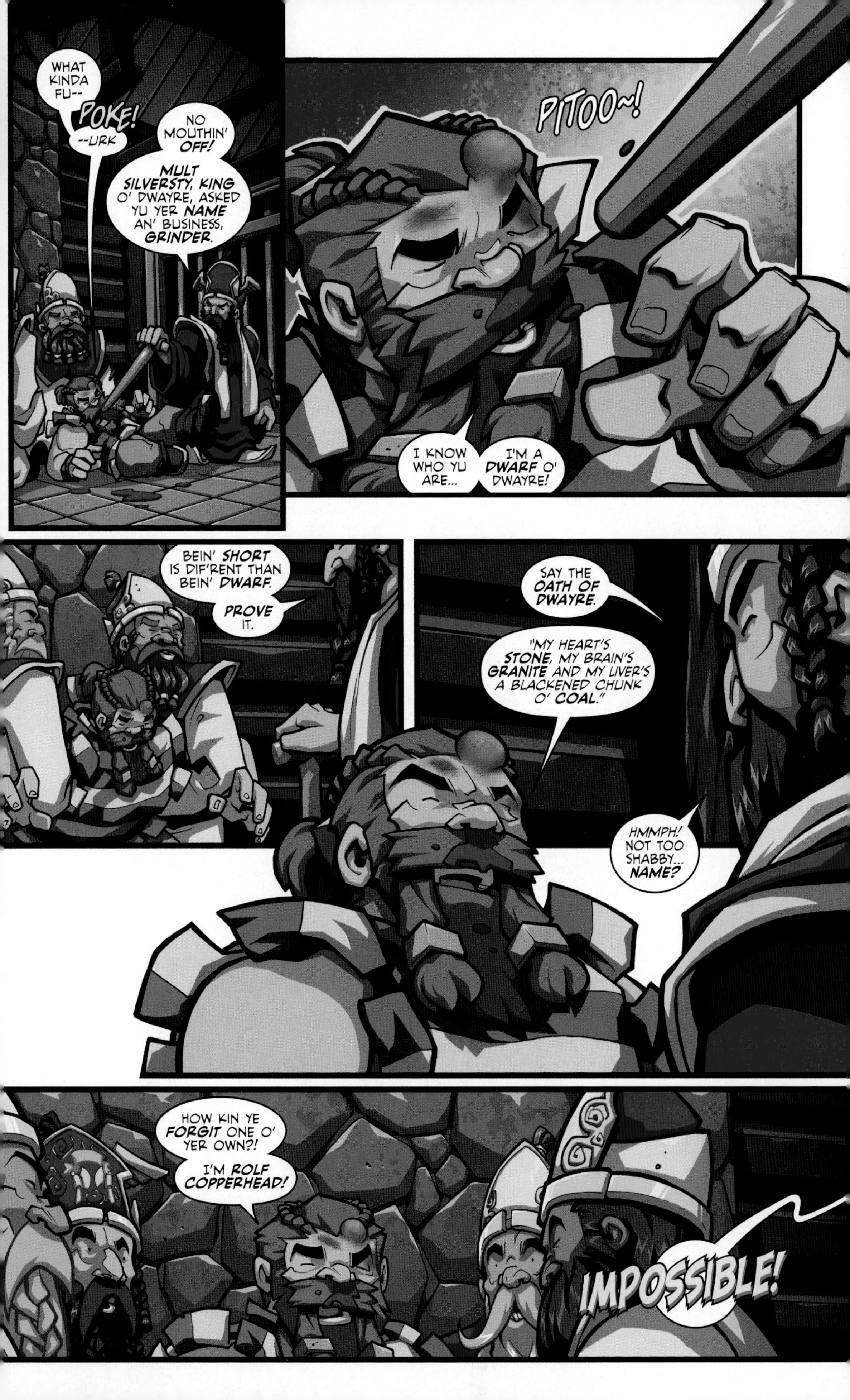
WHAT KINDA FU--
POKE!
--URK
NO MOUTHIN' OFF!
MULT SILVERSTY, KING O' DWAYRE, ASKED YU YER NAME AN' BUSINESS, GRINDER.
PITOO~!
I KNOW WHO YU ARE...
I'M A DWARF O' DWAYRE!
BEIN' SHORT IS DIF'RENT THAN BEIN' DWARF.
PROVE IT.
SAY THE OATH OF DWAYRE.
"MY HEART'S STONE, MY BRAIN'S GRANITE AND MY LIVER'S A BLACKENED CHUNK O' COAL."
HMMPH! NOT TOO SHABBY... NAME?
HOW KIN YE FORGIT ONE O' YER OWN?!
I'M ROLF COPPERHEAD!
IMPOSSIBLE!

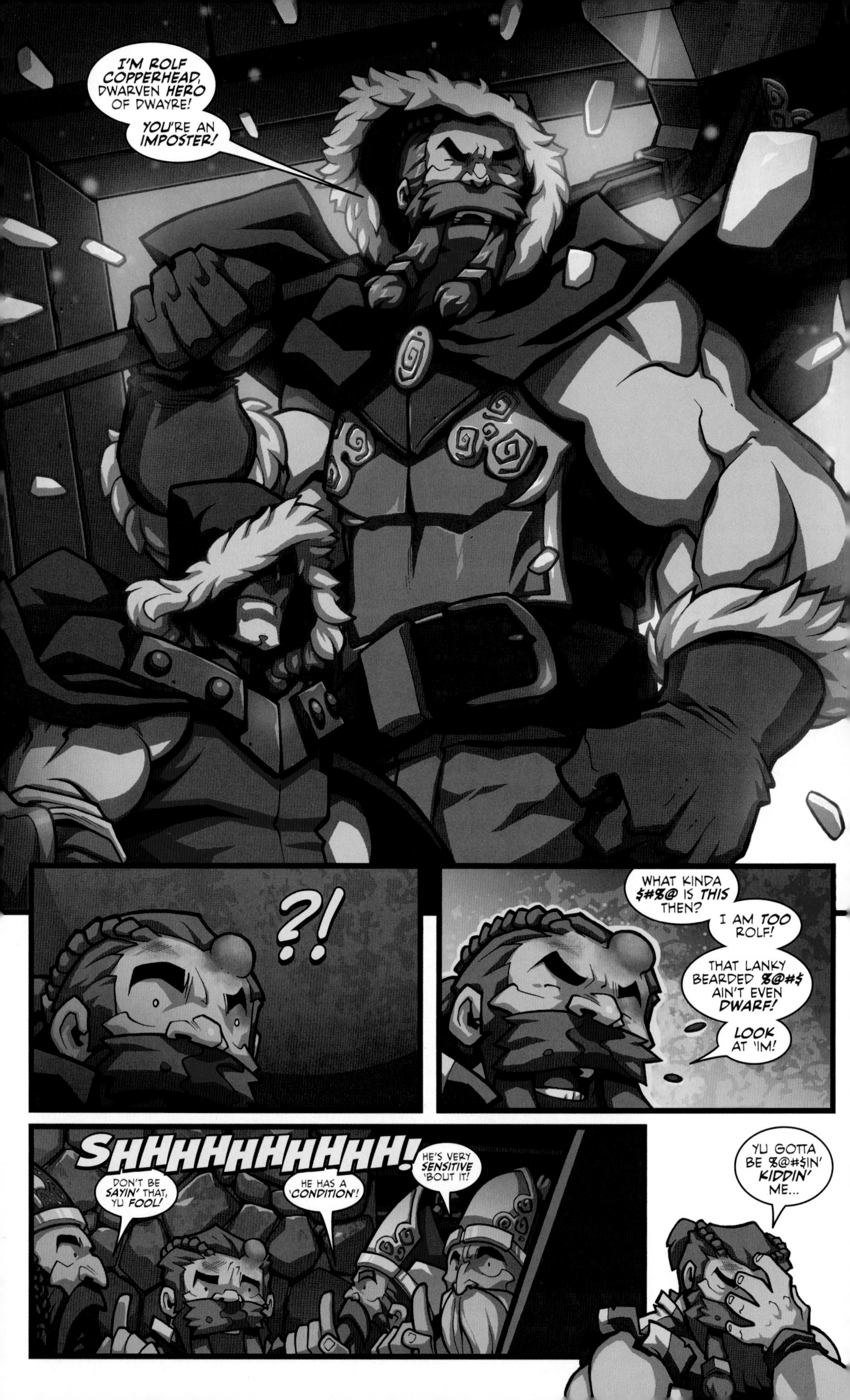
I'M ROLF COPPERHEAD, DWARVEN HERO OF DWAYRE!
YOU'RE AN IMPOSTER!
?!
WHAT KINDA $#%@ IS THIS THEN?
I AM TOO ROLF!
THAT LANKY BEARDED %@#$ AIN'T EVEN DWARF!
LOOK AT 'IM!
SHHHHHHHHHHH!
DON'T BE SAYIN' THAT, YU FOOL!
HE HAS A 'CONDITION'!
HE'S VERY SENSITIVE 'BOUT IT!
YU GOTTA BE %@#$IN' KIDDIN' ME...

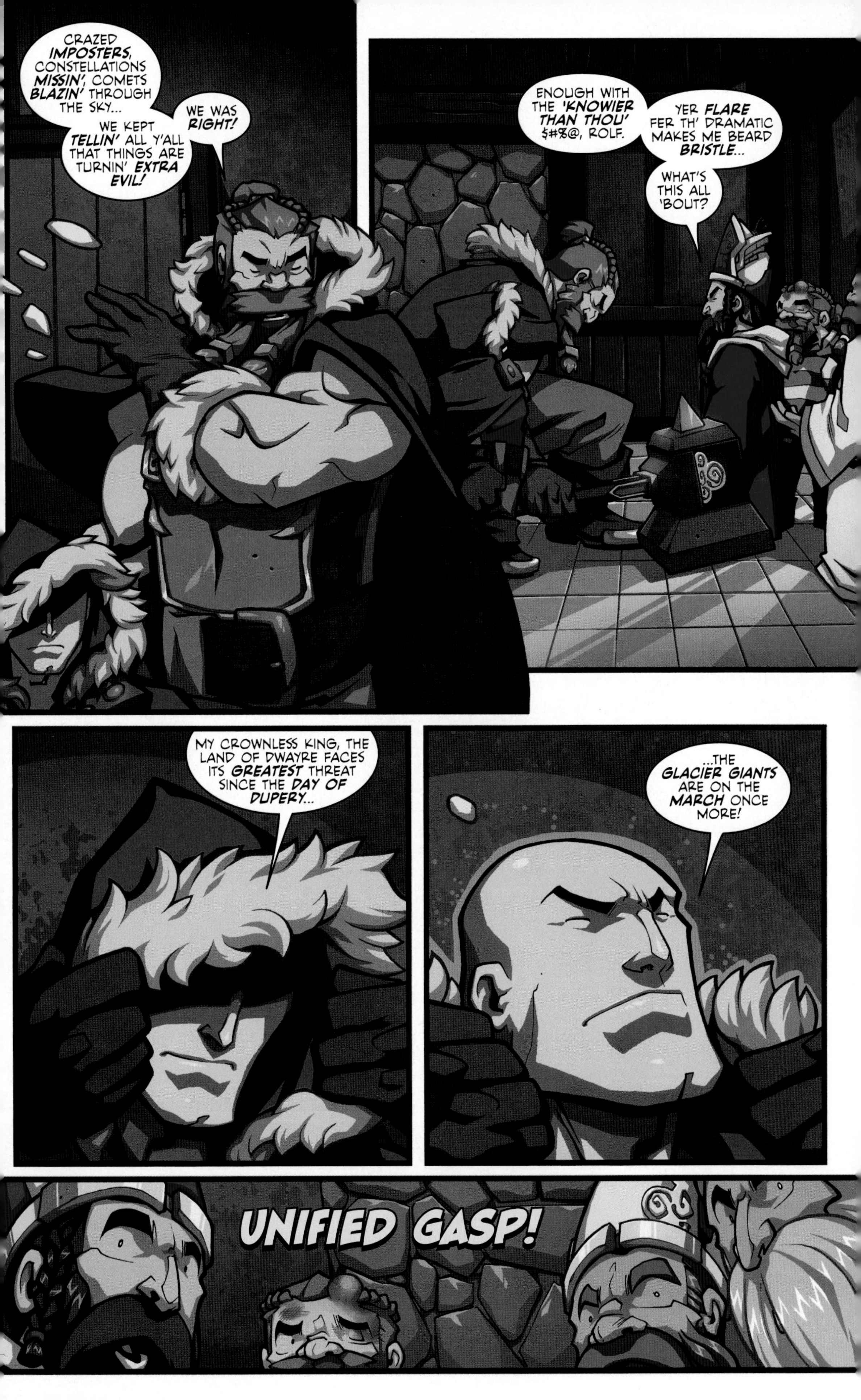
CRAZED IMPOSTERS, CONSTELLATIONS MISSIN', COMETS BLAZIN' THROUGH THE SKY...
WE KEPT TELLIN' ALL Y'ALL THAT THINGS ARE TURNIN' EXTRA EVIL!
WE WAS RIGHT!
ENOUGH WITH THE 'KNOWIER THAN THOU' $#%@, ROLF.
YER FLARE FER TH' DRAMATIC MAKES ME BEARD BRISTLE...
WHAT'S THIS ALL 'BOUT?
MY CROWNLESS KING, THE LAND OF DWAYRE FACES ITS GREATEST THREAT SINCE THE DAY OF DUPERY...
...THE GLACIER GIANTS ARE ON THE MARCH ONCE MORE!
UNIFIED GASP!

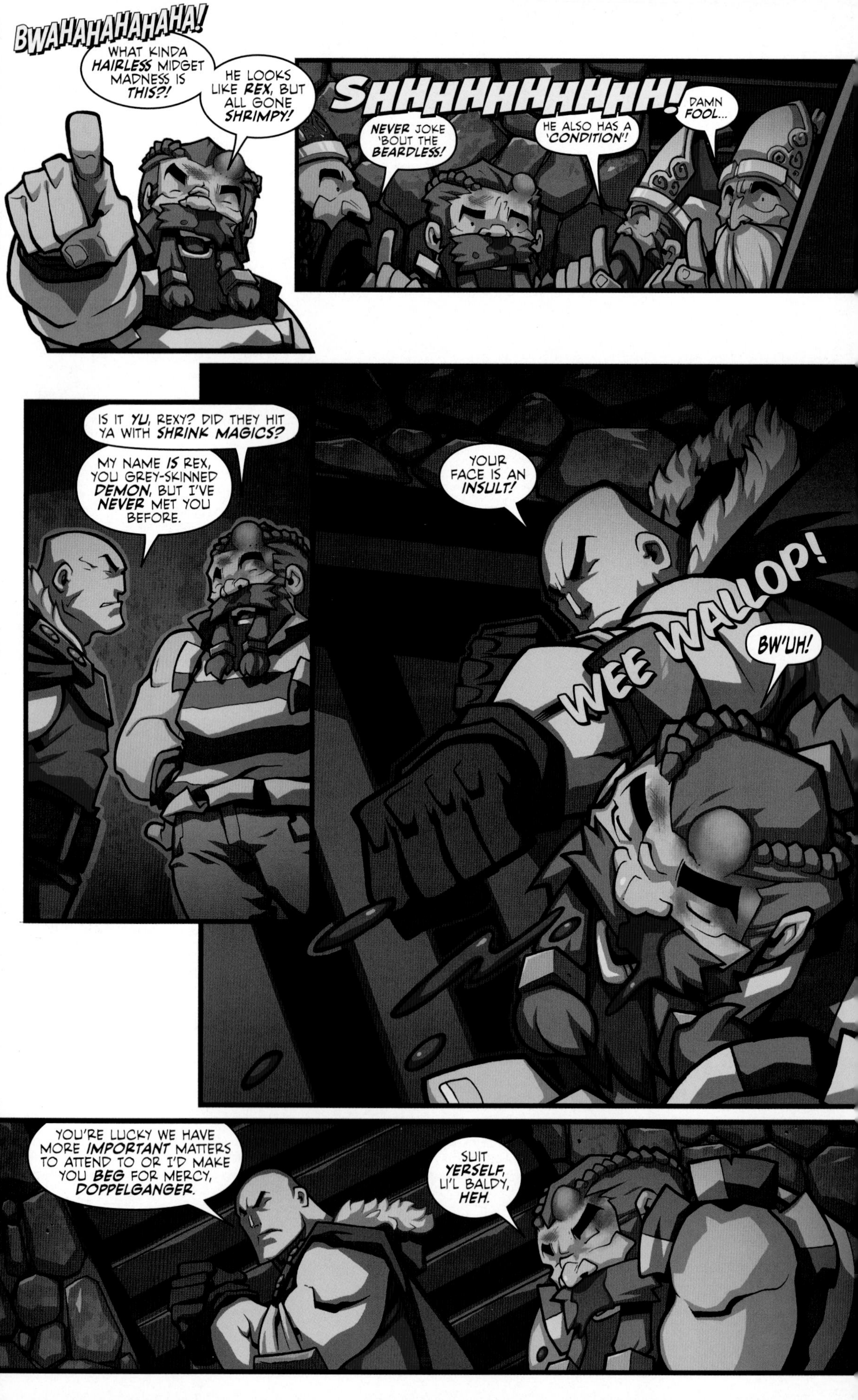
BWAHAHAHAHAHA!
WHAT KINDA HAIRLESS MIDGET MADNESS IS THIS?!
HE LOOKS LIKE REX, BUT ALL GONE SHRIMPY!
SHHHHHHHHHHH!
NEVER JOKE 'BOUT THE BEARDLESS!
HE ALSO HAS A 'CONDITION'!
DAMN FOOL...
IS IT YU, REXY? DID THEY HIT YA WITH SHRINK MAGICS?
MY NAME IS REX, YOU GREY-SKINNED DEMON, BUT I'VE NEVER MET YOU BEFORE.
YOUR FACE IS AN INSULT!
WEE WALLOP!
BW'UH!
YOU'RE LUCKY WE HAVE MORE IMPORTANT MATTERS TO ATTEND TO OR I'D MAKE YOU BEG FOR MERCY, DOPPELGANGER.
SUIT YERSELF, LI'L BALDY, HEH.

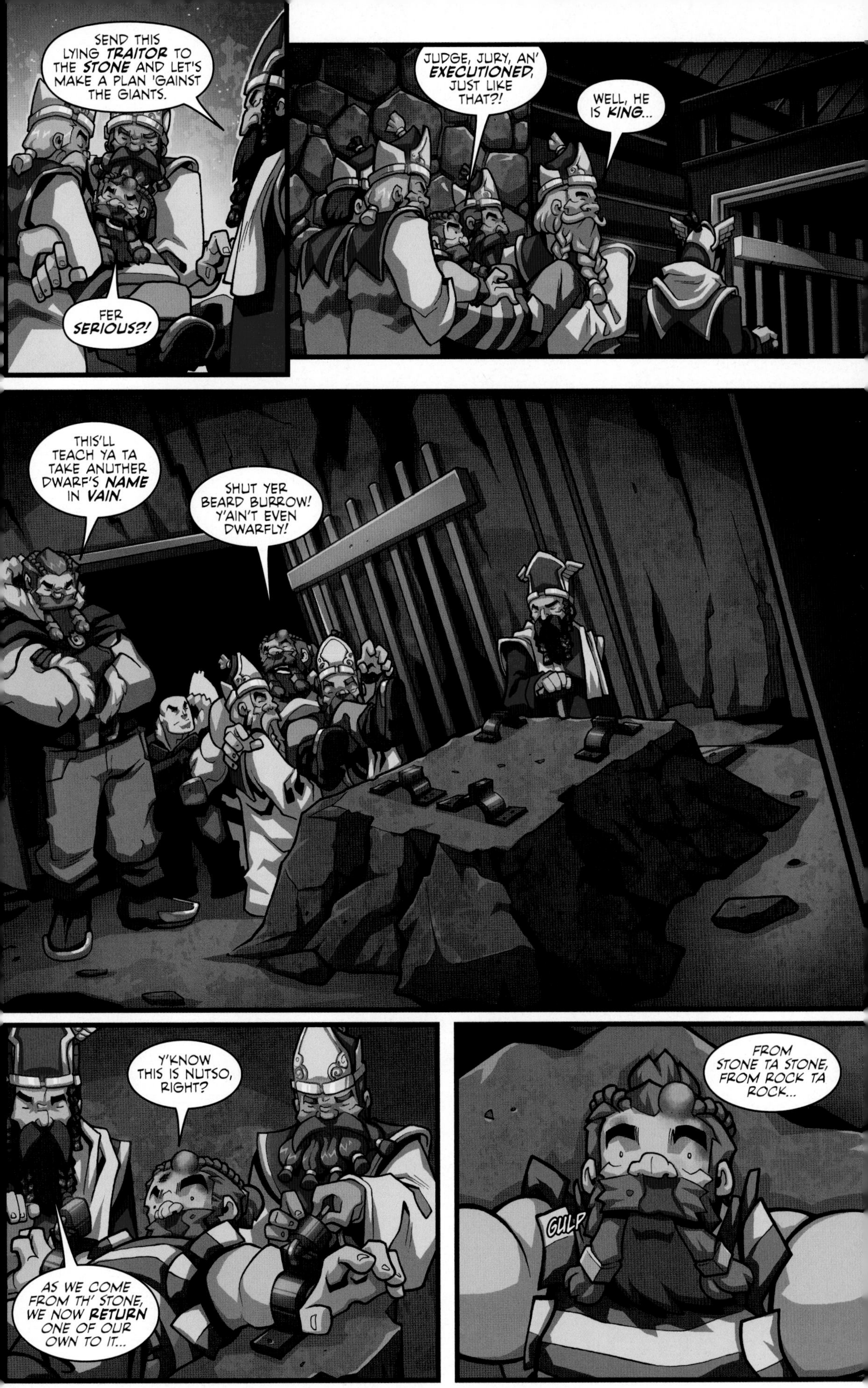
SEND THIS LYING TRAITOR TO THE STONE AND LET'S MAKE A PLAN 'GAINST THE GIANTS.
FER SERIOUS?!
JUDGE, JURY, AN' EXECUTIONED, JUST LIKE THAT?!
WELL, HE IS KING...
THIS'LL TEACH YA TA TAKE ANUTHER DWARF'S NAME IN VAIN.
SHUT YER BEARD BURROW! Y'AIN'T EVEN DWARFLY!
Y'KNOW THIS IS NUTSO, RIGHT?
AS WE COME FROM TH' STONE, WE NOW RETURN ONE OF OUR OWN TO IT...
FROM STONE TA STONE, FROM ROCK TA ROCK...
GULP

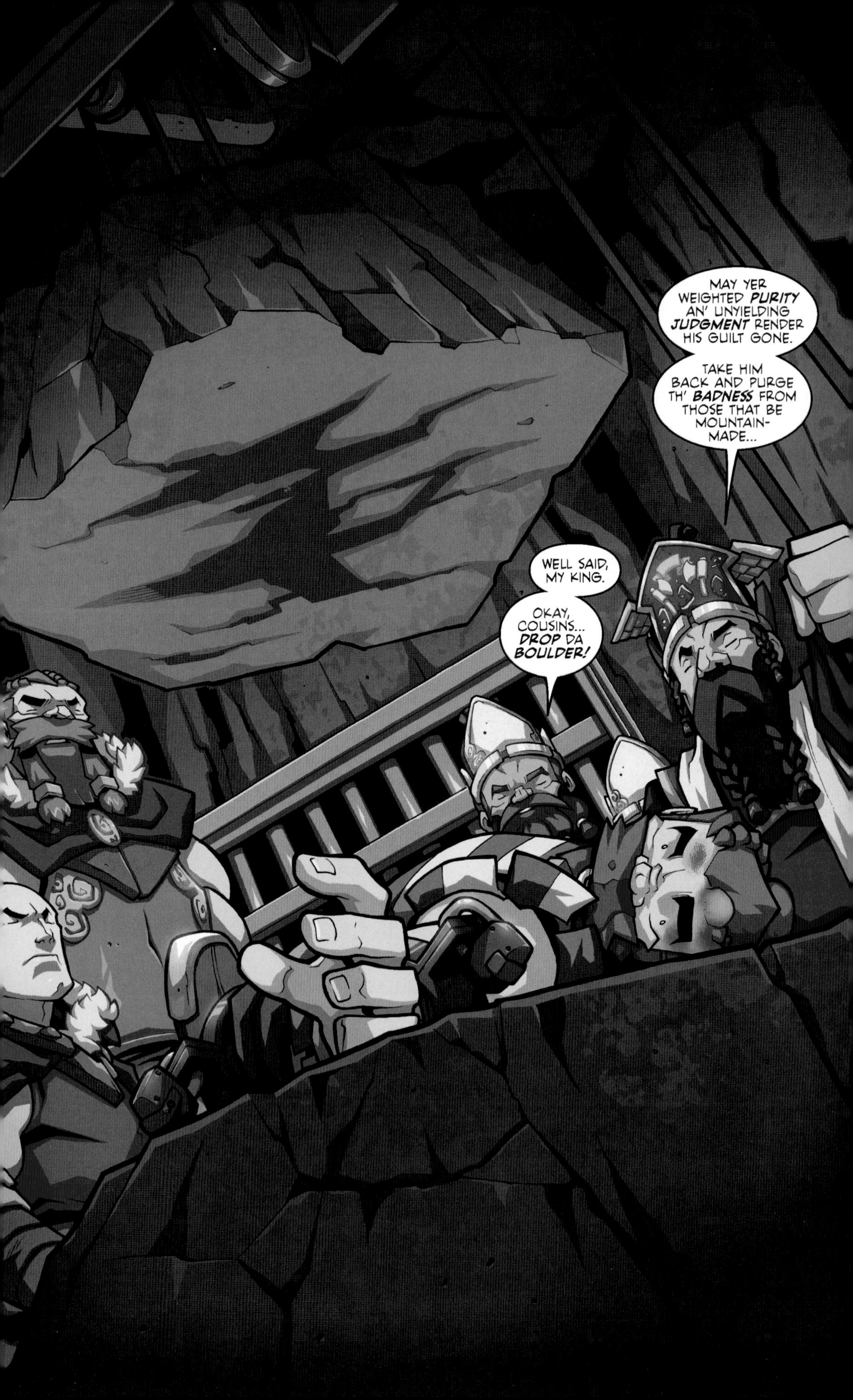
MAY YER WEIGHTED PURITY AN' UNYIELDING JUDGMENT RENDER HIS GUILT GONE.
TAKE HIM BACK AND PURGE TH' BADNESS FROM THOSE THAT BE MOUNTAIN-MADE...
WELL SAID, MY KING.
OKAY, COUSINS... DROP DA BOULDER!

CHAPTER TWO

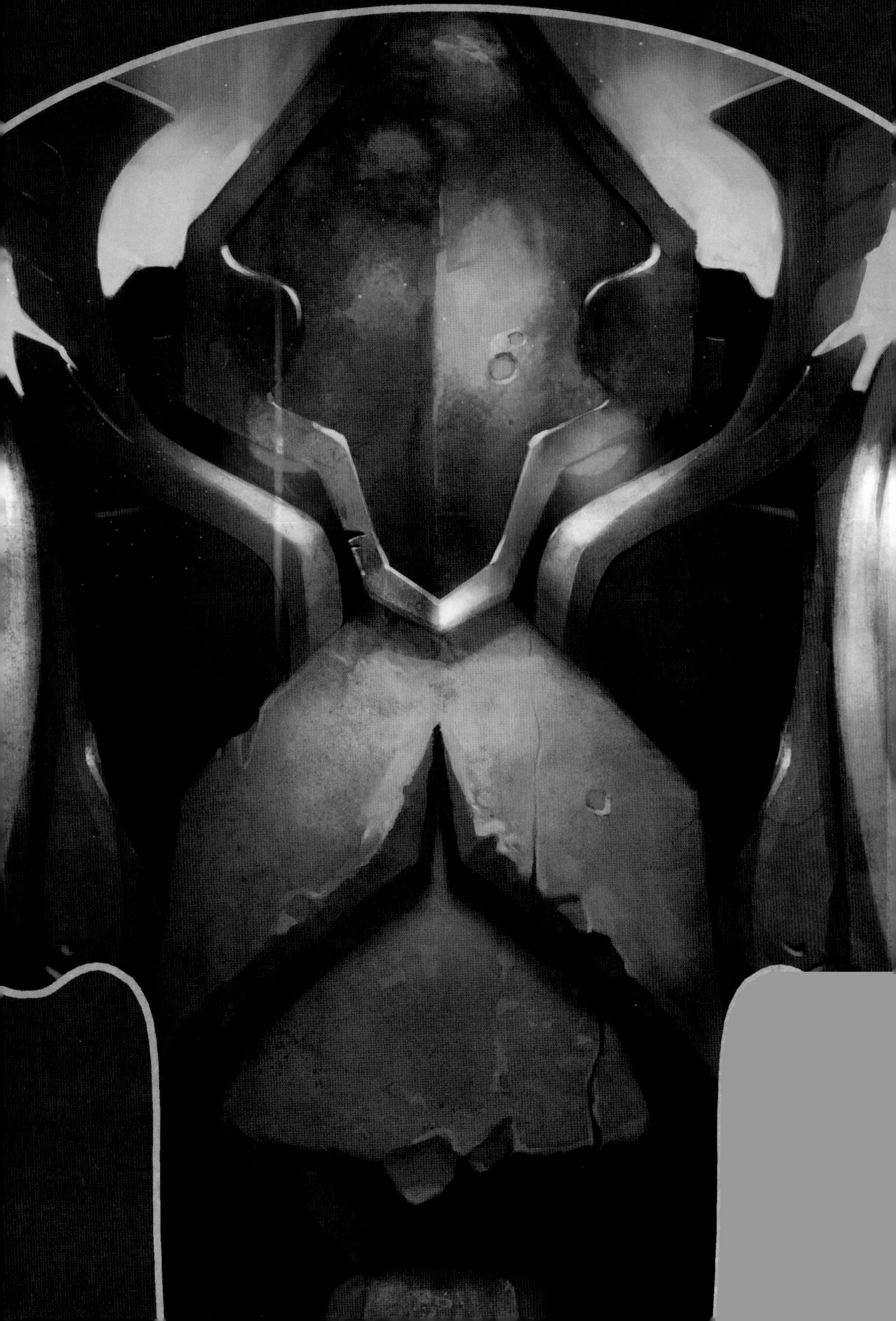

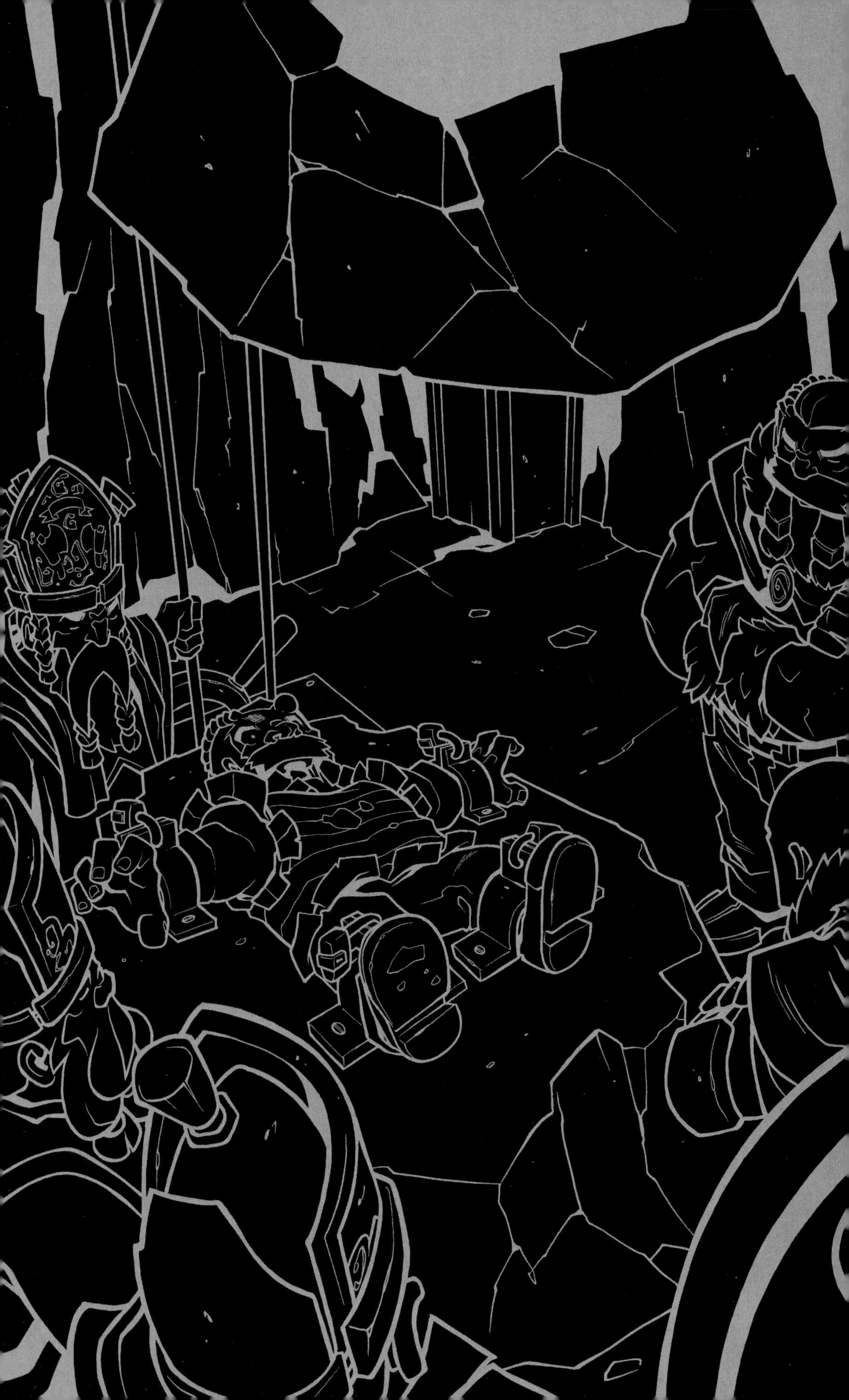

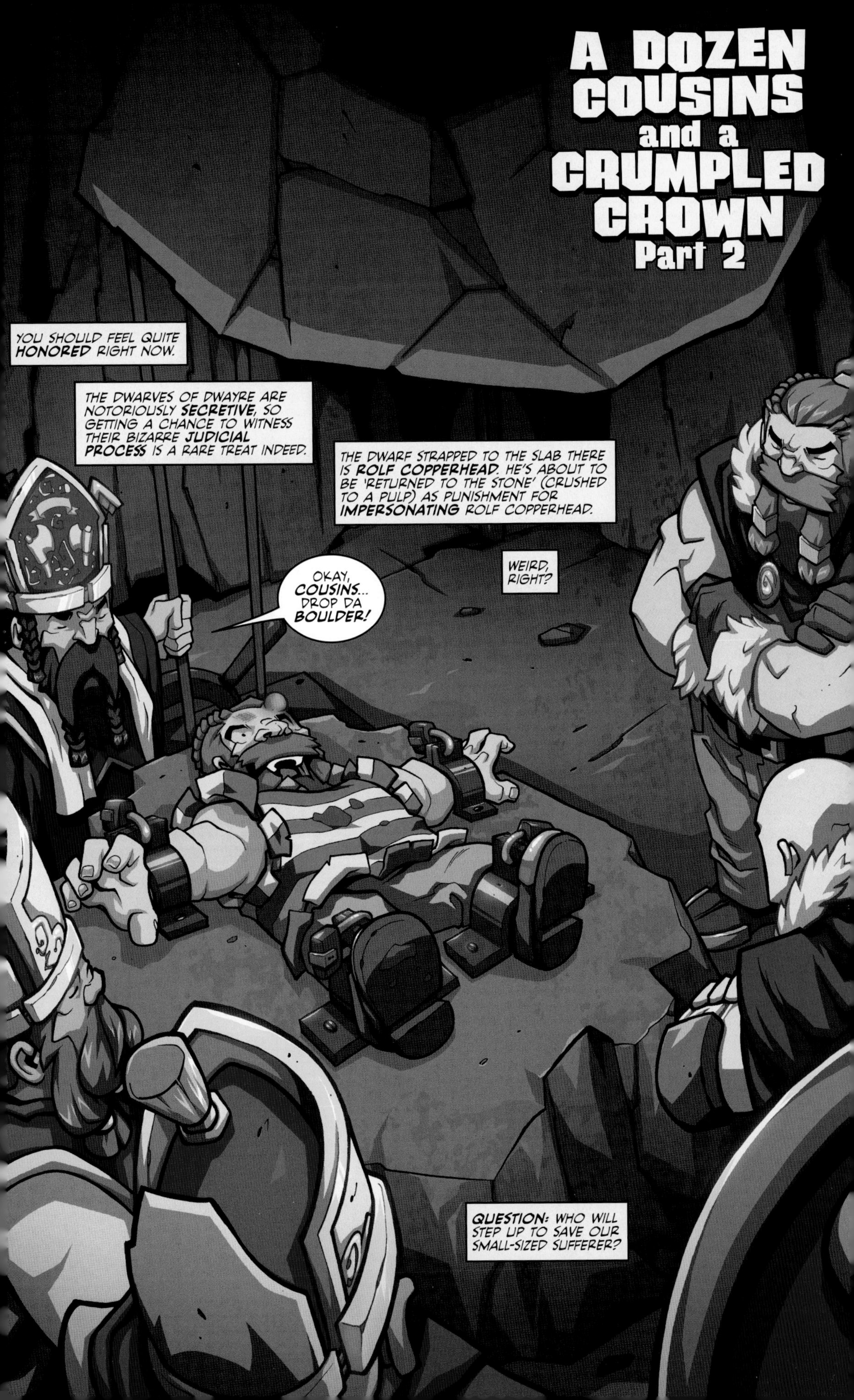
A DOZEN COUSINS and a CRUMPLED CROWN Part 2
YOU SHOULD FEEL QUITE HONORED RIGHT NOW.
THE DWARVES OF DWAYRE ARE NOTORIOUSLY SECRETIVE, SO GETTING A CHANCE TO WITNESS THEIR BIZARRE JUDICIAL PROCESS IS A RARE TREAT INDEED.
THE DWARF STRAPPED TO THE SLAB THERE IS ROLF COPPERHEAD. HE'S ABOUT TO BE 'RETURNED TO THE STONE' (CRUSHED TO A PULP) AS PUNISHMENT FOR IMPERSONATING ROLF COPPERHEAD.
WEIRD, RIGHT?
OKAY, COUSINS... DROP DA BOULDER!
QUESTION: WHO WILL STEP UP TO SAVE OUR SMALL-SIZED SUFFERER?

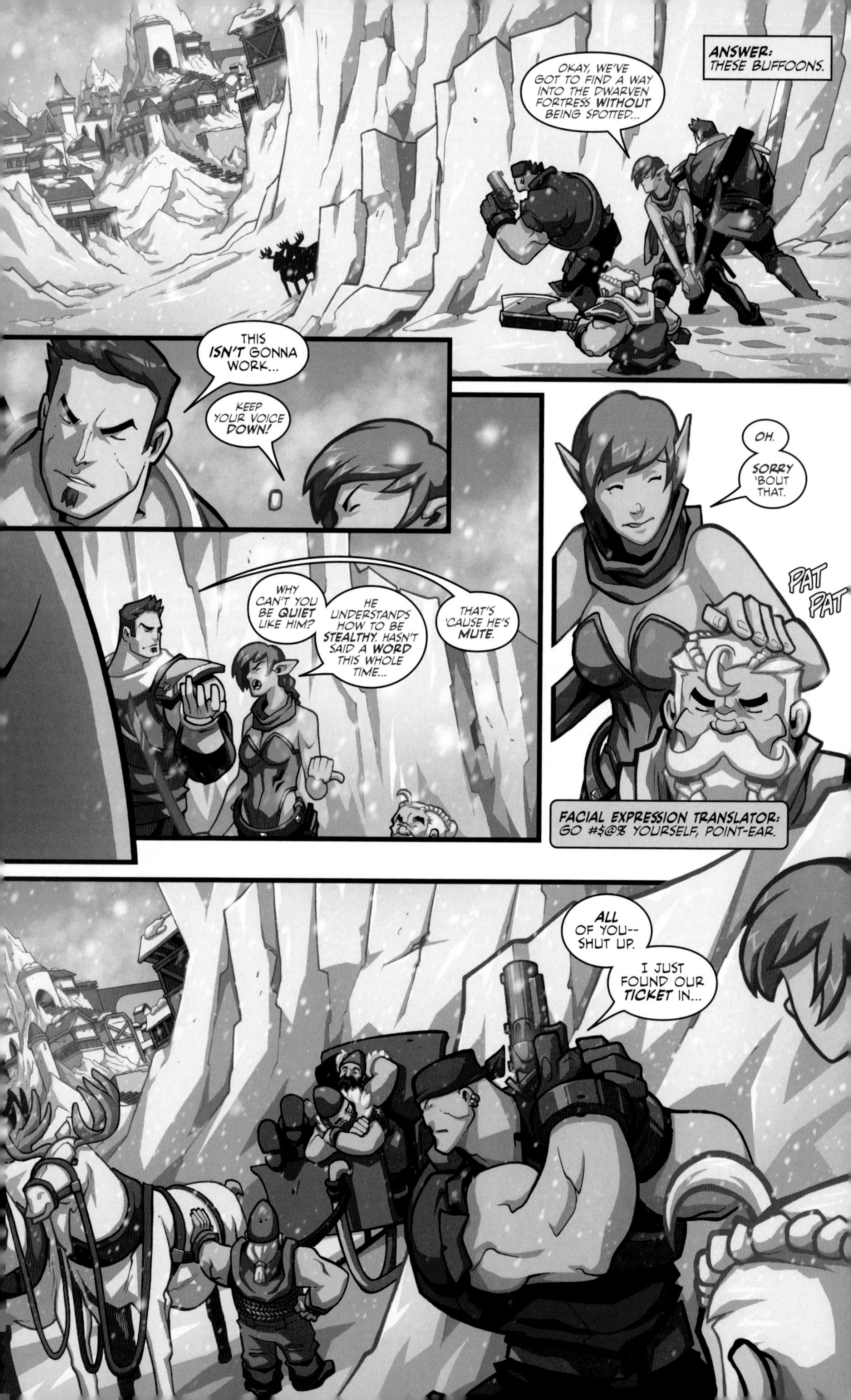
ANSWER: THESE BUFFOONS.
OKAY, WE'VE GOT TO FIND A WAY INTO THE DWARVEN FORTRESS WITHOUT BEING SPOTTED...
THIS ISN'T GONNA WORK...
KEEP YOUR VOICE DOWN!
OH.
SORRY 'BOUT THAT.
PAT PAT
WHY CAN'T YOU BE QUIET LIKE HIM?
HE UNDERSTANDS HOW TO BE STEALTHY. HASN'T SAID A WORD THIS WHOLE TIME...
THAT'S 'CAUSE HE'S MUTE.
FACIAL EXPRESSION TRANSLATOR: GO #$@% YOURSELF, POINT-EAR.
ALL OF YOU-- SHUT UP.
I JUST FOUND OUR TICKET IN...

SO, YEAH. NOT LOOKING TOO GOOD FOR OL' ROLF HERE, IS IT?

NOPE. NOT GOOD AT ALL.

GREEEAK

IF WE WANTED TO BE DOWNRIGHT CLICHÉ, WE'D SAY HIS LIFE IS FLASHING BEFORE HIS EYES.

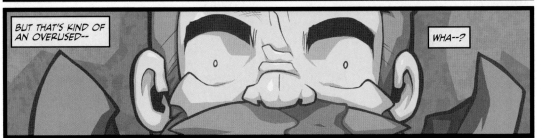

BUT THAT'S KIND OF AN OVERUSED--

WHA--?

WE'RE REALLY GOING TO DO THAT CORNY THING?

YEESH, THIS SERIES IS CREATIVELY BANKRUPT.

SAD...

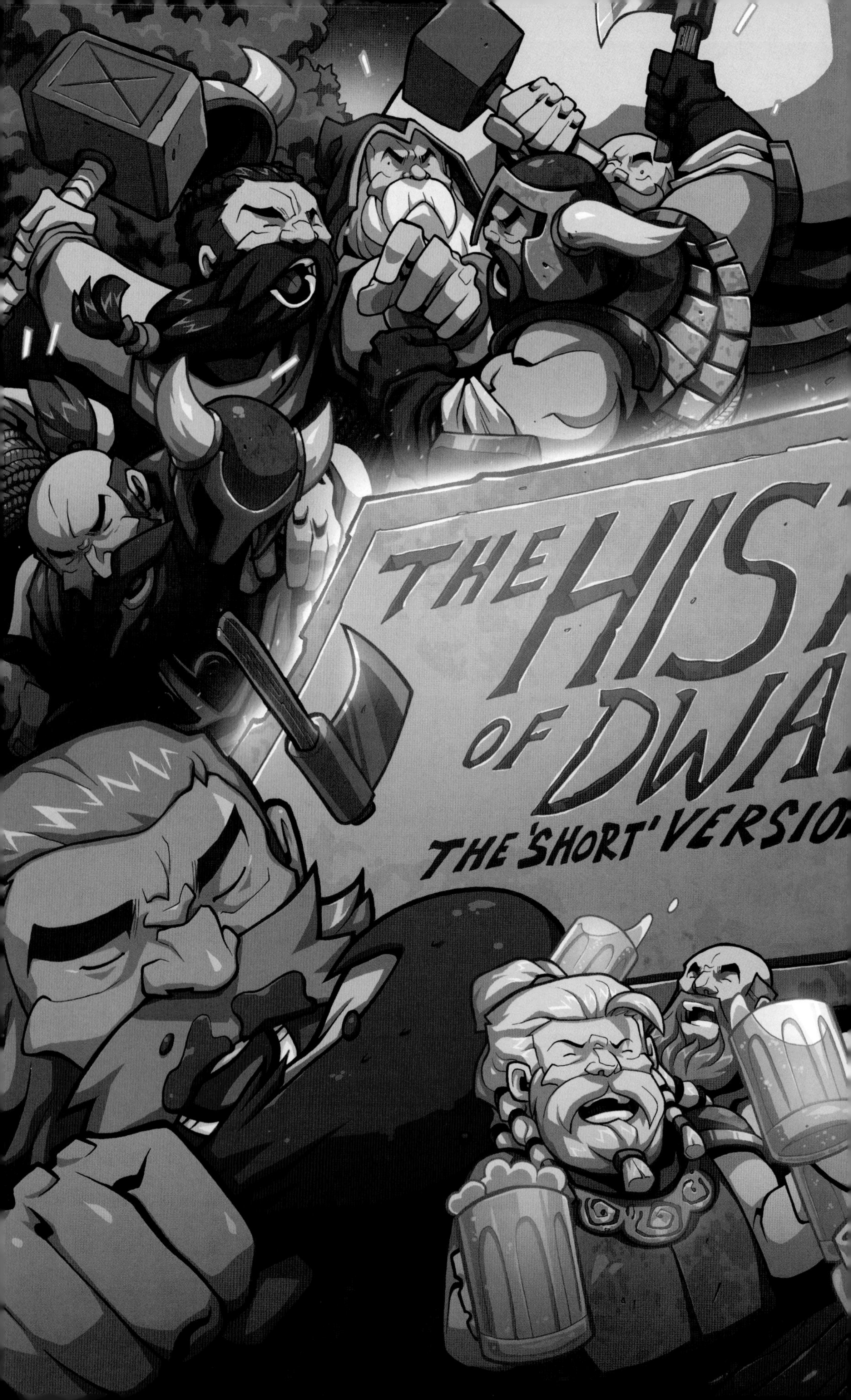
THE HIS
OF DWA
THE 'SHORT' VERSIO

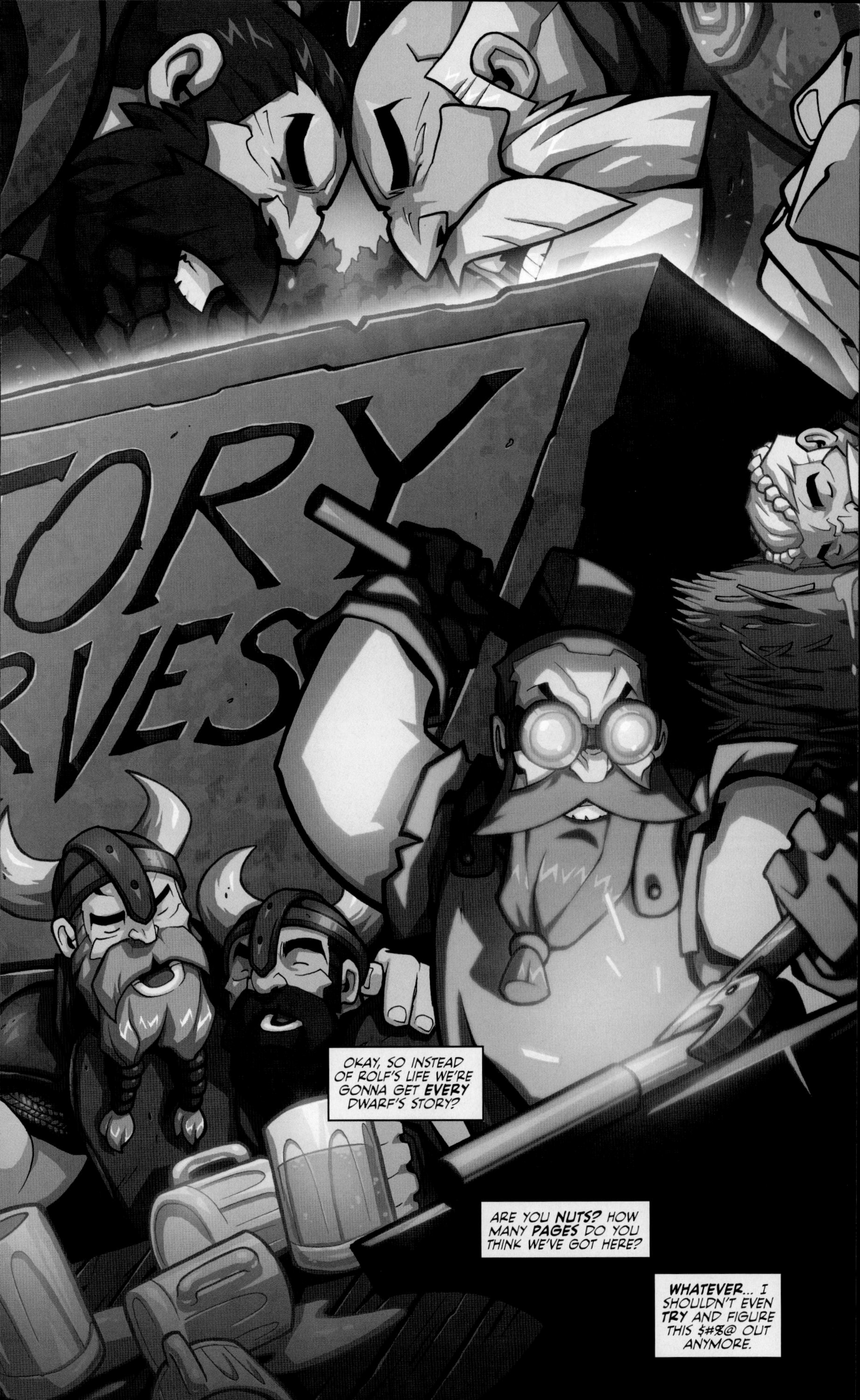

TORY
RVES
OKAY, SO INSTEAD OF ROLF'S LIFE WE'RE GONNA GET EVERY DWARF'S STORY?
ARE YOU NUTS? HOW MANY PAGES DO YOU THINK WE'VE GOT HERE?
WHATEVER... I SHOULDN'T EVEN TRY AND FIGURE THIS $#%@ OUT ANYMORE.

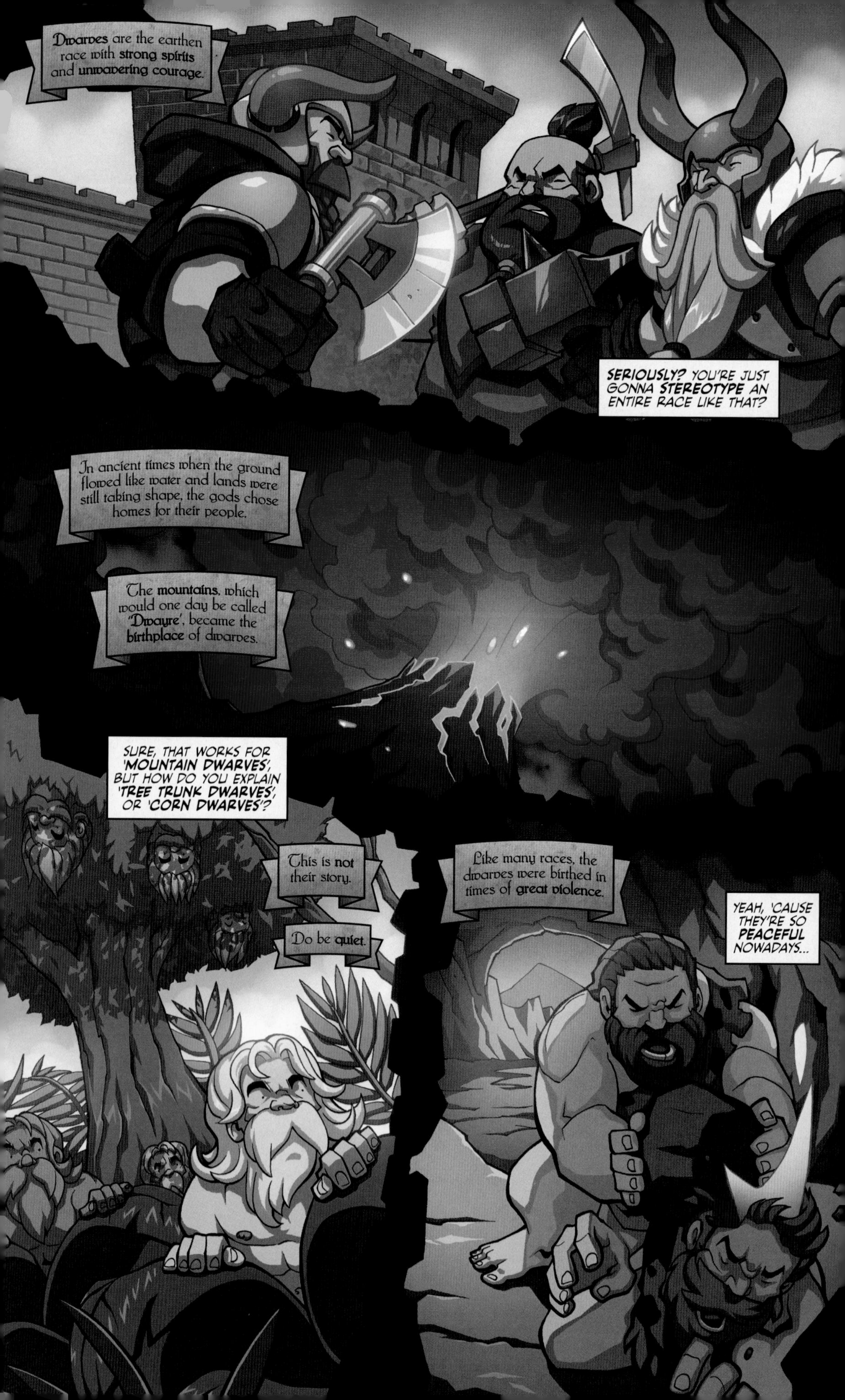
Dwarves are the earthen race with strong spirits and unwavering courage.
SERIOUSLY? YOU'RE JUST GONNA STEREOTYPE AN ENTIRE RACE LIKE THAT?
In ancient times when the ground flowed like water and lands were still taking shape, the gods chose homes for their people.
The mountains, which would one day be called 'Dwayre', became the birthplace of dwarves.
SURE, THAT WORKS FOR 'MOUNTAIN DWARVES', BUT HOW DO YOU EXPLAIN 'TREE TRUNK DWARVES', OR 'CORN DWARVES'?
This is not their story.
Do be quiet.
Like many races, the dwarves were birthed in times of great violence.
YEAH, 'CAUSE THEY'RE SO PEACEFUL NOWADAYS...

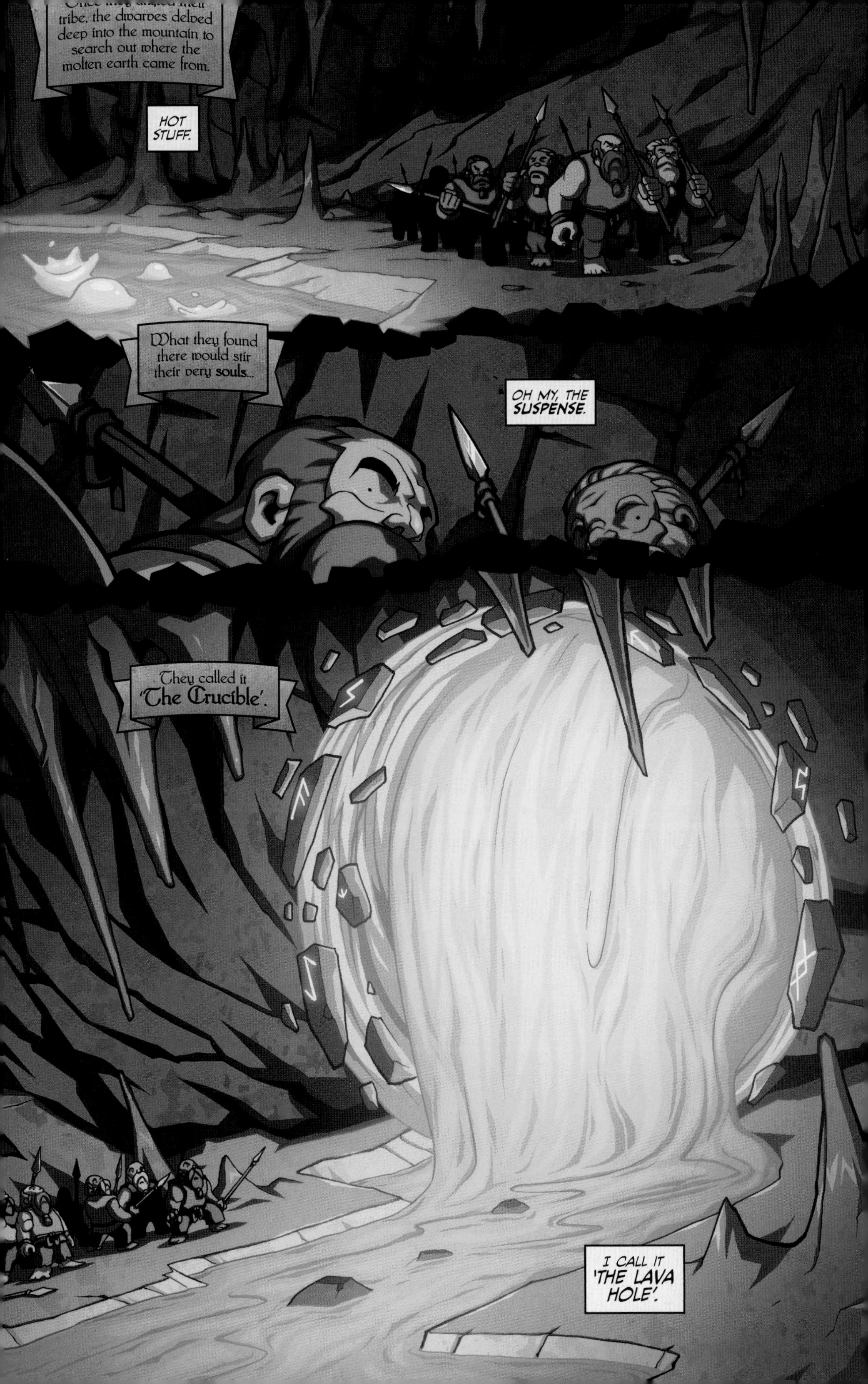
tribe, the dwarves delved deep into the mountain to search out where the molten earth came from.
HOT STUFF.
What they found there would stir their very souls...
OH MY, THE SUSPENSE.
They called it 'The Crucible'.
I CALL IT 'THE LAVA HOLE'.

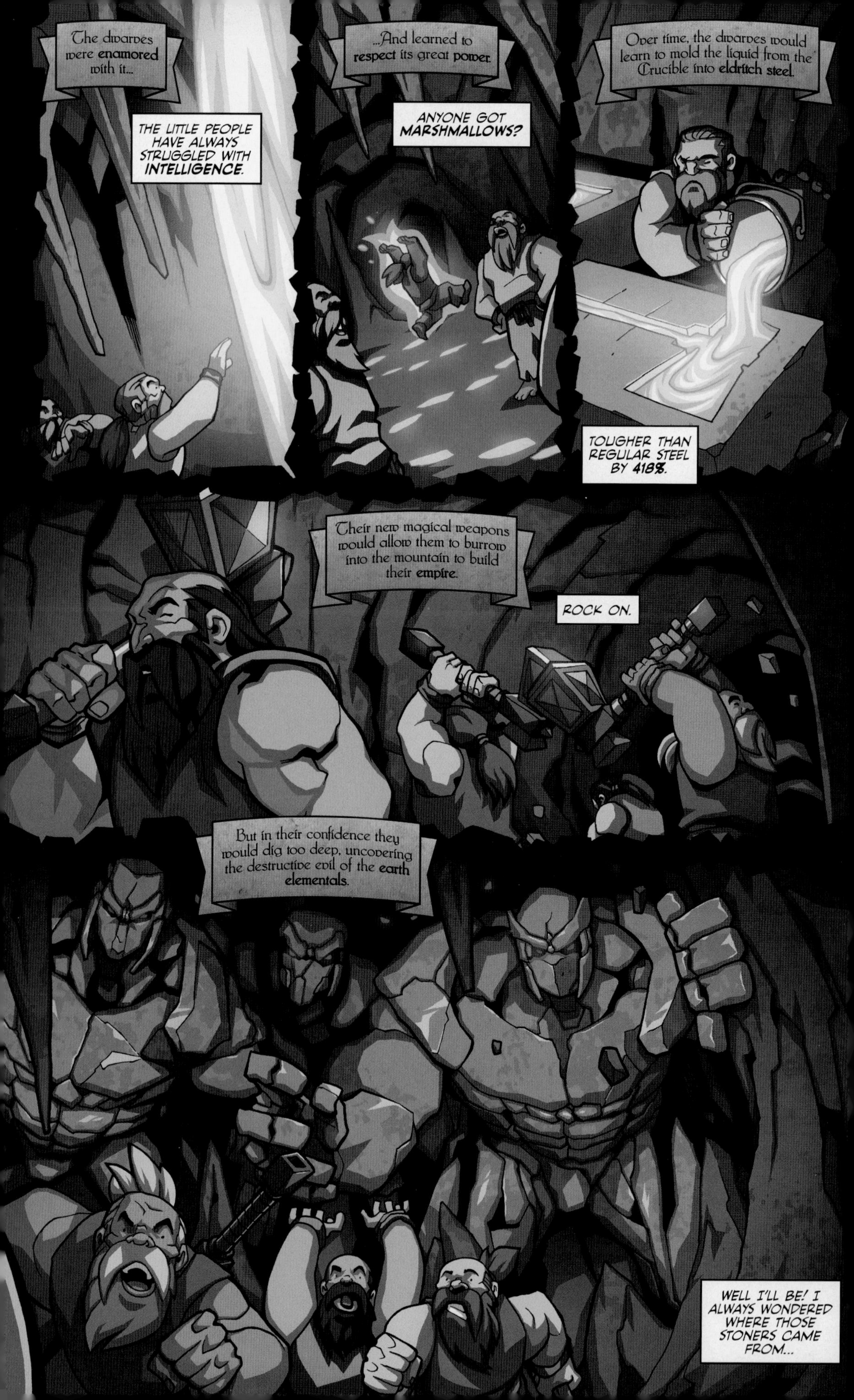
The dwarves were enamored with it...
THE LITTLE PEOPLE HAVE ALWAYS STRUGGLED WITH INTELLIGENCE.
...And learned to respect its great power.
ANYONE GOT MARSHMALLOWS?
Over time, the dwarves would learn to mold the liquid from the Crucible into eldritch steel.
TOUGHER THAN REGULAR STEEL BY 418%.
Their new magical weapons would allow them to burrow into the mountain to build their empire.
ROCK ON.
But in their confidence they would dig too deep, uncovering the destructive evil of the earth elementals.
WELL I'LL BE! I ALWAYS WONDERED WHERE THOSE STONERS CAME FROM...

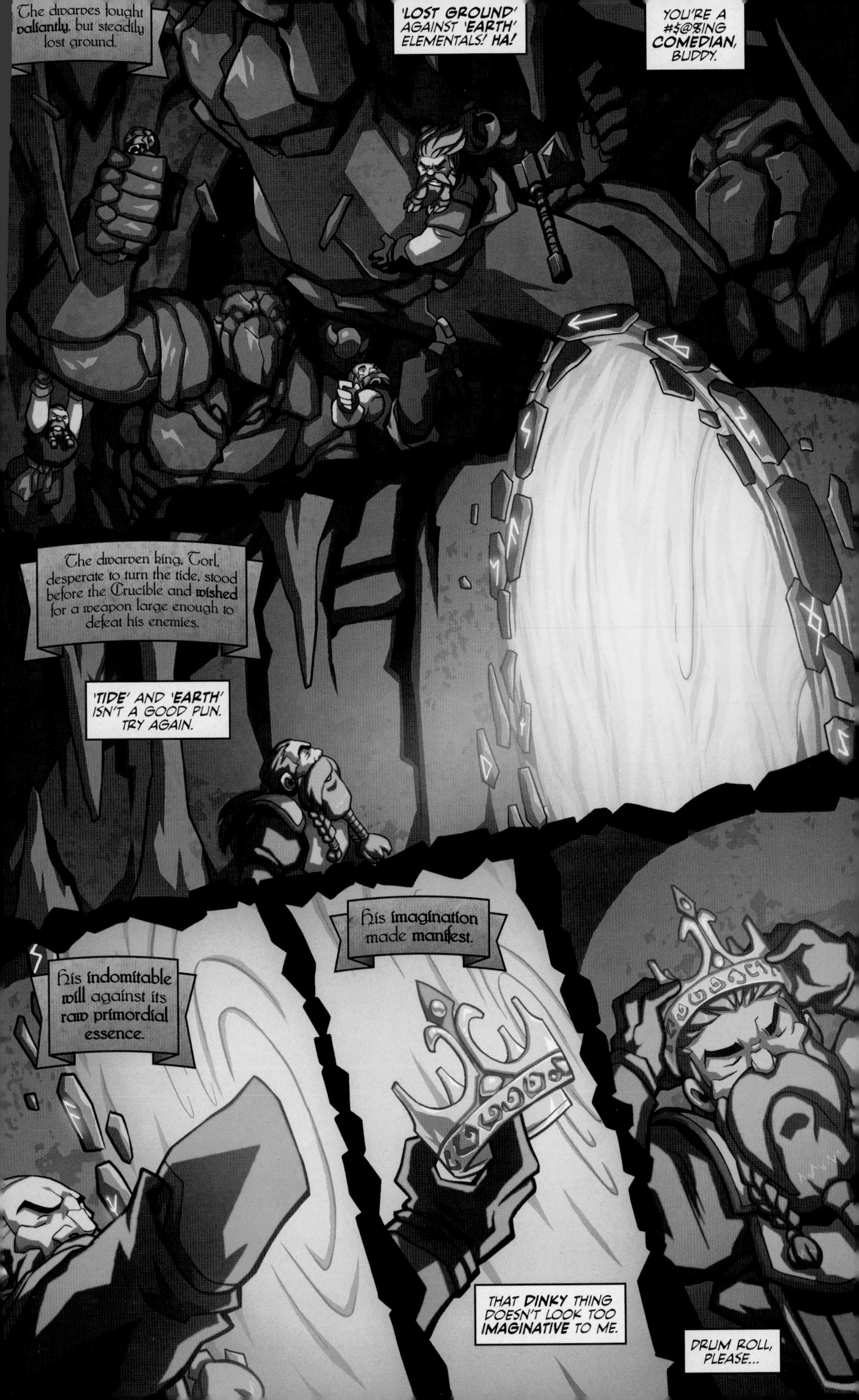
The dwarves fought valiantly, but steadily lost ground.
'LOST GROUND' AGAINST 'EARTH' ELEMENTALS! HA!
YOU'RE A #$@%ING COMEDIAN, BUDDY.
The dwarven king, Torl, desperate to turn the tide, stood before the Crucible and wished for a weapon large enough to defeat his enemies.
'TIDE' AND 'EARTH' ISN'T A GOOD PUN. TRY AGAIN.
His indomitable will against its raw primordial essence.
His imagination made manifest.
THAT DINKY THING DOESN'T LOOK TOO IMAGINATIVE TO ME.
DRUM ROLL, PLEASE...

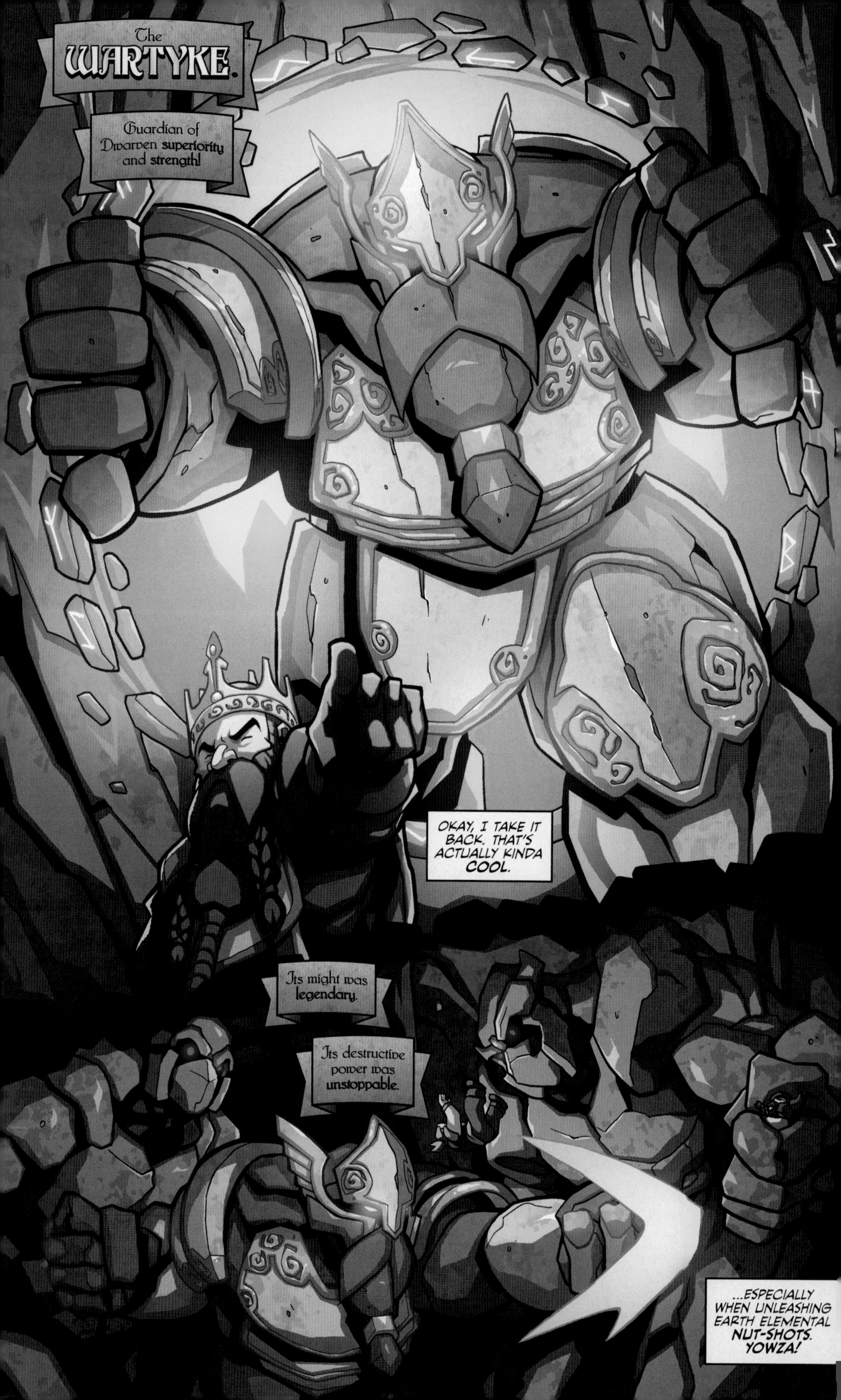
The WARTYKE.
Guardian of Dwarven superiority and strength!
OKAY, I TAKE IT BACK. THAT'S ACTUALLY KINDA COOL.
Its might was legendary.
Its destructive power was unstoppable.
...ESPECIALLY WHEN UNLEASHING EARTH ELEMENTAL NUT-SHOTS. YOWZA!

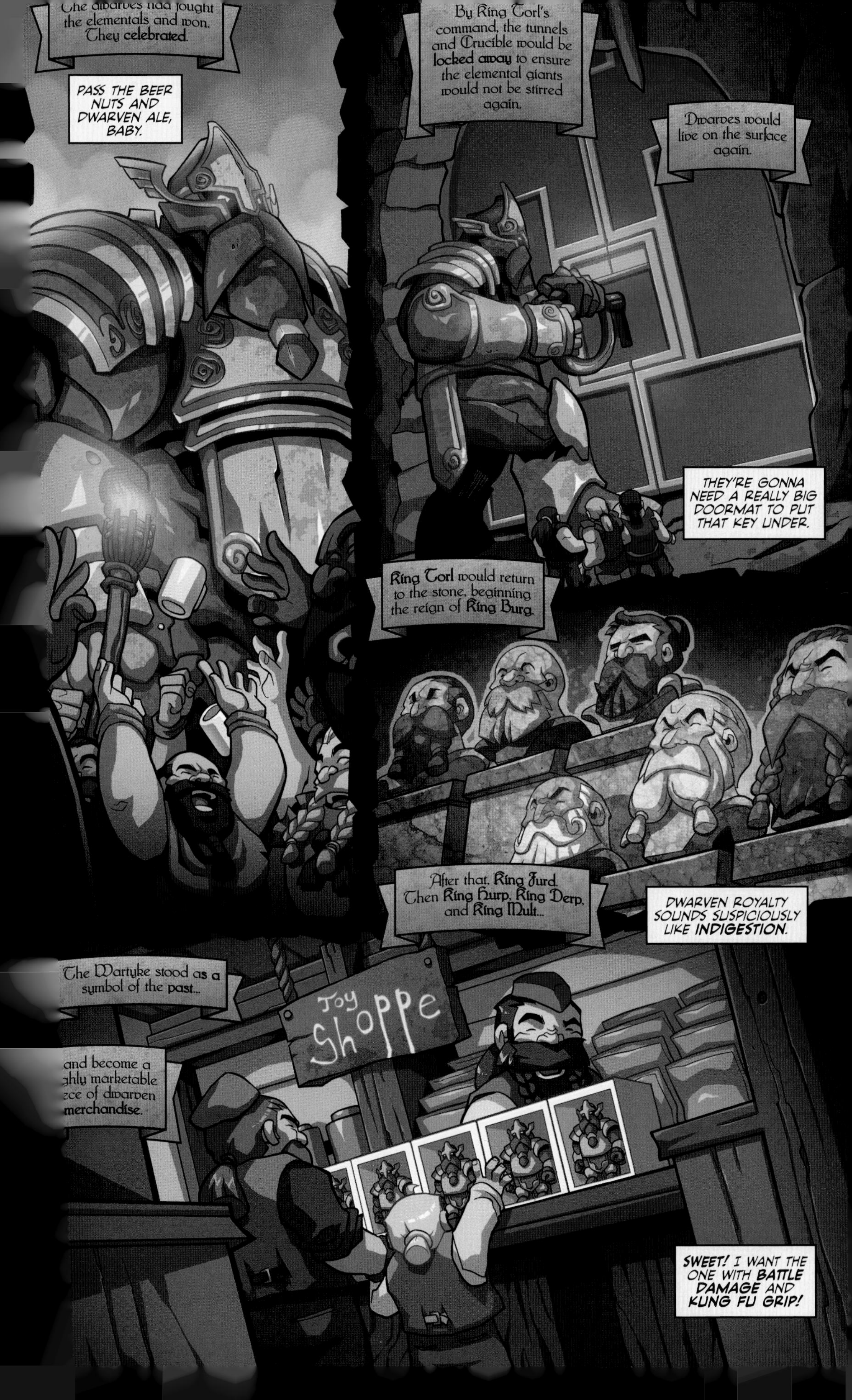

The dwarves had fought the elementals and won. They celebrated.
PASS THE BEER NUTS AND DWARVEN ALE, BABY.
By King Torl's command, the tunnels and Crucible would be locked away to ensure the elemental giants would not be stirred again.
Dwarves would live on the surface again.
THEY'RE GONNA NEED A REALLY BIG DOORMAT TO PUT THAT KEY UNDER.
King Torl would return to the stone, beginning the reign of King Burg.
After that, King Jurd. Then King Hurp, King Derp, and King Mult...
DWARVEN ROYALTY SOUNDS SUSPICIOUSLY LIKE INDIGESTION.
The Wartyke stood as a symbol of the past...
Toy Shoppe
and become a ghly marketable ece of dwarven merchandise.
SWEET! I WANT THE ONE WITH BATTLE DAMAGE AND KUNG FU GRIP!

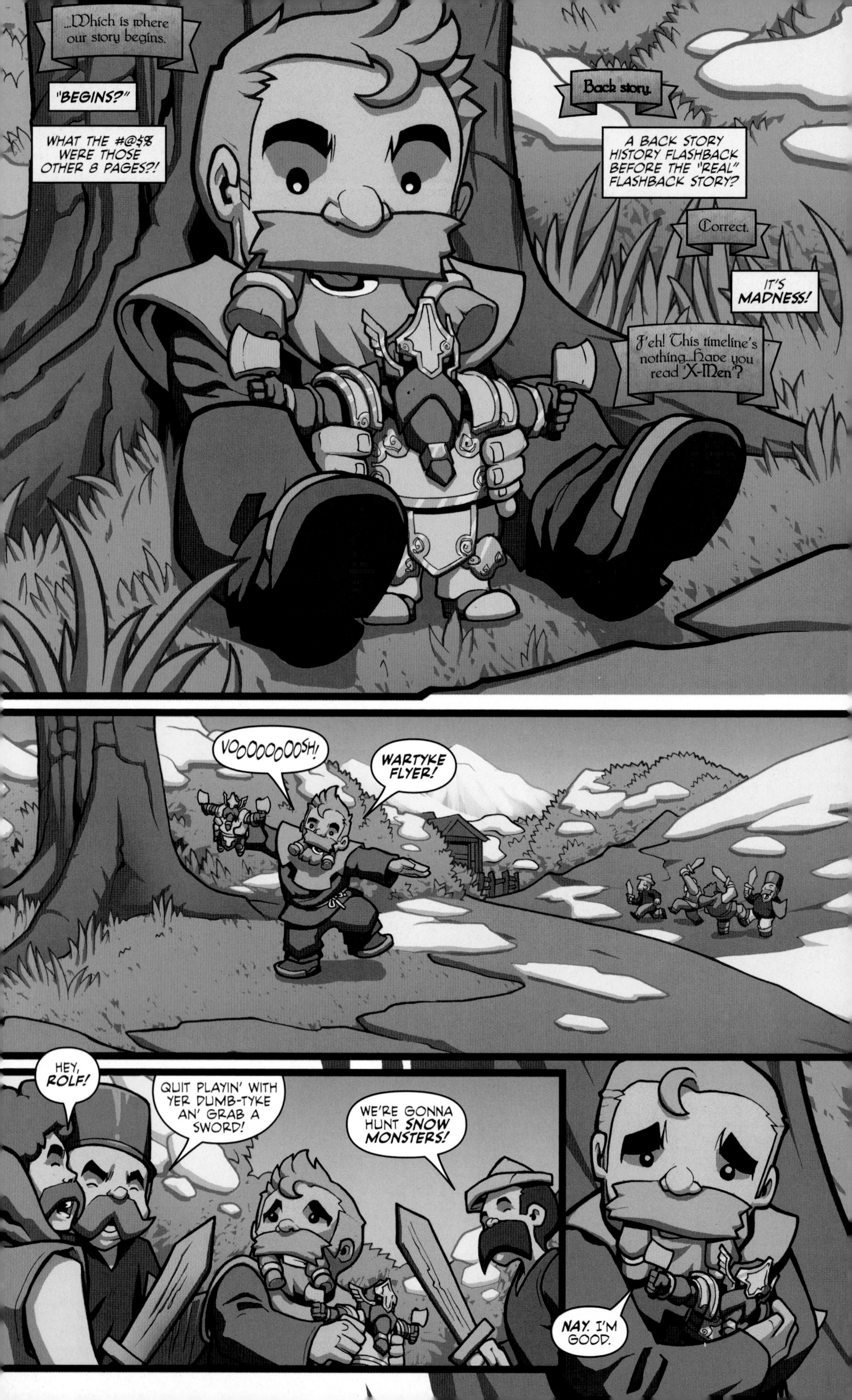
...Which is where our story begins.
"BEGINS?"
WHAT THE #@$% WERE THOSE OTHER 8 PAGES?!
Back story.
A BACK STORY HISTORY FLASHBACK BEFORE THE "REAL" FLASHBACK STORY?
Correct.
IT'S MADNESS!
Feh! This timeline's nothing...Have you read 'X-Men'?
VOOOOOOOOSH!
WARTYKE FLYER!
HEY, ROLF!
QUIT PLAYIN' WITH YER DUMB-TYKE AN' GRAB A SWORD!
WE'RE GONNA HUNT SNOW MONSTERS!
NAY. I'M GOOD.

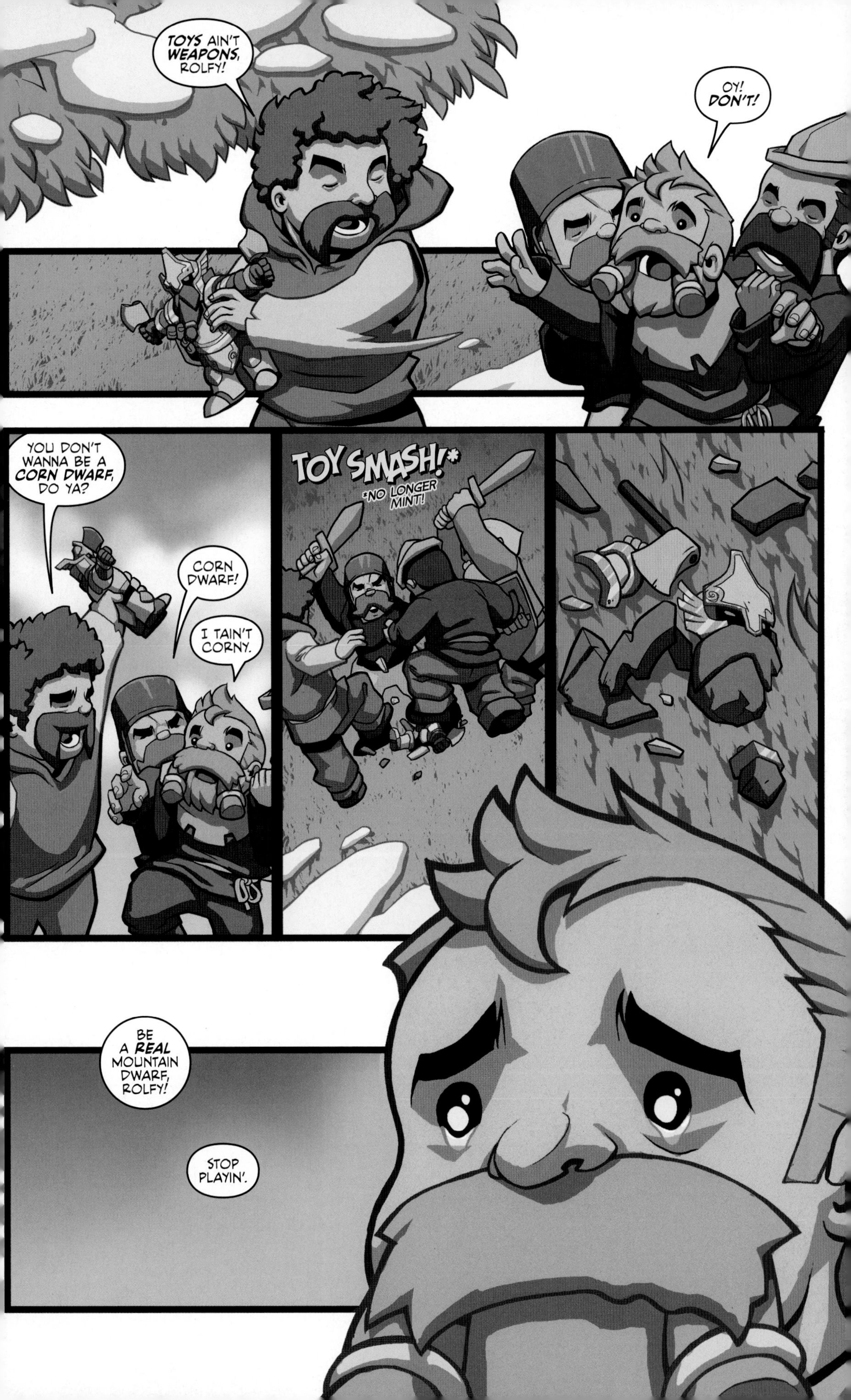
TOYS AIN'T WEAPONS, ROLFY!
OY! DON'T!
YOU DON'T WANNA BE A CORN DWARF, DO YA?
CORN DWARF!
I TAIN'T CORNY.
TOY SMASH!*
*NO LONGER MINT!
BE A REAL MOUNTAIN DWARF, ROLFY!
STOP PLAYIN'.

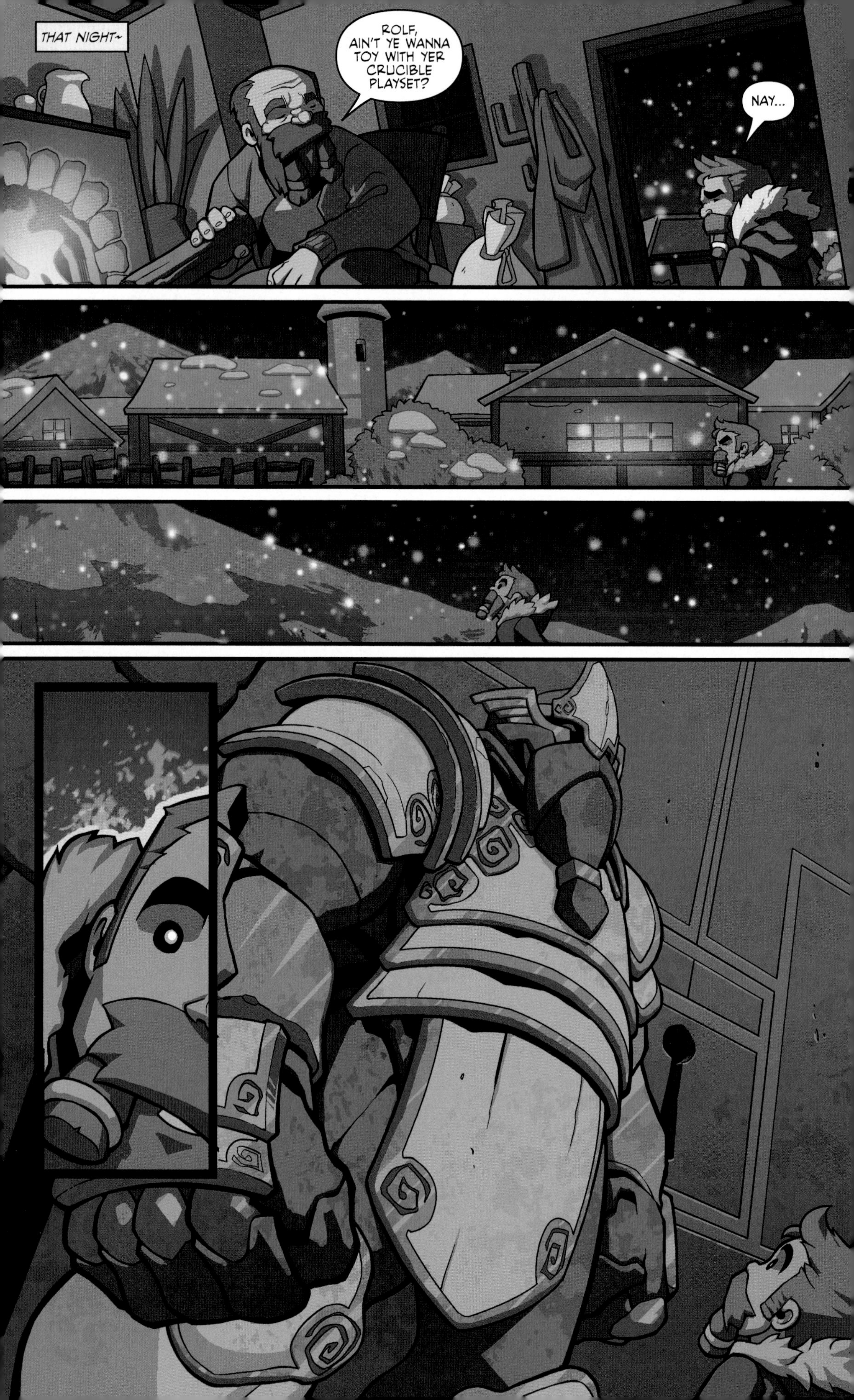
THAT NIGHT~
ROLF, AIN'T YE WANNA TOY WITH YER CRUCIBLE PLAYSET?
NAY...

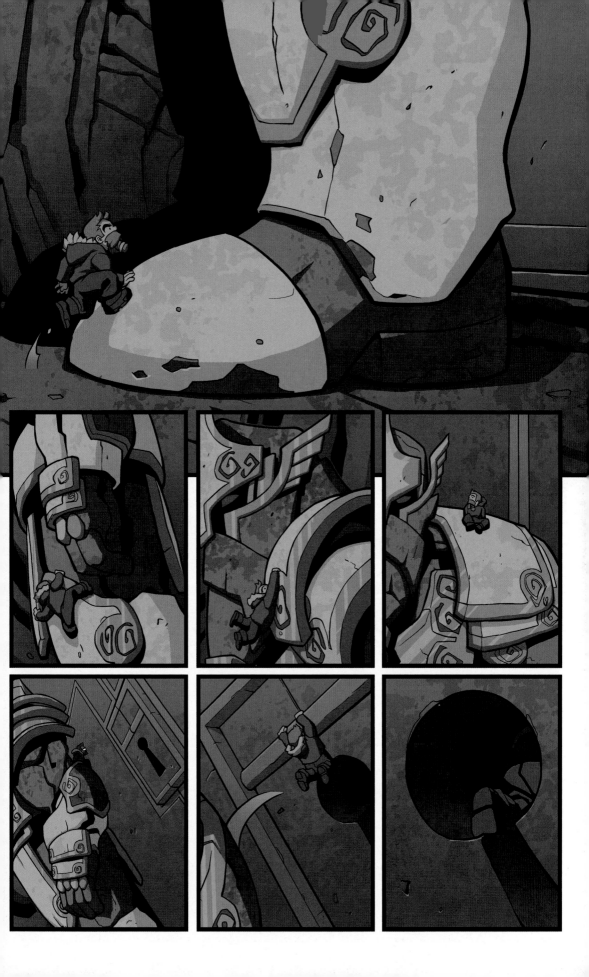

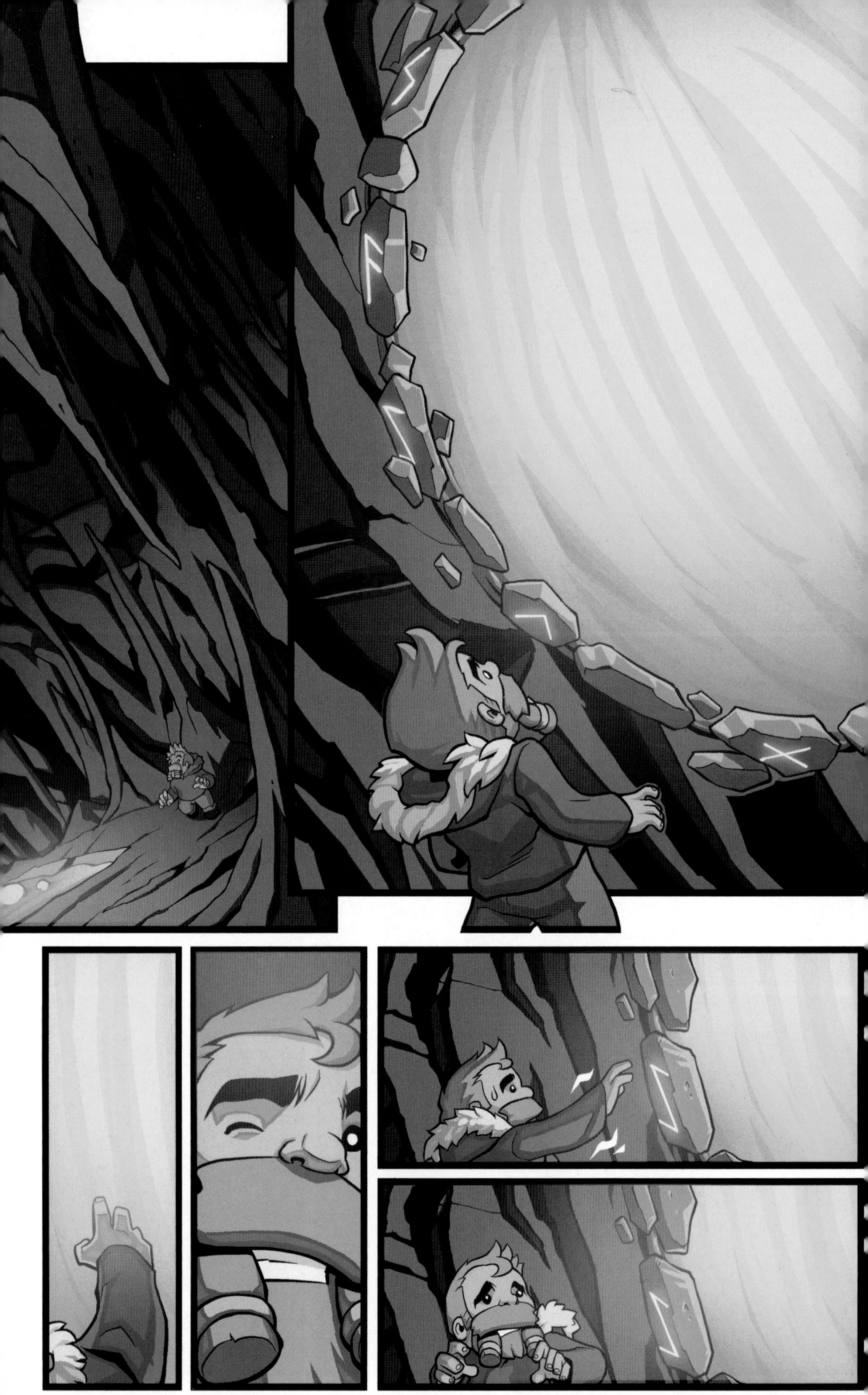

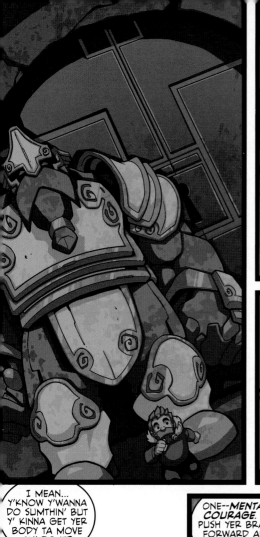

WHERE'D YA GO?

OUT.

DAD... DIDJA EVER GIT *SCARED?*

EH?

I MEAN... Y'KNOW Y'WANNA DO SUMTHIN' BUT Y' KINNA GET YER BODY TA MOVE AN' DO IT?

HEH.

AYE. I'VE HAD MY SHARE OF "*BONESHAKES*" NOW AN' AGAIN.

THERE'S A *COUPLE* WAYS TA *SOLVE* IT...

ONE--*MENTAL COURAGE.* Y' PUSH YER BRAIN FORWARD AN' DO THE SCARY THING.

TWO-- *LIQUID COURAGE.* Y' DROWN YER BRAIN 'TIL IT DON'T KNOW TA BE SCARED NO MORE.

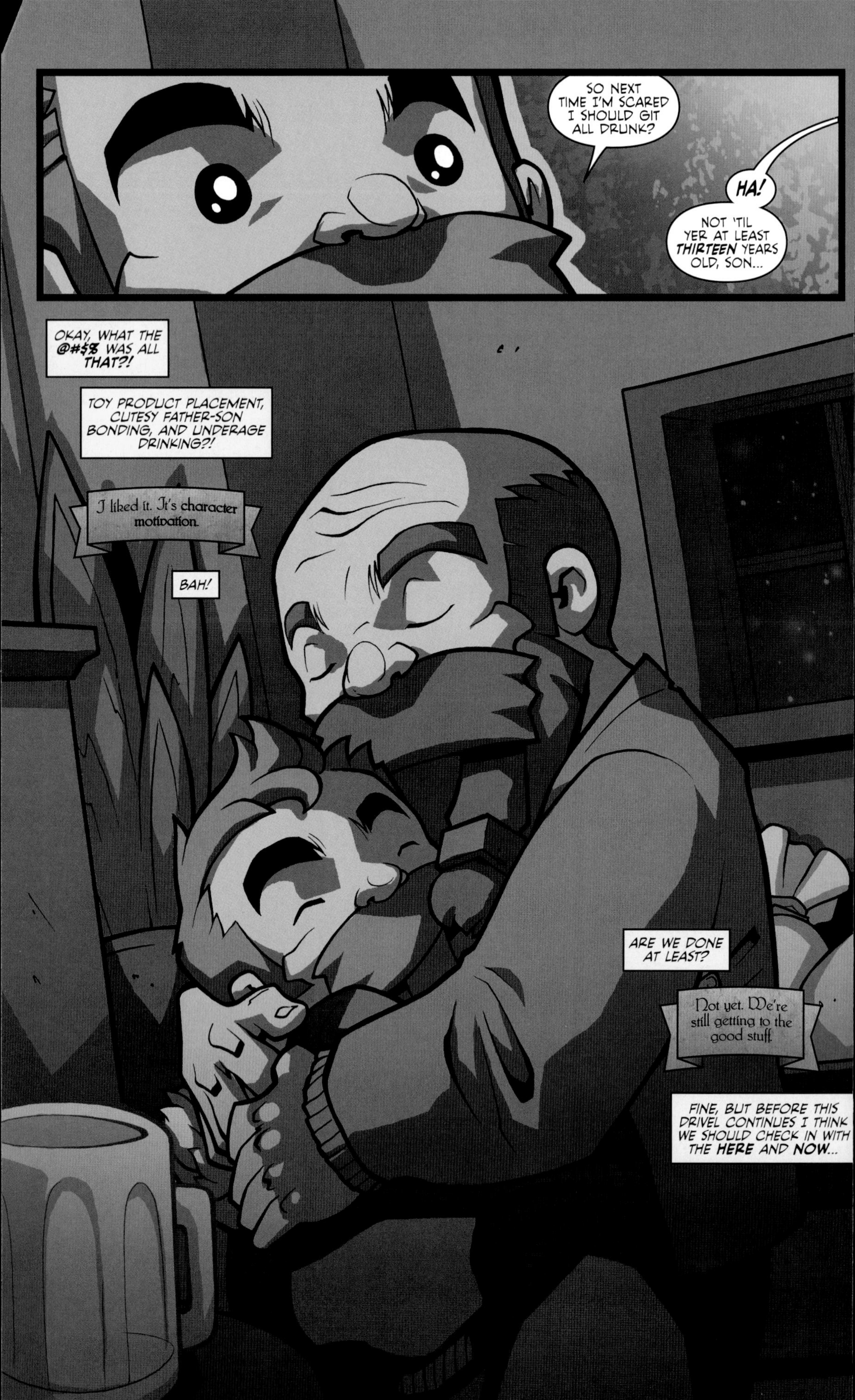
SO NEXT TIME I'M SCARED I SHOULD GIT ALL DRUNK?
HA!
NOT 'TIL YER AT LEAST THIRTEEN YEARS OLD, SON...
OKAY, WHAT THE @#$% WAS ALL THAT?!
TOY PRODUCT PLACEMENT, CUTESY FATHER-SON BONDING, AND UNDERAGE DRINKING?!
I liked it. It's character motivation.
BAH!
ARE WE DONE AT LEAST?
Not yet. We're still getting to the good stuff.
FINE, BUT BEFORE THIS DRIVEL CONTINUES I THINK WE SHOULD CHECK IN WITH THE HERE AND NOW...

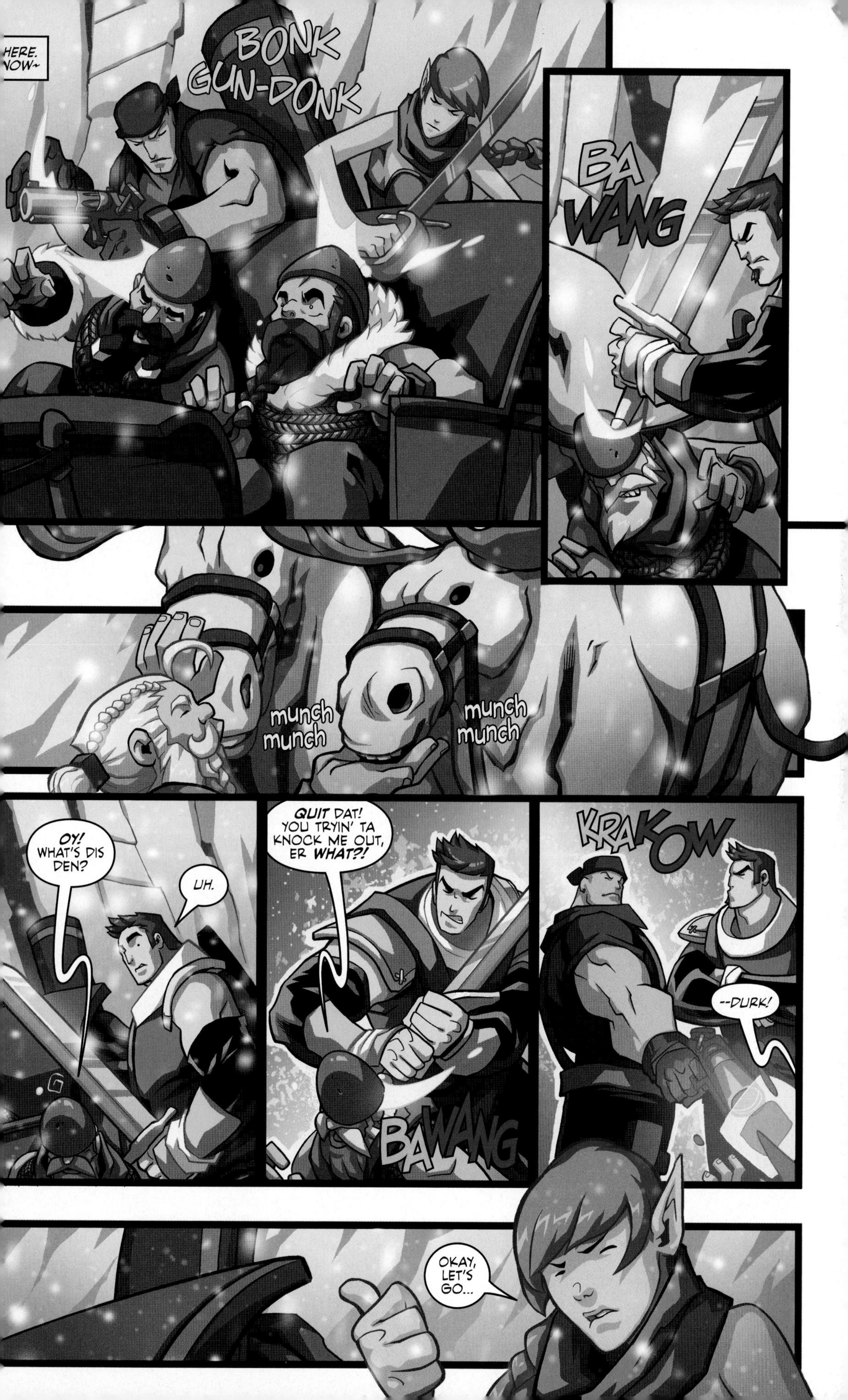
HERE.
NOW-
BONK
GUN-DONK
BA
WANG
munch
munch
munch
munch
OY! WHAT'S DIS DEN?
UH.
QUIT DAT! YOU TRYIN' TA KNOCK ME OUT, ER WHAT?!
BAWANG
KRAKOW
--DURK!
OKAY, LET'S GO...

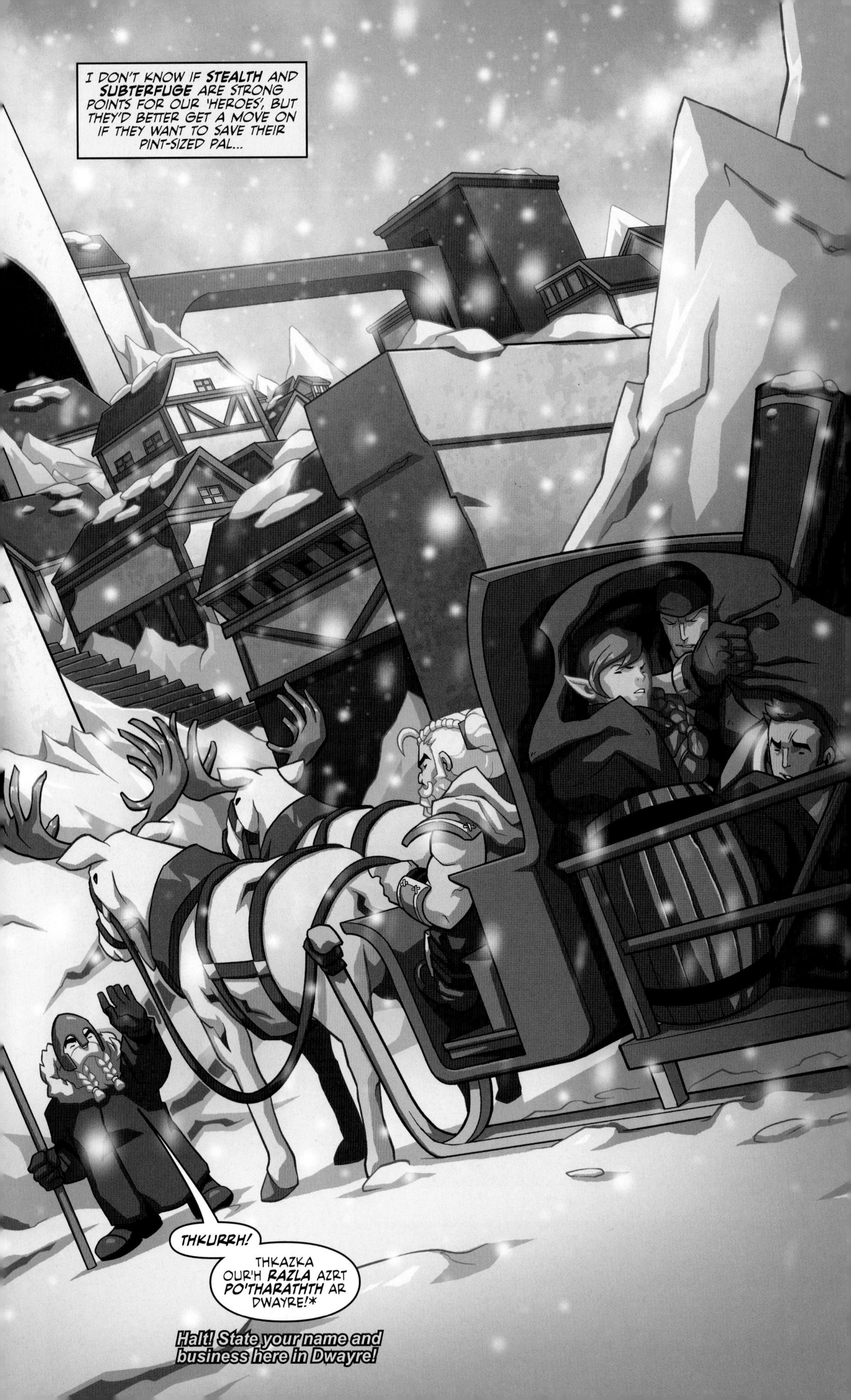
I DON'T KNOW IF STEALTH AND SUBTERFUGE ARE STRONG POINTS FOR OUR 'HEROES', BUT THEY'D BETTER GET A MOVE ON IF THEY WANT TO SAVE THEIR PINT-SIZED PAL...
THKURRH!
THKAZKA OUR'H RAZLA AZRT PO'THARATHTH AR DWAYRE!*
Halt! State your name and business here in Dwayre!

CHAPTER THREE

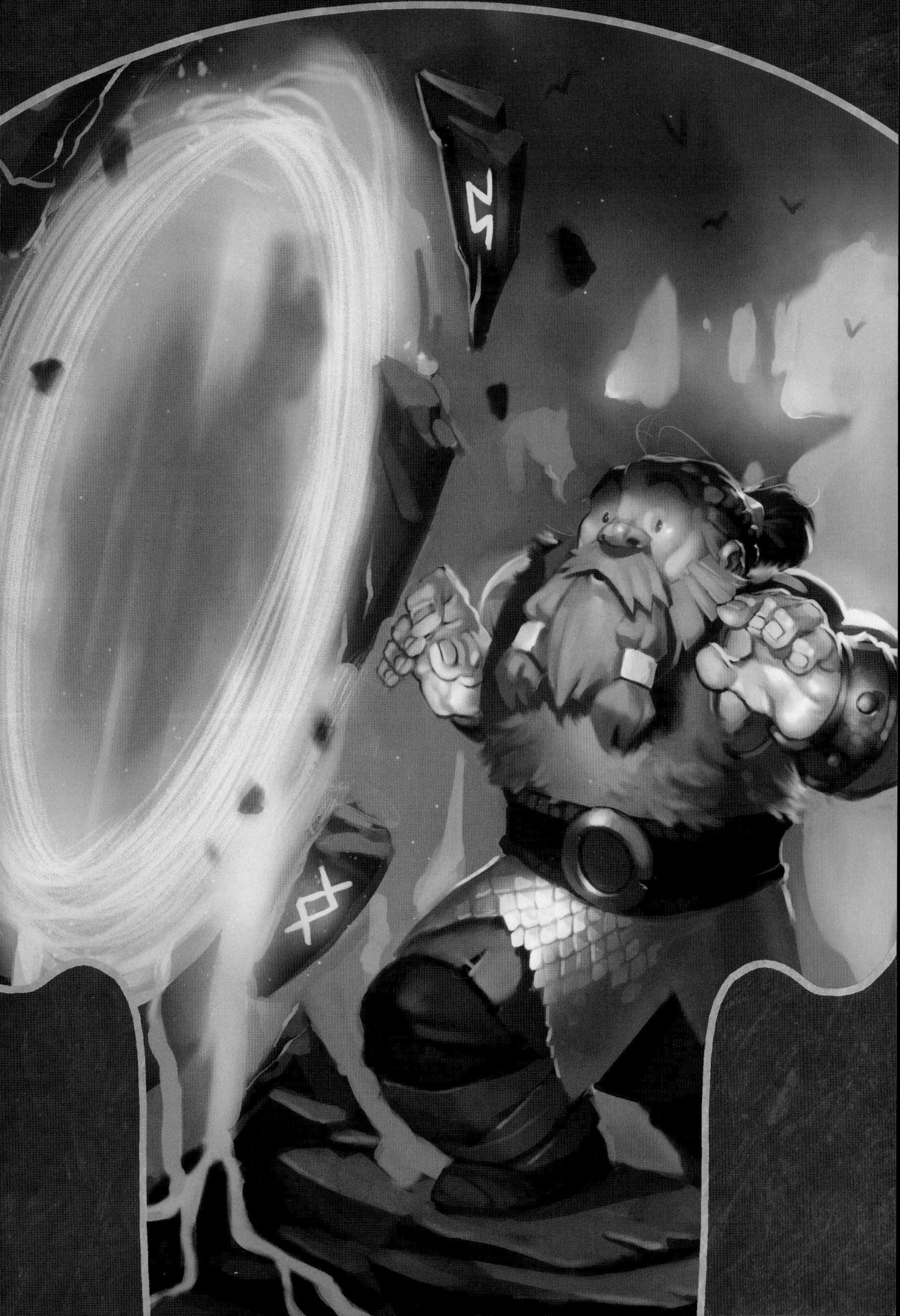

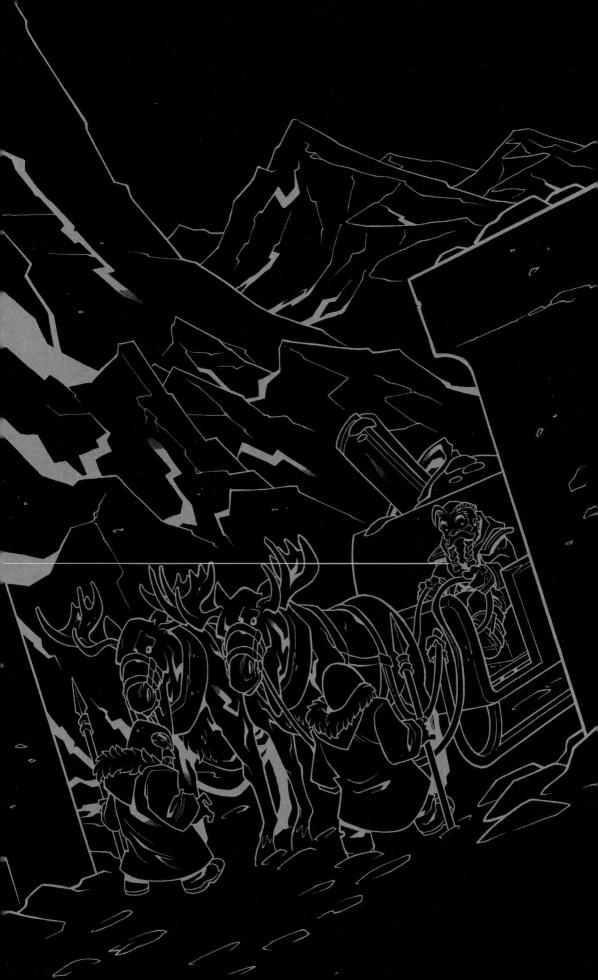

A DOZEN COUSINS and a CRUMPLED CROWN Part 3
AH, YES... OUR HEROES ARE USING THE OL' "WE'LL SNEAK IN PRETENDING TO BE MERCHANTS" TRICK. A TIME-HONORED CLASSIC...
THKURRH!
THKAZKA OUR'H RAZLA AZRT PO'THARATHTH AR DWAYRE!
Halt! State your name and business here in Dwayre!

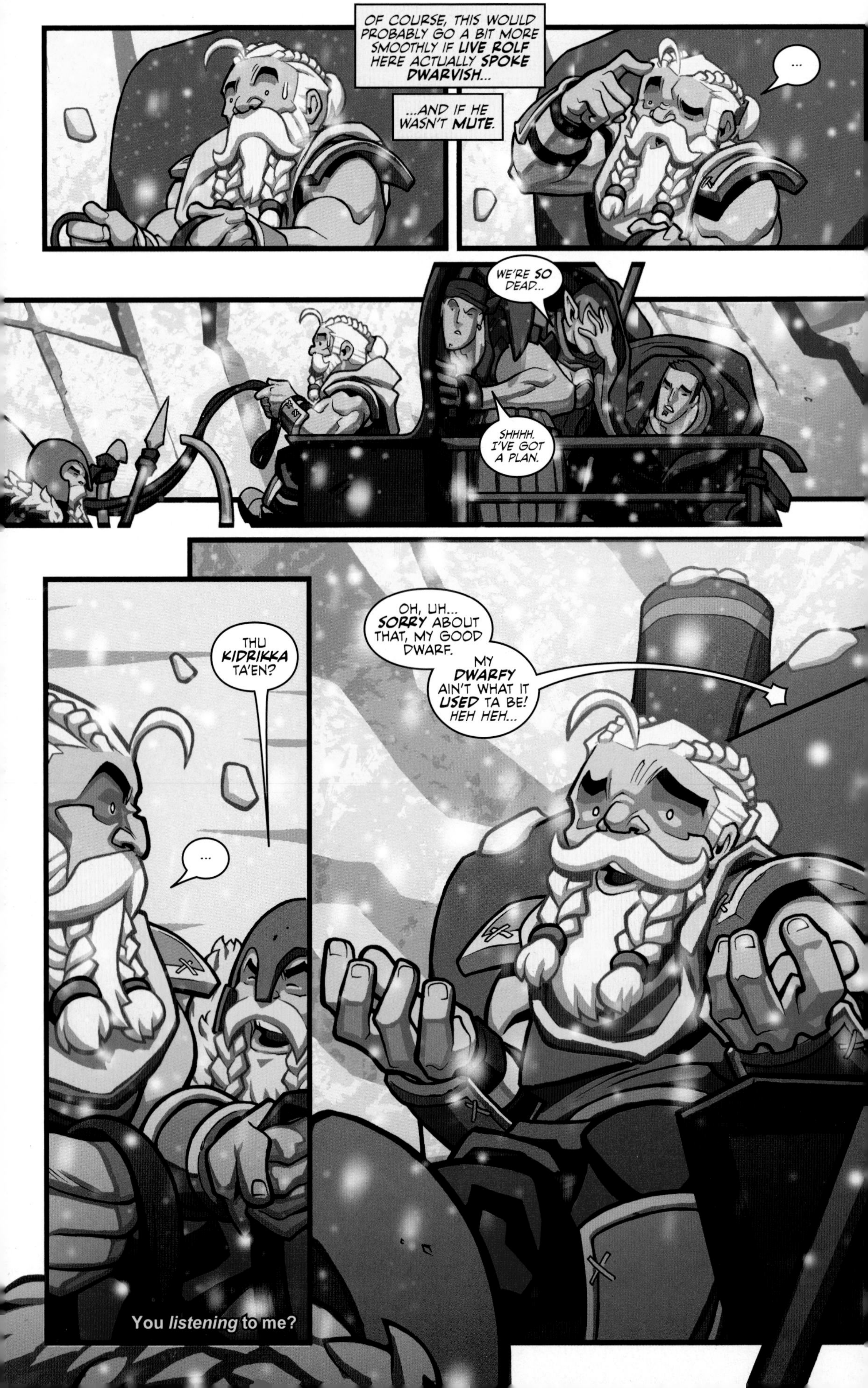
OF COURSE, THIS WOULD PROBABLY GO A BIT MORE SMOOTHLY IF LIVE ROLF HERE ACTUALLY SPOKE DWARVISH...
...AND IF HE WASN'T MUTE.
...
WE'RE SO DEAD...
SHHHH. I'VE GOT A PLAN.
THU KIDRIKKA TA'EN?
...
OH, UH... SORRY ABOUT THAT, MY GOOD DWARF.
MY DWARFY AIN'T WHAT IT USED TA BE! HEH HEH...
You listening to me?

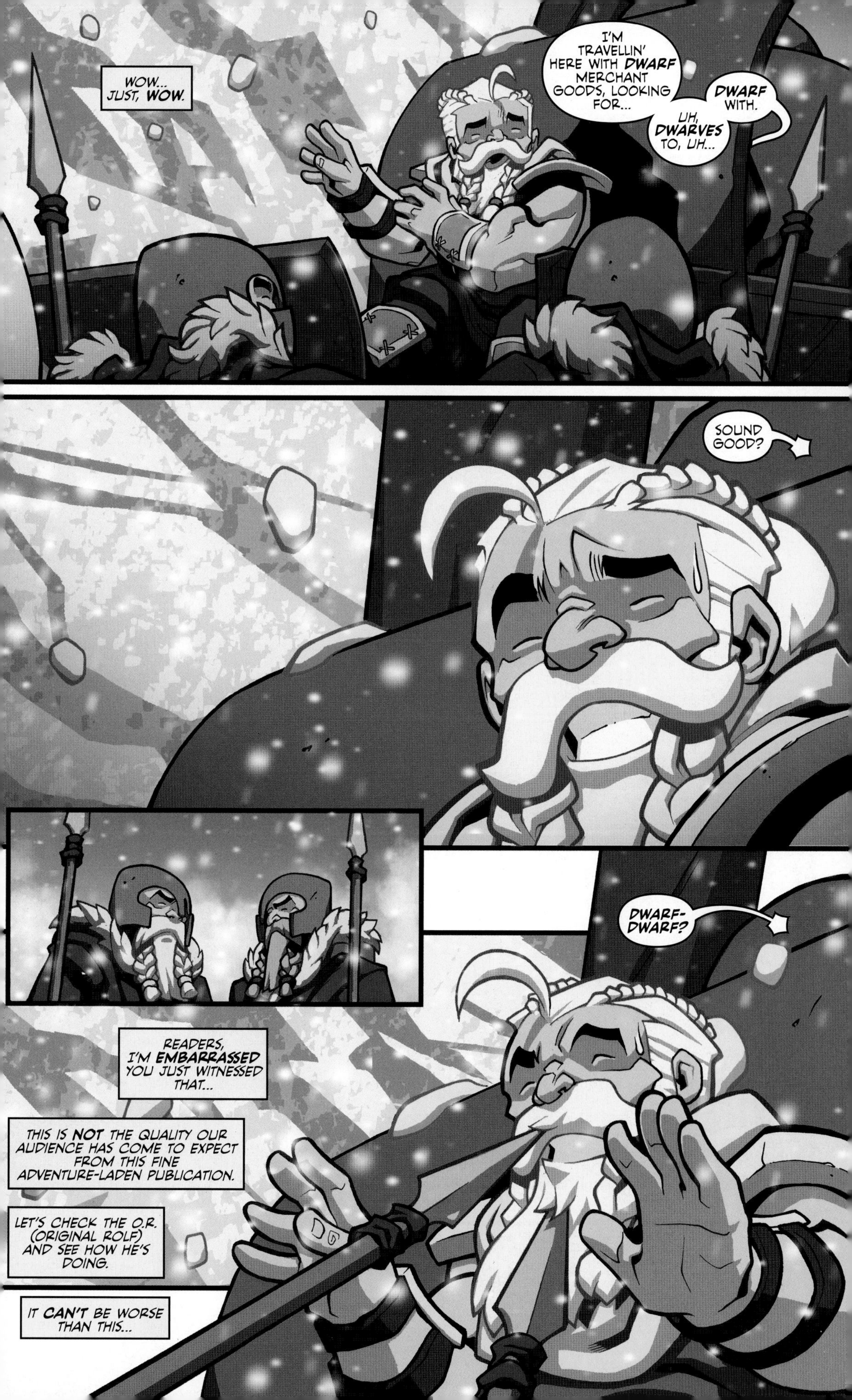
WOW... JUST, WOW.
I'M TRAVELLIN' HERE WITH DWARF MERCHANT GOODS, LOOKING FOR...
UH, DWARVES TO, UH...
DWARF WITH.
SOUND GOOD?
DWARF-DWARF?
READERS, I'M EMBARRASSED YOU JUST WITNESSED THAT...
THIS IS NOT THE QUALITY OUR AUDIENCE HAS COME TO EXPECT FROM THIS FINE ADVENTURE-LADEN PUBLICATION.
LET'S CHECK THE O.R. (ORIGINAL ROLF) AND SEE HOW HE'S DOING.
IT CAN'T BE WORSE THAN THIS...

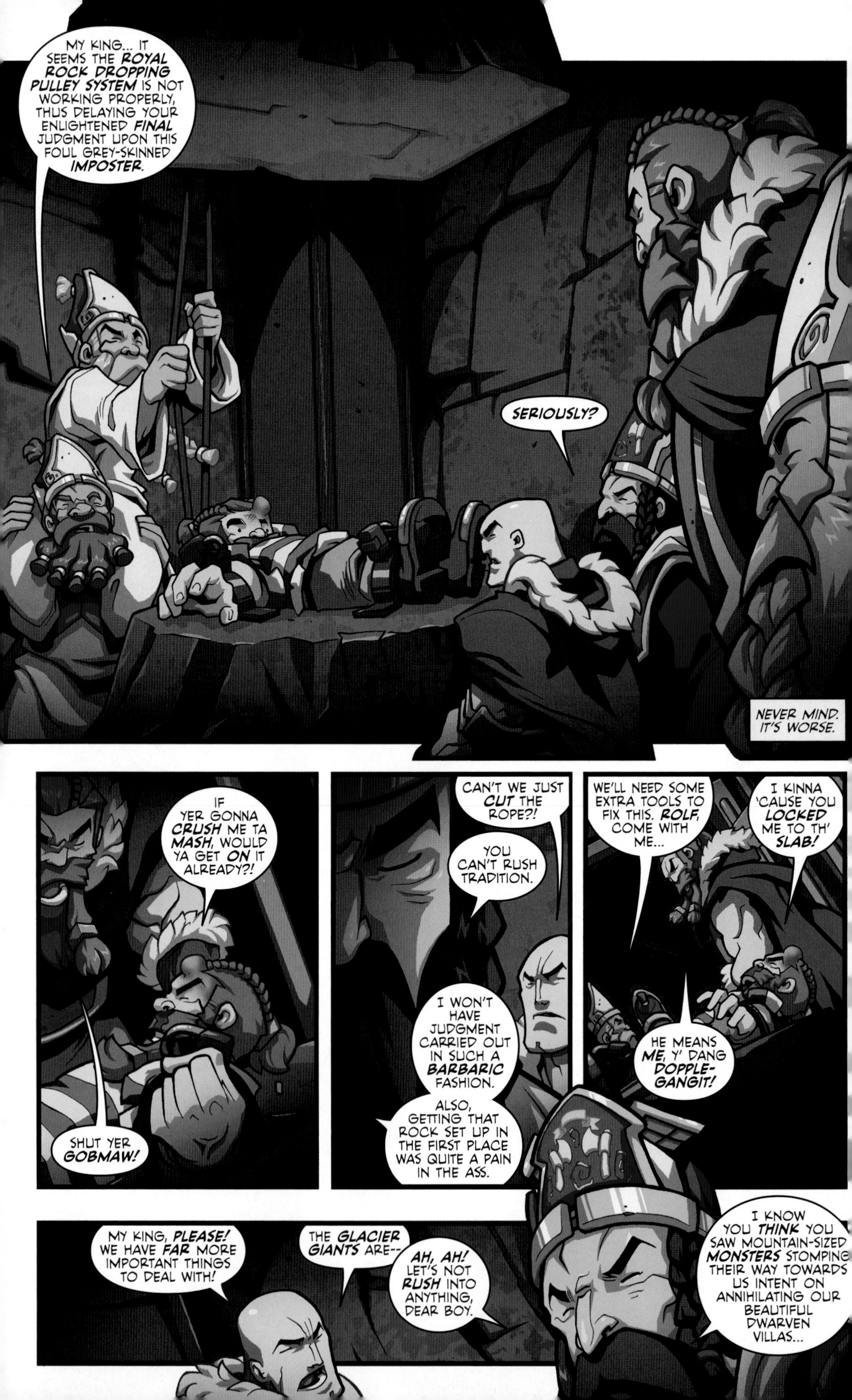
MY KING... IT SEEMS THE ROYAL ROCK DROPPING PULLEY SYSTEM IS NOT WORKING PROPERLY, THUS DELAYING YOUR ENLIGHTENED FINAL JUDGMENT UPON THIS FOUL GREY-SKINNED IMPOSTER.
SERIOUSLY?
NEVER MIND. IT'S WORSE.
IF YER GONNA CRUSH ME TA MASH, WOULD YA GET ON IT ALREADY?!
SHUT YER GOBMAW!
CAN'T WE JUST CUT THE ROPE?!
YOU CAN'T RUSH TRADITION.
I WON'T HAVE JUDGMENT CARRIED OUT IN SUCH A BARBARIC FASHION.
ALSO, GETTING THAT ROCK SET UP IN THE FIRST PLACE WAS QUITE A PAIN IN THE ASS.
WE'LL NEED SOME EXTRA TOOLS TO FIX THIS. ROLF, COME WITH ME...
I KINNA 'CAUSE YOU LOCKED ME TO TH' SLAB!
HE MEANS ME, Y' DANG DOPPLE-GANGIT!
MY KING, PLEASE! WE HAVE FAR MORE IMPORTANT THINGS TO DEAL WITH!
THE GLACIER GIANTS ARE--
AH, AH! LET'S NOT RUSH INTO ANYTHING, DEAR BOY.
I KNOW YOU THINK YOU SAW MOUNTAIN-SIZED MONSTERS STOMPING THEIR WAY TOWARDS US INTENT ON ANNIHILATING OUR BEAUTIFUL DWARVEN VILLAS...

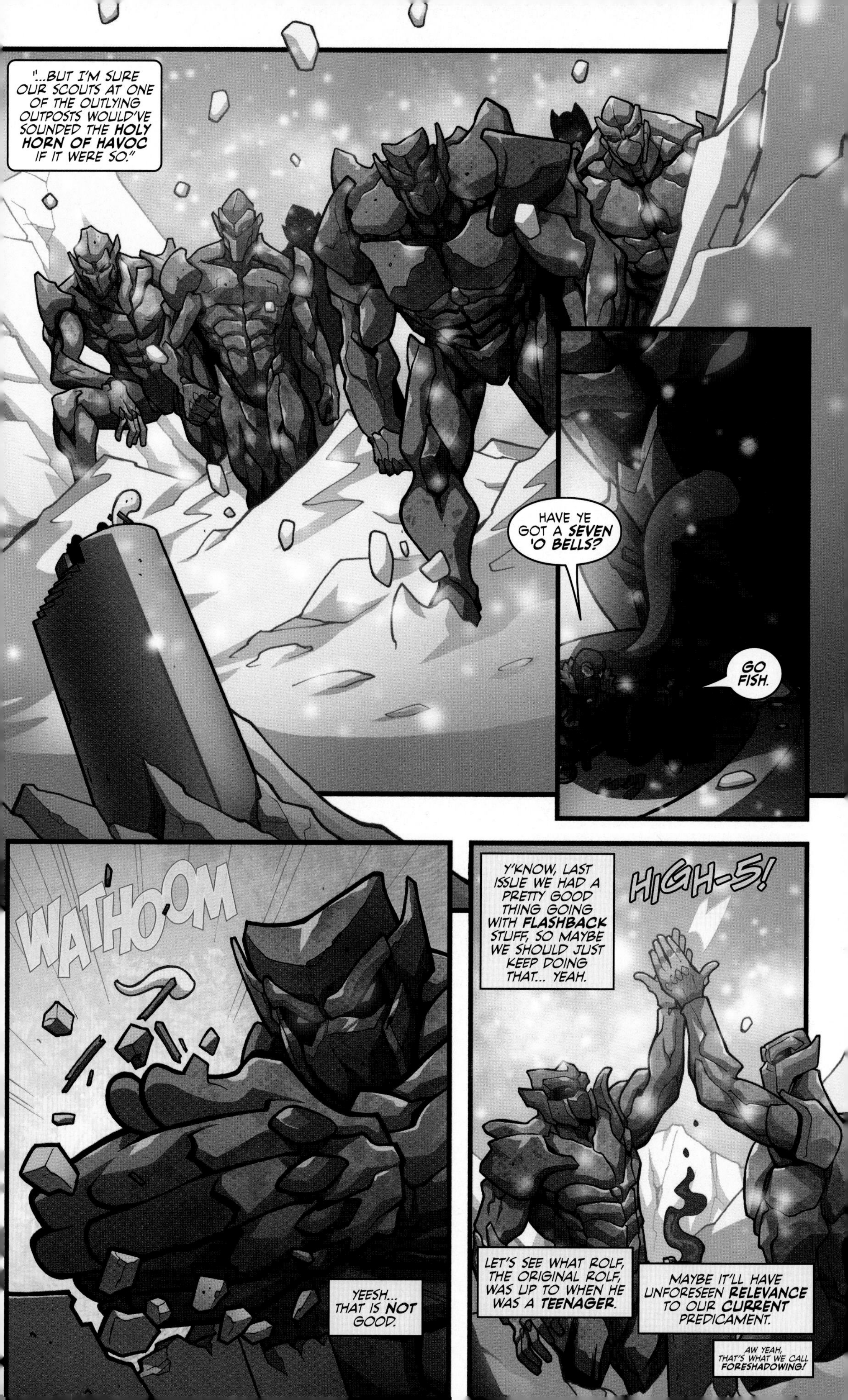
"...BUT I'M SURE OUR SCOUTS AT ONE OF THE OUTLYING OUTPOSTS WOULD'VE SOUNDED THE **HOLY HORN OF HAVOC** IF IT WERE SO."
HAVE YE GOT A **SEVEN 'O BELLS?**
GO FISH.
WATHOOM
YEESH... THAT IS **NOT** GOOD.
Y'KNOW, LAST ISSUE WE HAD A PRETTY GOOD THING GOING WITH **FLASHBACK** STUFF, SO MAYBE WE SHOULD JUST KEEP DOING THAT... YEAH.
HIGH-5!
LET'S SEE WHAT ROLF, THE ORIGINAL ROLF, WAS UP TO WHEN HE WAS A **TEENAGER**.
MAYBE IT'LL HAVE UNFORESEEN **RELEVANCE** TO OUR **CURRENT** PREDICAMENT.
AW YEAH, THAT'S WHAT WE CALL **FORESHADOWING!**

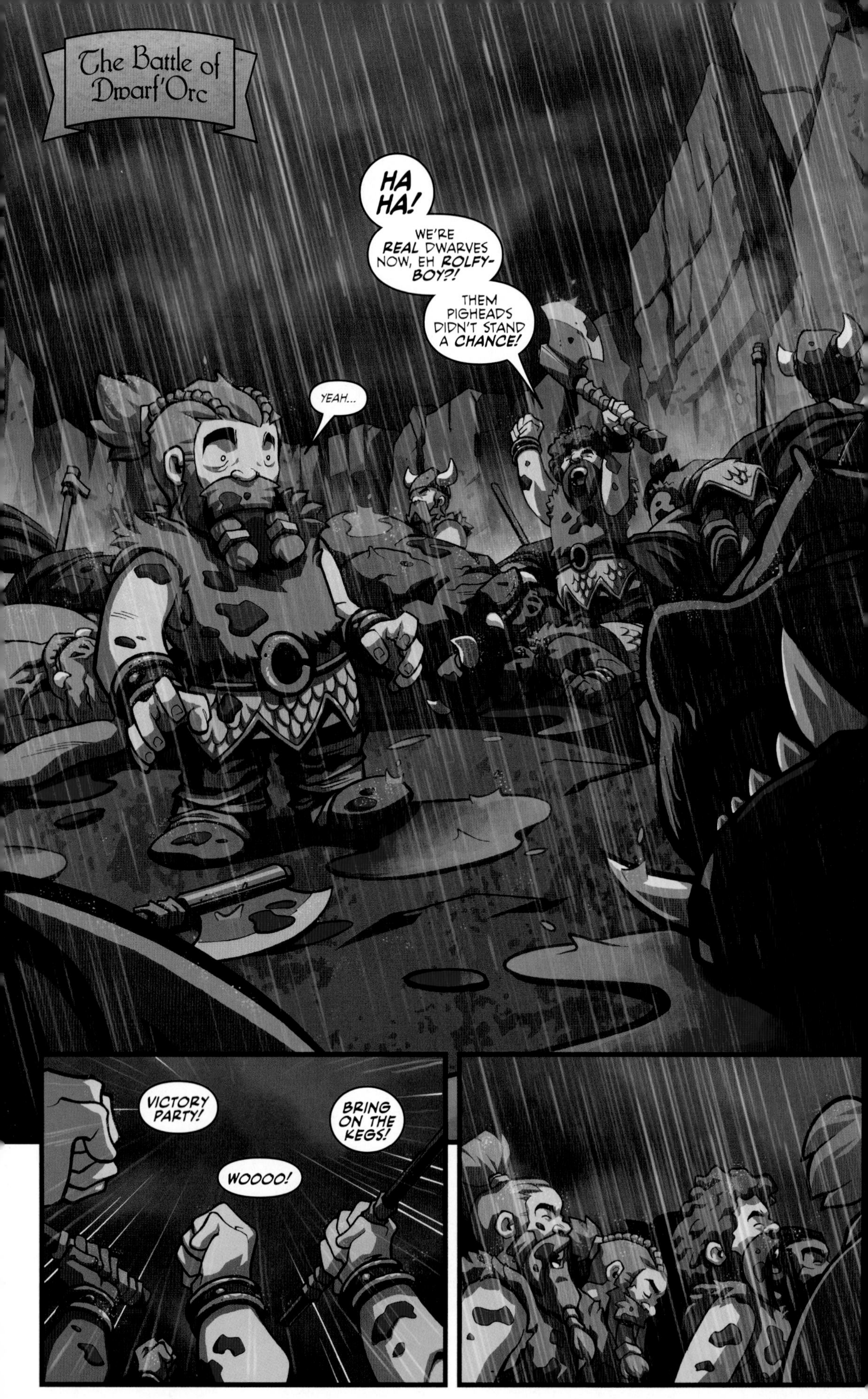

The Battle of Dwarf'Orc
HA HA!
WE'RE **REAL** DWARVES NOW, EH **ROLFY-BOY?!**
THEM PIGHEADS DIDN'T STAND A **CHANCE!**
YEAH...
VICTORY PARTY!
BRING ON THE KEGS!
WOOOO!

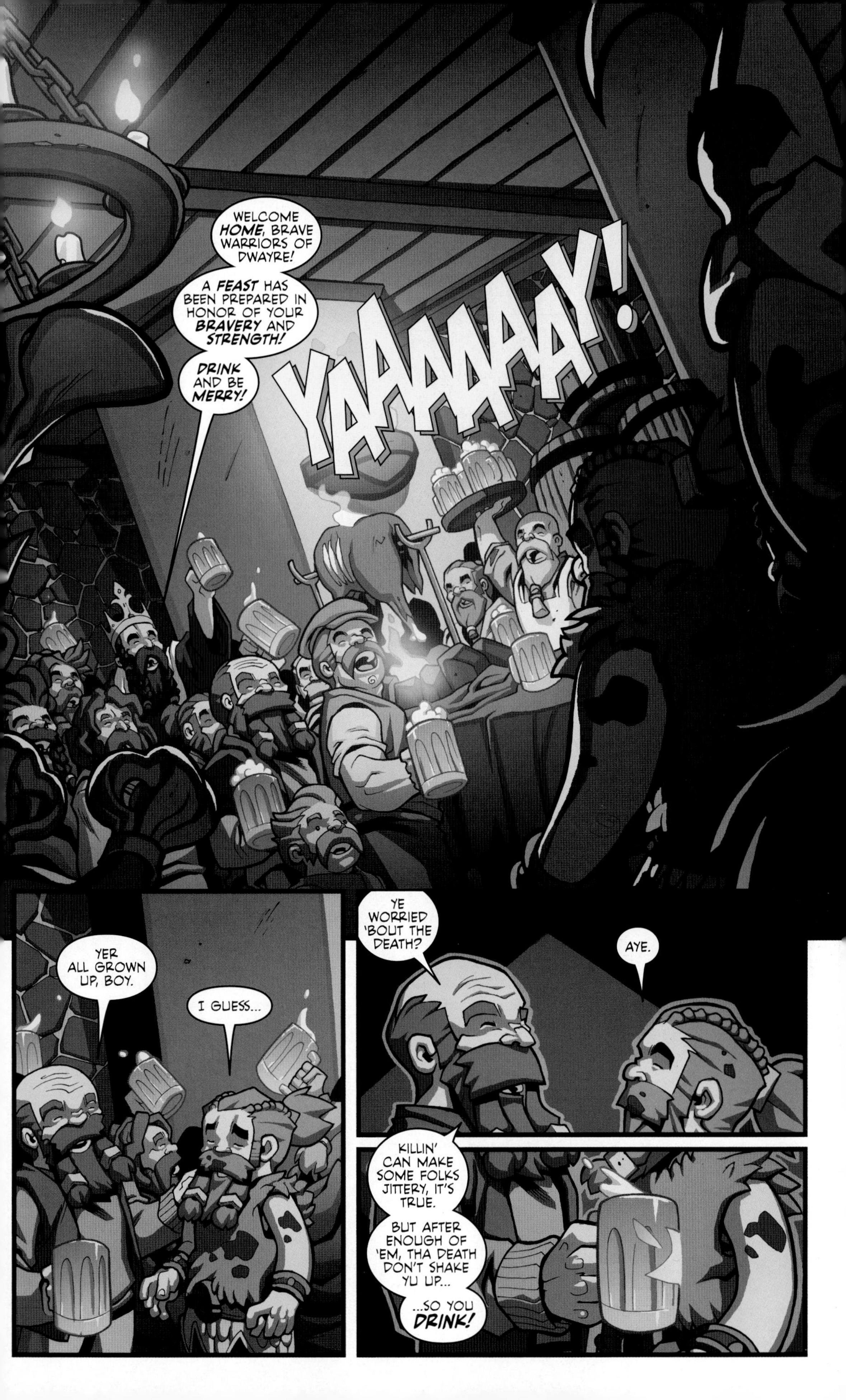
WELCOME HOME, BRAVE WARRIORS OF DWAYRE!
A FEAST HAS BEEN PREPARED IN HONOR OF YOUR BRAVERY AND STRENGTH!
DRINK AND BE MERRY!
YAAAAAY!
YER ALL GROWN UP, BOY.
I GUESS...
YE WORRIED 'BOUT THE DEATH?
AYE.
KILLIN' CAN MAKE SOME FOLKS JITTERY, IT'S TRUE.
BUT AFTER ENOUGH OF 'EM, THA DEATH DON'T SHAKE YU UP...
...SO YOU DRINK!

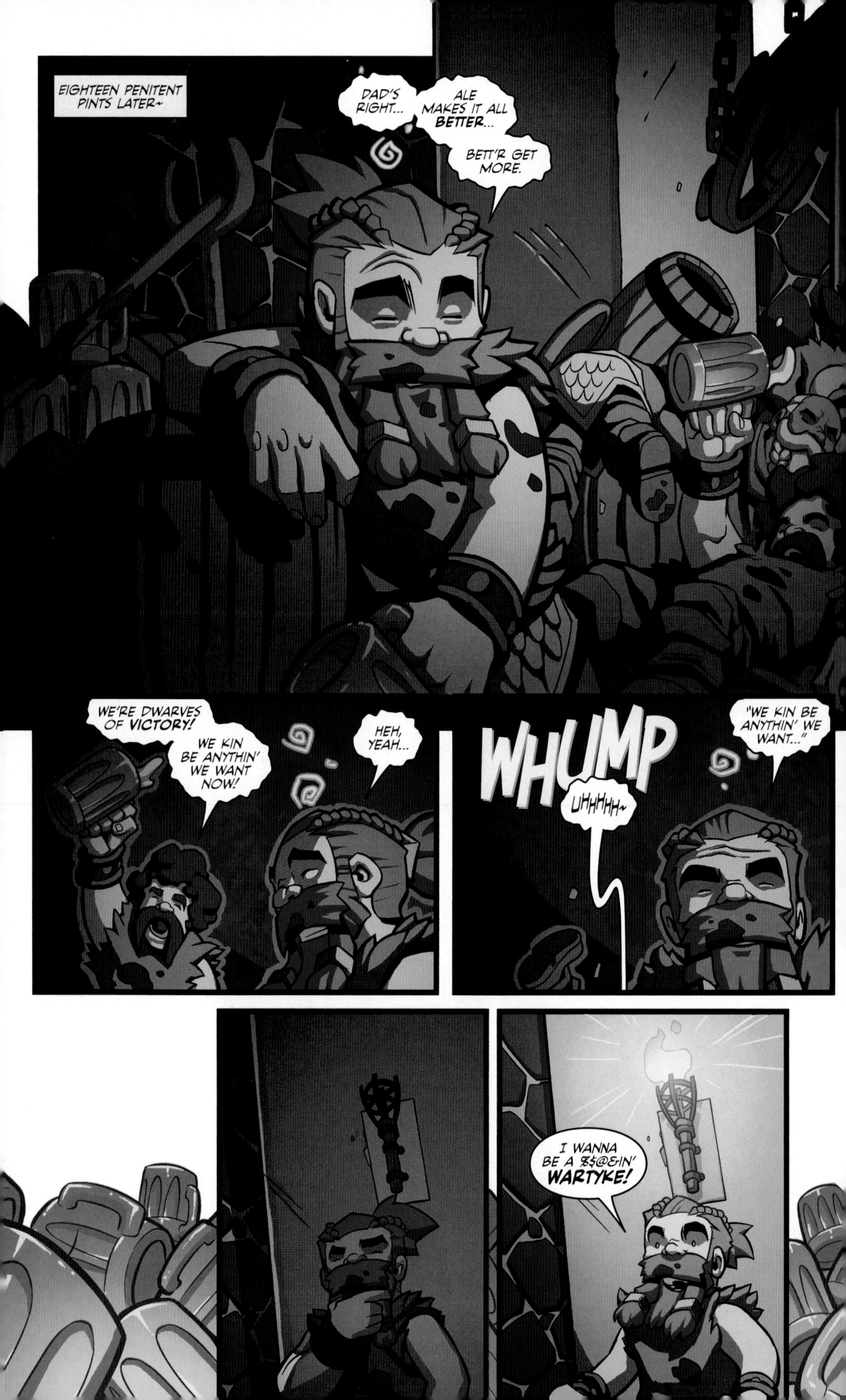
EIGHTEEN PENITENT PINTS LATER~
DAD'S RIGHT...
ALE MAKES IT ALL **BETTER**...
BETT'R GET MORE.
WE'RE DWARVES OF **VICTORY**!
WE KIN BE ANYTHIN' WE WANT NOW!
HEH, YEAH...
WHUMP
UHHHHH~
"WE KIN BE ANYTHIN' WE WANT..."
I WANNA BE A %$@&IN' **WARTYKE**!

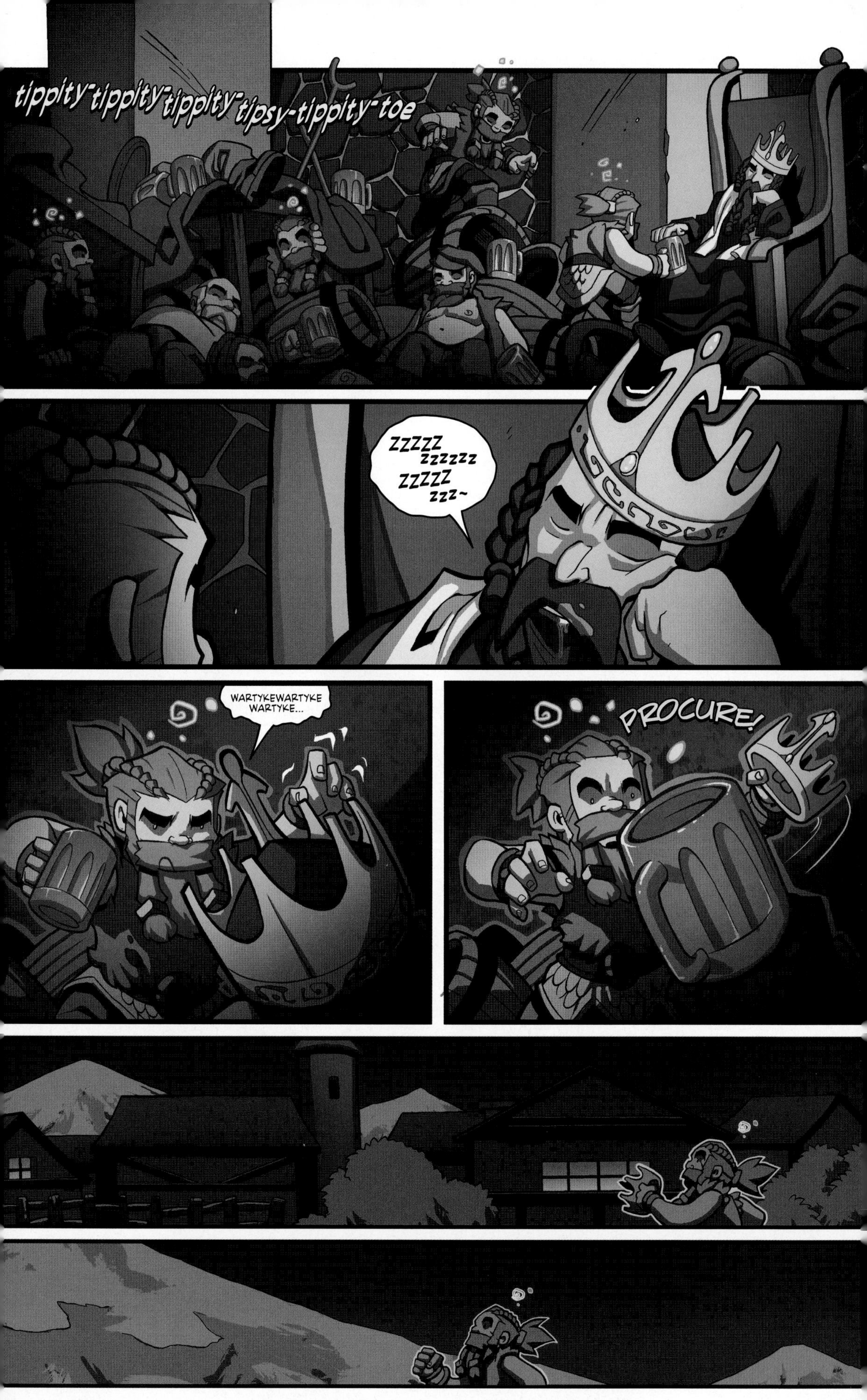
tippity-tippity-tippity-tipsy-tippity-toe
ZZZZZ zzzzzz ZZZZZ zzz~
WARTYKEWARTYKE WARTYKE...
PROCURE!

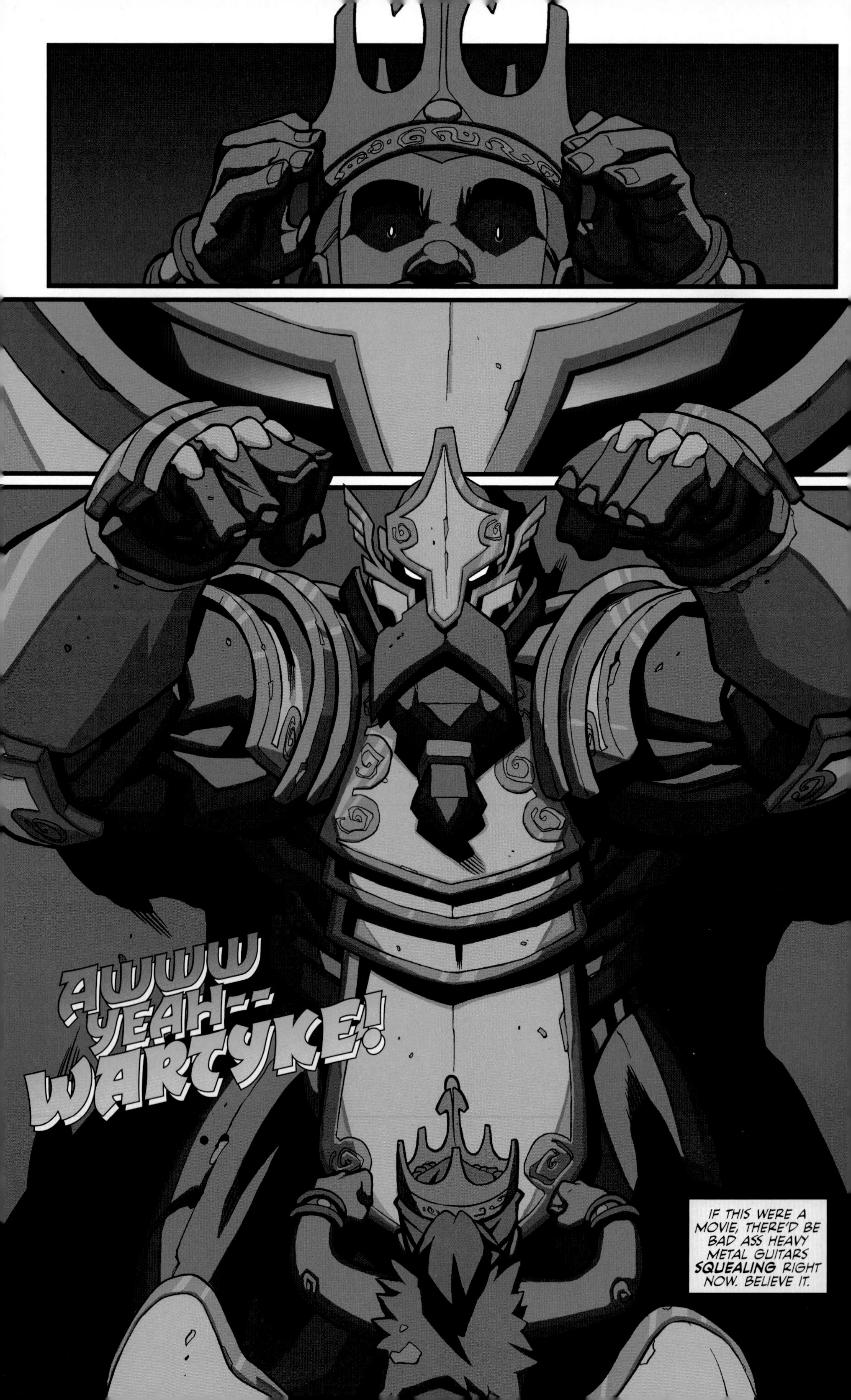
AWWW YEAH-- WARTYKE!
IF THIS WERE A MOVIE, THERE'D BE BAD ASS HEAVY METAL GUITARS SQUEALING RIGHT NOW. BELIEVE IT.

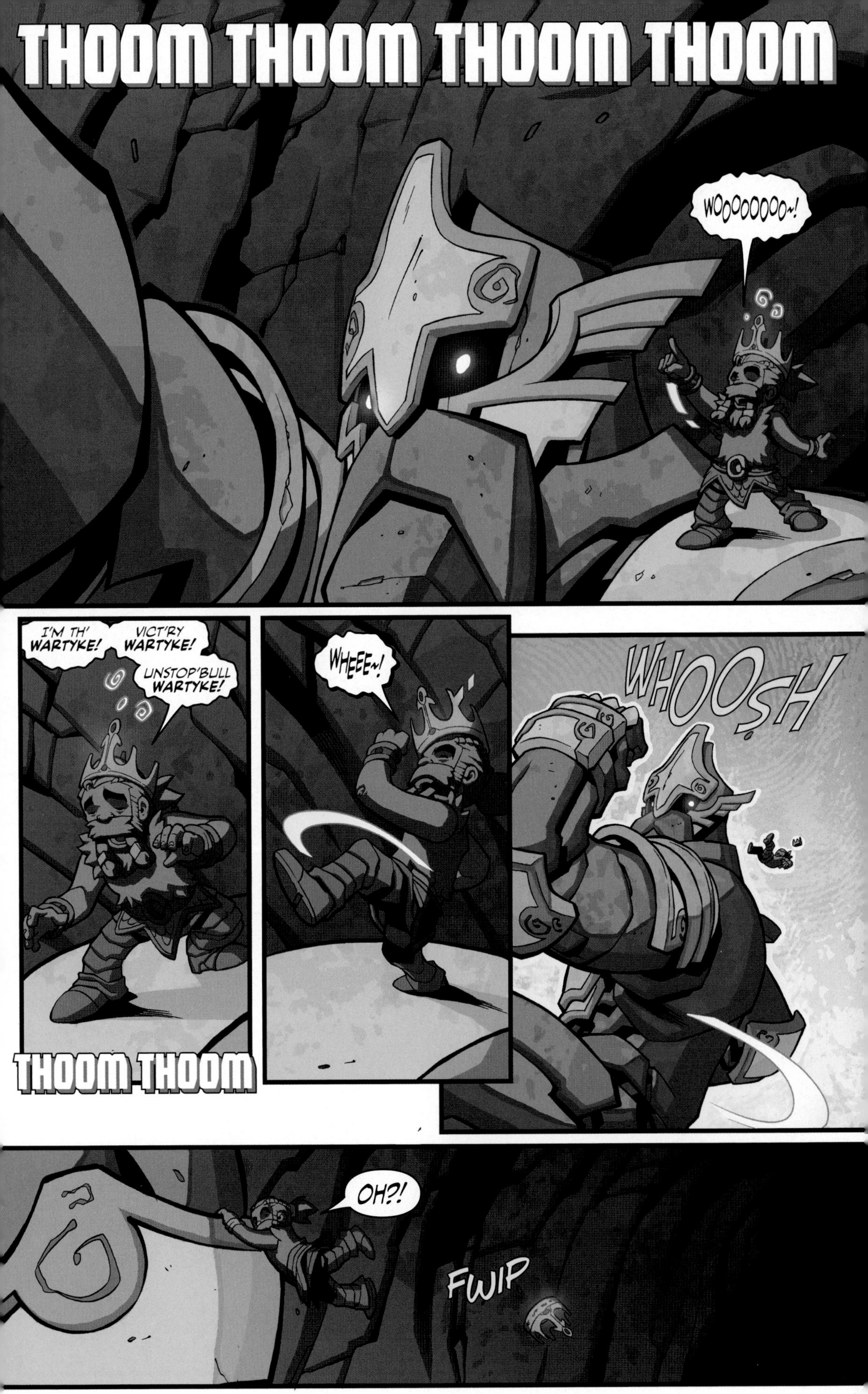
THOOM THOOM THOOM THOOM
WOOOOOOOO~!
I'M TH' WARTYKE!
VICT'RY WARTYKE!
UNSTOP'BULL WARTYKE!
THOOM THOOM
WHEEE~!
WHOOSH
OH?!
FWIP

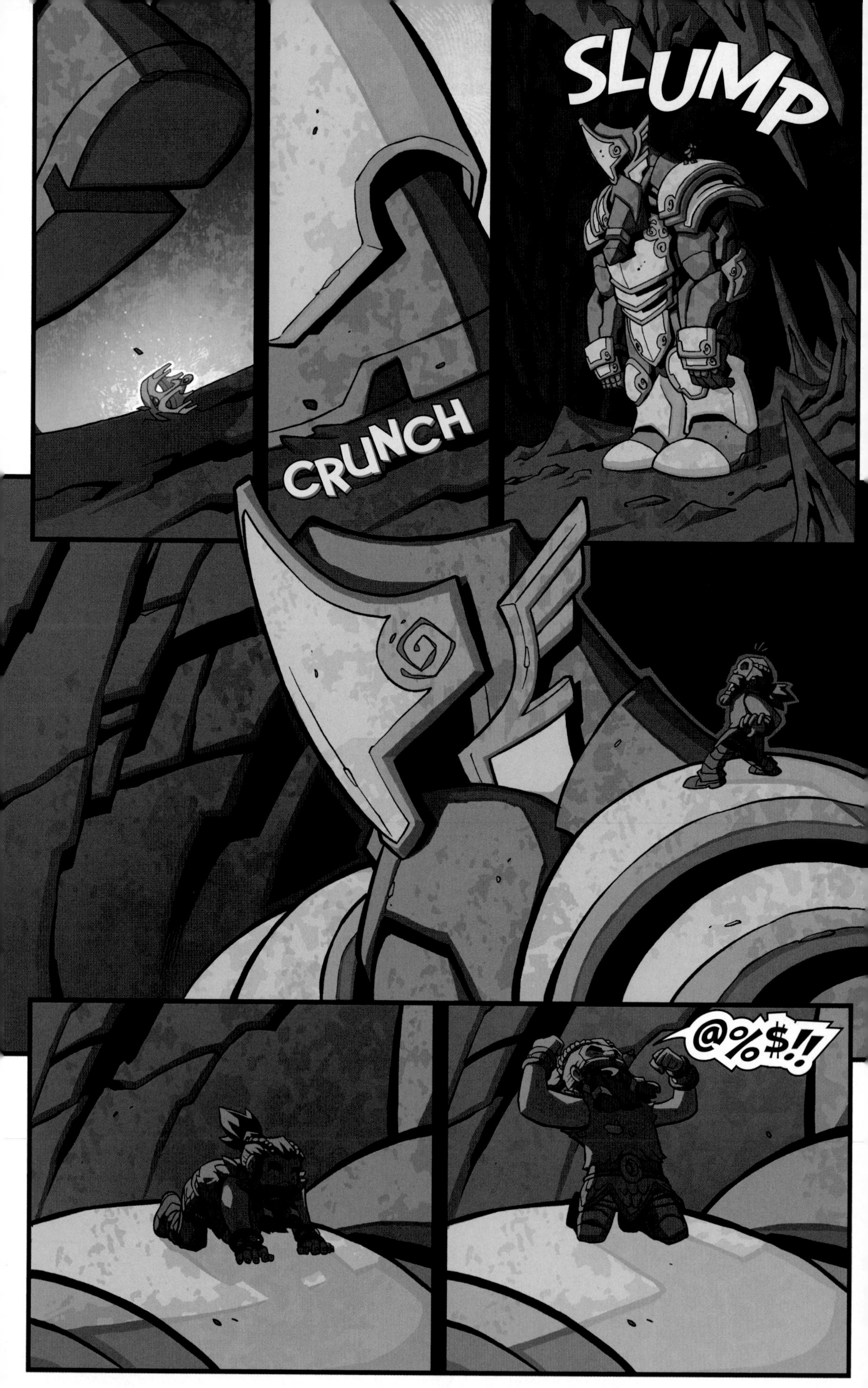
CRUNCH
SLUMP
@%$!!

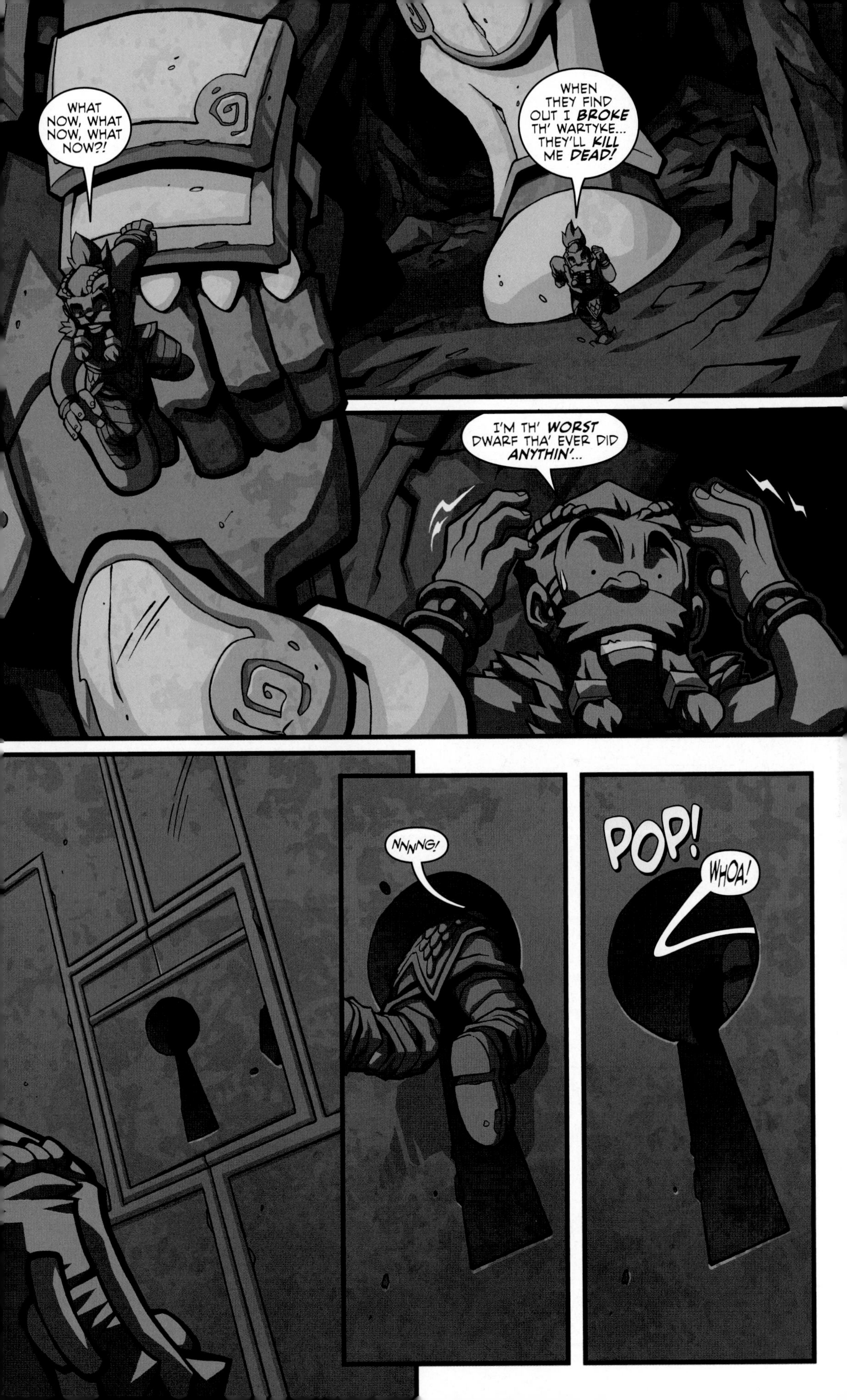
WHAT NOW, WHAT NOW, WHAT NOW?!
WHEN THEY FIND OUT I BROKE TH' WARTYKE... THEY'LL KILL ME DEAD!
I'M TH' WORST DWARF THA' EVER DID ANYTHIN'...
NNNNG!
POP!
WHOA!

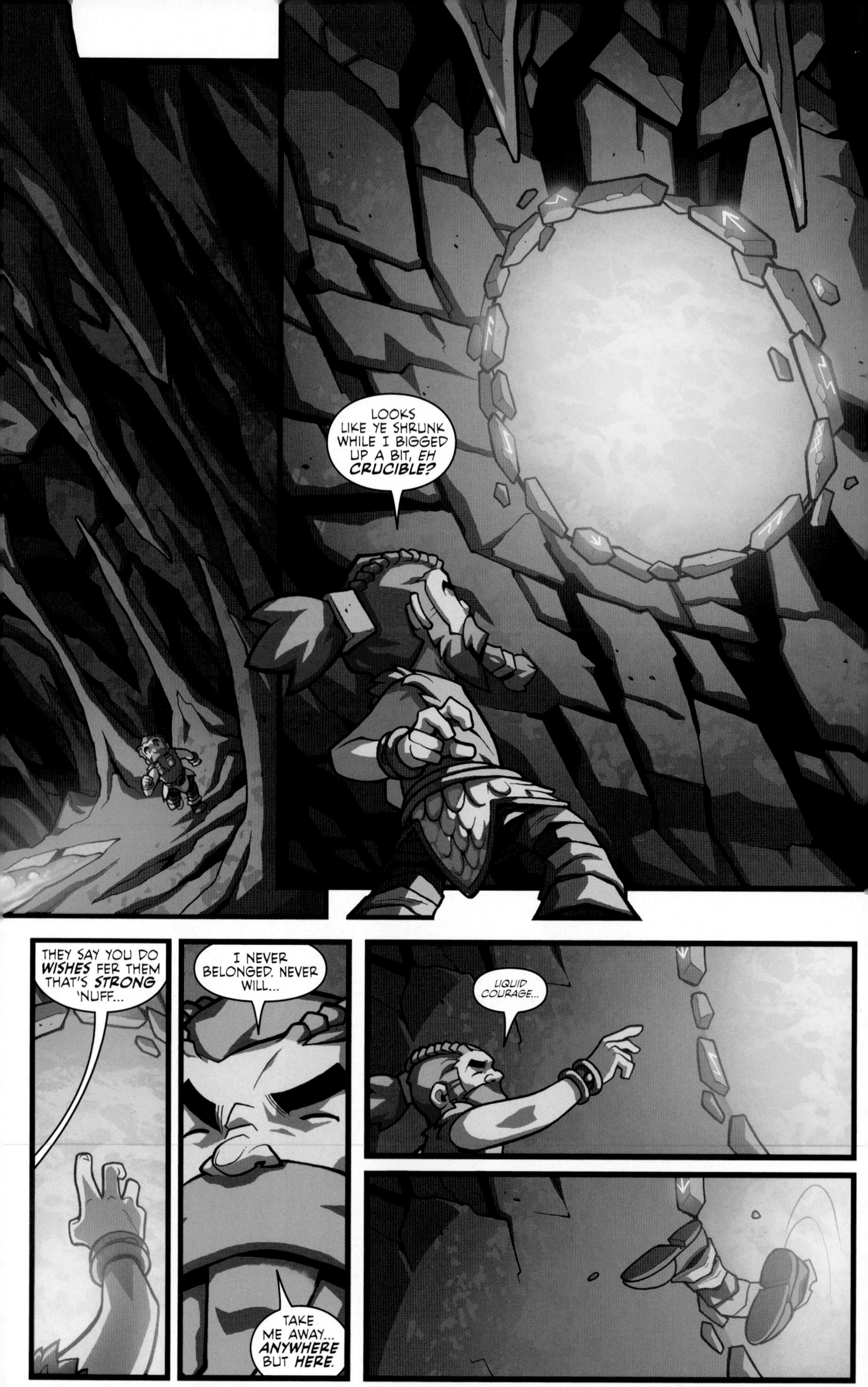
LOOKS LIKE YE SHRUNK WHILE I BIGGED UP A BIT, EH *CRUCIBLE?*
THEY SAY YOU DO *WISHES* FER THEM THAT'S *STRONG* 'NUFF...
I NEVER BELONGED. NEVER WILL...
TAKE ME AWAY... *ANYWHERE* BUT *HERE*.
LIQUID COURAGE...

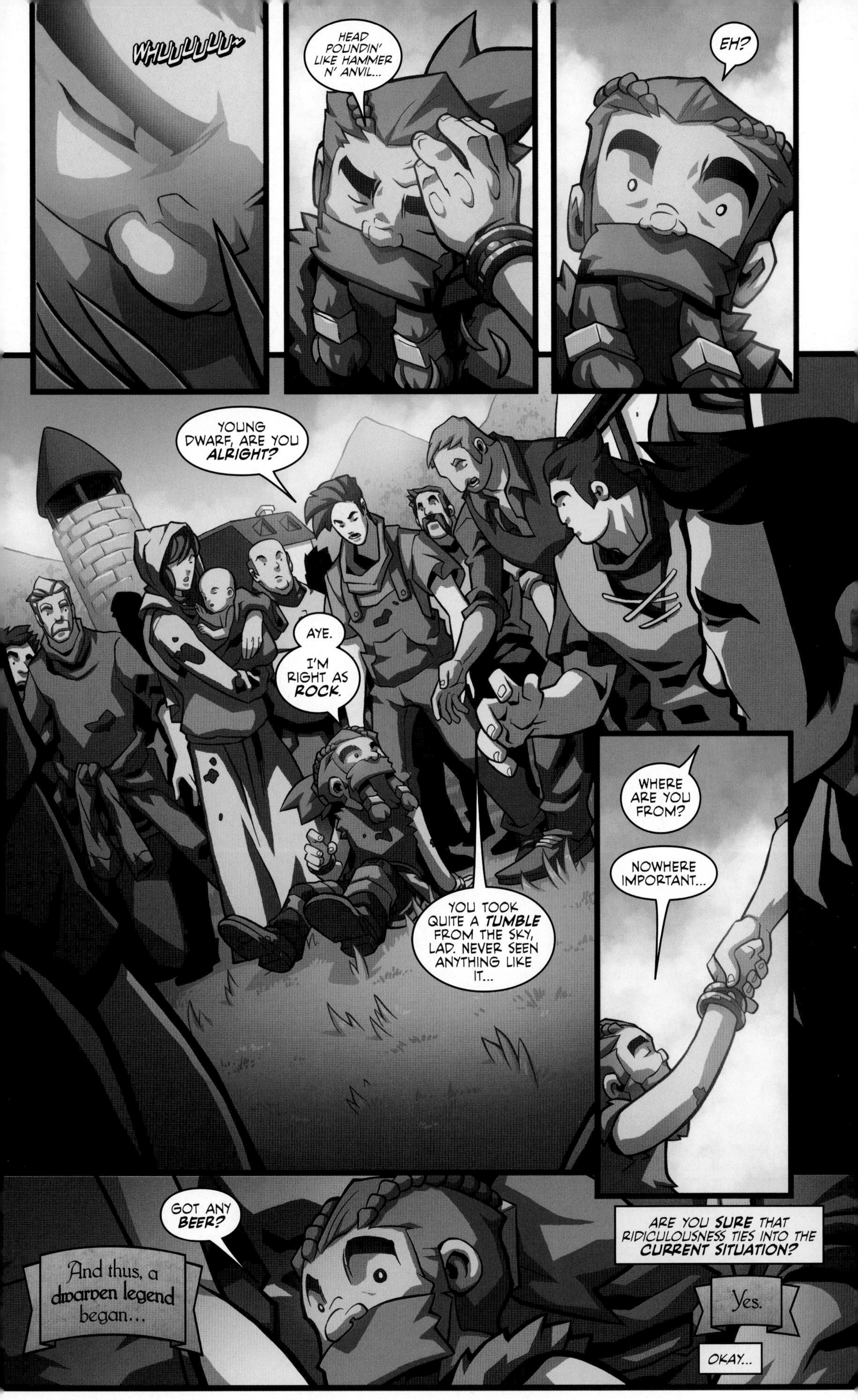

WHLUUUUU~
HEAD POUNDIN' LIKE HAMMER N' ANVIL...
EH?
YOUNG DWARF, ARE YOU ALRIGHT?
AYE.
I'M RIGHT AS ROCK.
YOU TOOK QUITE A TUMBLE FROM THE SKY, LAD. NEVER SEEN ANYTHING LIKE IT...
WHERE ARE YOU FROM?
NOWHERE IMPORTANT...
GOT ANY BEER?
And thus, a dwarven legend began...
ARE YOU SURE THAT RIDICULOUSNESS TIES INTO THE CURRENT SITUATION?
Yes.
OKAY...

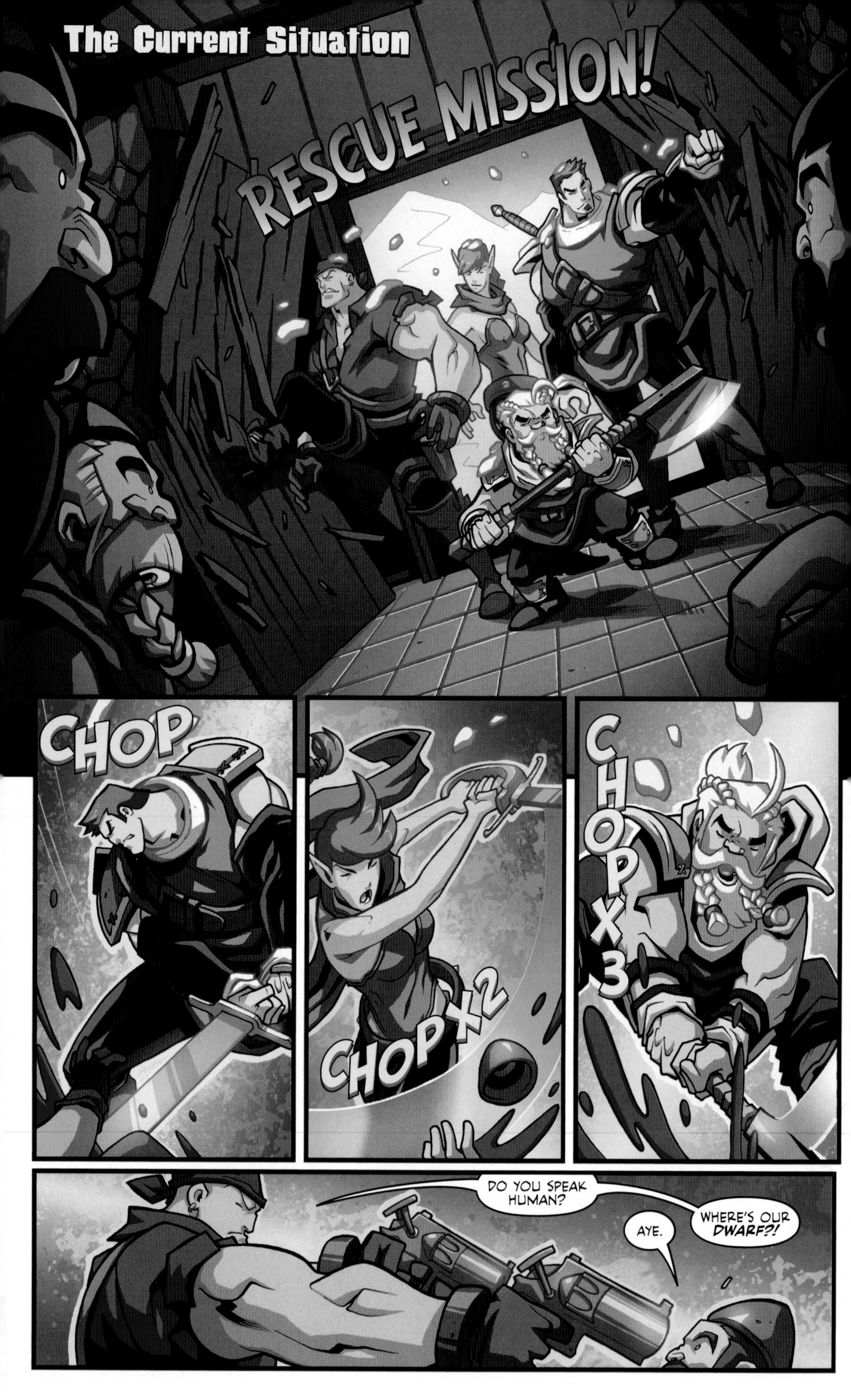

The Current Situation
RESCUE MISSION!
CHOP
CHOP X2
CHOP X3
DO YOU SPEAK HUMAN?
AYE.
WHERE'S OUR DWARF?!

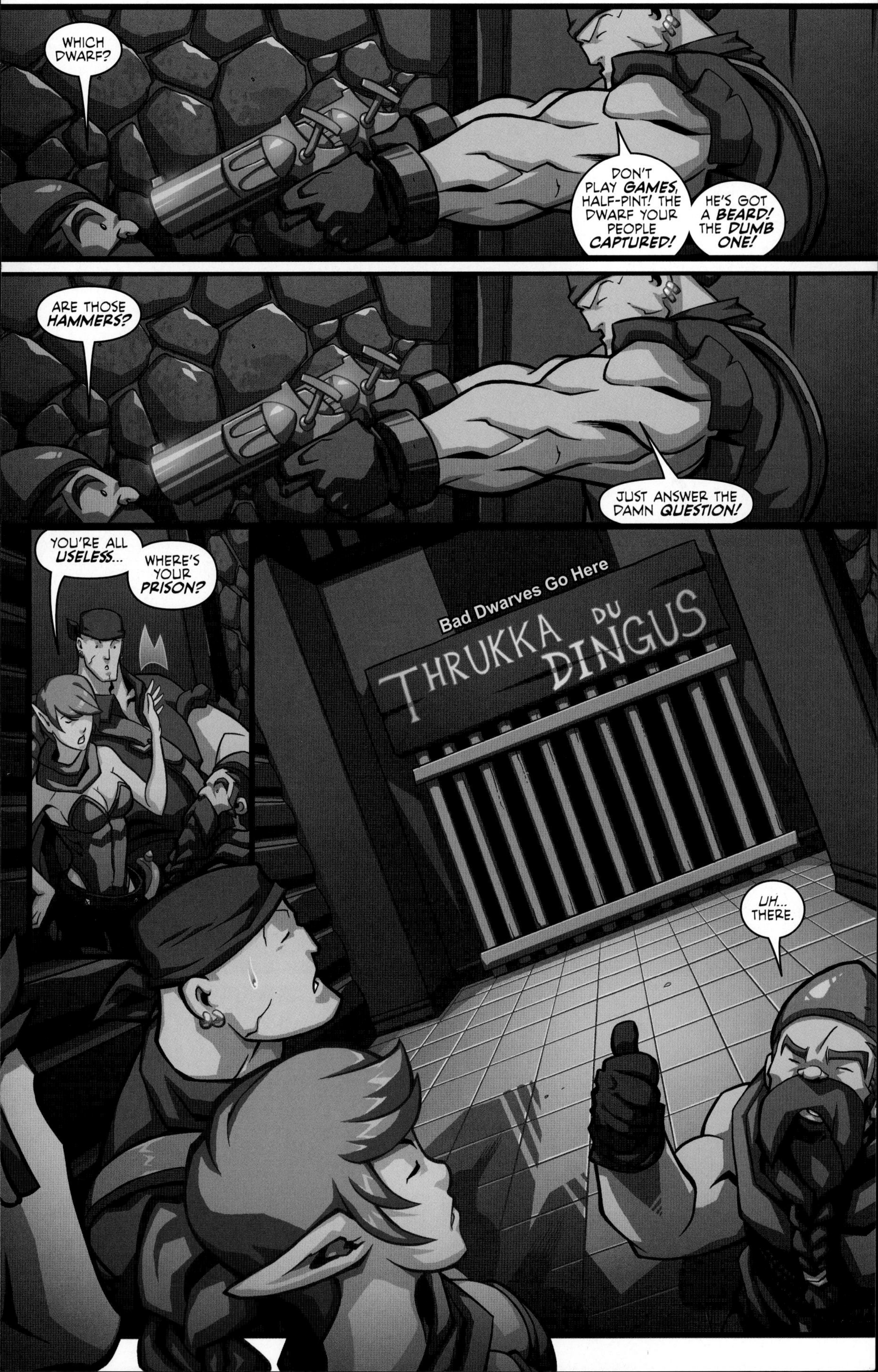

WHICH DWARF?
DON'T PLAY GAMES, HALF-PINT! THE DWARF YOUR PEOPLE CAPTURED!
HE'S GOT A BEARD! THE DUMB ONE!
ARE THOSE HAMMERS?
JUST ANSWER THE DAMN QUESTION!
YOU'RE ALL USELESS...
WHERE'S YOUR PRISON?
Bad Dwarves Go Here
THRUKKA DU DINGUS
UH... THERE.

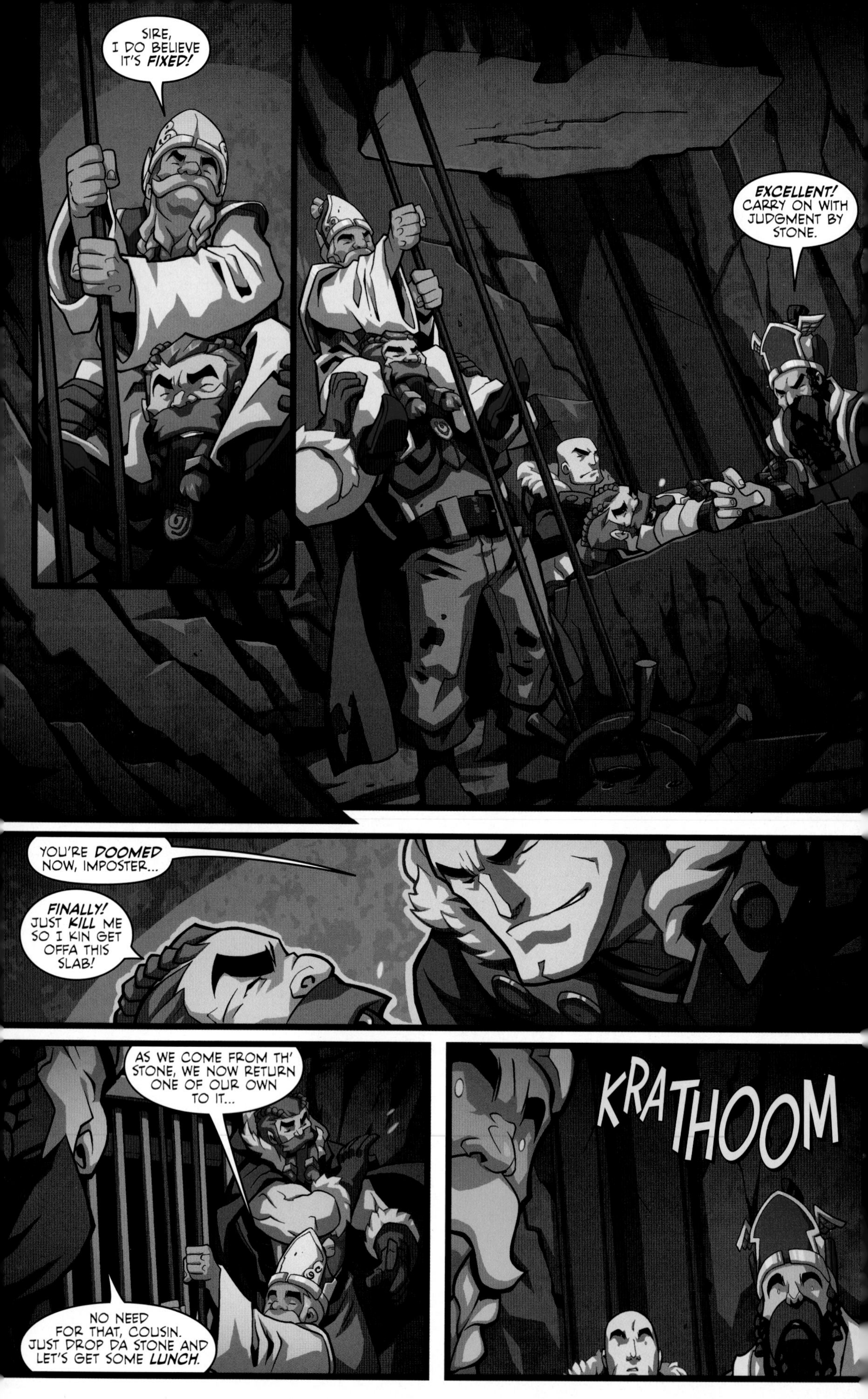
SIRE, I DO BELIEVE IT'S FIXED!
EXCELLENT! CARRY ON WITH JUDGMENT BY STONE.
YOU'RE DOOMED NOW, IMPOSTER...
FINALLY! JUST KILL ME SO I KIN GET OFFA THIS SLAB!
AS WE COME FROM TH' STONE, WE NOW RETURN ONE OF OUR OWN TO IT...
NO NEED FOR THAT, COUSIN. JUST DROP DA STONE AND LET'S GET SOME LUNCH.
KRATHOOM

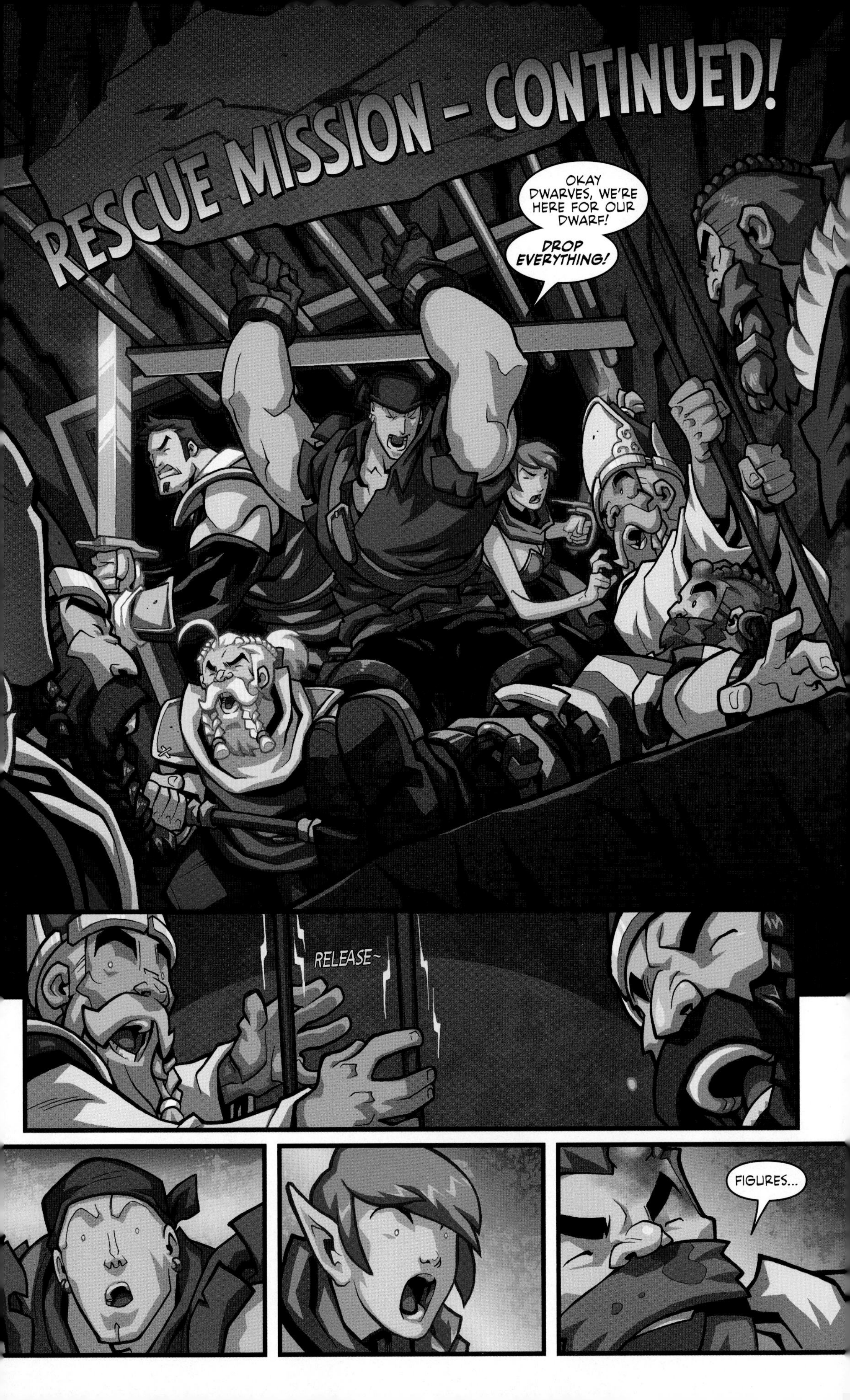
RESCUE MISSION – CONTINUED!
OKAY DWARVES, WE'RE HERE FOR OUR DWARF!
DROP EVERYTHING!
RELEASE~
FIGURES...

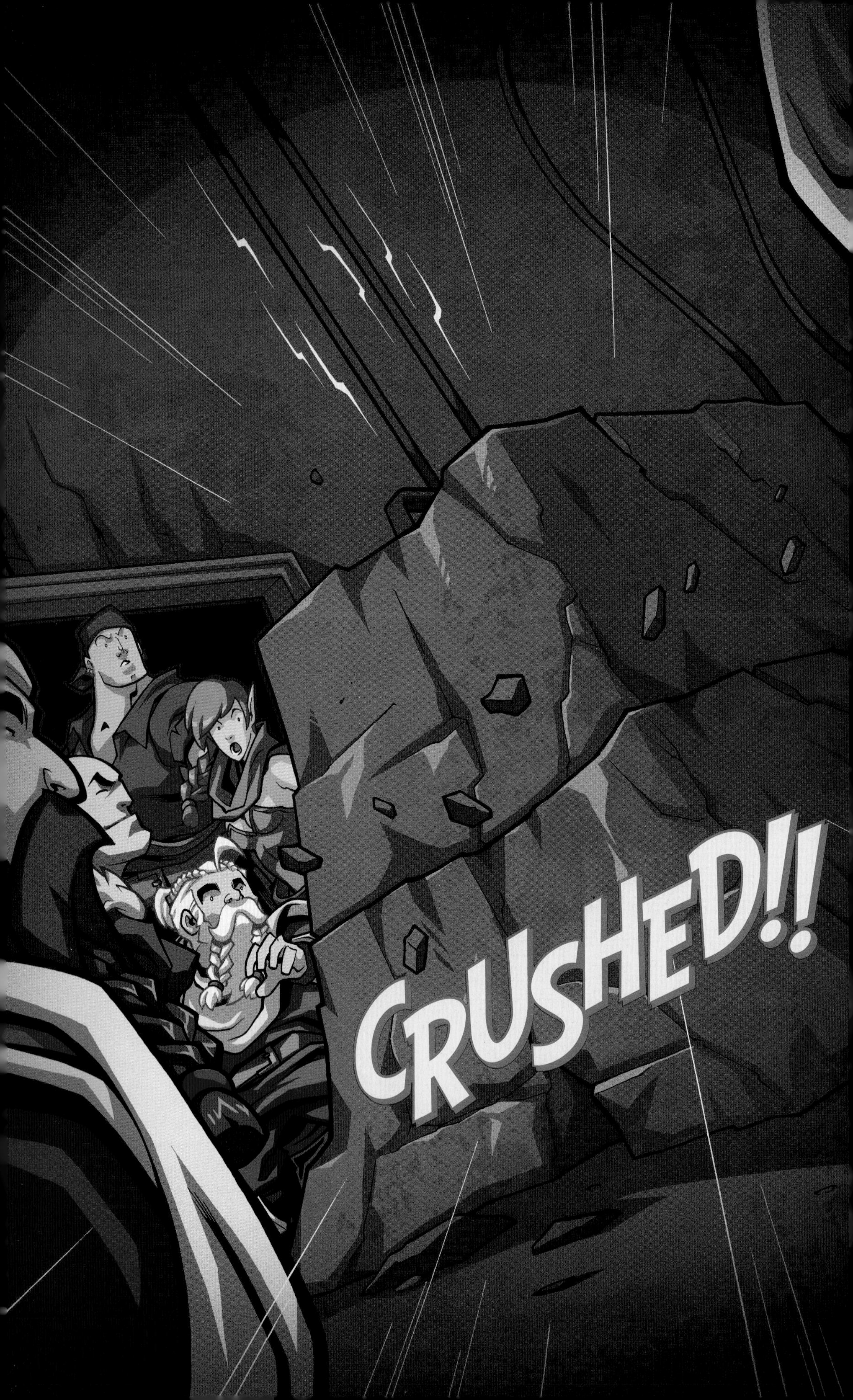
CRUSHED!!

CHAPTER FOUR

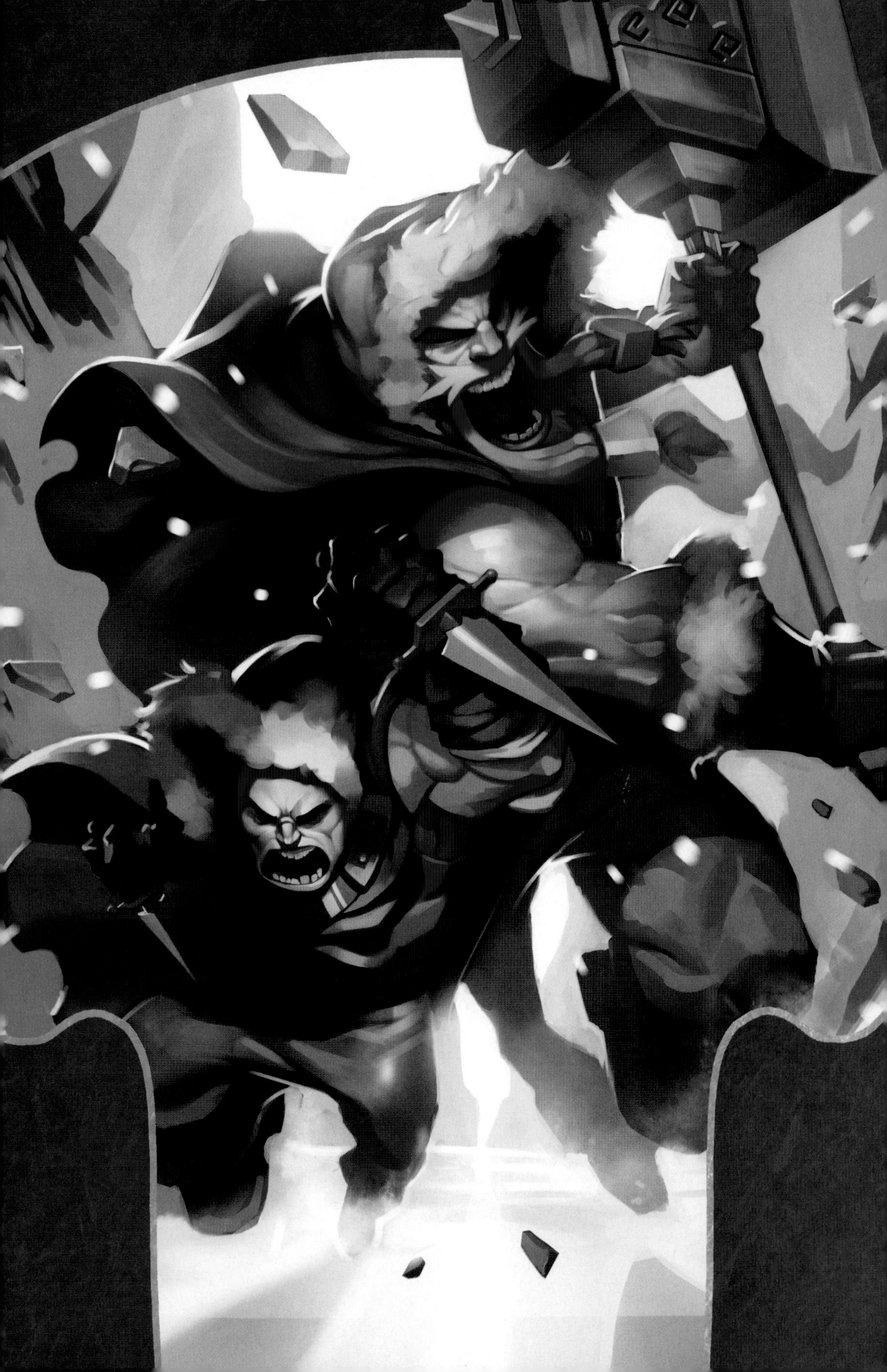

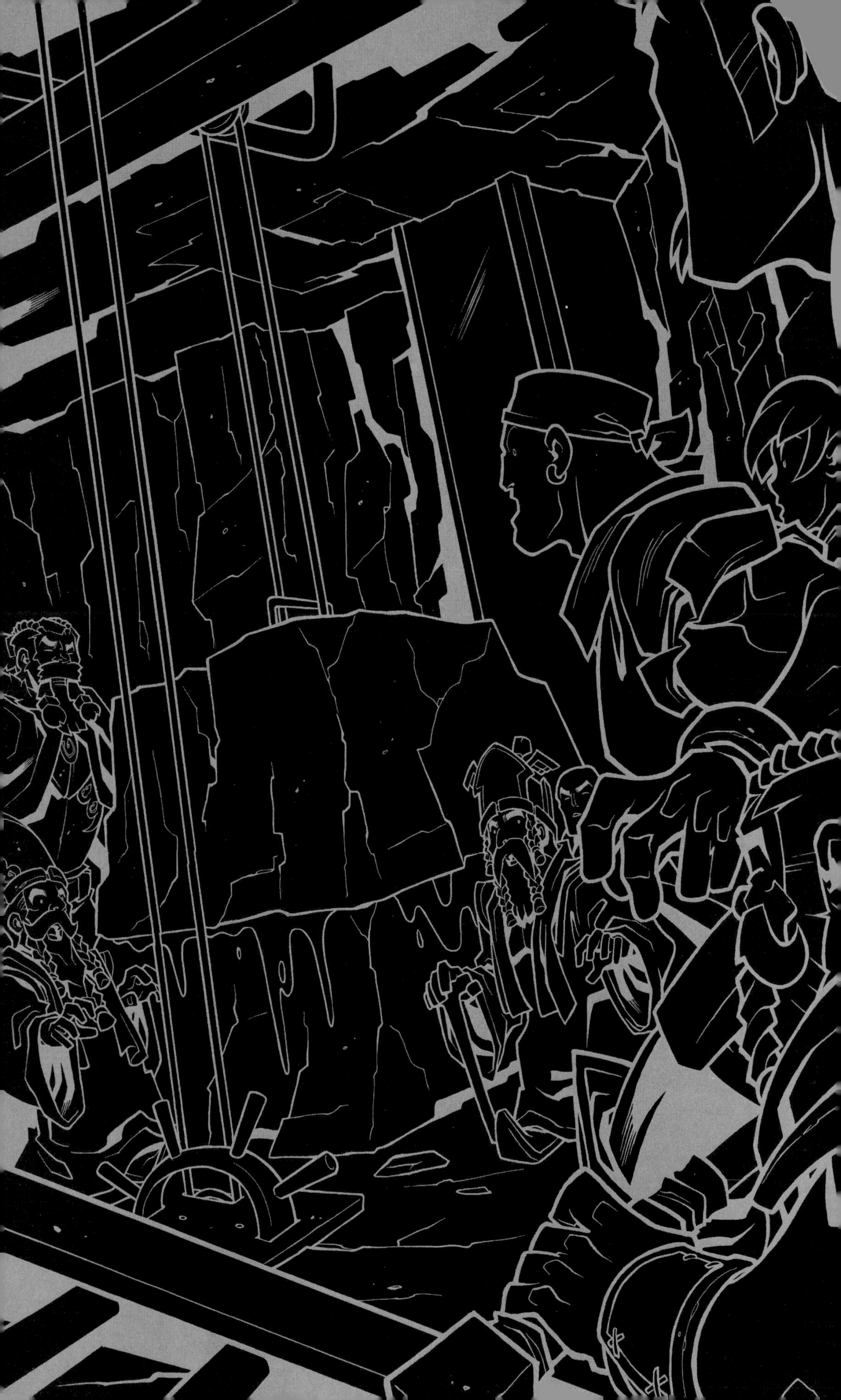

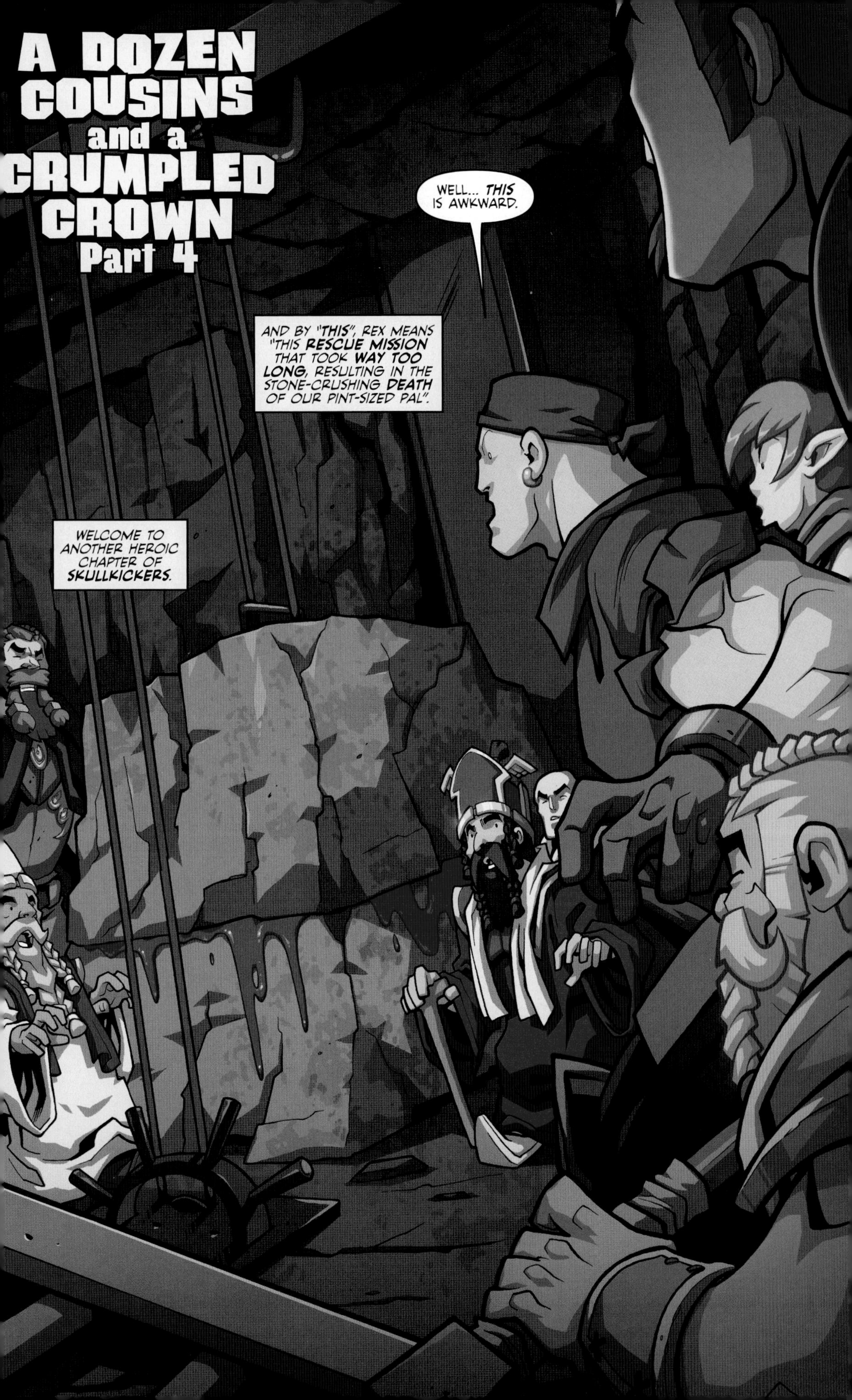
A DOZEN COUSINS and a CRUMPLED CROWN Part 4
WELL... THIS IS AWKWARD.
AND BY "THIS", REX MEANS "THIS RESCUE MISSION THAT TOOK WAY TOO LONG, RESULTING IN THE STONE-CRUSHING DEATH OF OUR PINT-SIZED PAL".
WELCOME TO ANOTHER HEROIC CHAPTER OF SKULLKICKERS.

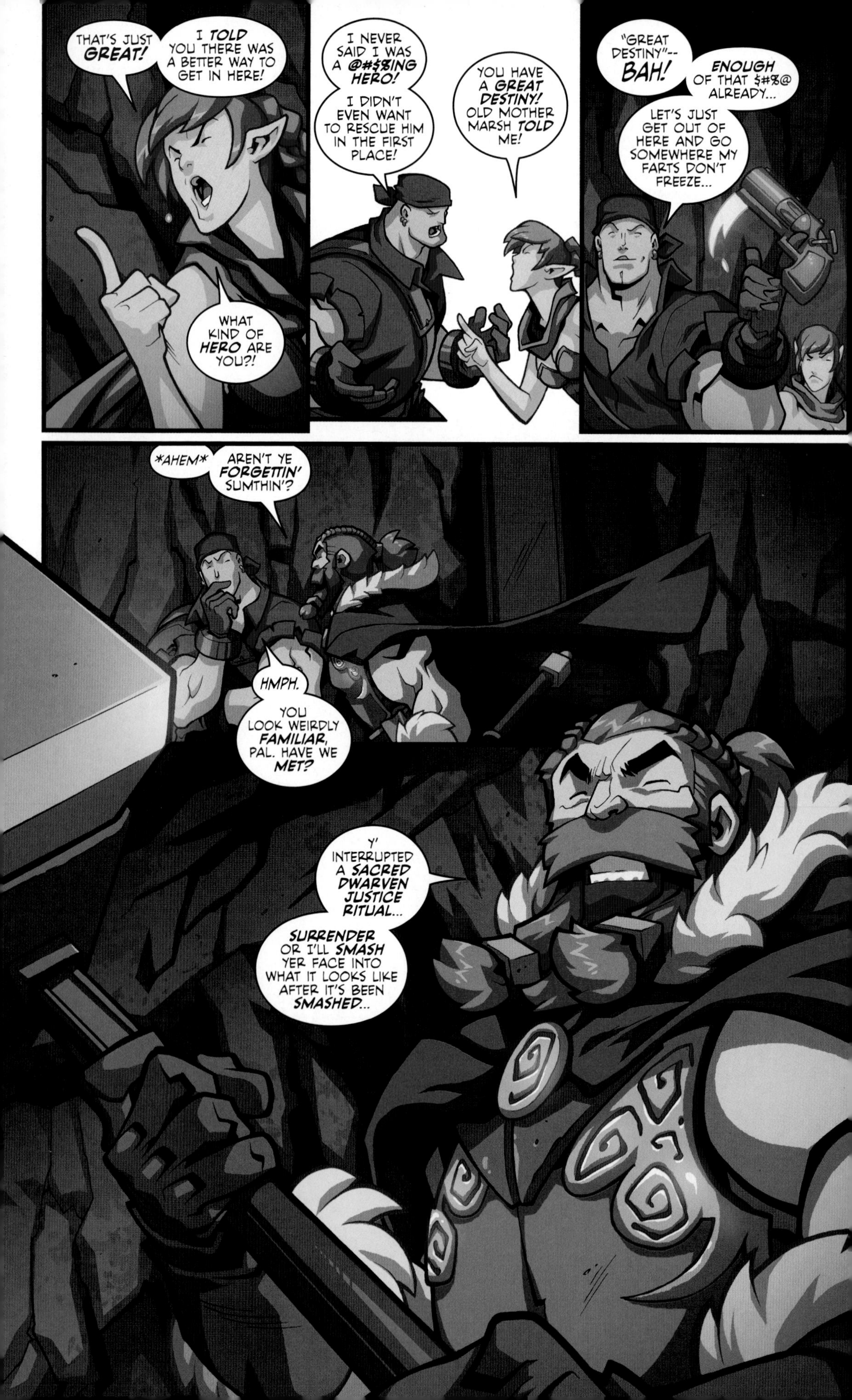
THAT'S JUST GREAT!
I TOLD YOU THERE WAS A BETTER WAY TO GET IN HERE!
WHAT KIND OF HERO ARE YOU?!
I NEVER SAID I WAS A @#$%ING HERO!
I DIDN'T EVEN WANT TO RESCUE HIM IN THE FIRST PLACE!
YOU HAVE A GREAT DESTINY! OLD MOTHER MARSH TOLD ME!
"GREAT DESTINY"-- BAH!
ENOUGH OF THAT $#%@ ALREADY...
LET'S JUST GET OUT OF HERE AND GO SOMEWHERE MY FARTS DON'T FREEZE...
AHEM
AREN'T YE FORGETTIN' SUMTHIN'?
HMPH.
YOU LOOK WEIRDLY FAMILIAR, PAL. HAVE WE MET?
Y' INTERRUPTED A SACRED DWARVEN JUSTICE RITUAL...
SURRENDER OR I'LL SMASH YER FACE INTO WHAT IT LOOKS LIKE AFTER IT'S BEEN SMASHED...

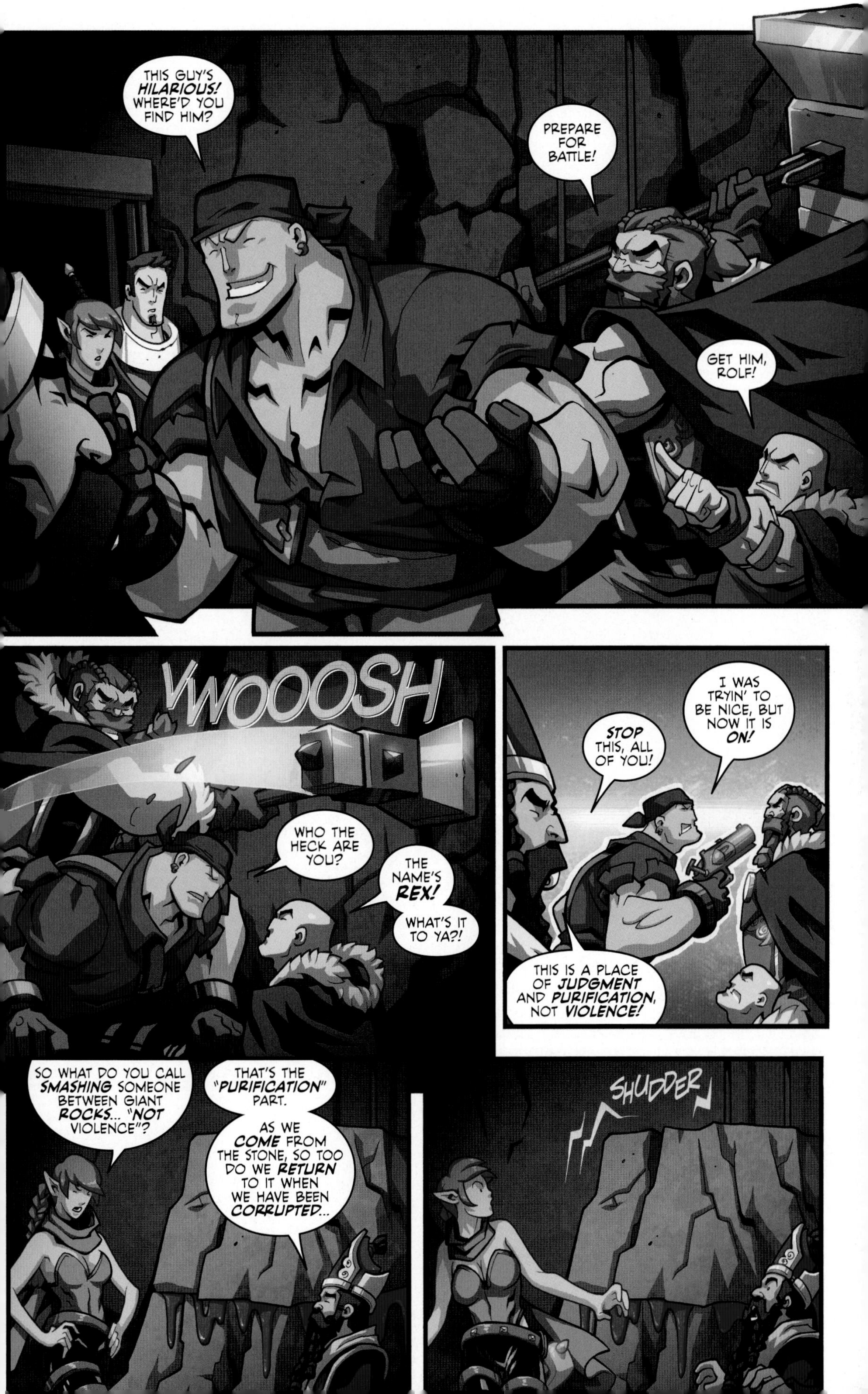

THIS GUY'S HILARIOUS! WHERE'D YOU FIND HIM?
PREPARE FOR BATTLE!
GET HIM, ROLF!
VWOOOSH
WHO THE HECK ARE YOU?
THE NAME'S REX!
WHAT'S IT TO YA?!
I WAS TRYIN' TO BE NICE, BUT NOW IT IS ON!
STOP THIS, ALL OF YOU!
THIS IS A PLACE OF JUDGMENT AND PURIFICATION, NOT VIOLENCE!
SO WHAT DO YOU CALL SMASHING SOMEONE BETWEEN GIANT ROCKS... "NOT VIOLENCE"?
THAT'S THE "PURIFICATION" PART.
AS WE COME FROM THE STONE, SO TOO DO WE RETURN TO IT WHEN WE HAVE BEEN CORRUPTED...
SHUDDER

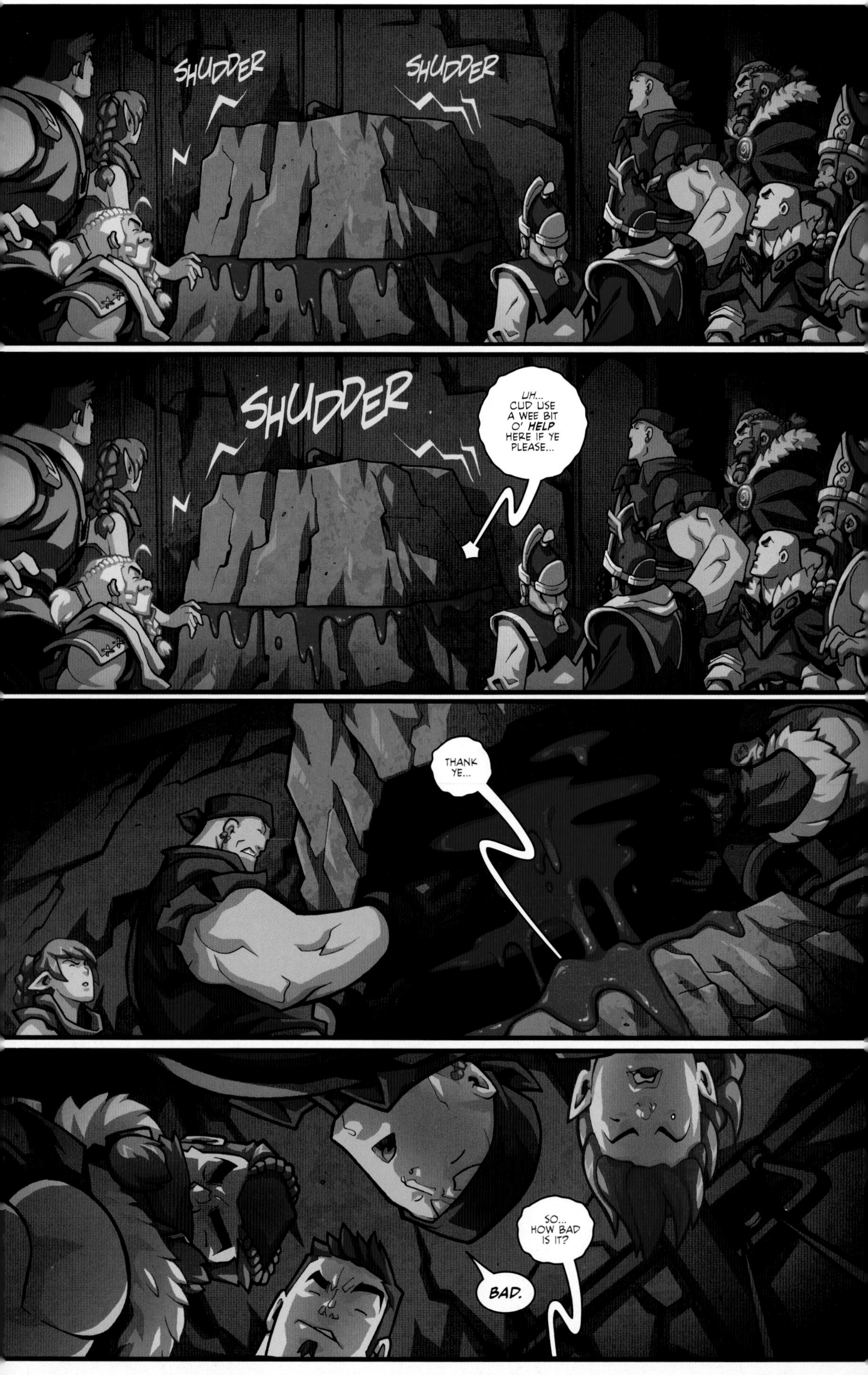
SHUDDER
SHUDDER
SHUDDER
UH... CUD USE A WEE BIT O' **HELP** HERE IF YE PLEASE...
THANK YE...
SO... HOW BAD IS IT?
BAD.

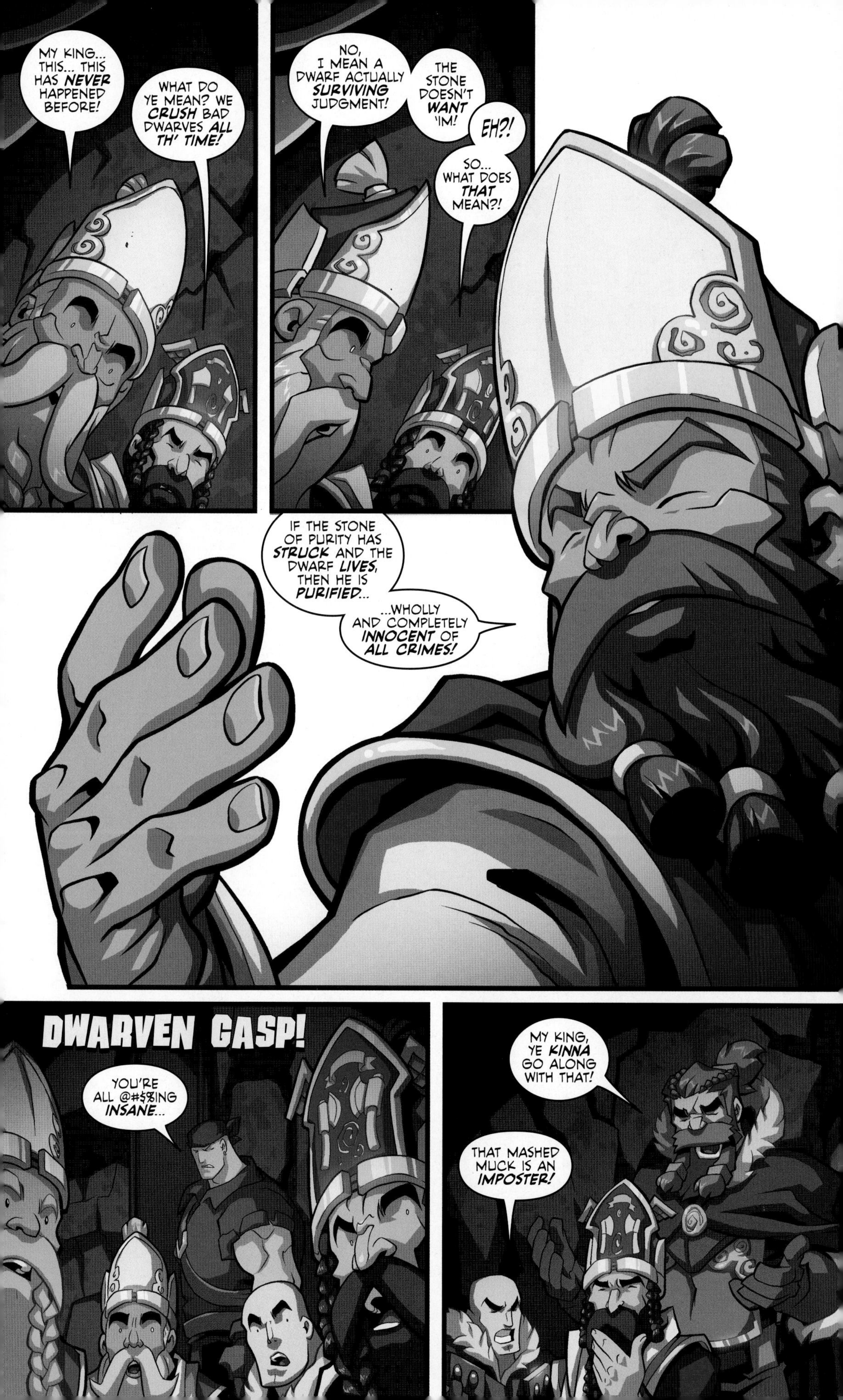

MY KING... THIS... THIS HAS NEVER HAPPENED BEFORE!
WHAT DO YE MEAN? WE CRUSH BAD DWARVES ALL TH' TIME!
NO, I MEAN A DWARF ACTUALLY SURVIVING JUDGMENT!
THE STONE DOESN'T WANT 'IM!
EH?!
SO... WHAT DOES THAT MEAN?!
IF THE STONE OF PURITY HAS STRUCK AND THE DWARF LIVES, THEN HE IS PURIFIED...
...WHOLLY AND COMPLETELY INNOCENT OF ALL CRIMES!
DWARVEN GASP!
YOU'RE ALL @#$%ING INSANE...
MY KING, YE KINNA GO ALONG WITH THAT!
THAT MASHED MUCK IS AN IMPOSTER!

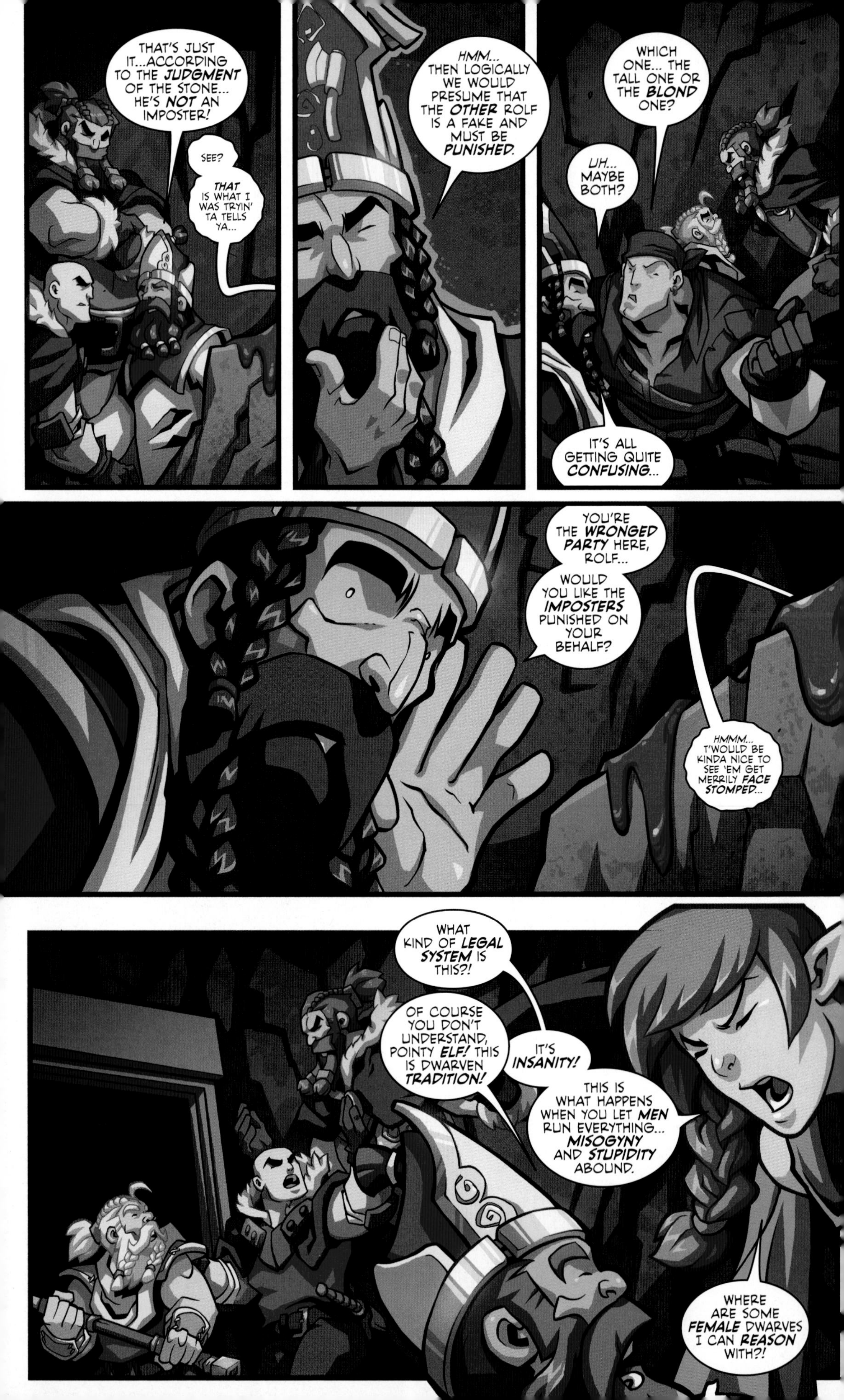

THAT'S JUST IT...ACCORDING TO THE JUDGMENT OF THE STONE... HE'S NOT AN IMPOSTER!
SEE?
THAT IS WHAT I WAS TRYIN' TA TELLS YA...
HMM... THEN LOGICALLY WE WOULD PRESUME THAT THE OTHER ROLF IS A FAKE AND MUST BE PUNISHED.
WHICH ONE... THE TALL ONE OR THE BLOND ONE?
UH... MAYBE BOTH?
IT'S ALL GETTING QUITE CONFUSING...
YOU'RE THE WRONGED PARTY HERE, ROLF...
WOULD YOU LIKE THE IMPOSTERS PUNISHED ON YOUR BEHALF?
HMMM... T'WOULD BE KINDA NICE TO SEE 'EM GET MERRILY FACE STOMPED...
WHAT KIND OF LEGAL SYSTEM IS THIS?!
OF COURSE YOU DON'T UNDERSTAND, POINTY ELF! THIS IS DWARVEN TRADITION!
IT'S INSANITY!
THIS IS WHAT HAPPENS WHEN YOU LET MEN RUN EVERYTHING... MISOGYNY AND STUPIDITY ABOUND.
WHERE ARE SOME FEMALE DWARVES I CAN REASON WITH?!

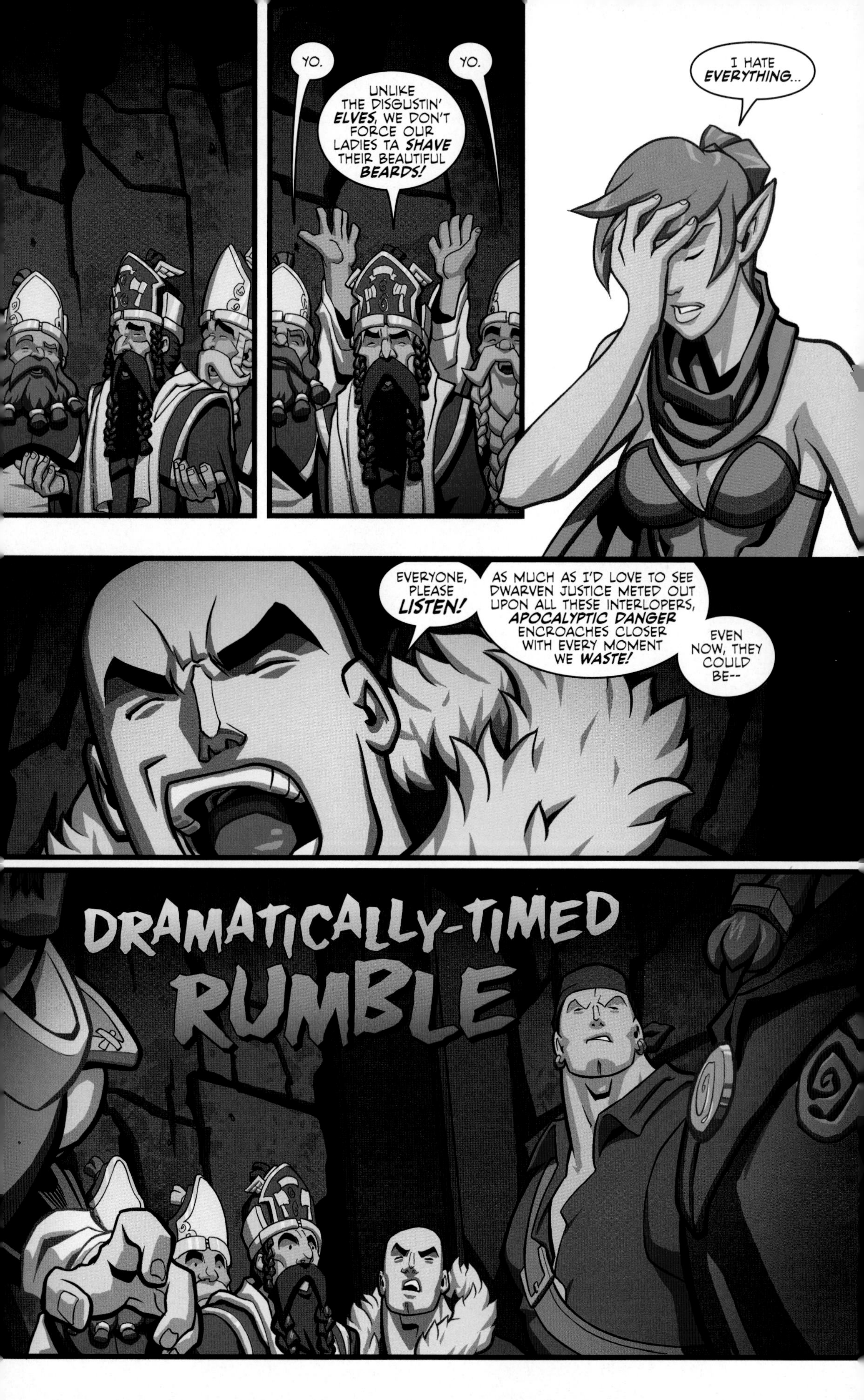
YO.
UNLIKE THE DISGUSTIN' ELVES, WE DON'T FORCE OUR LADIES TA SHAVE THEIR BEAUTIFUL BEARDS!
YO.
I HATE EVERYTHING...
EVERYONE, PLEASE LISTEN!
AS MUCH AS I'D LOVE TO SEE DWARVEN JUSTICE METED OUT UPON ALL THESE INTERLOPERS, APOCALYPTIC DANGER ENCROACHES CLOSER WITH EVERY MOMENT WE WASTE!
EVEN NOW, THEY COULD BE--
DRAMATICALLY-TIMED RUMBLE

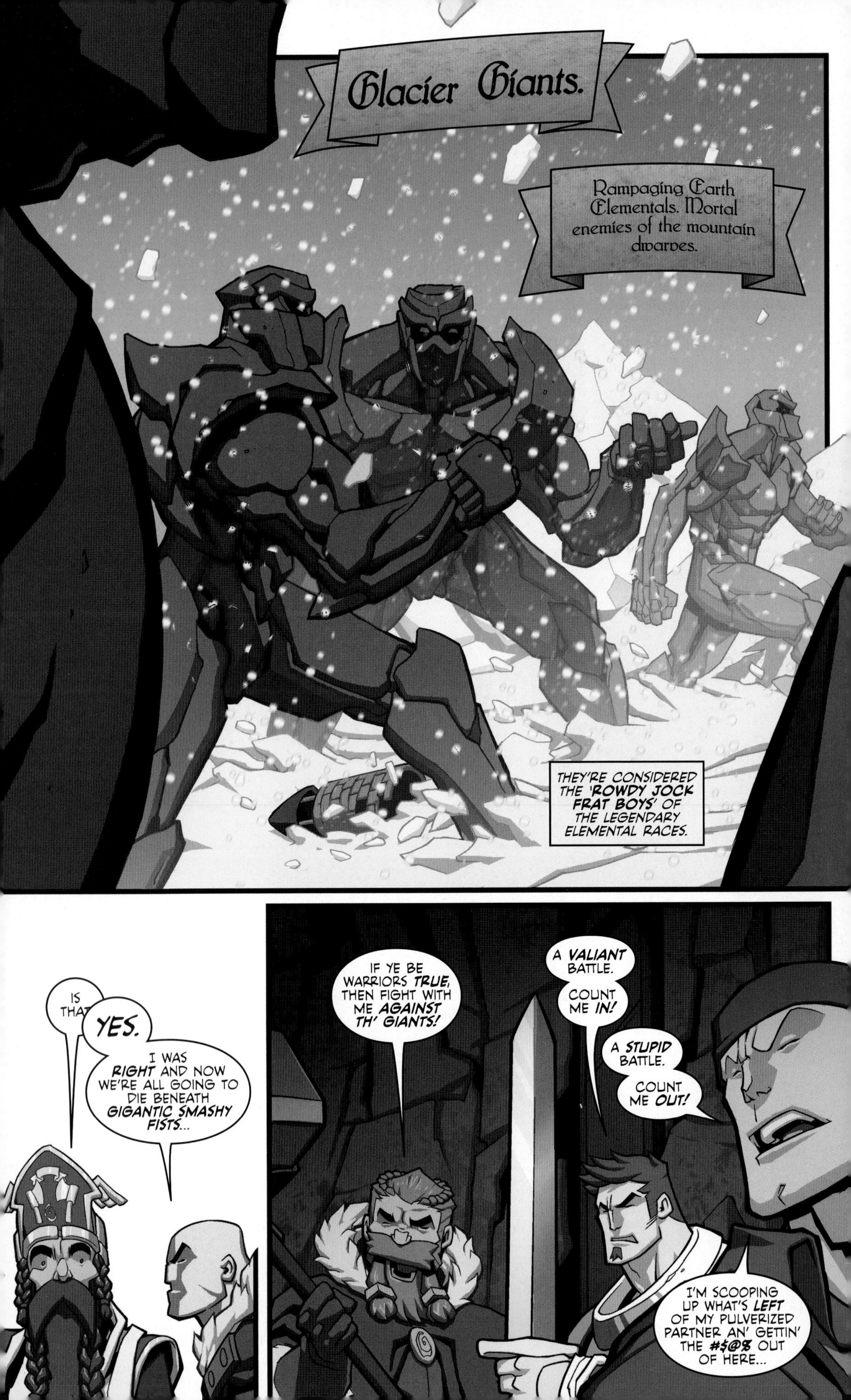
Glacier Giants.
Rampaging Earth Elementals. Mortal enemies of the mountain dwarves.
THEY'RE CONSIDERED THE 'ROWDY JOCK FRAT BOYS' OF THE LEGENDARY ELEMENTAL RACES.
IS THAT
YES.
I WAS RIGHT AND NOW WE'RE ALL GOING TO DIE BENEATH GIGANTIC SMASHY FISTS...
IF YE BE WARRIORS TRUE, THEN FIGHT WITH ME AGAINST TH' GIANTS!
A VALIANT BATTLE.
COUNT ME IN!
A STUPID BATTLE.
COUNT ME OUT!
I'M SCOOPING UP WHAT'S LEFT OF MY PULVERIZED PARTNER AN' GETTIN' THE #$@% OUT OF HERE...

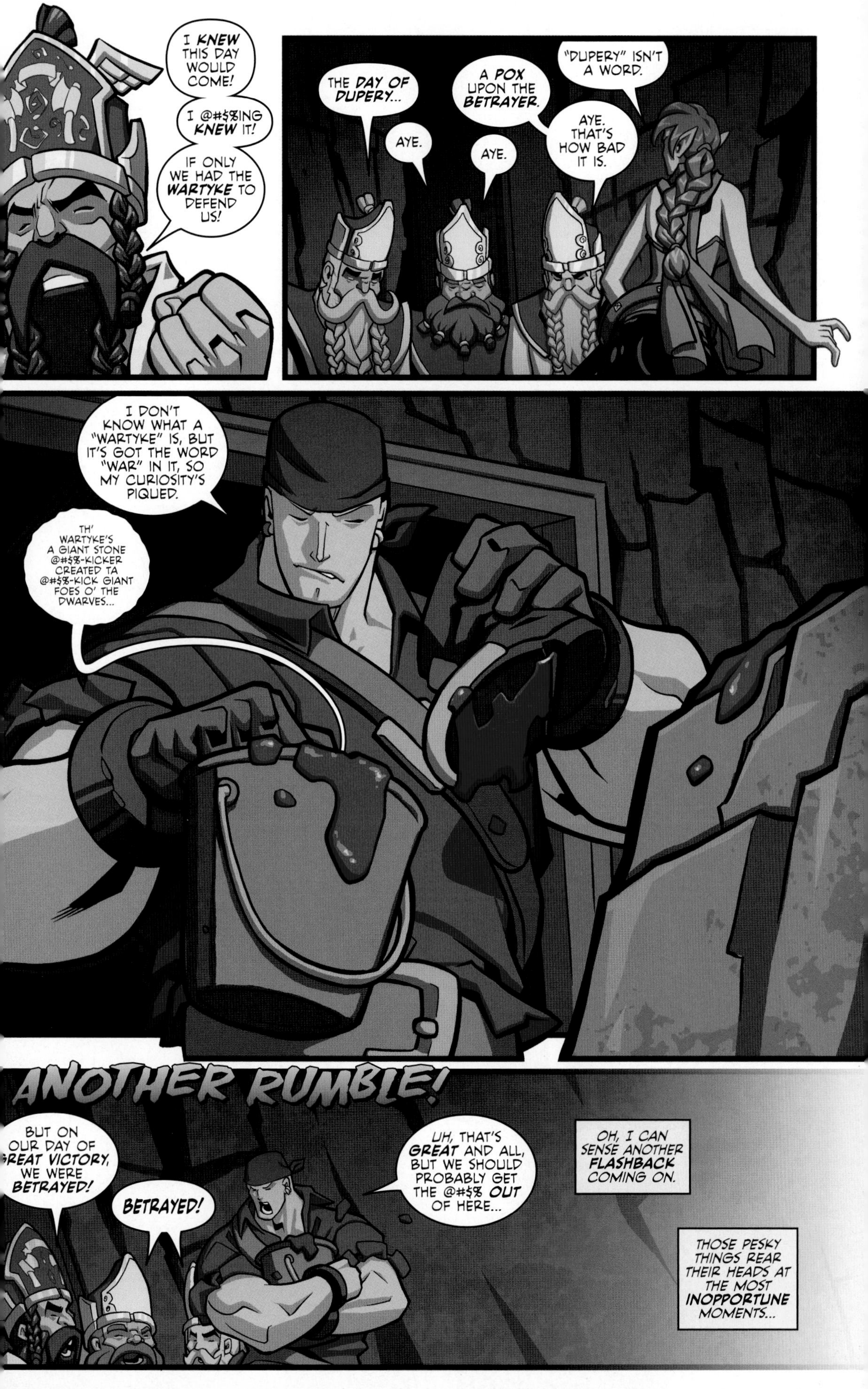

I KNEW THIS DAY WOULD COME!
I @#$%ING KNEW IT!
IF ONLY WE HAD THE WARTYKE TO DEFEND US!
THE DAY OF DUPERY...
AYE.
A POX UPON THE BETRAYER.
AYE.
"DUPERY" ISN'T A WORD.
AYE. THAT'S HOW BAD IT IS.
I DON'T KNOW WHAT A "WARTYKE" IS, BUT IT'S GOT THE WORD "WAR" IN IT, SO MY CURIOSITY'S PIQUED.
TH' WARTYKE'S A GIANT STONE @#$%-KICKER CREATED TA @#$%-KICK GIANT FOES O' THE DWARVES...
ANOTHER RUMBLE!
BUT ON OUR DAY OF GREAT VICTORY, WE WERE BETRAYED!
BETRAYED!
UH, THAT'S GREAT AND ALL, BUT WE SHOULD PROBABLY GET THE @#$% OUT OF HERE...
OH, I CAN SENSE ANOTHER FLASHBACK COMING ON.
THOSE PESKY THINGS REAR THEIR HEADS AT THE MOST INOPPORTUNE MOMENTS...

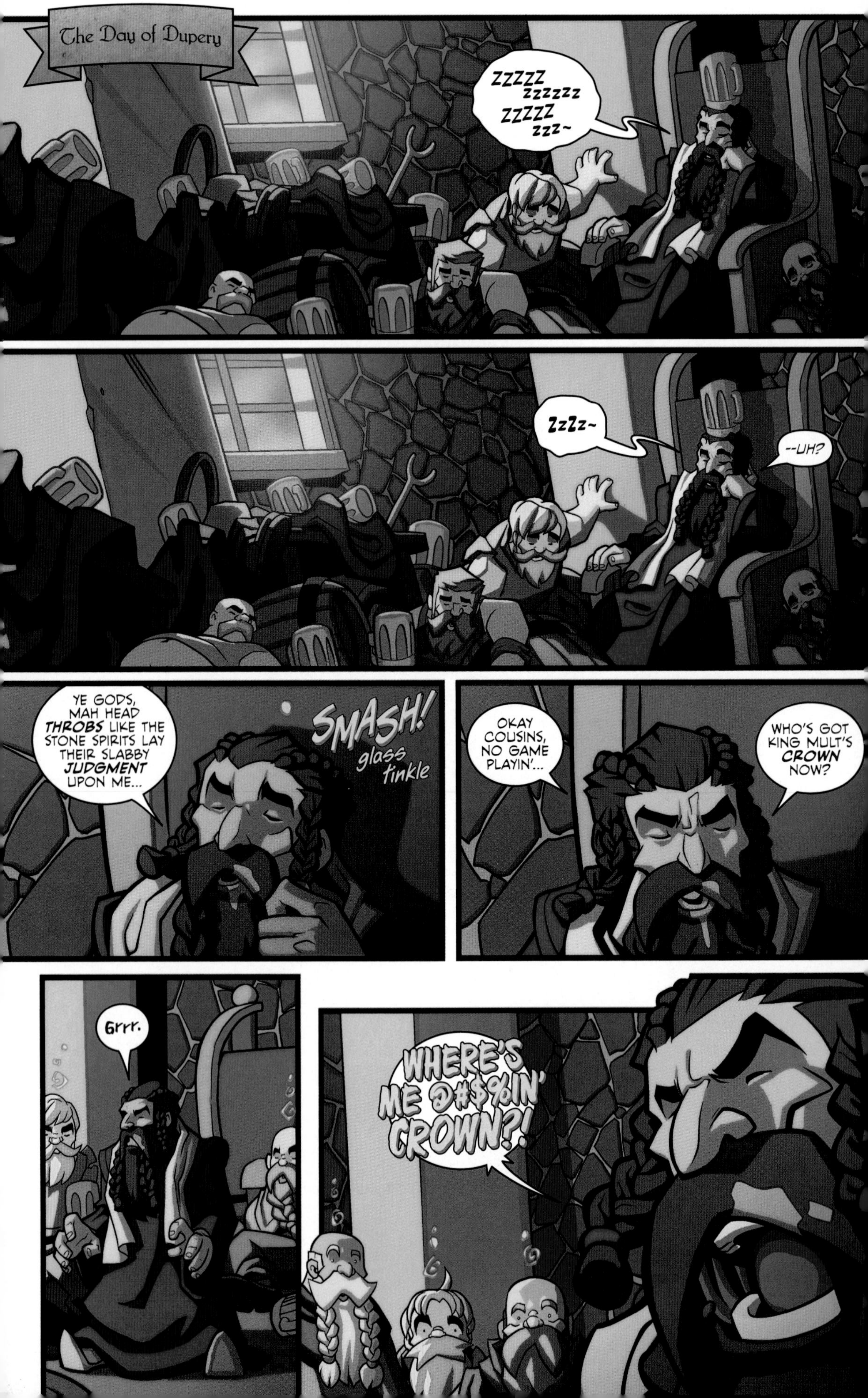
The Day of Dupery
ZZZZZ ZZZZZZ ZZZZZ ZZZ~
ZzZz~
--UH?
YE GODS, MAH HEAD THROBS LIKE THE STONE SPIRITS LAY THEIR SLABBY JUDGMENT UPON ME...
SMASH!
glass tinkle
OKAY COUSINS, NO GAME PLAYIN'...
WHO'S GOT KING MULT'S CROWN NOW?
Grrr.
WHERE'S ME @#$%IN' CROWN?!

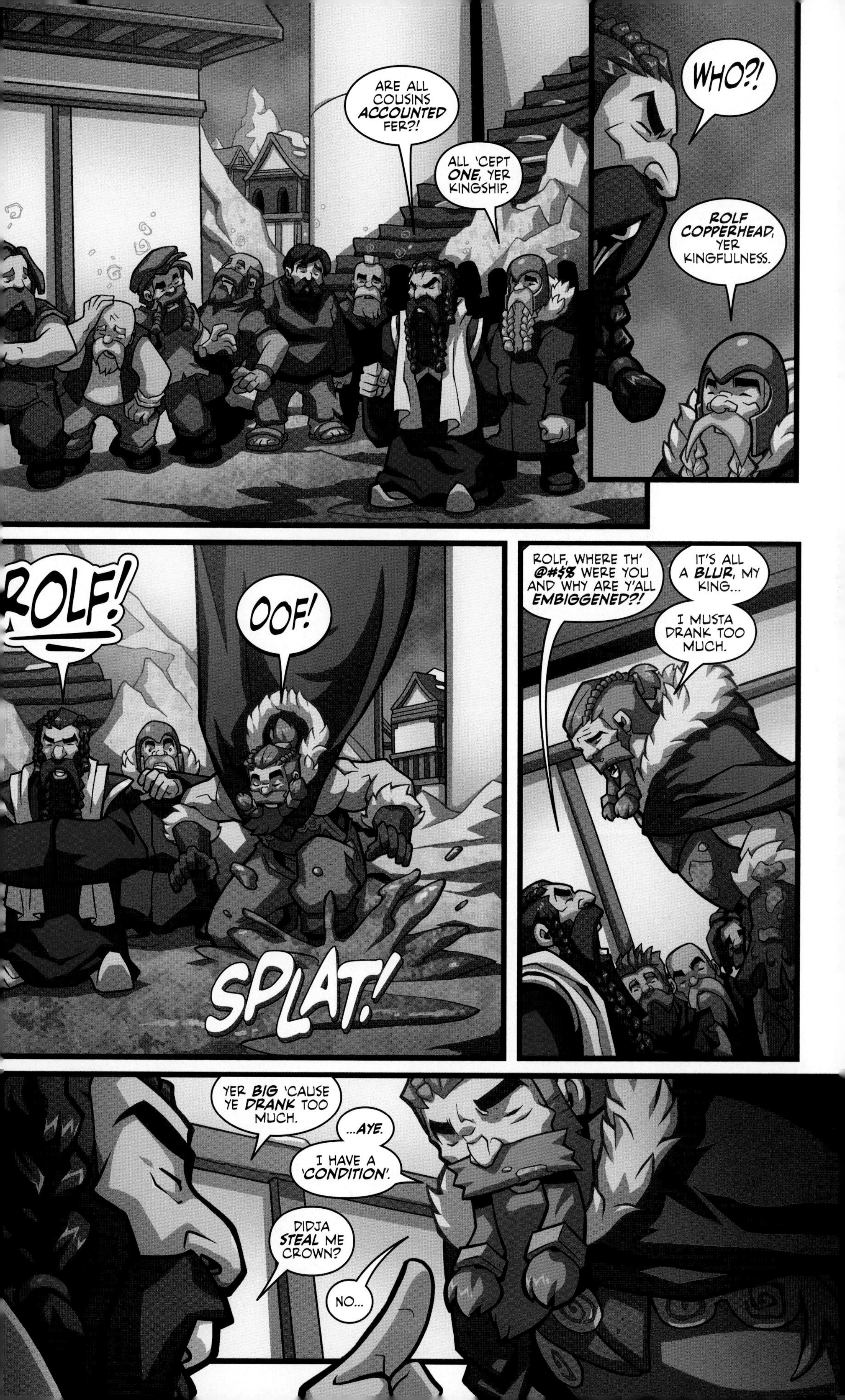

ARE ALL COUSINS ACCOUNTED FER?!
ALL 'CEPT ONE, YER KINGSHIP.
WHO?!
ROLF COPPERHEAD, YER KINGFULNESS.
ROLF!
OOF!
SPLAT!
ROLF, WHERE TH' @#$% WERE YOU AND WHY ARE Y'ALL EMBIGGENED?!
IT'S ALL A BLUR, MY KING...
I MUSTA DRANK TOO MUCH.
YER BIG 'CAUSE YE DRANK TOO MUCH.
...AYE.
I HAVE A 'CONDITION'.
DIDJA STEAL ME CROWN?
NO...

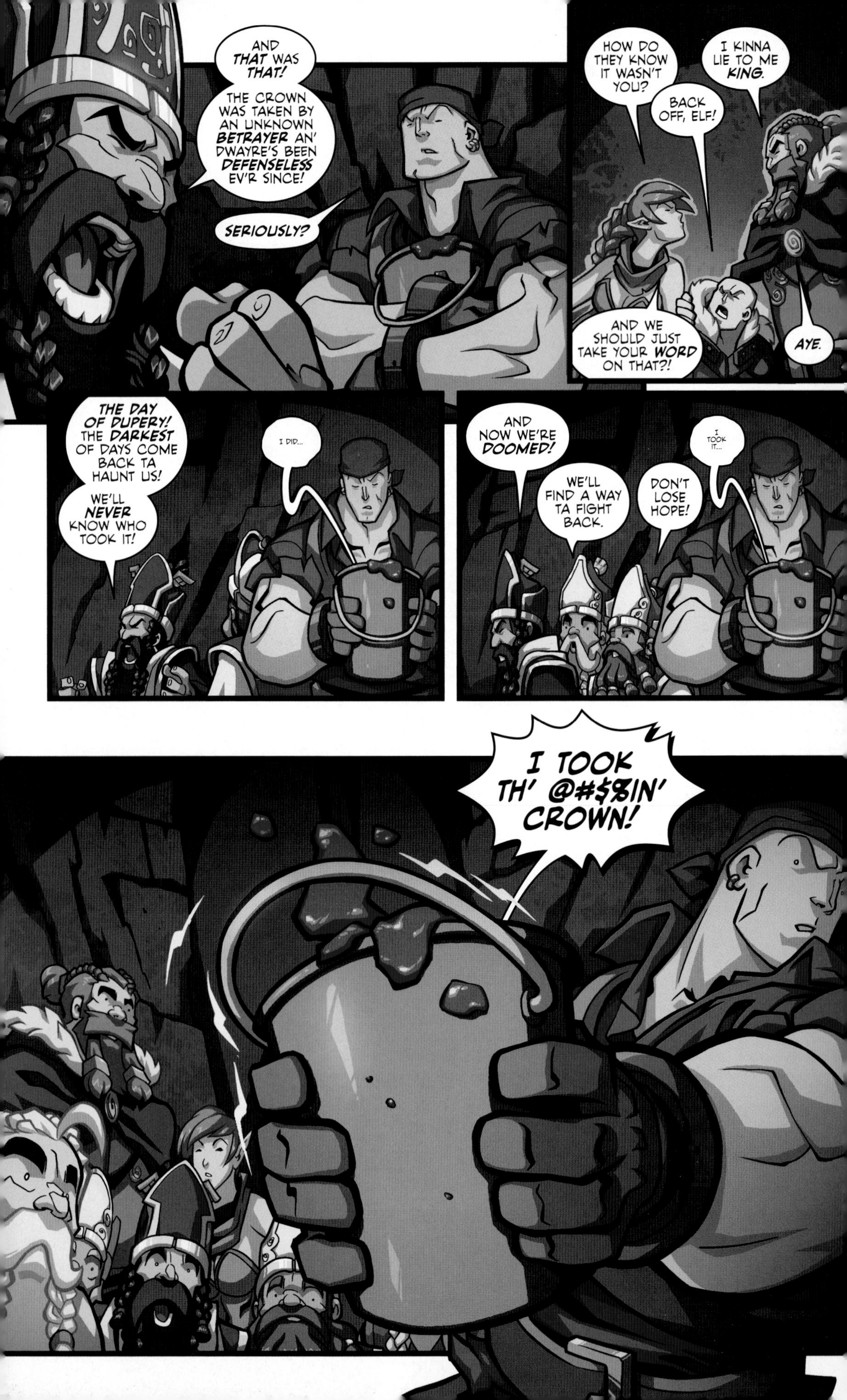
AND THAT WAS THAT!
THE CROWN WAS TAKEN BY AN UNKNOWN BETRAYER AN' DWAYRE'S BEEN DEFENSELESS EV'R SINCE!
SERIOUSLY?
HOW DO THEY KNOW IT WASN'T YOU?
I KINNA LIE TO ME KING.
BACK OFF, ELF!
AND WE SHOULD JUST TAKE YOUR WORD ON THAT?!
AYE.
THE DAY OF DUPERY! THE DARKEST OF DAYS COME BACK TA HAUNT US!
WE'LL NEVER KNOW WHO TOOK IT!
I DID...
AND NOW WE'RE DOOMED!
WE'LL FIND A WAY TA FIGHT BACK.
DON'T LOSE HOPE!
I TOOK IT...
I TOOK TH' @#$%IN' CROWN!

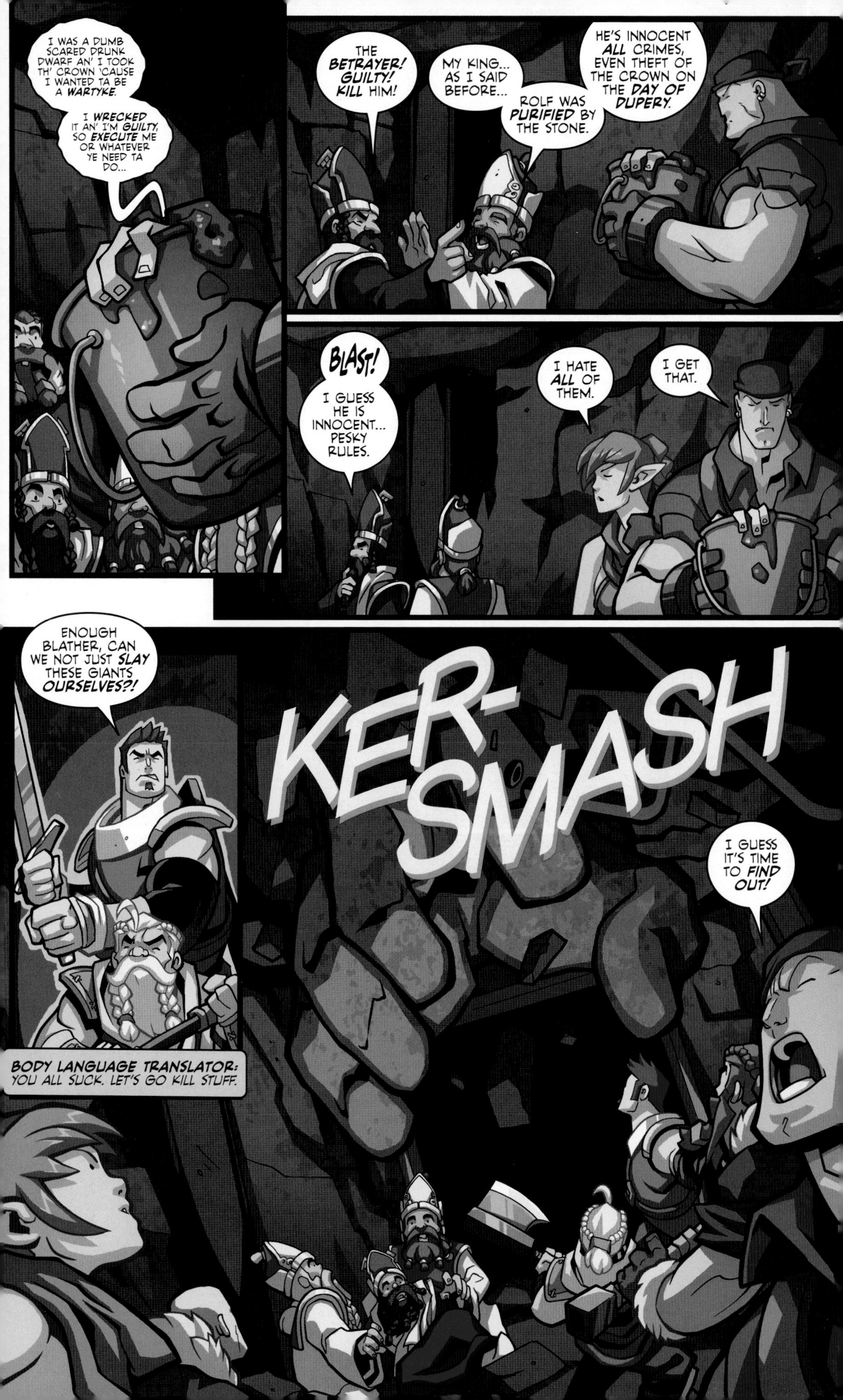

I WAS A DUMB SCARED DRUNK DWARF AN' I TOOK TH' CROWN 'CAUSE I WANTED TA BE A WARTYKE.
I WRECKED IT AN' I'M GUILTY, SO EXECUTE ME OR WHATEVER YE NEED TA DO...
THE BETRAYER! GUILTY! KILL HIM!
MY KING... AS I SAID BEFORE...
ROLF WAS PURIFIED BY THE STONE.
HE'S INNOCENT ALL CRIMES, EVEN THEFT OF THE CROWN ON THE DAY OF DUPERY.
BLAST!
I GUESS HE IS INNOCENT... PESKY RULES.
I HATE ALL OF THEM.
I GET THAT.
ENOUGH BLATHER, CAN WE NOT JUST SLAY THESE GIANTS OURSELVES?!
BODY LANGUAGE TRANSLATOR: YOU ALL SUCK. LET'S GO KILL STUFF.
KER-SMASH
I GUESS IT'S TIME TO FIND OUT!

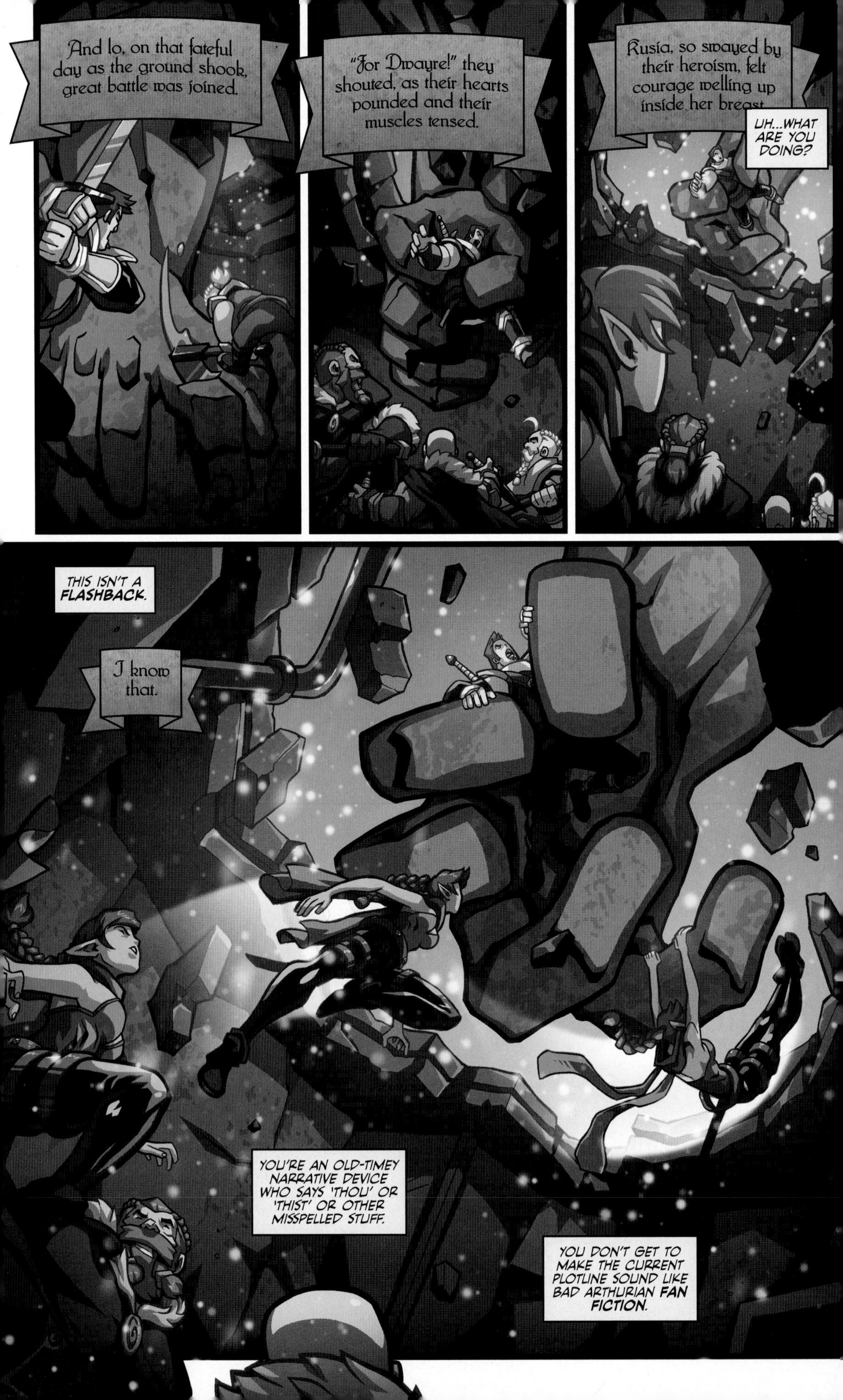

And lo, on that fateful day as the ground shook, great battle was joined.
"For Dwayre!" they shouted, as their hearts pounded and their muscles tensed.
Kusia, so swayed by their heroism, felt courage welling up inside her breast
UH...WHAT ARE YOU DOING?
THIS ISN'T A FLASHBACK.
I know that.
YOU'RE AN OLD-TIMEY NARRATIVE DEVICE WHO SAYS 'THOU' OR 'THIST' OR OTHER MISSPELLED STUFF.
YOU DON'T GET TO MAKE THE CURRENT PLOTLINE SOUND LIKE BAD ARTHURIAN FAN FICTION.

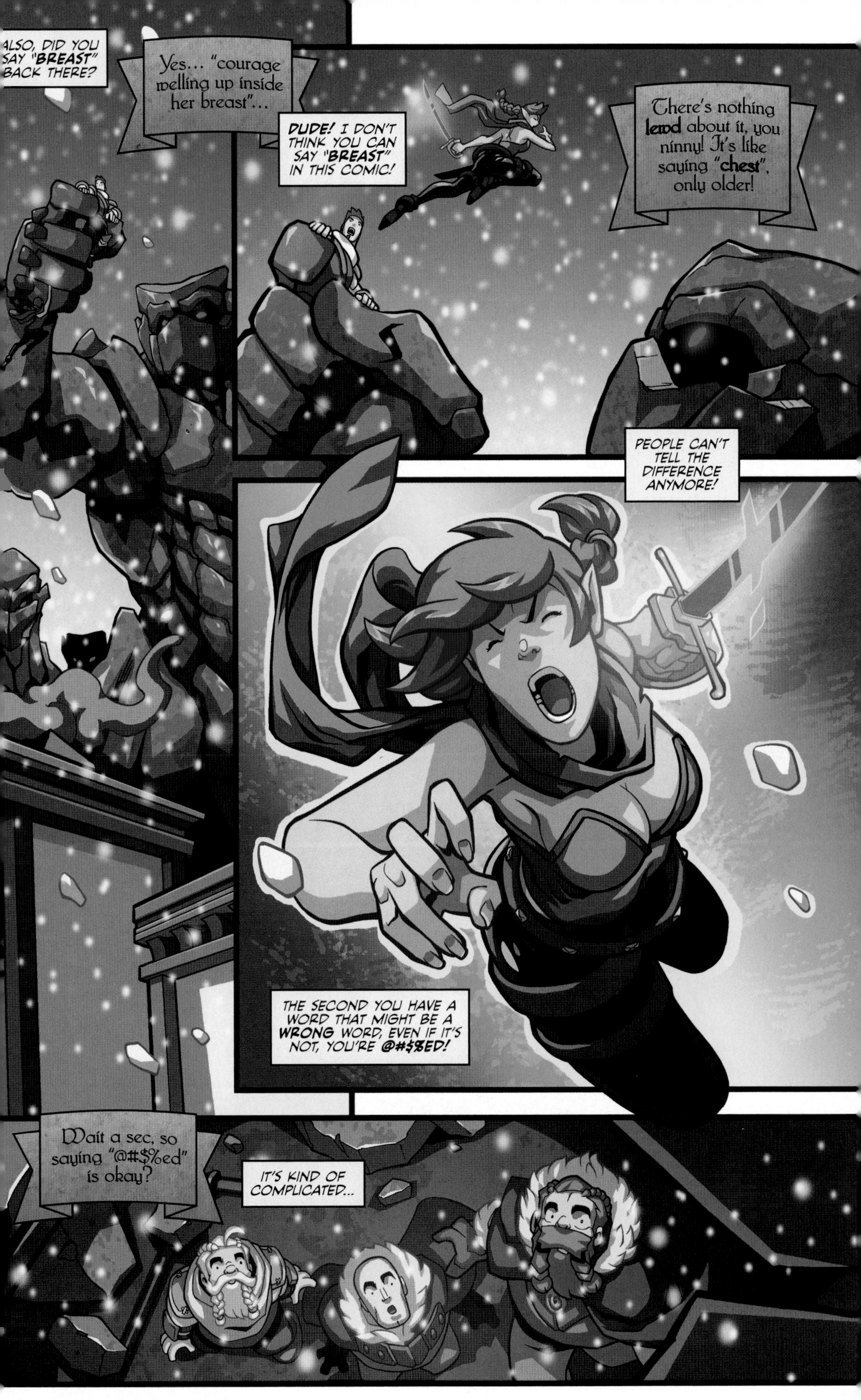
ALSO, DID YOU SAY "BREAST" BACK THERE?
Yes... "courage welling up inside her breast"...
DUDE! I DON'T THINK YOU CAN SAY "BREAST" IN THIS COMIC!
There's nothing lewd about it, you ninny! It's like saying "chest", only older!
PEOPLE CAN'T TELL THE DIFFERENCE ANYMORE!
THE SECOND YOU HAVE A WORD THAT MIGHT BE A WRONG WORD, EVEN IF IT'S NOT, YOU'RE @#$%ED!
Wait a sec, so saying "@#$%ed" is okay?
IT'S KIND OF COMPLICATED...

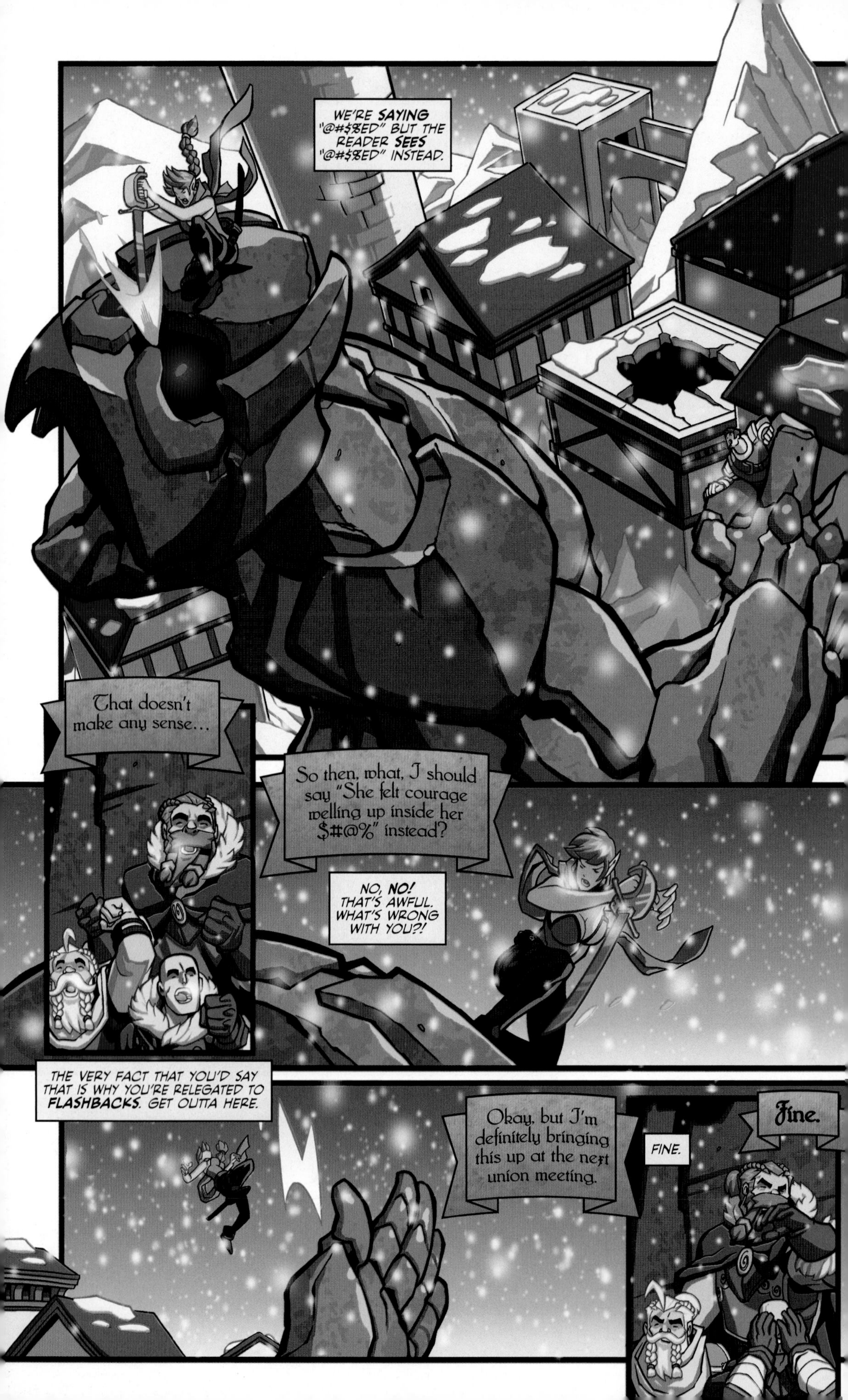
WE'RE SAYING "@#$%ED" BUT THE READER SEES "@#$%ED" INSTEAD.
That doesn't make any sense...
So then, what, I should say "She felt courage welling up inside her $#@%" instead?
NO, NO! THAT'S AWFUL. WHAT'S WRONG WITH YOU?!
THE VERY FACT THAT YOU'D SAY THAT IS WHY YOU'RE RELEGATED TO FLASHBACKS. GET OUTTA HERE.
Okay, but I'm definitely bringing this up at the next union meeting.
Fine.
FINE.

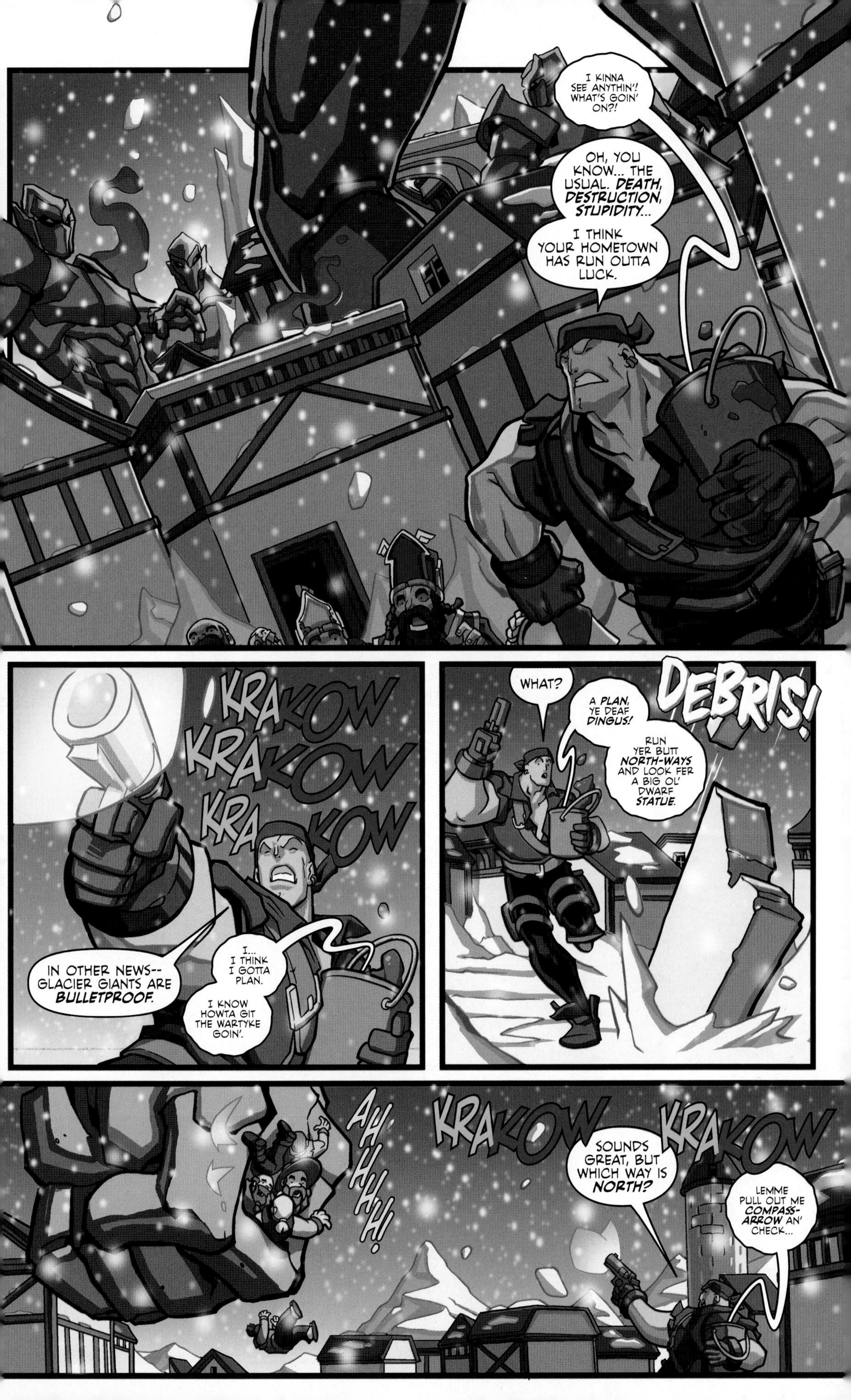
I KINNA SEE ANYTHIN'! WHAT'S GOIN' ON?!
OH, YOU KNOW... THE USUAL. DEATH, DESTRUCTION, STUPIDITY...
I THINK YOUR HOMETOWN HAS RUN OUTTA LUCK.
KRAKOW
KRAKOW
KRAKOW
IN OTHER NEWS-- GLACIER GIANTS ARE BULLETPROOF.
I... I THINK I GOTTA PLAN.
I KNOW HOWTA GIT THE WARTYKE GOIN'.
DEBRIS!
WHAT?
A PLAN, YE DEAF DINGUS!
RUN YER BUTT NORTH-WAYS AND LOOK FER A BIG OL' DWARF STATUE.
AHHHHH!
KRAKOW
KRAKOW
SOUNDS GREAT, BUT WHICH WAY IS NORTH?
LEMME PULL OUT ME COMPASS-ARROW AN' CHECK...

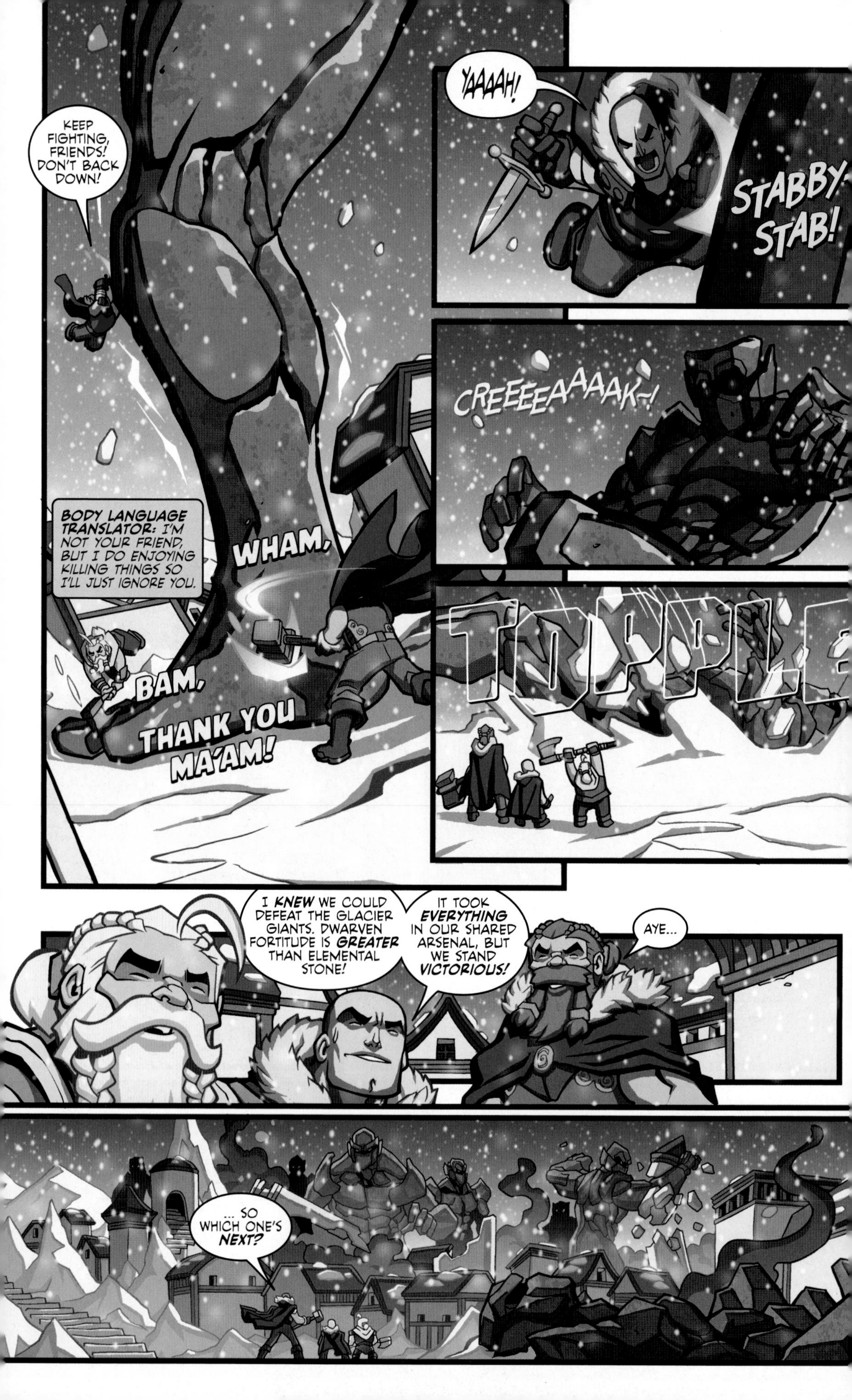
KEEP FIGHTING, FRIENDS! DON'T BACK DOWN!
YAAAAH!
STABBY-STAB!
CREEEEAAAAK~!
BODY LANGUAGE TRANSLATOR: I'M NOT YOUR FRIEND, BUT I DO ENJOYING KILLING THINGS SO I'LL JUST IGNORE YOU.
WHAM,
BAM,
THANK YOU MA'AM!
TOPPLE
I KNEW WE COULD DEFEAT THE GLACIER GIANTS. DWARVEN FORTITUDE IS GREATER THAN ELEMENTAL STONE!
IT TOOK EVERYTHING IN OUR SHARED ARSENAL, BUT WE STAND VICTORIOUS!
AYE...
... SO WHICH ONE'S NEXT?

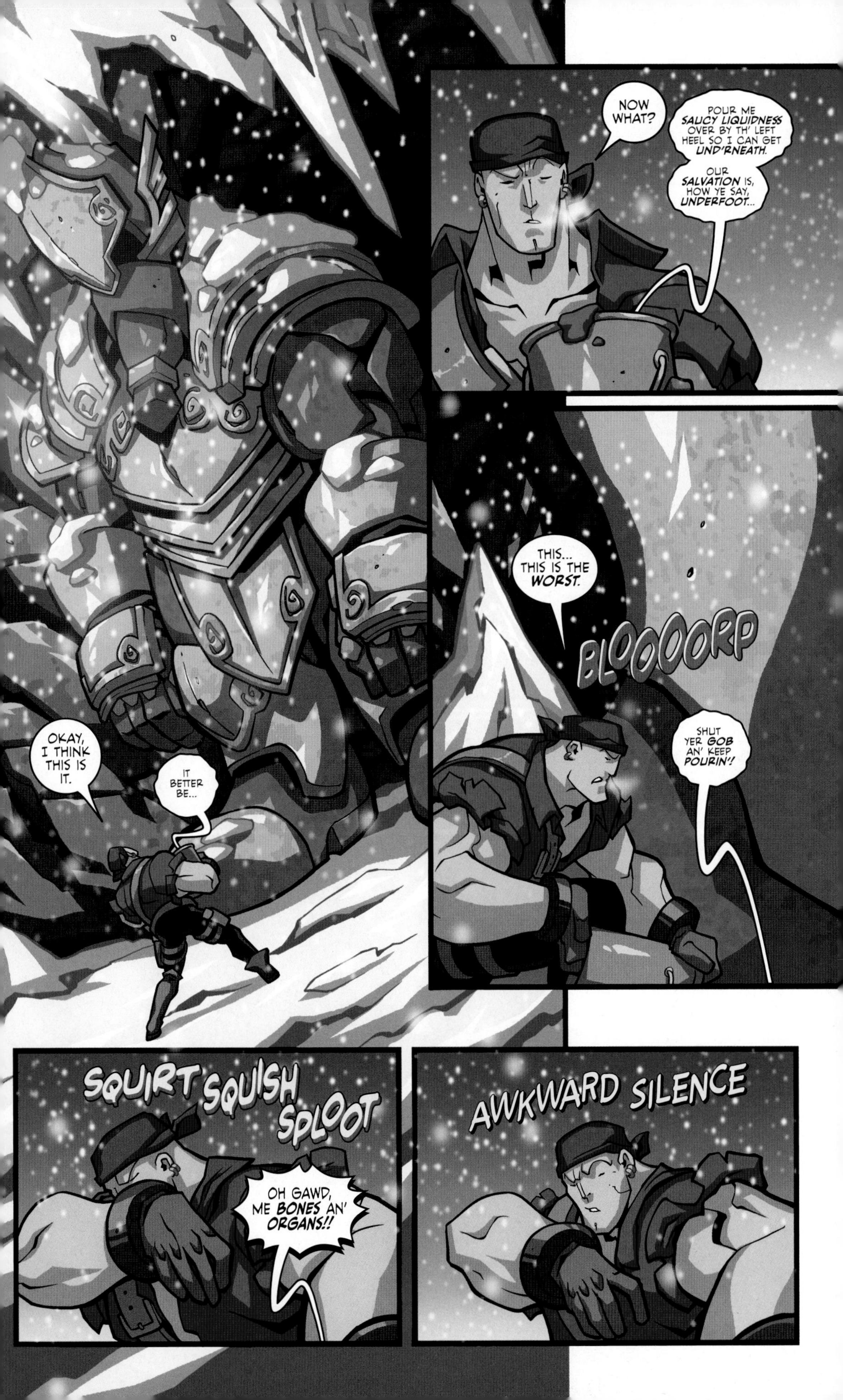
NOW WHAT?
POUR ME SAUCY LIQUIDNESS OVER BY TH' LEFT HEEL SO I CAN GET UND'RNEATH.
OUR SALVATION IS, HOW YE SAY, UNDERFOOT...
OKAY, I THINK THIS IS IT.
IT BETTER BE...
THIS... THIS IS THE WORST.
BLOOOORP
SHUT YER GOB AN' KEEP POURIN'!
SQUIRT SQUISH SPLOOT
OH GAWD, ME BONES AN' ORGANS!!
AWKWARD SILENCE

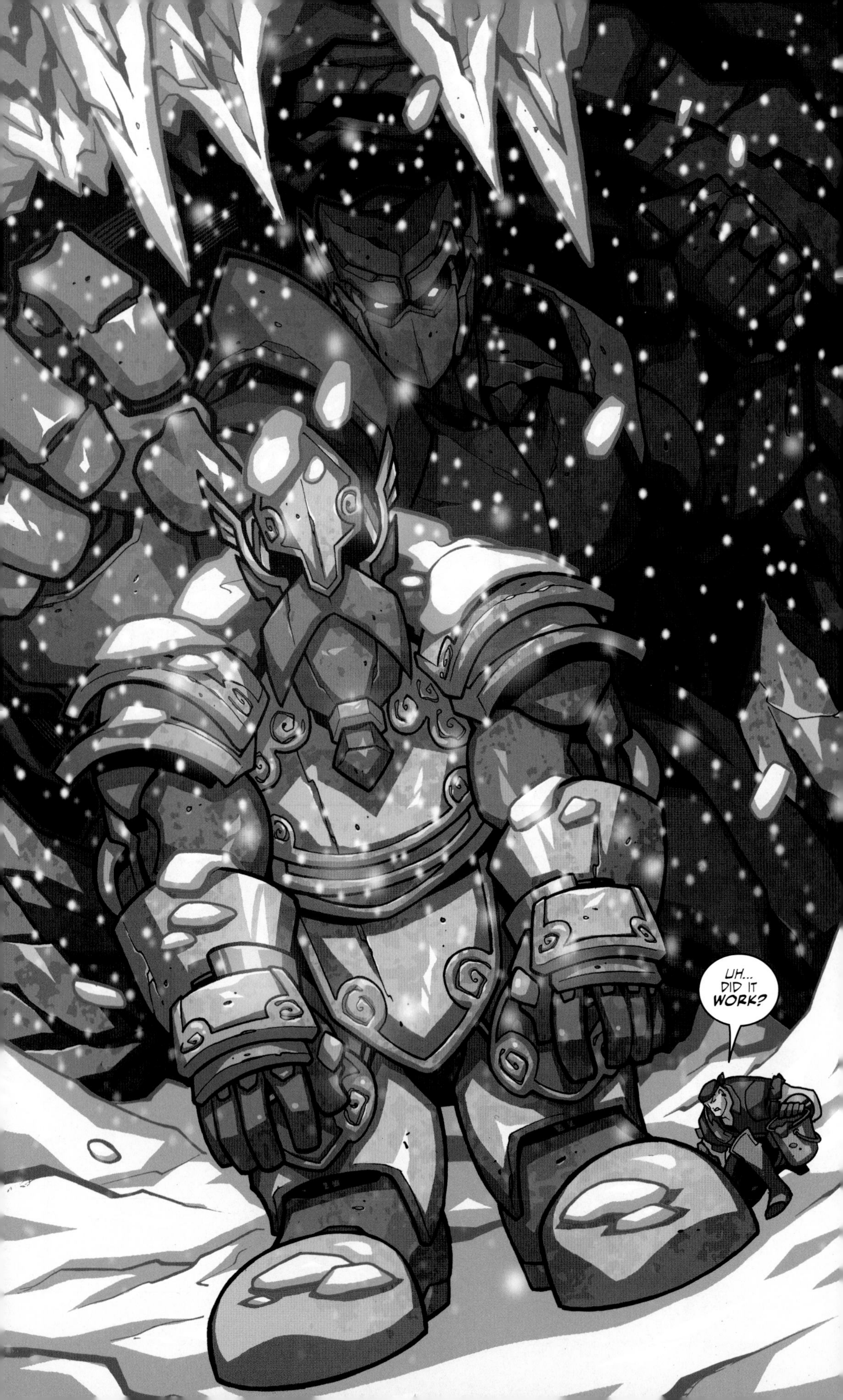
UH... DID IT WORK?

CHAPTER FIVE

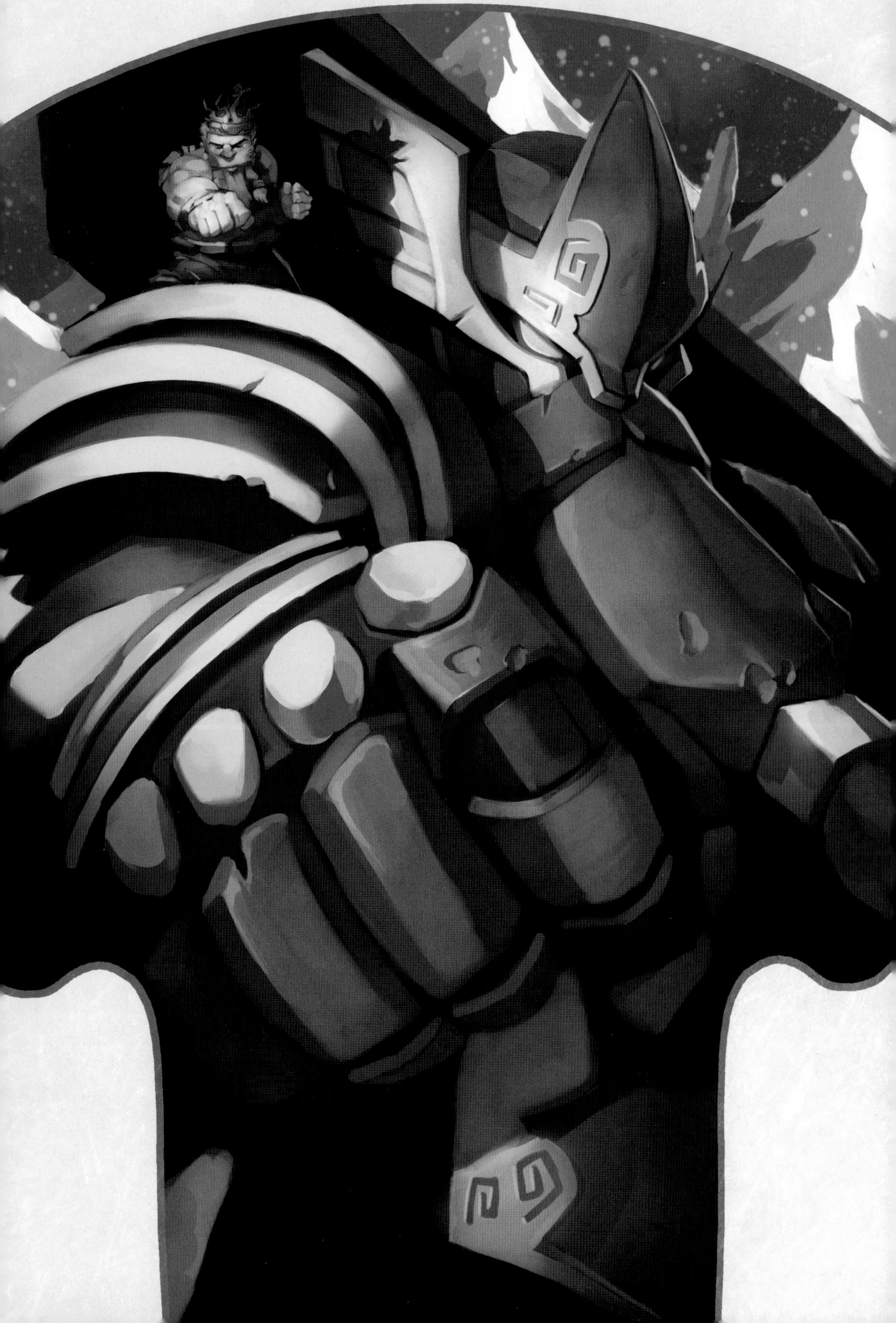

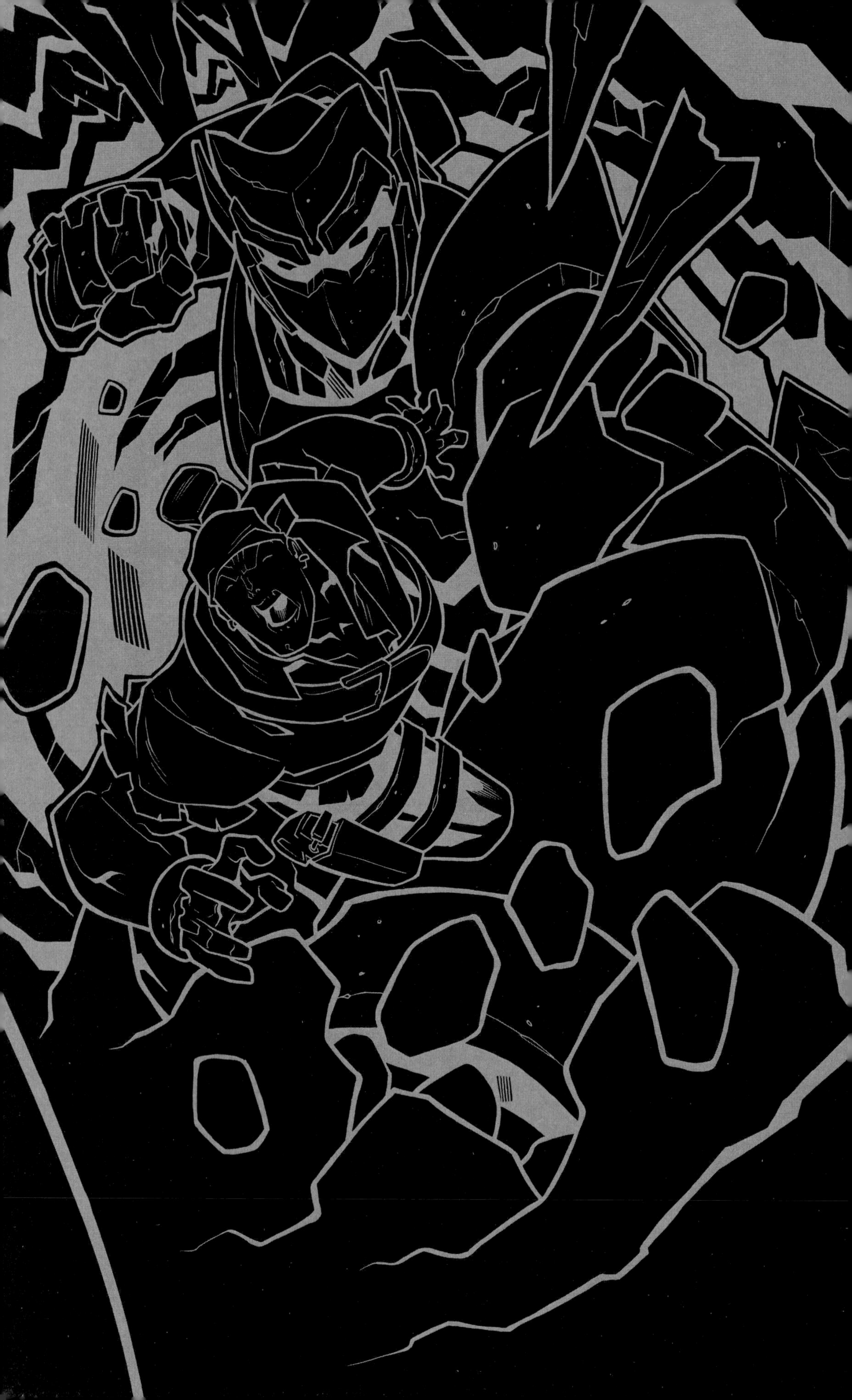

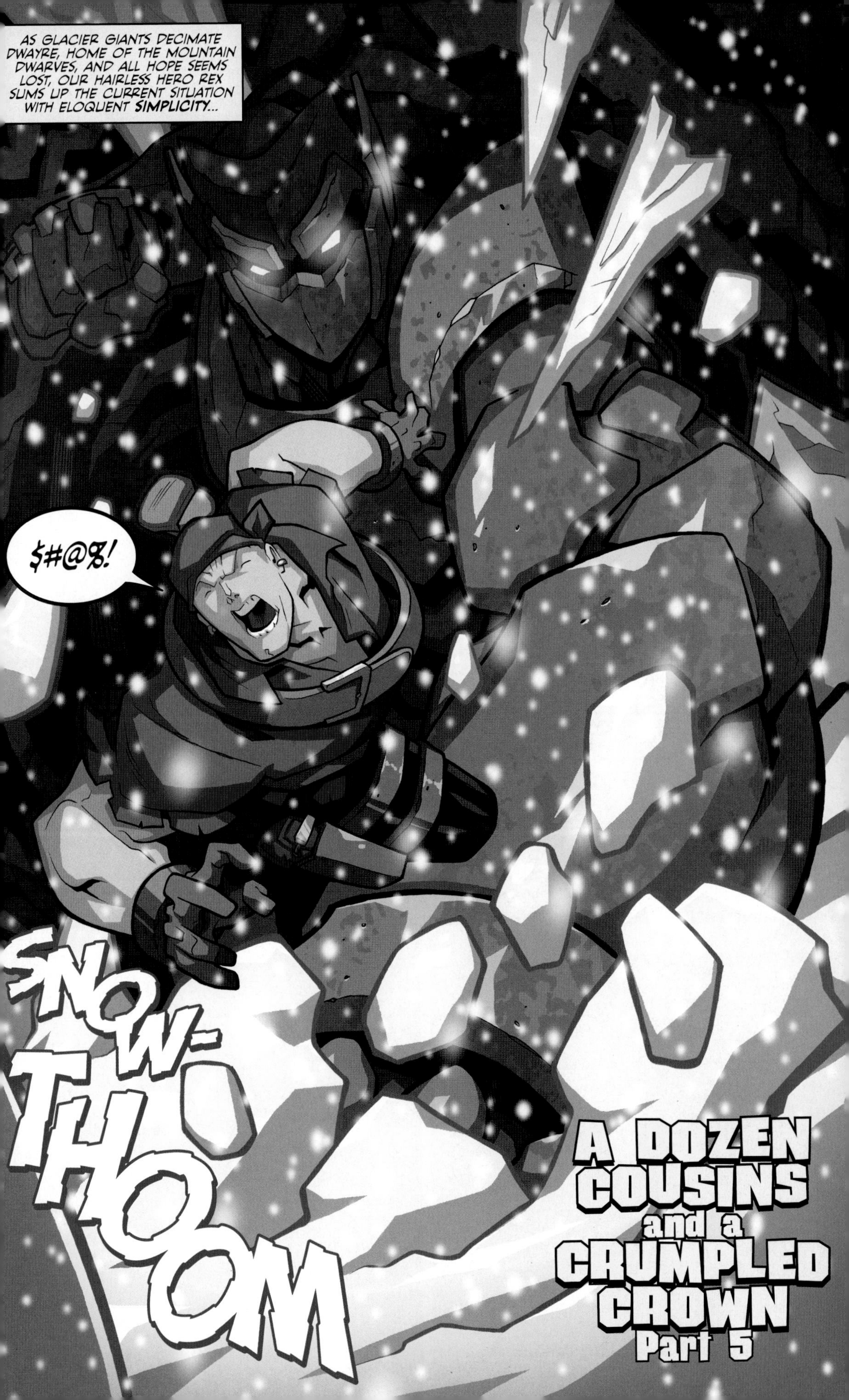
AS GLACIER GIANTS DECIMATE DWAYRE, HOME OF THE MOUNTAIN DWARVES, AND ALL HOPE SEEMS LOST, OUR HAIRLESS HERO REX SUMS UP THE CURRENT SITUATION WITH ELOQUENT SIMPLICITY...
$#@%!
SNOW-THOOOM
A DOZEN COUSINS and a CRUMPLED CROWN Part 5

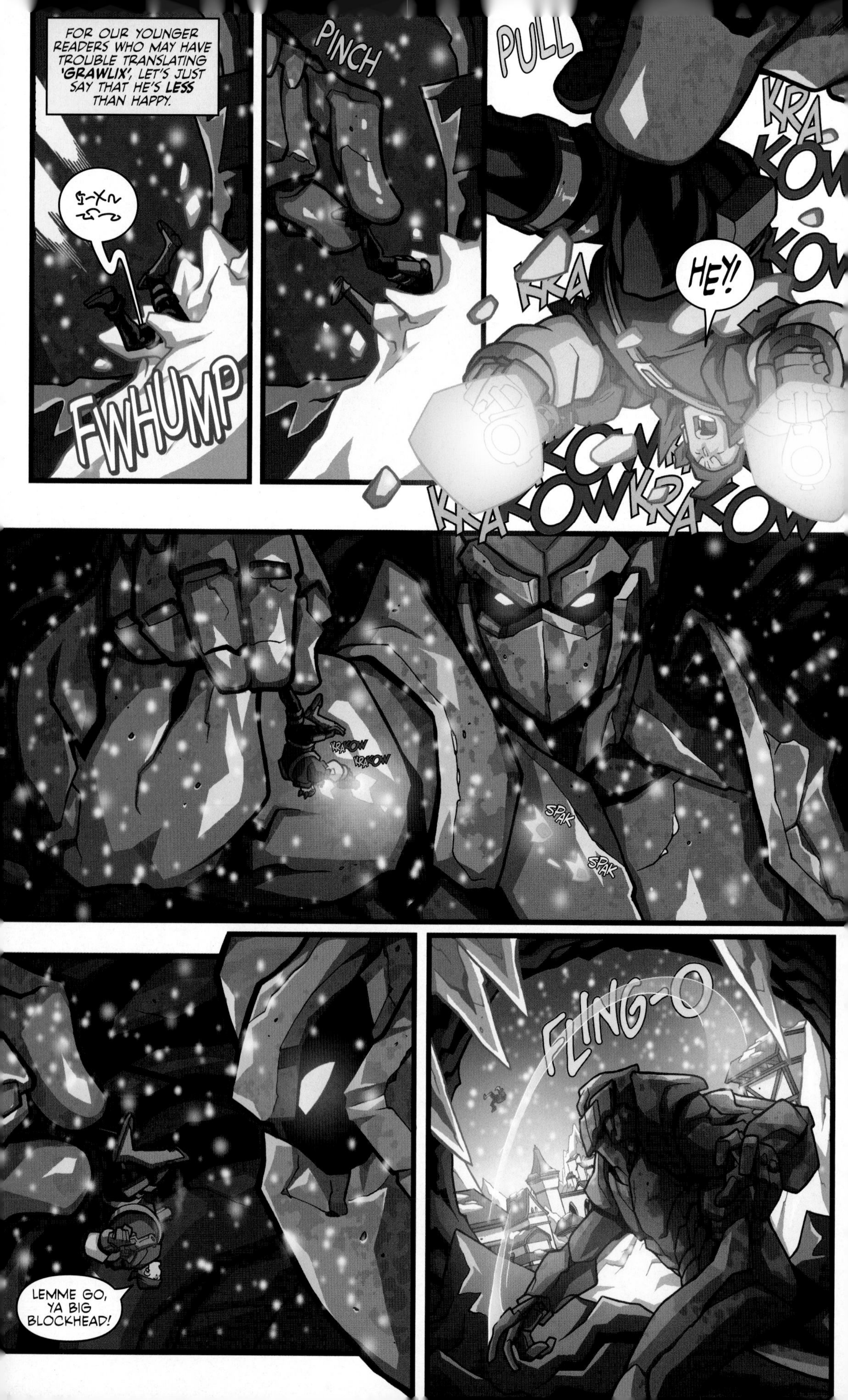
FOR OUR YOUNGER READERS WHO MAY HAVE TROUBLE TRANSLATING 'GRAWLIX', LET'S JUST SAY THAT HE'S LESS THAN HAPPY.
FWHUMP
PINCH
PULL
KRAKOW
KRAKOW
KRA
HEY!
KRAKOWKRAKOW
KRAKOW
KRAKOW
SPAK
SPAK
LEMME GO, YA BIG BLOCKHEAD!
FLING-O

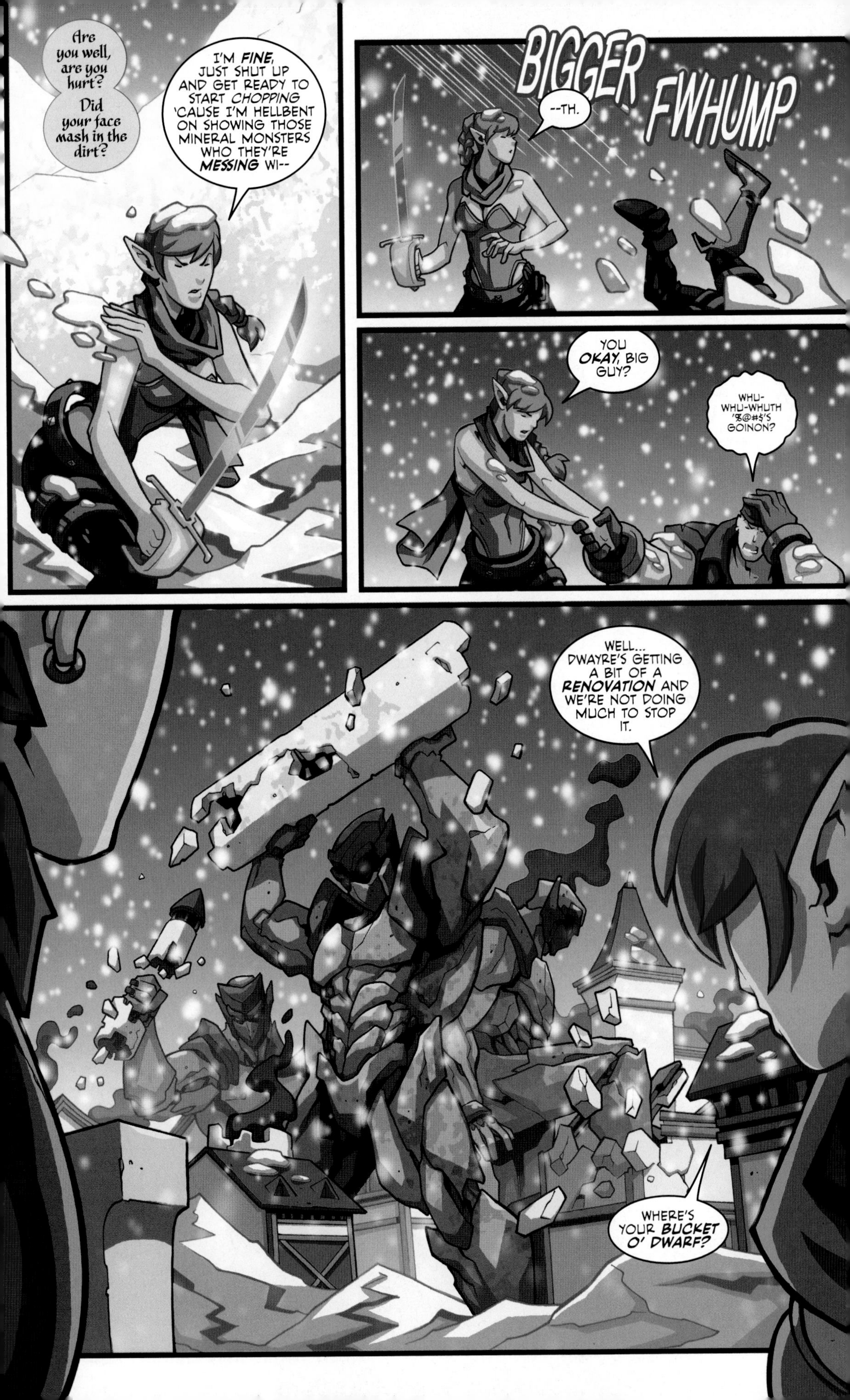
Are you well, are you hurt?
Did your face mash in the dirt?
I'M FINE, JUST SHUT UP AND GET READY TO START CHOPPING 'CAUSE I'M HELLBENT ON SHOWING THOSE MINERAL MONSTERS WHO THEY'RE MESSING WI--
BIGGER FWHUMP
--TH.
YOU OKAY, BIG GUY?
WHU-WHU-WHUTH '%@#$'S GOINON?
WELL... DWAYRE'S GETTING A BIT OF A RENOVATION AND WE'RE NOT DOING MUCH TO STOP IT.
WHERE'S YOUR BUCKET O' DWARF?

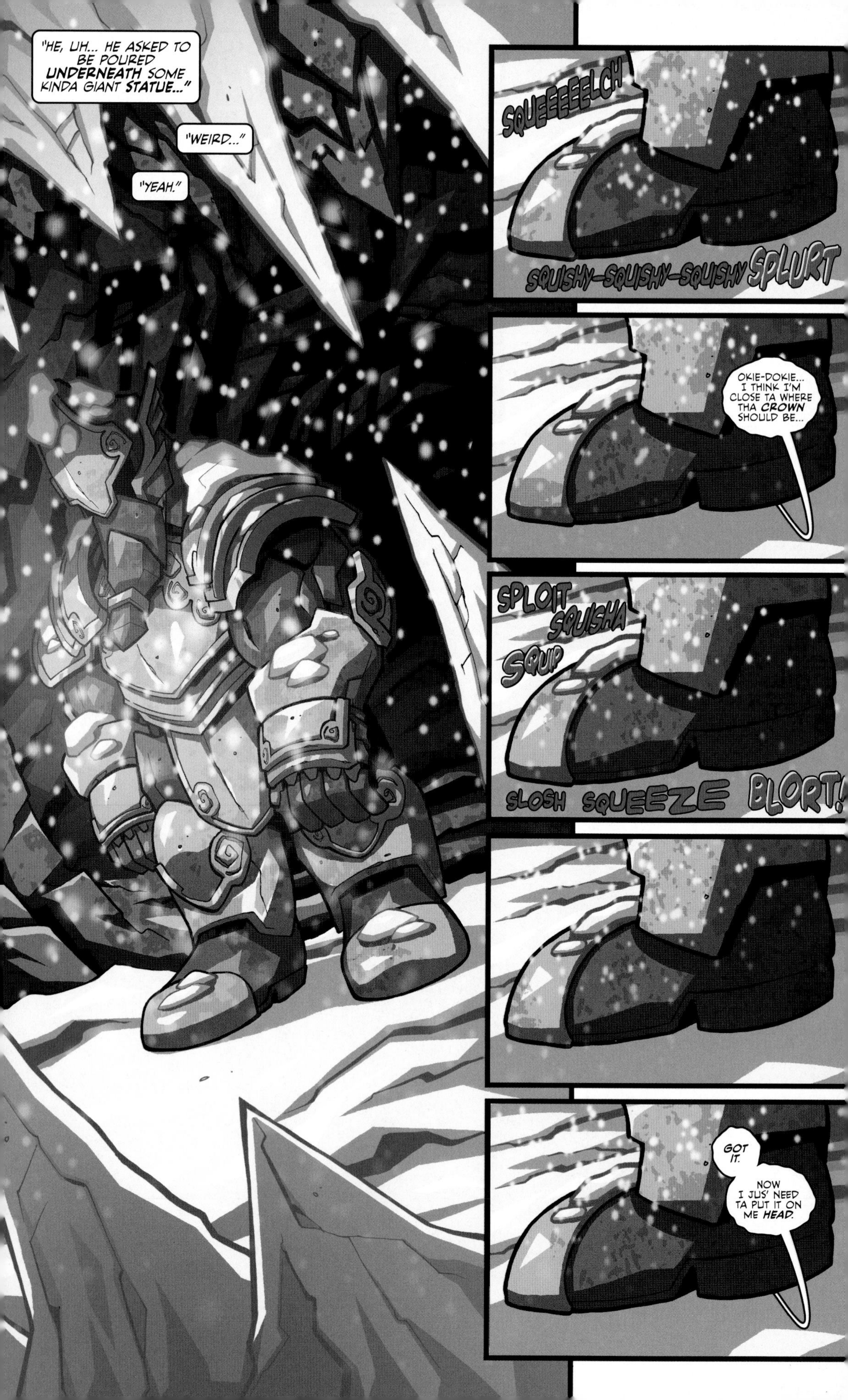
"HE, UH... HE ASKED TO BE POURED UNDERNEATH SOME KINDA GIANT STATUE..."
"WEIRD..."
"YEAH."
SQUEEEEEELCH
SQUISHY-SQUISHY-SQUISHY SPLURT
OKIE-DOKIE... I THINK I'M CLOSE TA WHERE THA CROWN SHOULD BE...
SPLOIT
SQUISHA
SQUIP
SLOSH SQUEEZE BLORT!
GOT IT.
NOW I JUS' NEED TA PUT IT ON ME HEAD.

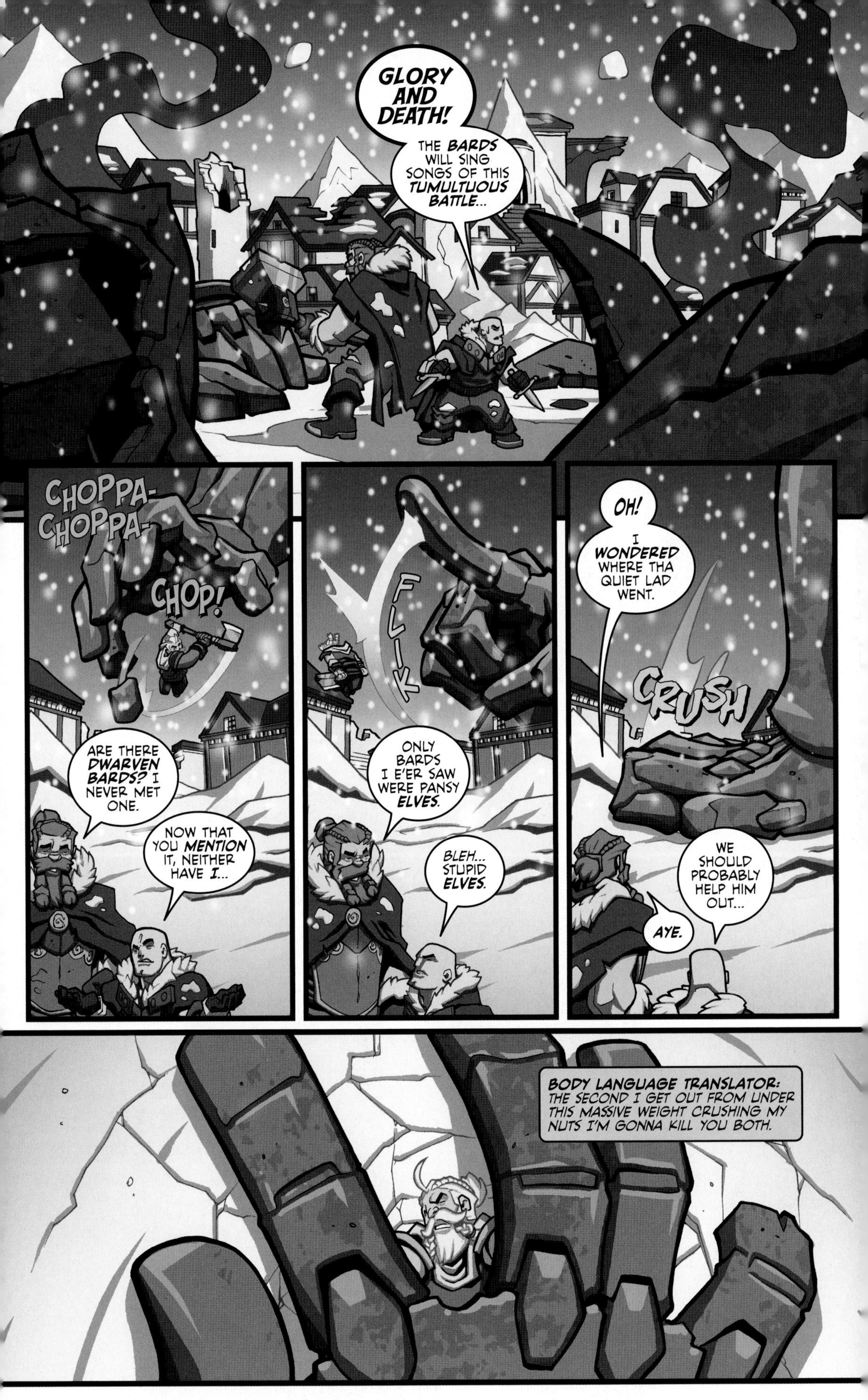
GLORY AND DEATH!
THE BARDS WILL SING SONGS OF THIS TUMULTUOUS BATTLE...
CHOPPA-CHOPPA-
CHOP!
ARE THERE DWARVEN BARDS? I NEVER MET ONE.
NOW THAT YOU MENTION IT, NEITHER HAVE I...
FLIK
ONLY BARDS I E'ER SAW WERE PANSY ELVES.
BLEH... STUPID ELVES.
OH!
I WONDERED WHERE THA QUIET LAD WENT.
CRUSH
WE SHOULD PROBABLY HELP HIM OUT...
AYE.
BODY LANGUAGE TRANSLATOR: THE SECOND I GET OUT FROM UNDER THIS MASSIVE WEIGHT CRUSHING MY NUTS I'M GONNA KILL YOU BOTH.

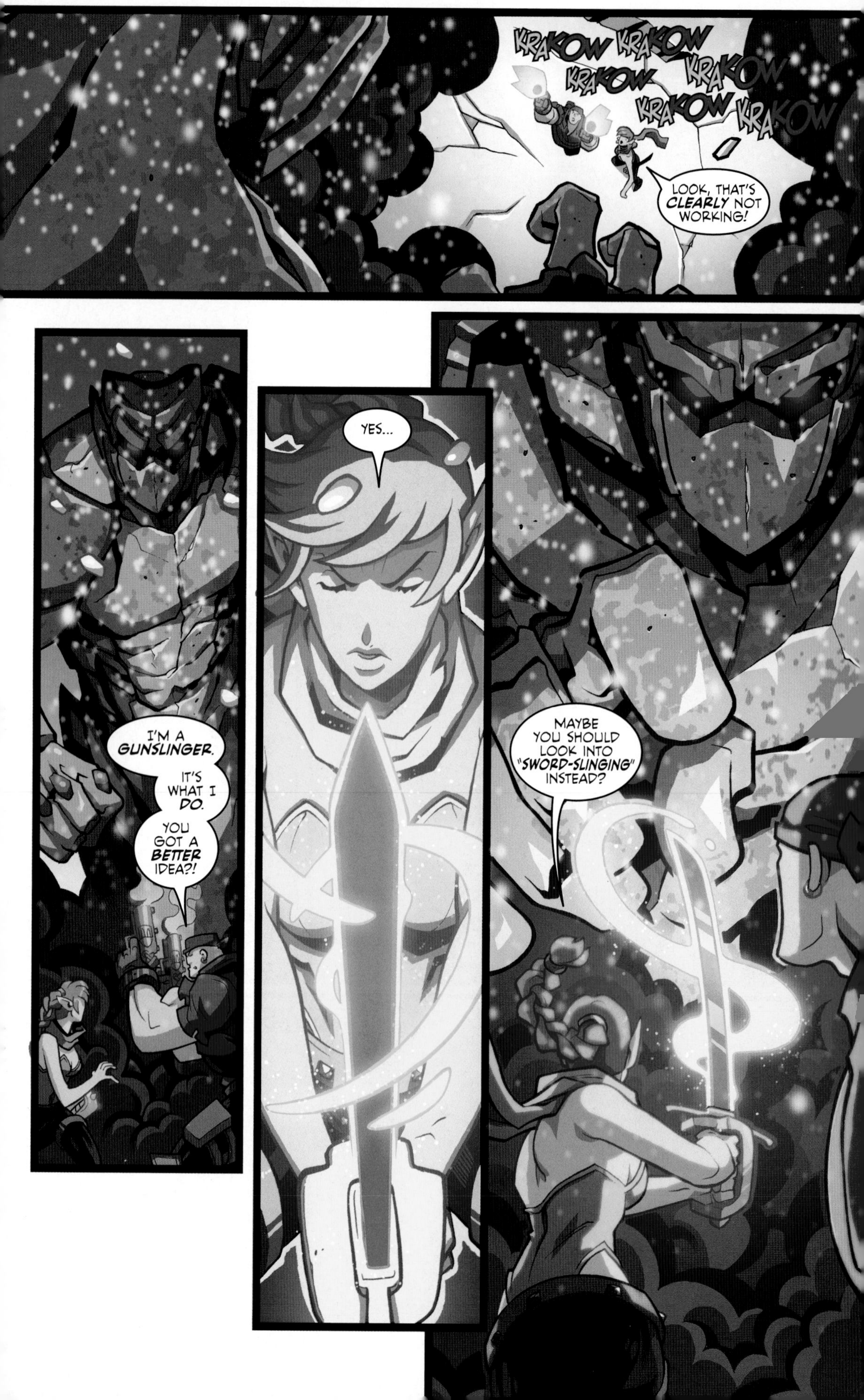
KRAKOW KRAKOW KRAKOW KRAKOW KRAKOW KRAKOW
LOOK, THAT'S CLEARLY NOT WORKING!
I'M A GUNSLINGER.
IT'S WHAT I DO.
YOU GOT A BETTER IDEA?!
YES...
MAYBE YOU SHOULD LOOK INTO "SWORD-SLINGING" INSTEAD?

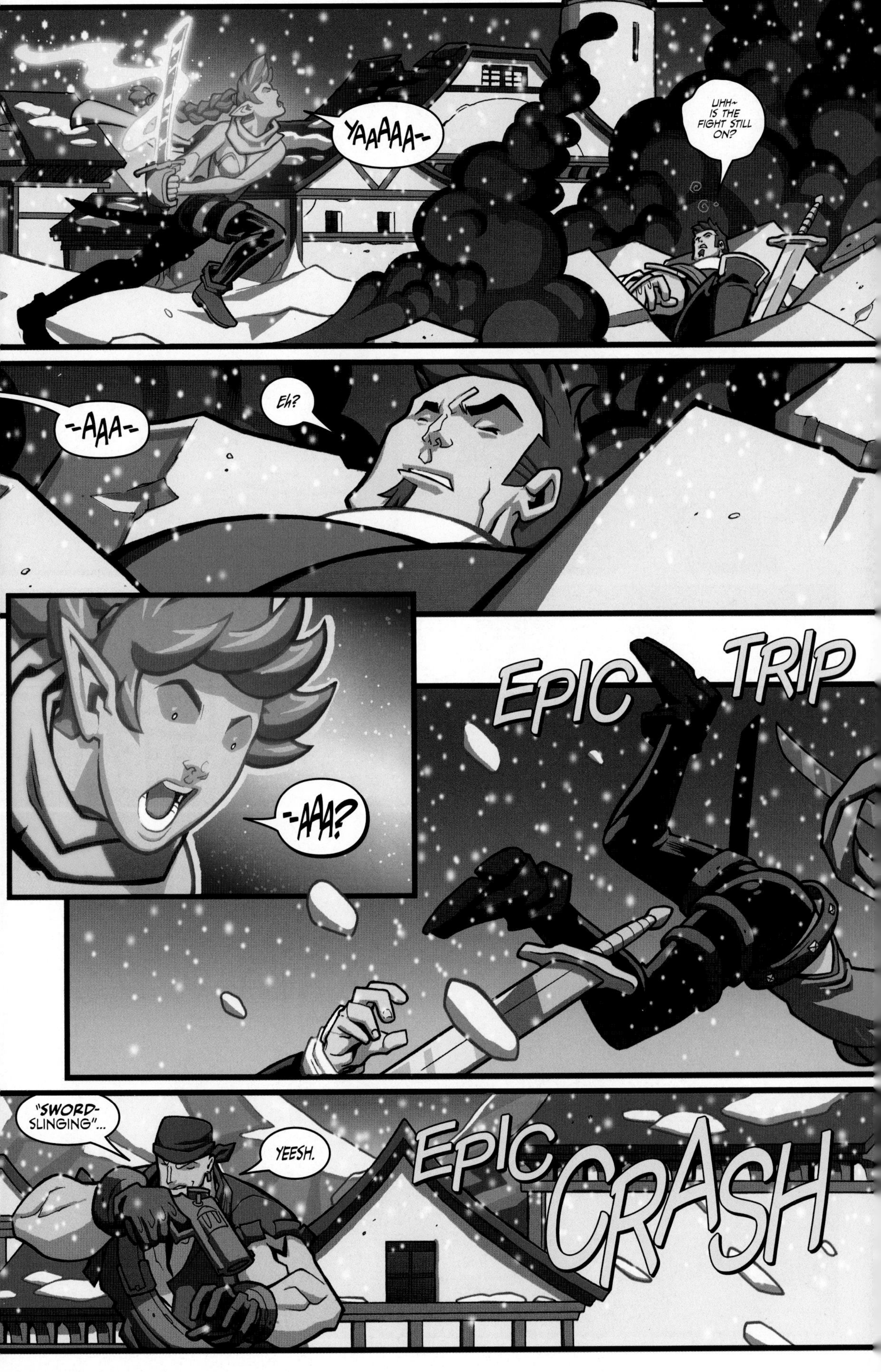
YAAAAA--
UHH~ IS THE FIGHT STILL ON?
--AAA--
Eh?
--AAA?
EPIC TRIP
"SWORD-SLINGING"...
YEESH.
EPIC CRASH

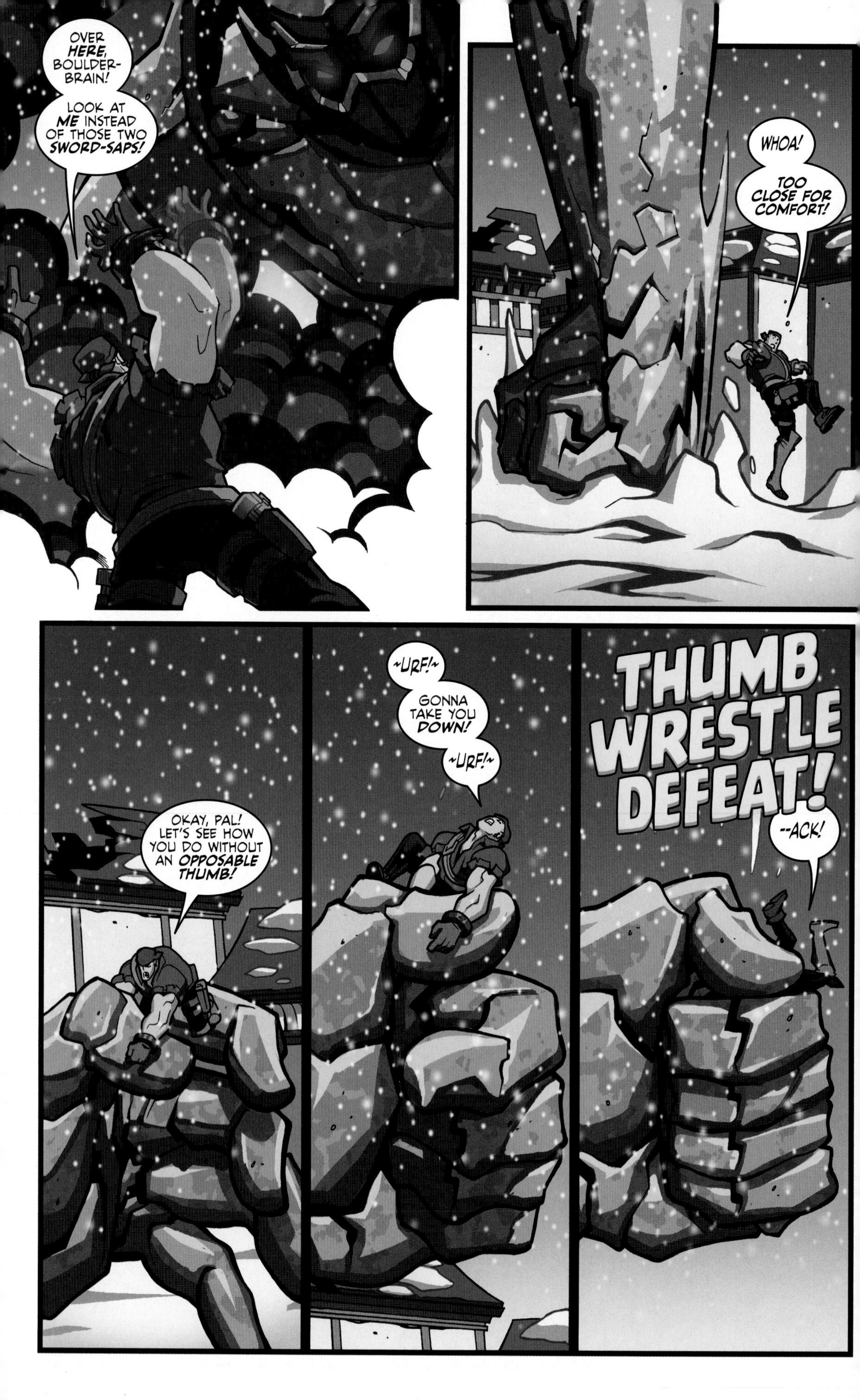
OVER HERE, BOULDER-BRAIN!
LOOK AT ME INSTEAD OF THOSE TWO SWORD-SAPS!
WHOA!
TOO CLOSE FOR COMFORT!
OKAY, PAL! LET'S SEE HOW YOU DO WITHOUT AN OPPOSABLE THUMB!
~URF!~
GONNA TAKE YOU DOWN!
~URF!~
THUMB WRESTLE DEFEAT!
--ACK!

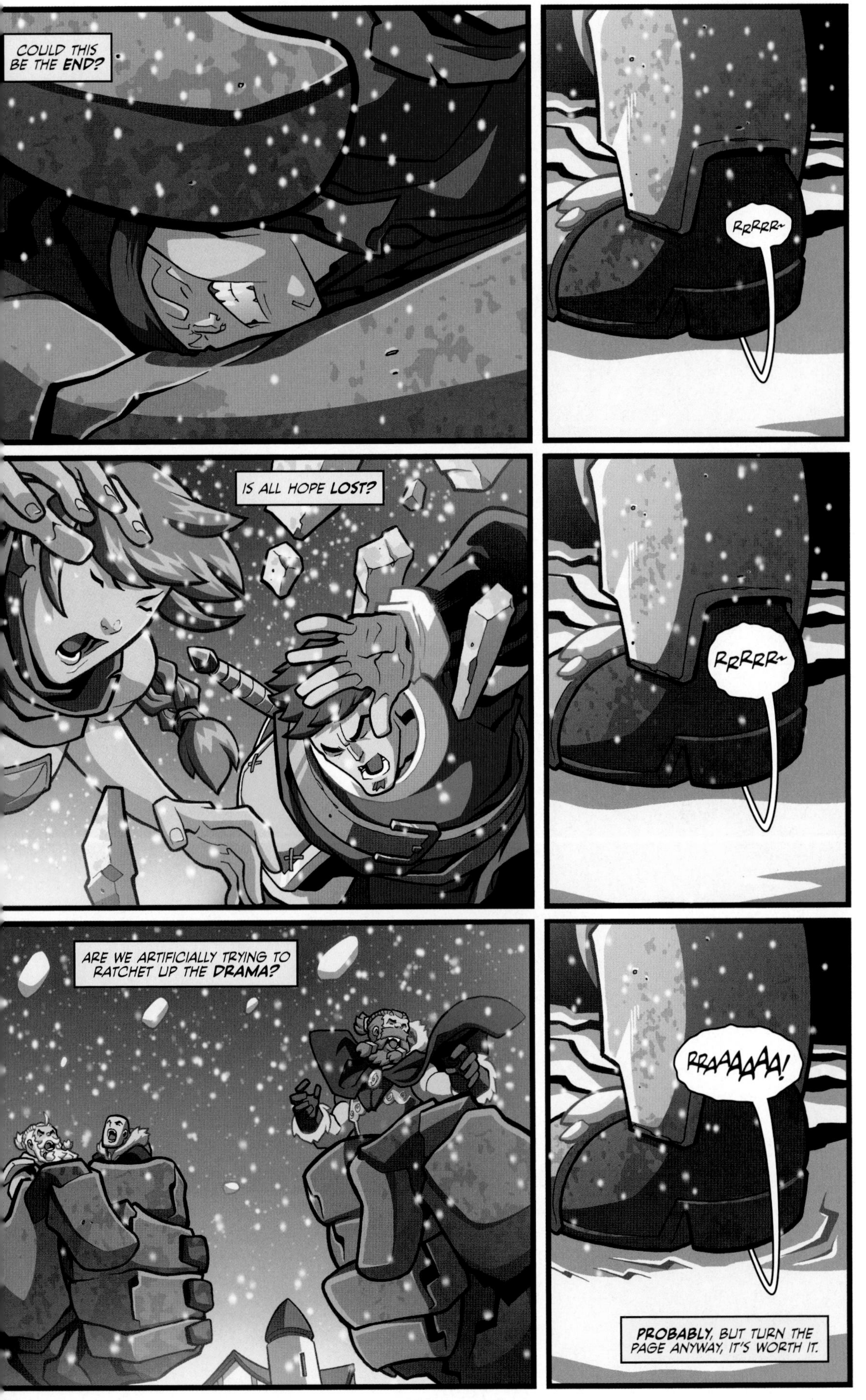
COULD THIS BE THE END?
RRRRR~
IS ALL HOPE LOST?
RRRRR~
ARE WE ARTIFICIALLY TRYING TO RATCHET UP THE DRAMA?
RRAAAAAAA!
PROBABLY, BUT TURN THE PAGE ANYWAY, IT'S WORTH IT.

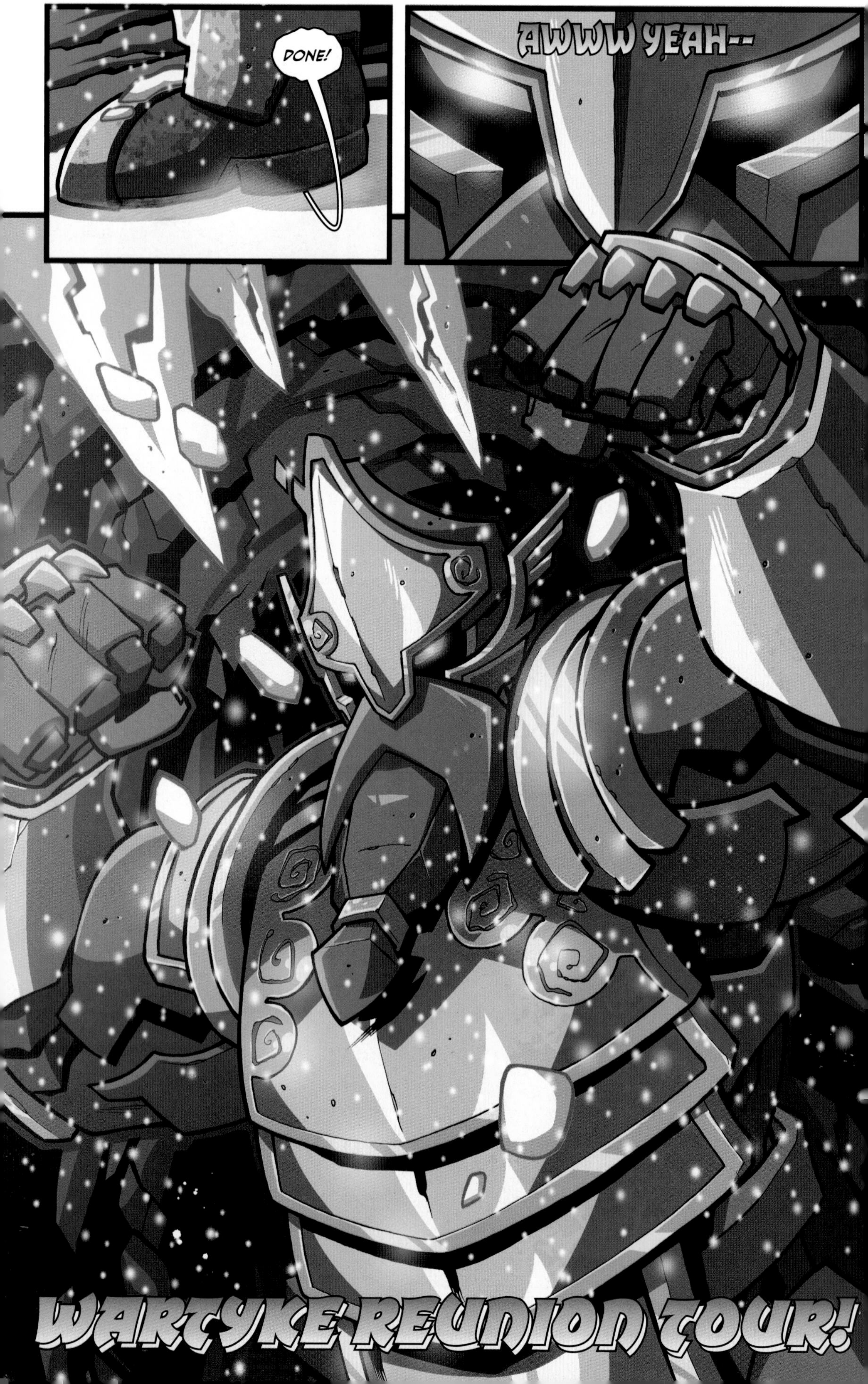
DONE!
AWWW YEAH--
WARTYKE REUNION TOUR!

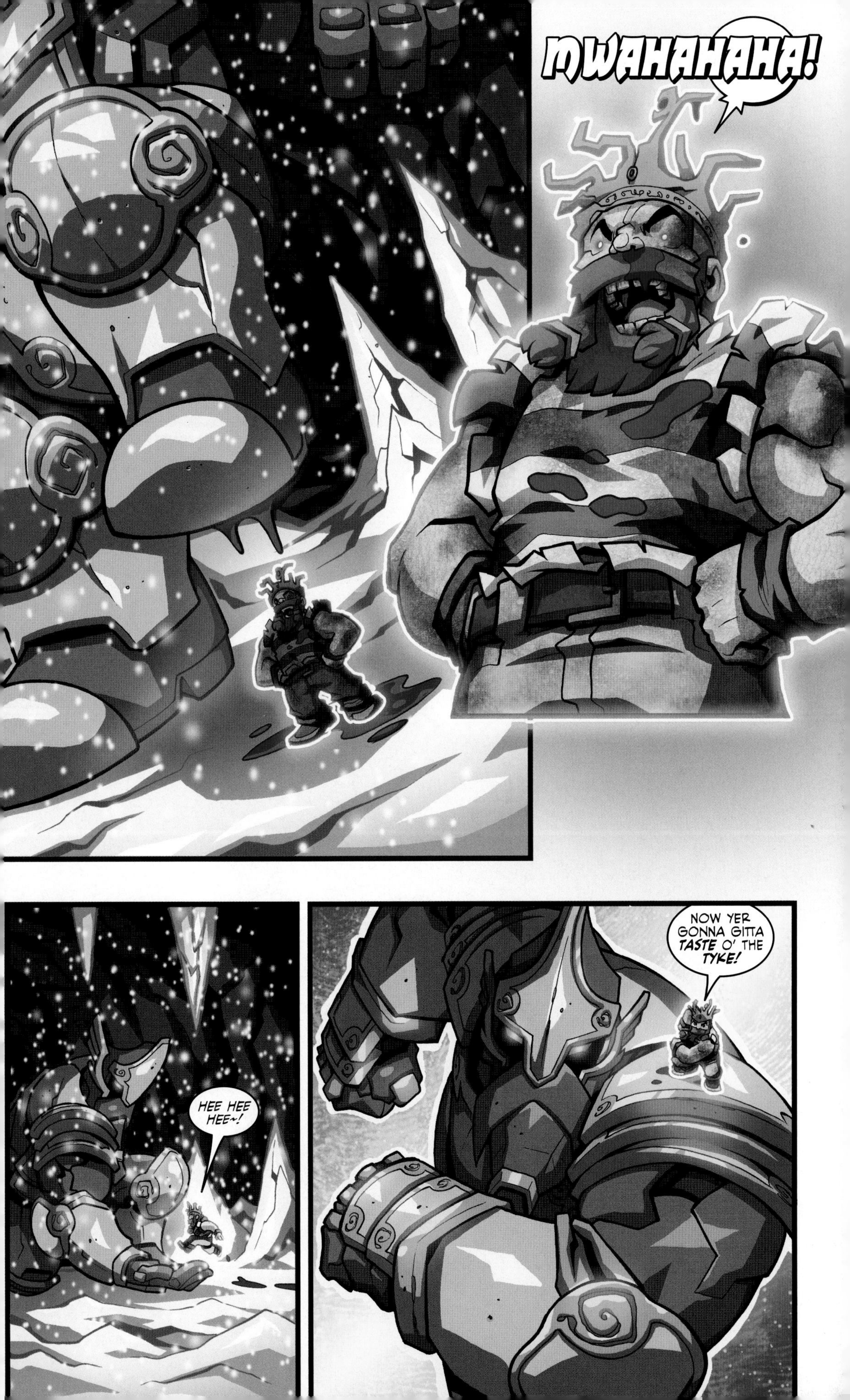
MWAHAHAHA!
HEE HEE HEE~!
NOW YER GONNA GITTA TASTE O' THE TYKE!

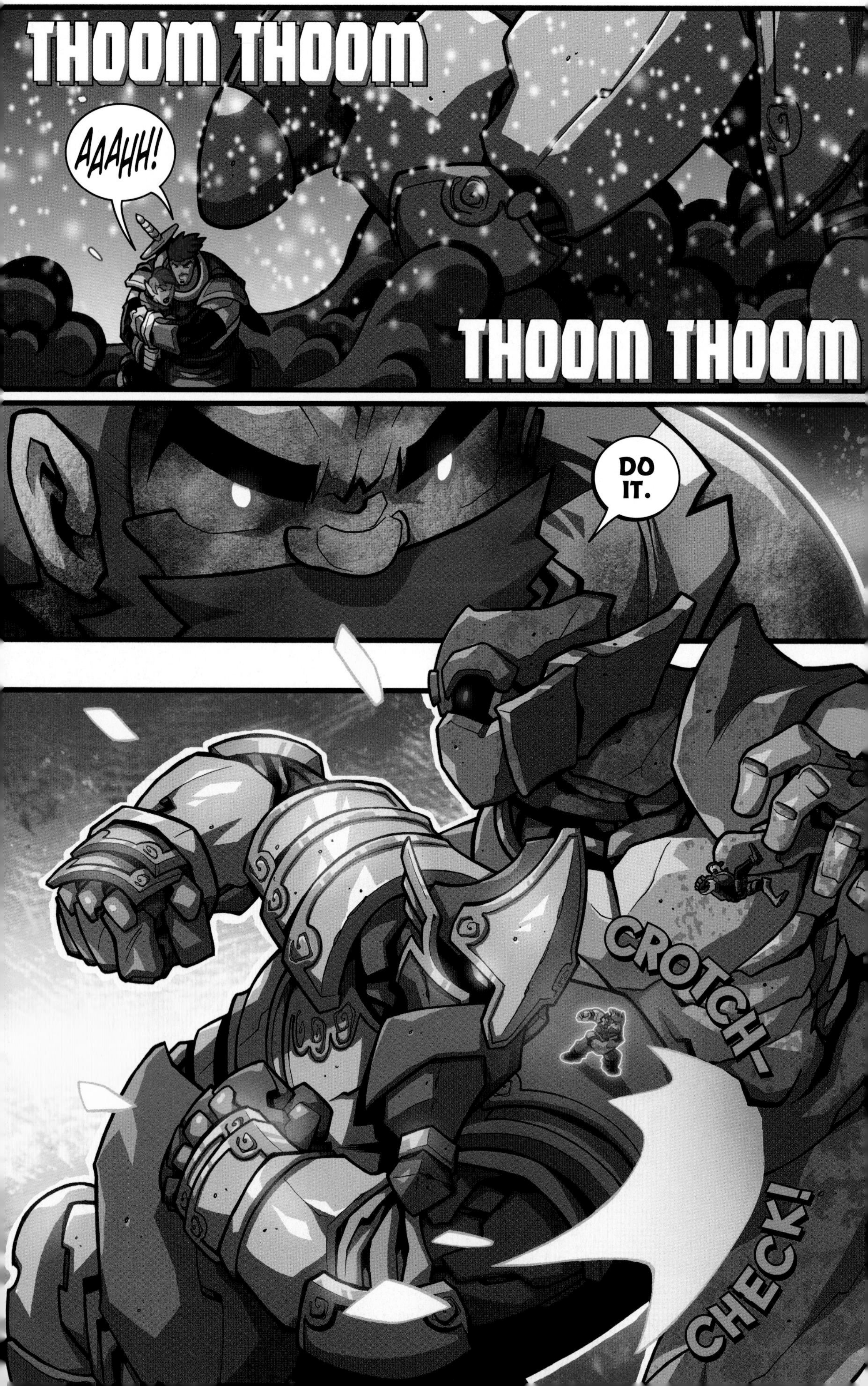
THOOM THOOM
AAAHH!
THOOM THOOM
DO IT.
CROTCH-
CHECK!

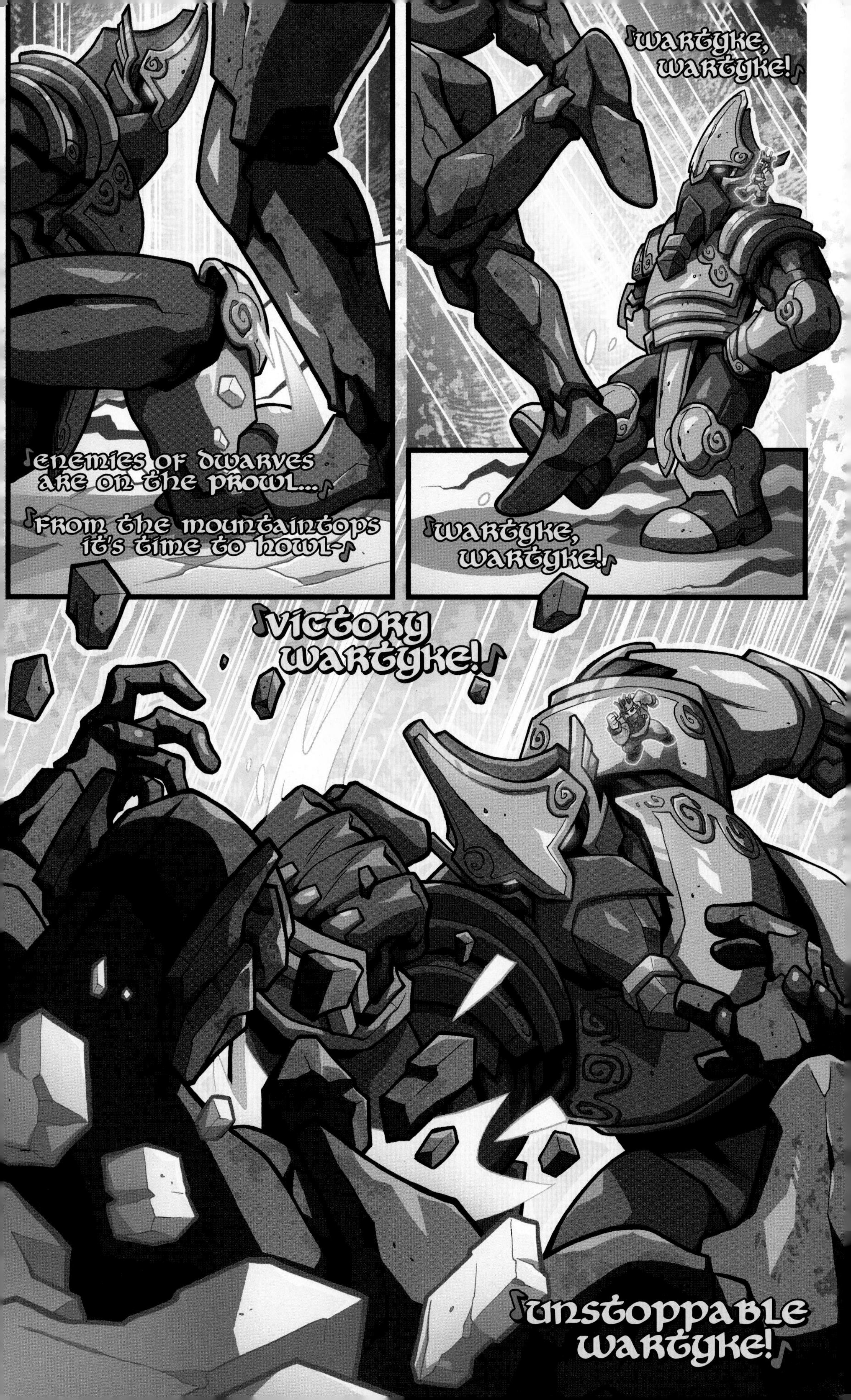

ENEMIES OF DWARVES ARE ON THE PROWL...
FROM THE MOUNTAINTOPS IT'S TIME TO HOWL-
WARTYKE, WARTYKE!
WARTYKE, WARTYKE!
VICTORY WARTYKE!
UNSTOPPABLE WARTYKE!

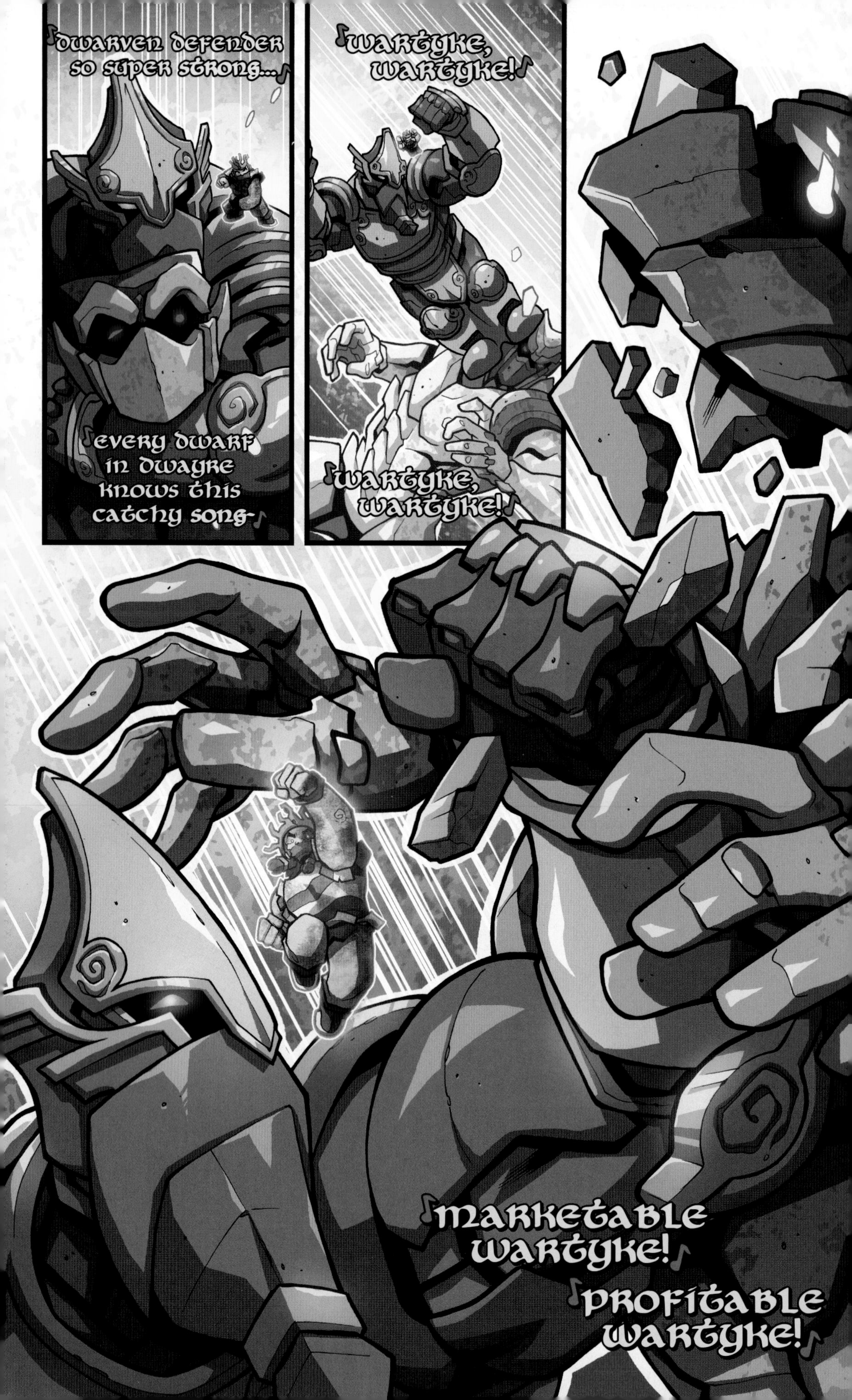
DWARVEN DEFENDER SO SUPER STRONG...
EVERY DWARF IN DWAYRE KNOWS THIS CATCHY SONG-
WARTYKE, WARTYKE!
WARTYKE, WARTYKE!
MARKETABLE WARTYKE!
PROFITABLE WARTYKE!

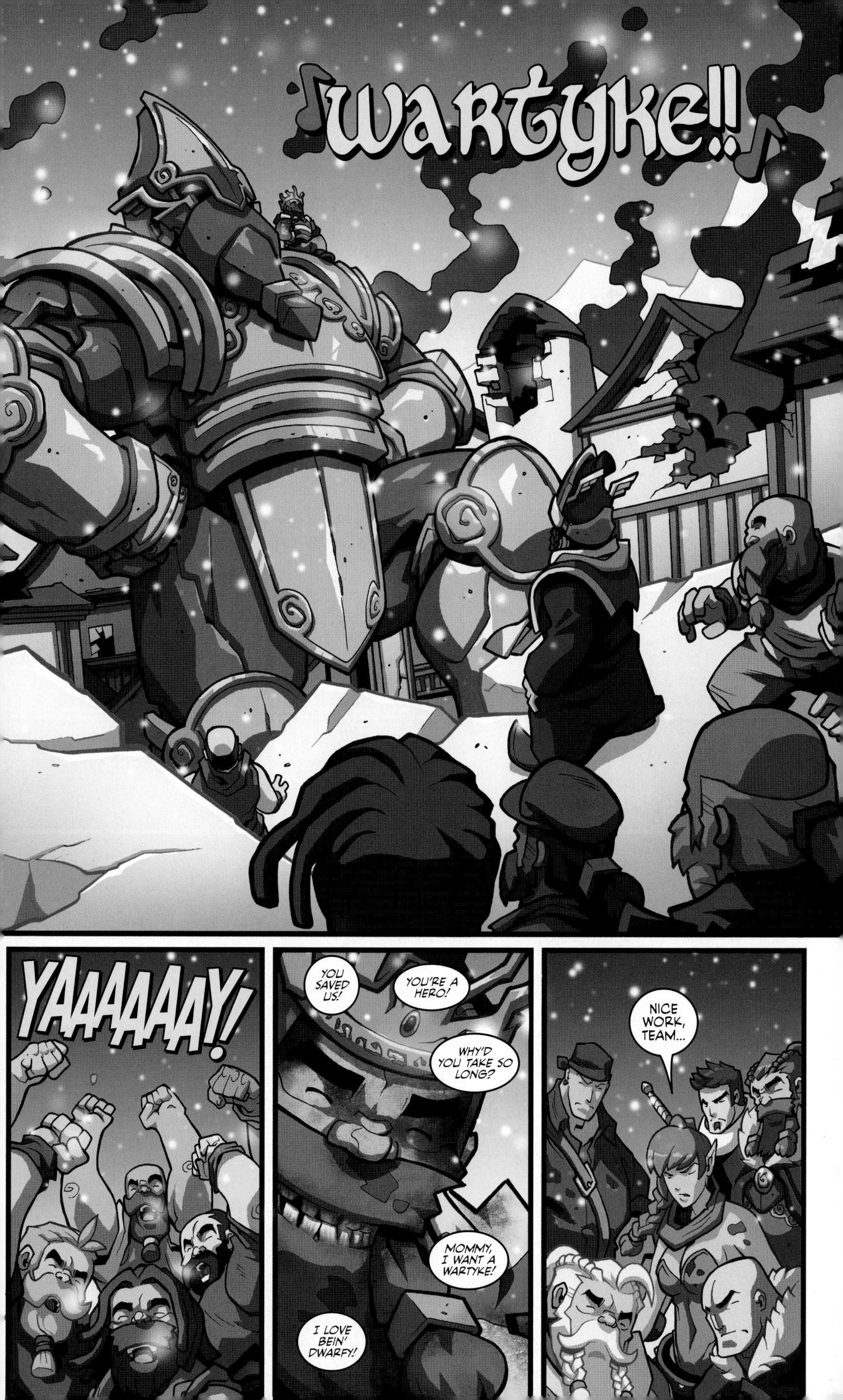
WARTYKE!!
YAAAAAAY!
YOU SAVED US!
YOU'RE A HERO!
WHY'D YOU TAKE SO LONG?
MOMMY, I WANT A WARTYKE!
I LOVE BEIN' DWARFY!
NICE WORK, TEAM...

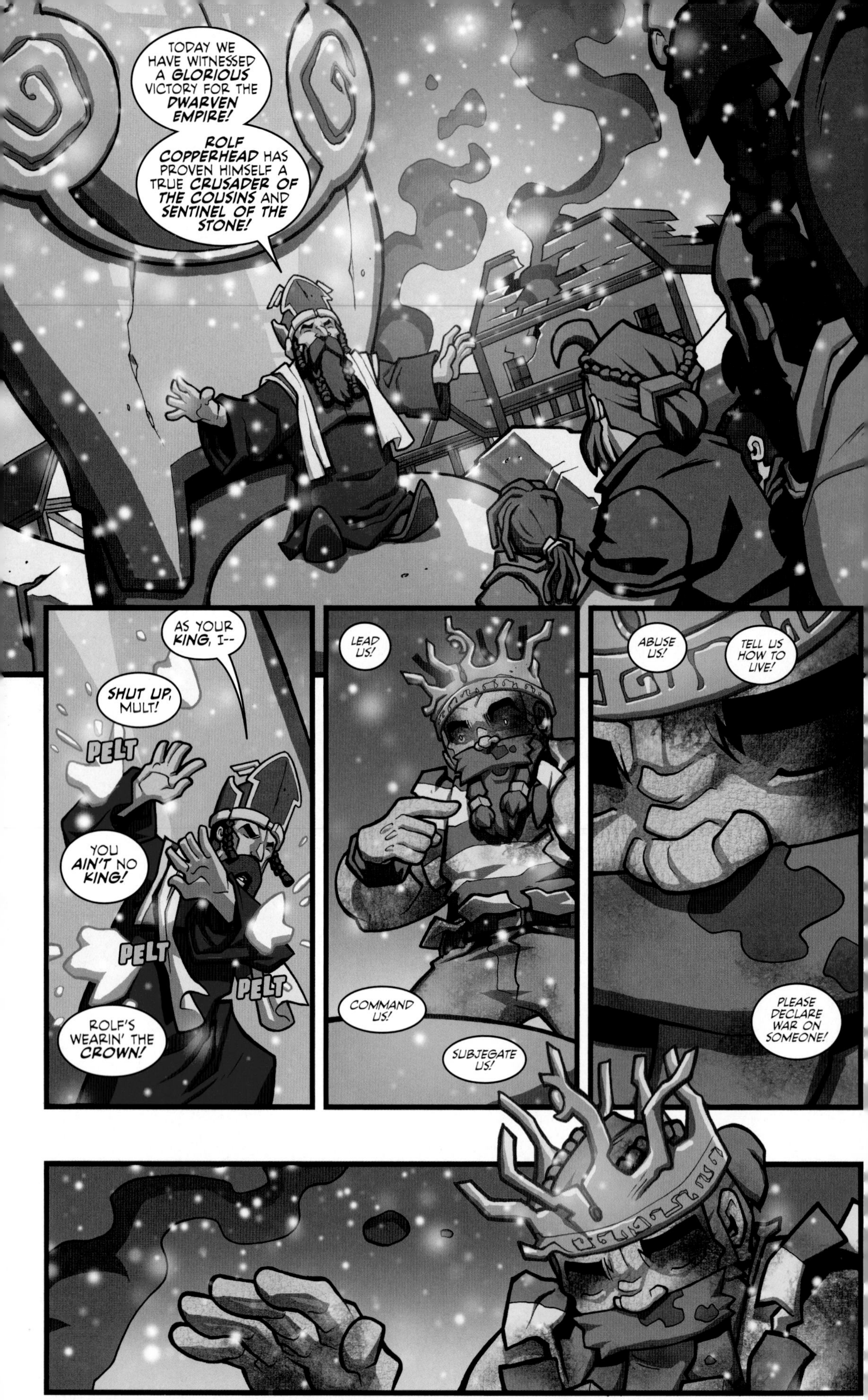
TODAY WE HAVE WITNESSED A GLORIOUS VICTORY FOR THE DWARVEN EMPIRE!
ROLF COPPERHEAD HAS PROVEN HIMSELF A TRUE CRUSADER OF THE COUSINS AND SENTINEL OF THE STONE!
AS YOUR KING, I--
SHUT UP, MULT!
PELT
YOU AIN'T NO KING!
PELT
PELT
ROLF'S WEARIN' THE CROWN!
LEAD US!
COMMAND US!
SUBJEGATE US!
ABUSE US!
TELL US HOW TO LIVE!
PLEASE DECLARE WAR ON SOMEONE!

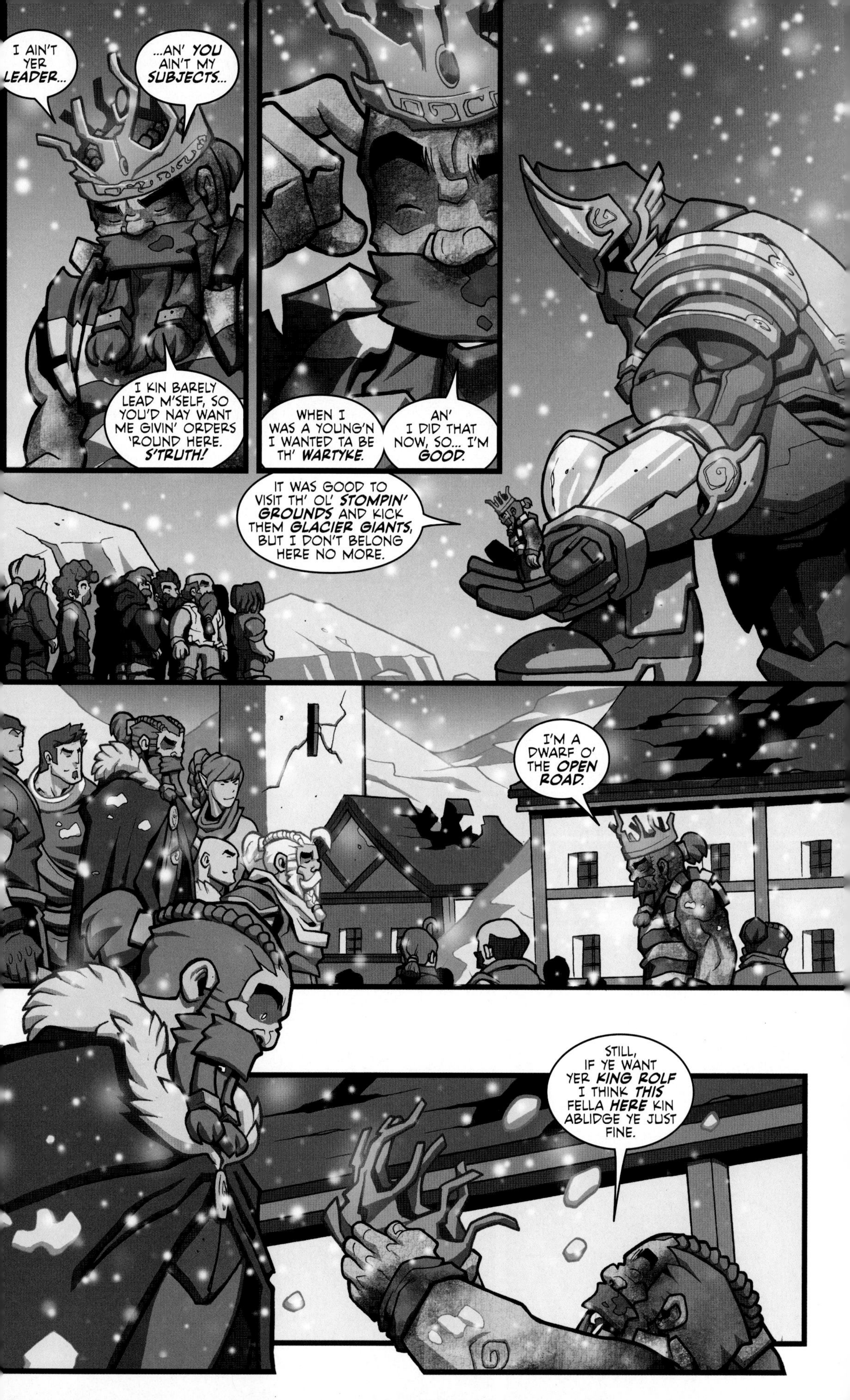

I AIN'T YER LEADER...
...AN' YOU AIN'T MY SUBJECTS...
I KIN BARELY LEAD M'SELF, SO YOU'D NAY WANT ME GIVIN' ORDERS 'ROUND HERE. S'TRUTH!
WHEN I WAS A YOUNG'N I WANTED TA BE TH' WARTYKE.
AN' I DID THAT NOW, SO... I'M GOOD.
IT WAS GOOD TO VISIT TH' OL' STOMPIN' GROUNDS AND KICK THEM GLACIER GIANTS, BUT I DON'T BELONG HERE NO MORE.
I'M A DWARF O' THE OPEN ROAD.
STILL, IF YE WANT YER KING ROLF I THINK THIS FELLA HERE KIN ABLIDGE YE JUST FINE.

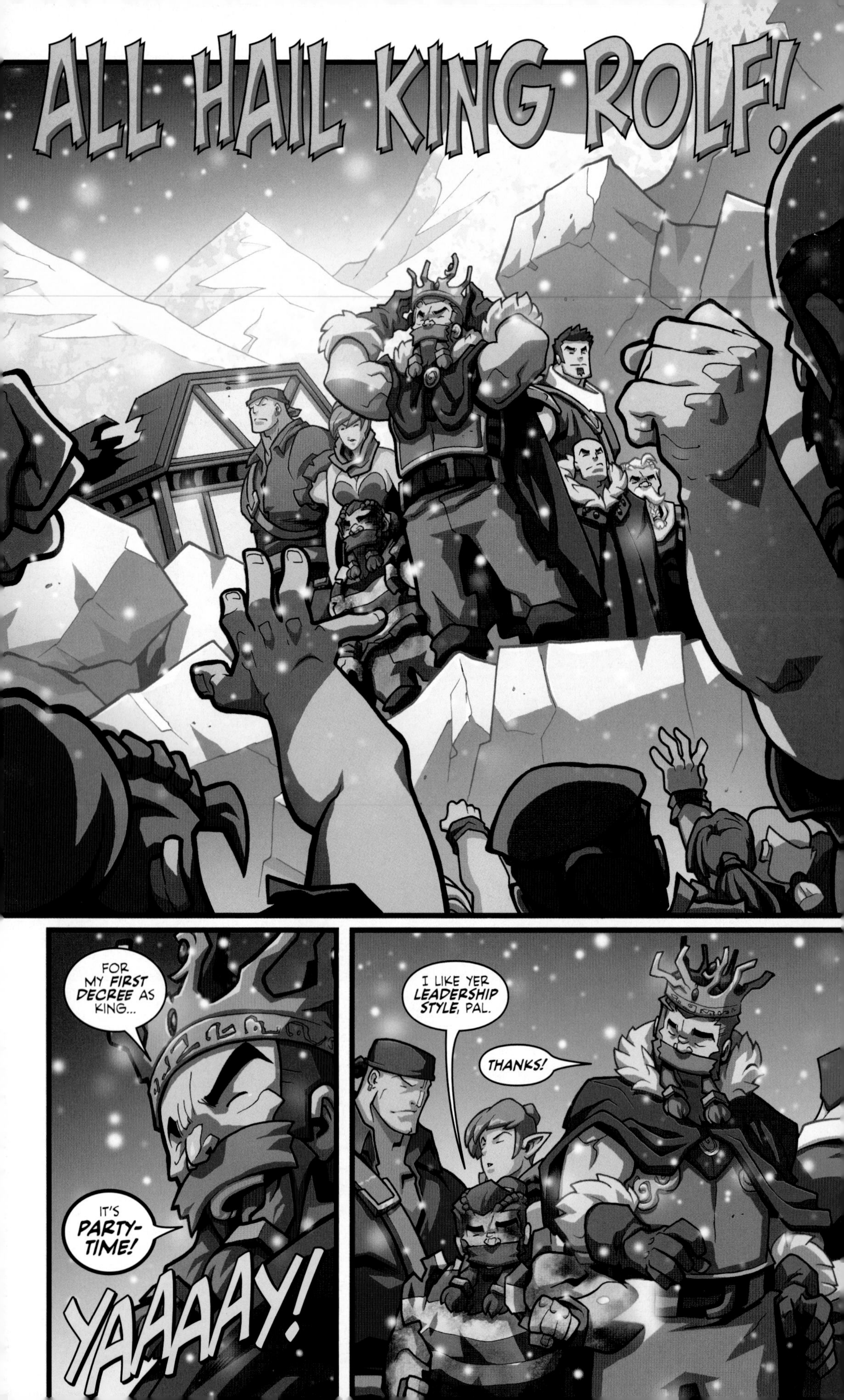
ALL HAIL KING ROLF!
FOR MY FIRST DECREE AS KING...
IT'S PARTY-TIME!
YAAAAY!
I LIKE YER LEADERSHIP STYLE, PAL.
THANKS!

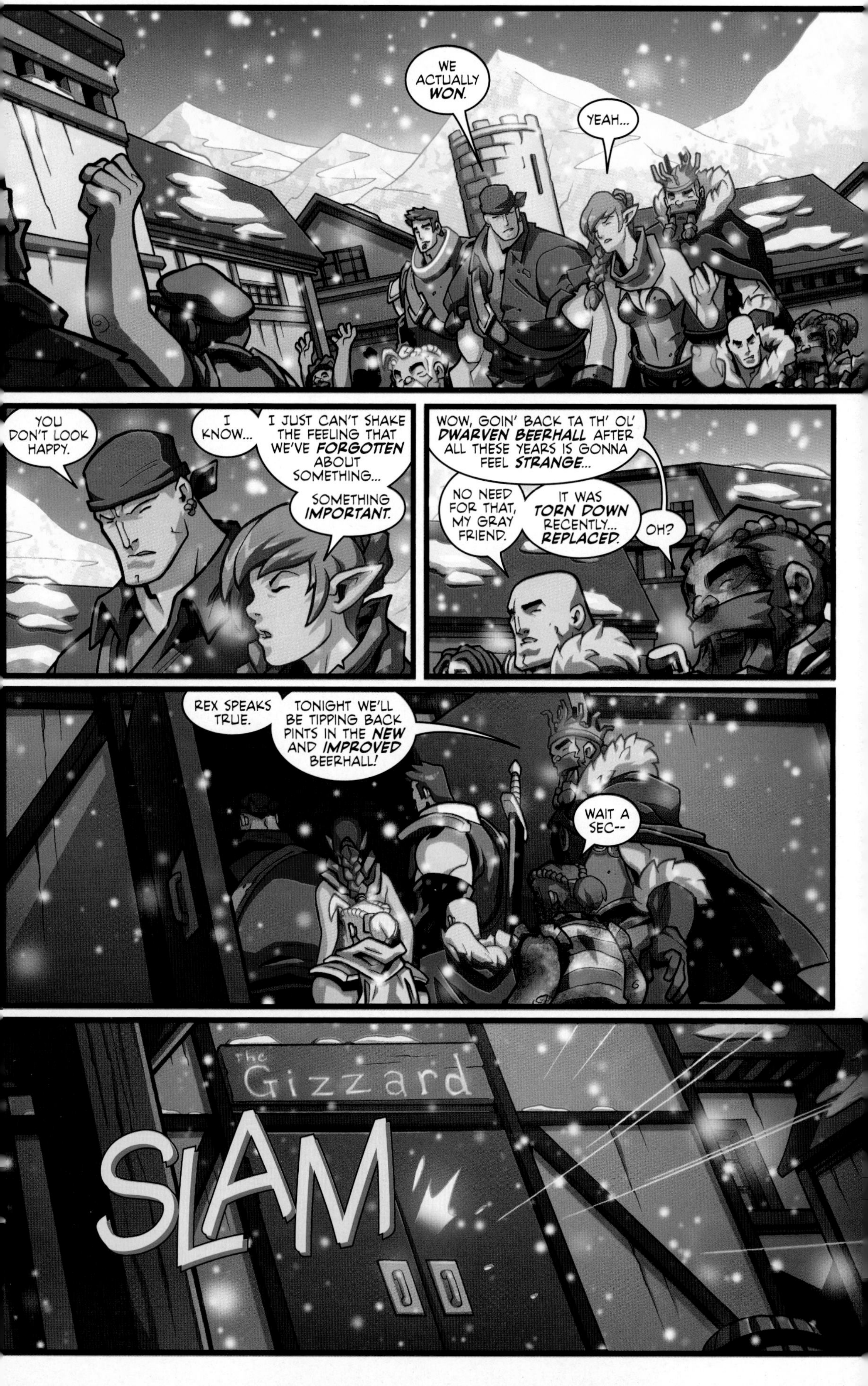

WE ACTUALLY WON.
YEAH...
YOU DON'T LOOK HAPPY.
I KNOW...
I JUST CAN'T SHAKE THE FEELING THAT WE'VE FORGOTTEN ABOUT SOMETHING...
SOMETHING IMPORTANT.
WOW, GOIN' BACK TA TH' OL' DWARVEN BEERHALL AFTER ALL THESE YEARS IS GONNA FEEL STRANGE...
NO NEED FOR THAT, MY GRAY FRIEND.
IT WAS TORN DOWN RECENTLY... REPLACED.
OH?
REX SPEAKS TRUE.
TONIGHT WE'LL BE TIPPING BACK PINTS IN THE NEW AND IMPROVED BEERHALL!
WAIT A SEC--
The Gizzard
SLAM

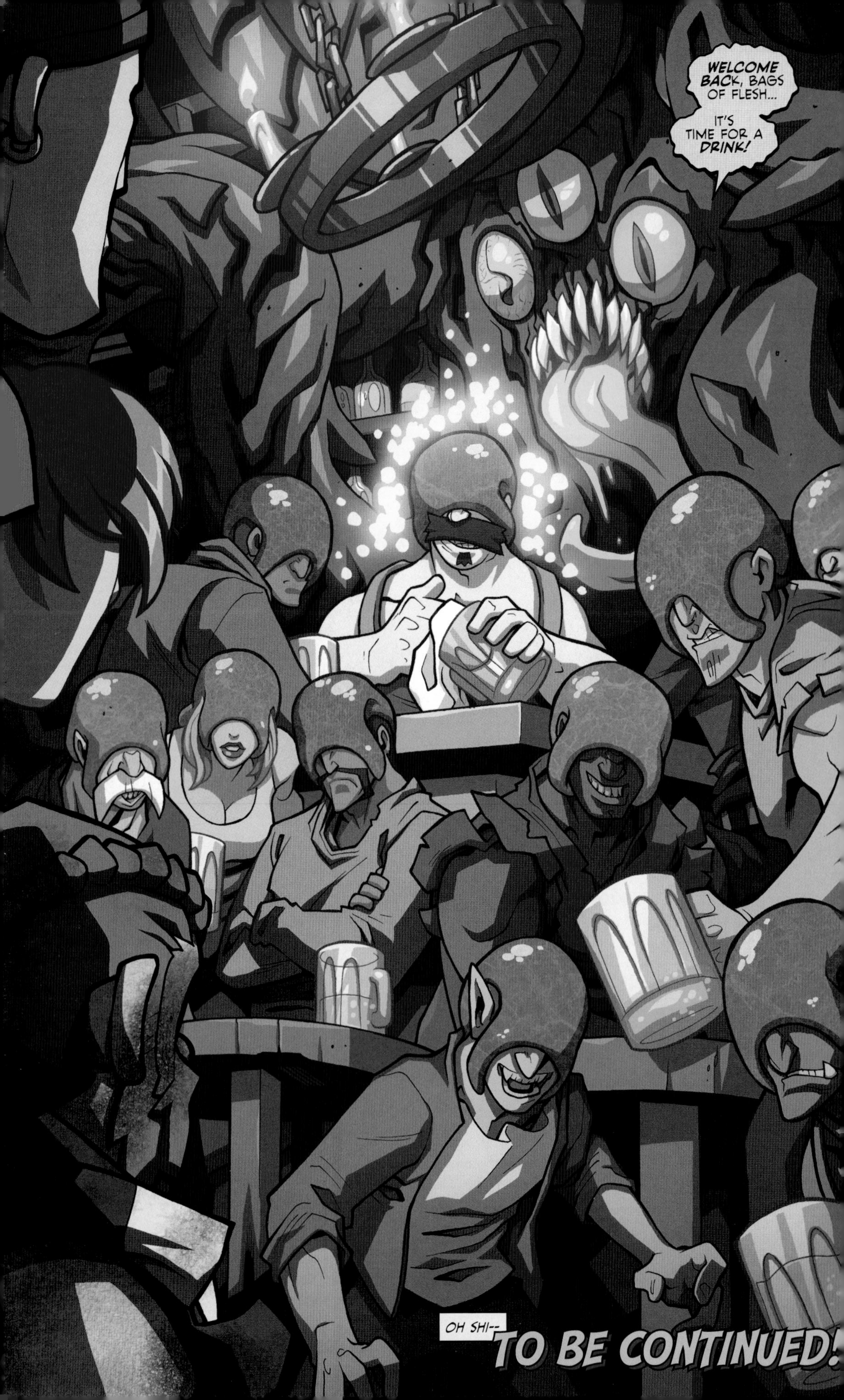
WELCOME BACK, BAGS OF FLESH...
IT'S TIME FOR A DRINK!
OH SHI--
TO BE CONTINUED!

SKETCHES

As each story arc of Skullkickers wraps up I look back at the ridiculous things I ask Edwin and Misty to put together and I'm amazed it comes together as well as it does.

Juggling multiple designs for the same characters, illustrating wanton destruction with a comedic flare, none of the fun story stuff would work without the tireless work of the art team.

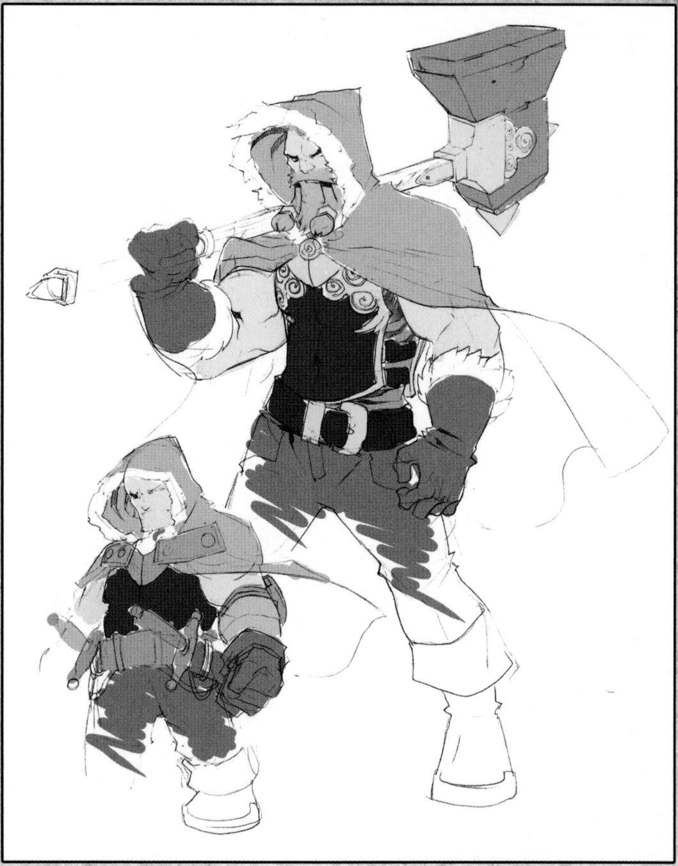

Top-Right: Dwarf Rex and Tall Rolf design sketch by Edwin.

Bottom-Left: Mighty Wartyke design sketch by Edwin.

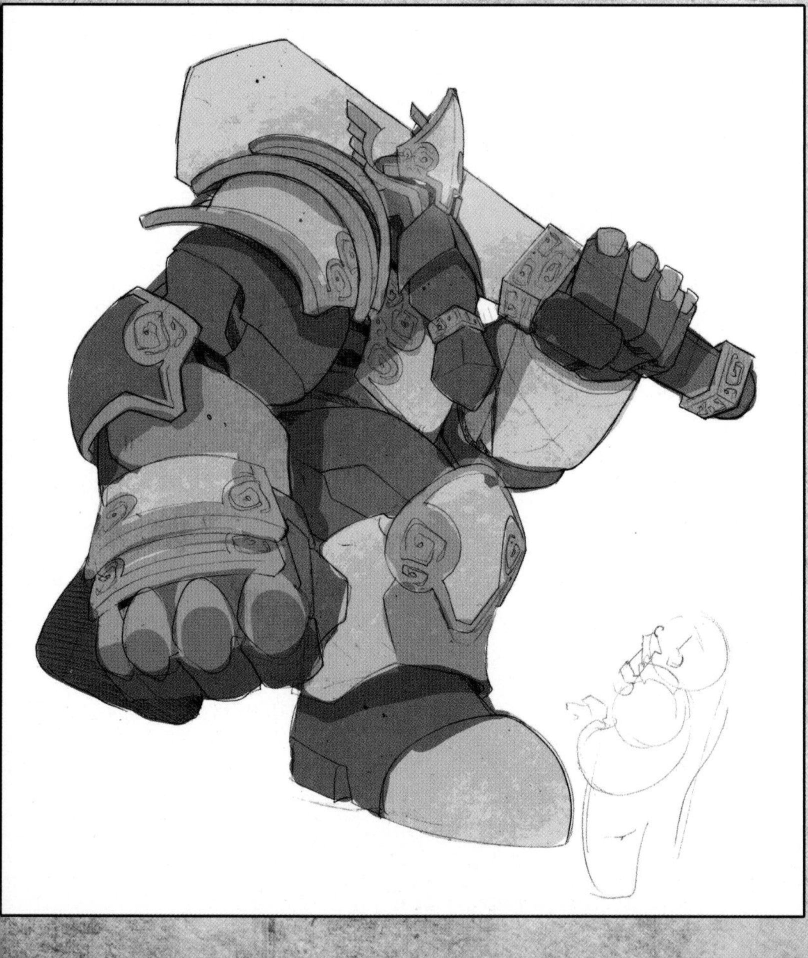

Even though the overall story we're telling is planned out through to the end, inspiration can strike at weird moments and there are many times where I email Edwin out of the blue with an excited "Okay, I need you to design this new last minute thing because I think it'll be funny."

Within a few hours he's sketched it all up and, surprising no one at all, it looks incredible.

When you work with people this skilled, you try not to take it for granted, but then my next big stupid idea hits and I'm asking for something even more difficult. What I'm really trying to say here is that I'm a monster.

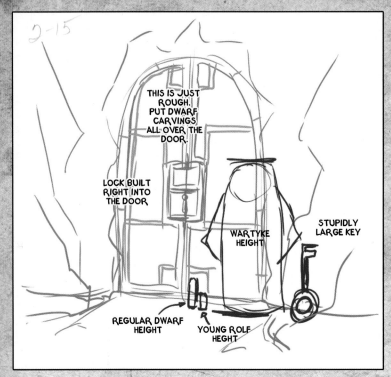

Within the doodle:

2-15

THIS IS JUST ROUGH. PUT DWARF CARVINGS ALL OVER THE DOOR.

LOCK BUILT RIGHT INTO THE DOOR

WARTYKE HEIGHT

STUPIDLY LARGE KEY

REGULAR DWARF HEIGHT

YOUNG ROLF HEIGHT

When my location descriptions get vague (and, when deadlines are tight, you better believe they do) I'll sometimes send along quick doodles or reference photos to explain what I'm talking about.

The entrance to the tunnels of the mountain dwarves was a cross between giant cathedral doors and the silver age-era entrance door to Superman's Fortress of Solitude, complete with a goofy giant key.

Top-Left: Mountain door doodle by Zub.

Bottom-Right: Young Rolf sketches by Edwin.

When I asked Edwin to design up a kid version of Rolf and the other young dwarves (I think my copious design notes consisted of "just draw kids with beards and moustaches") I didn't anticipate that he'd melt the hearts of Skullkickers readers with a ridiculously adorable wide-eyed dwarf child. I mean, seriously, just look at that!

Look at it!

Adorbs.

This character grows up to become an ornery murderous mercenary. You can't do that!

Anyway, it's a pure delight bringing you these low-brow high-fantasy stories and have them so well received. Skullkickers Volume 6, egotistically titled "Infinite Icons of the Endless Epic", has a lot to live up to, but we'll do our best to deliver the goods.

-ZUB